THE
HEART
OF
RESISTANCE

THE DREADNOUGHT

A shape caught her eye from within the mass, something large and dark looming just at the edge of sight. She squinted, shielding her eyes against the sun, trying to decipher what it could be. Then the storm parted suddenly as the shape broke through, shedding wisps of vapor from its hull as it blotted out the golden clouds.

Elsie's mouth dropped open. She had never seen anything so massive, nor so terrifying. The *thing*, the ship, did not look like any other airship she knew. It was built around a metal mound in the center, like a balloon but rigid and heavy, its angular hull bristling with cannons and walkways and cables. She saw figures climbing up and down, appearing antlike in comparison to the massive structure. Black smoke billowed out behind as it lumbered through the air towards them.

"Arthur," she said, her voice almost a whisper at first, then rising into a shriek of terror. "Arthur!"

Arthur broke from the embrace and ran down the stairs to join her on the main deck, his grin erased by a look of grave concern. She pointed breathlessly at the enormous ship, her hand trembling in the air.

"What is that?"

Arthur stared, his face falling into an indecipherable mask as he took it in. At length, he spoke.

"Kid, *that* is an imperial dreadnought."

THE
HEART
OF
RESISTANCE
BOOK ONE

A.D. GRIFFEY

To Ezra
To whom the name Pendington is owed.

Table of Contents

PART 5: THE STORM

Maps

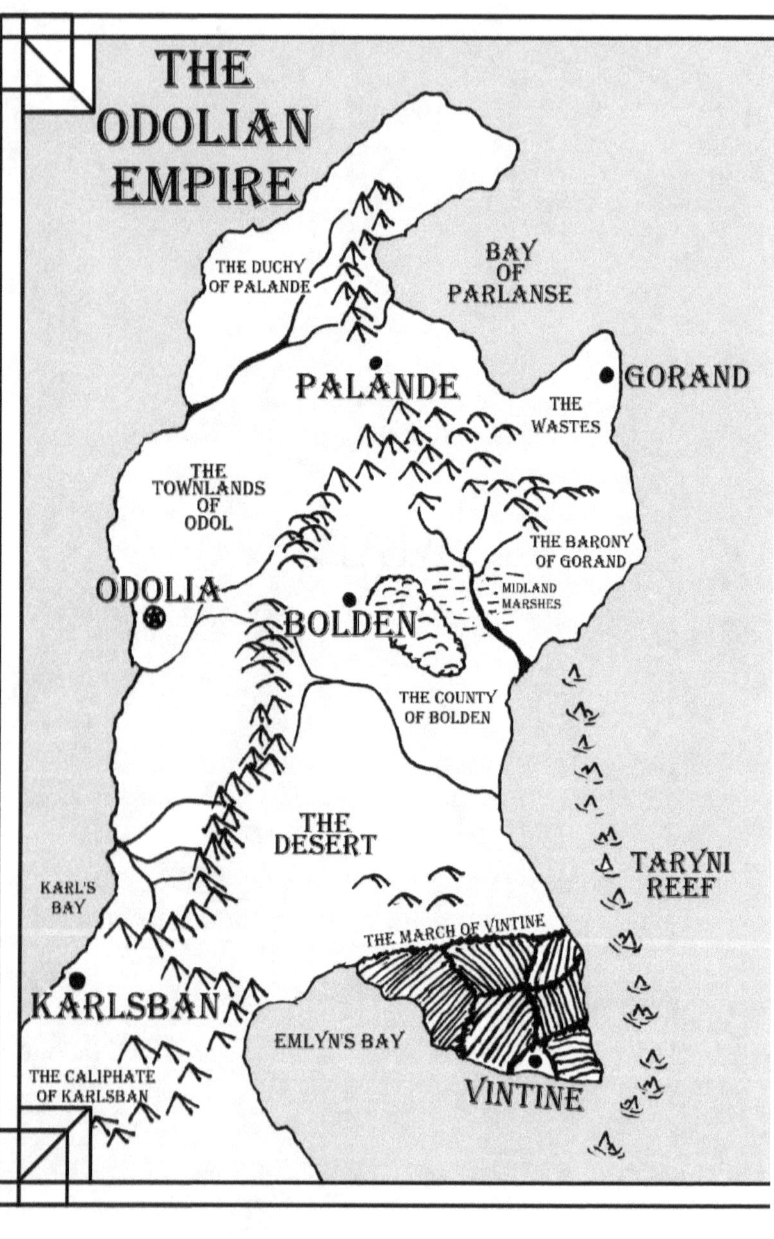

THE ODOLIAN EMPIRE
THE DUCHY OF PALANDE
BAY OF PARLANSE
PALANDE
GORAND
THE WASTES
THE TOWNLANDS OF ODOL
THE BARONY OF GORAND
MIDLAND MARSHES
ODOLIA
BOLDEN
THE COUNTY OF BOLDEN
THE DESERT
TARYNI REEF
KARL'S BAY
THE MARCH OF VINTINE
KARLSBAN
EMLYN'S BAY
VINTINE
THE CALIPHATE OF KARLSBAN

THE
KINGDOM
OF
SIAL
YNARUS
SIALI JUNGLE
ALDIA
SIALI DESERT
JENTIA
JENTI GULF
THE GREAT PLATEAU
N
W
E
S

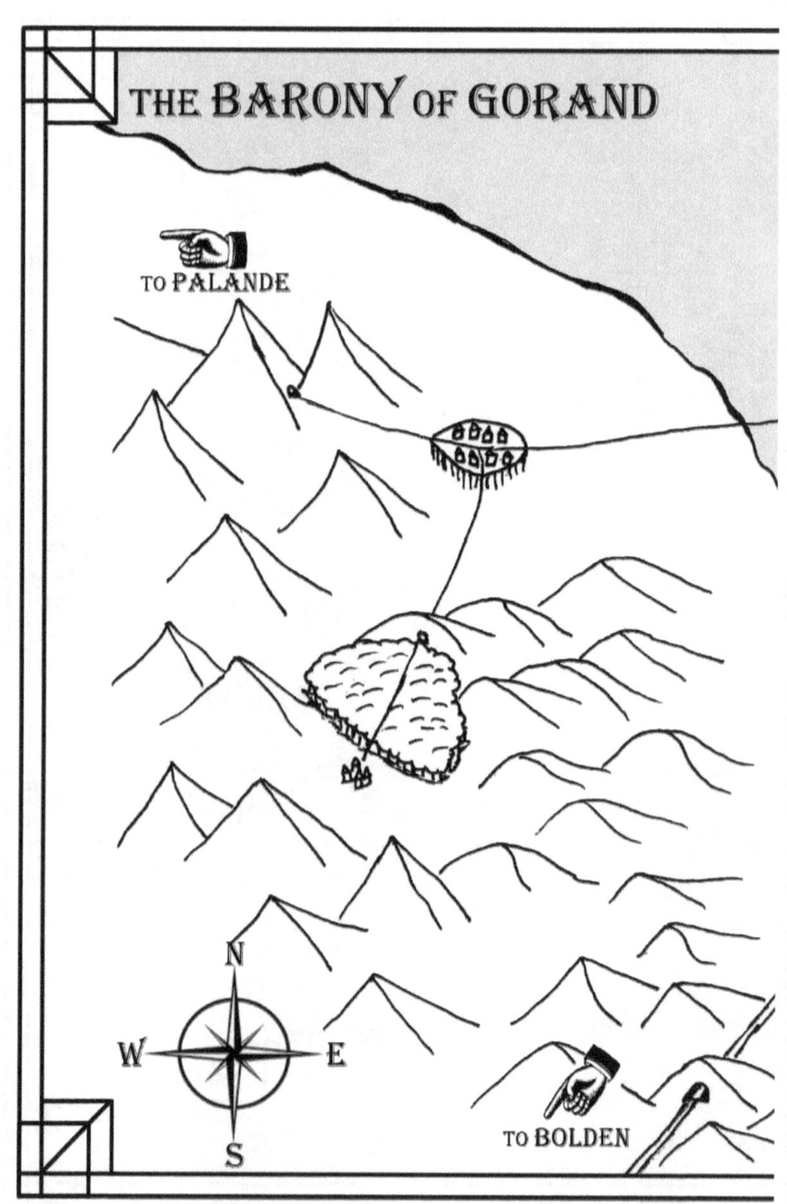

THE BARONY OF GORAND
TO PALANDE
TO BOLDEN
N
W
E
S

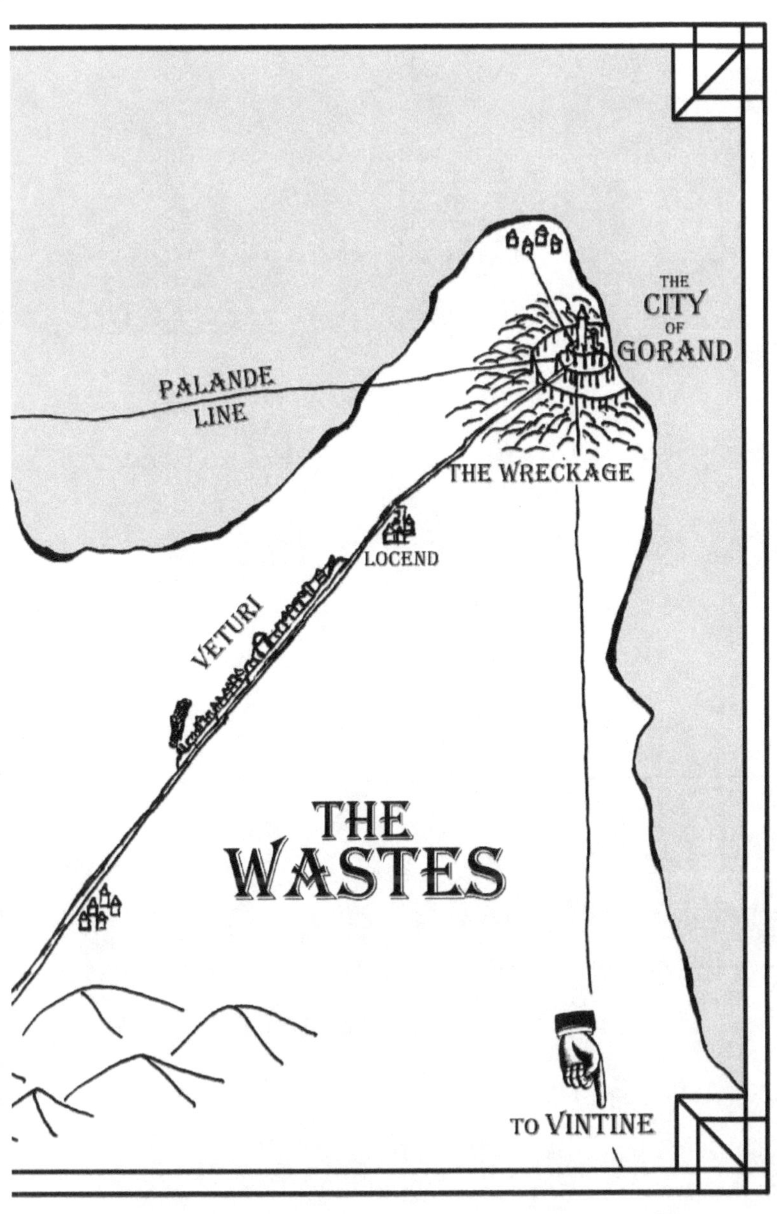

THE CITY OF GORAND
PALANDE LINE
THE WRECKAGE
LOCEND
VETURI
THE WASTES
TO VINTINE

PART 1:
THE ENGINEER

JANNA

Beer was beer and Janna had learned that with enough time and persistence even the worst brew from the worst pub in Gorand could take the edge off old memories. She glanced around the smoky, ill-lit bar before taking another swig from her mug. It was watered down. The tables and booths were beginning to clear as the dockworkers and other laborers made their way home to bed before another hard day's work. The only remnant were bums who likely wouldn't pay their tab at the end of the night. The bartender was betting that everyone who remained was too drunk to notice the diminishing quality of their drinks.

Of course, Janna did notice. It would take far more than a few splashes of weak beer to get her tipsy. She was too tired to care now, and in a foul mood besides, though not in a way that would cause her to make a scene. Unlike earlier that day.

Warily, she glanced around the room again, though without moving from her resting position: leaned back in her corner booth with her tall, oil-stained boots resting on the unwashed table. She didn't recognize anyone at the bar tonight. That was good. Better still, no one seemed to recognize her either. She glanced at the evening edition of the *Gorand Standard* rolled neatly on the table by her dirty plate and mugs, a castoff from some previous patron. The headline marched across the smudgy newsprint in stark, bold letters:

"GREYER'S REBELLION EXTERMINATED!"

Feeling the heat of guilt in her chest, she turned the paper over, revealing innocuous ads for hair products and the latest opera, words that weren't an indictment on her.

Janna Tulli had spent her life with the words 'Greyer's rebellion' hanging like an albatross around her neck. When she was born, her father, Greyer Tulli, was a freedom fighter in the Twenty Year's War, a conflict between the independent state of Karlsban and the long arm of the Odolian Empire. Eventually, Odol had bombed Karlsban into submission, annexing it like every other nation on the continent.

But her father was not one to be deterred by little things like treaties and annexation. Along with a number of like-minded men and women, as well as his reluctant daughter, Greyer began burning a path from the Karlsban mountains straight to Bolden, the heart of the empire. They recruited others along the way, scattering small groups of fanatics like shrapnel to every corner of the empire, where they dug in and caused trouble both small and large. It took two long years and the firepower of Odol's feared dreadnoughts to finally destroy Greyer himself. But the rebellion had not died, merely dispersed. Pockets of desperate men still harassed the Odolians from time to time even now. *Despite what that headline would have me believe. I know they're still out there.*

Janna shuddered, remembering those miserable last days. She had been raised as a fiery Karlsban patriot by both her parents and was more than willing to fight for her homeland. Her engineering skills were second to none among her father's men. When the war ended, though, she saw a change, an increase in desperation and brutality. She saw the rebellion commit crimes against Odolian citizens that still curdled her stomach. She tried to leave, only managing it when Greyer's madness cost him his life and nearly her own. But her time in the rebellion still plagued her.

Running from the remnants of her father's tattered dream, she moved to the Odolian city of Gorand, where jobs on the skydocks were plentiful. She existed on a first name basis, using a fake surname when absolutely necessary. But the time when that was enough to cover her tracks had passed.

The memory of that morning's fight was foggy in Janna's mind. Perhaps the beer was finally doing its job. She had been consistently employed for a little over a month loading cargo ships, which was a record for her, but one of the guys had gotten a little too fresh with her in the back of the clipper's hold. A punch to the jaw solved that problem, but he shouted "rebel wench" at her as a form of weak retaliation. Even the word was dangerous when said too loudly and heard by the wrong set of ears, but that wasn't the worst of it. She'd been drinking on the job, of course, and was too riled up to think straight. Her response had been something along the lines of "My father has nothing to do with this!"

Once he told someone higher up, it wouldn't be difficult for them to put two and two together. Three years of careful anonymity washed away in an instant. She'd stormed off the job and leapt onto a train taking workers back into Gorand proper, where she'd gone to ground and ended up at one of her least favorite dives. She was now spending the last money she would ever earn in this city, or anywhere in Odol for that matter, on crappy food and laughable beer. Tomorrow, she would be found and taken to one of the garrisons, probed and prodded and perhaps tortured for information she didn't have. But that was tomorrow.

Her misery was interrupted by the creak of the street door as it swung open. Heavy boots clomped on the dusty wooden floor. *No one comes here so close to curfew. The bar closes in half an hour!* Carefully, she moved her head to peek at whoever had just come in. It was a man, taller than average with red hair and, more disconcertingly, the burgundy overcoat of an Odolian officer. His face was stern as he glared around the room. He was searching hard for something. Or someone.

She tried to hide in her now empty mug of beer, pulling her feet off the table and sliding subtly back into the booth. Quickly, she realized how conspicuous the corner booth was and the stranger's sharp eyes caught her an instant later. Janna cursed under her breath and set the mug down as casually as she could, faking a sigh of satisfaction. She snatched up the newspaper and buried her nose in the headline, praying he hadn't already seen the evening edition. She didn't want any needless association between her and her father; her darker complexion, brown-black hair, and lean physique betrayed her Karlsban heritage, making her stick out among the pale Gorandis regardless of circumstance.

Staring intently at a blank space on the front page, she nearly jumped as a hand gripped the top of the paper. The man pushed the paper down firmly and suddenly they were face to face.

"Are you Janna?" the man asked.

"Just Janna, that's me," she said with a hollow smile. Her heart was thrumming in the back of her throat. *It's over.*

"Good, I've been looking for you," he said as he sat down.

The sounds of the bar had been dying down already, but now it seemed deadly silent. Janna swallowed, eyeing the man up and down for a brief moment. His overcoat had certainly once been an officer's, but the insignia and rank had been ripped off. Beneath, he wore a simple cotton shirt instead of the scarlet jacket of an officer's dress uniform. His eyes, however, were still commanding. *Ex-military, then. I hope.*

"You've been looking for me? Why?" Janna stretched the words so she didn't have to hear the answer.

"I'm looking to hire a mechanic. You were... recommended to me. I was told you're the best."

"Who told you that?" Janna hedged.

"Unimportant. Are you the best?"

"I am," Janna said too quickly. *Careful...this could still be a trap.* Pausing, she searched for a way to determine his motives without revealing more about herself than necessary. "But even with the flattery, I won't work for free. Full time, or just a quick repair job? I need something long term."

"That was the idea. Can you manage engineering duties as far as Bolden?"

Her heart began to pound. It was an effort to keep her voice steady. Bolden would be safer than Gorand, at least. Given her situation, she had little choice... "Depends on the ship. Depends on the engine. Probably."

He nodded. "Good. We can discuss the details at my place."

Janna blinked. "Just like that? No credentials, no inquiry, nothing?" She realized her voice was growing too loud and she nearly bit her tongue. She shrank back against the cracked leather of the booth, dropping her eyes. "I don't even know your name and you expect me to accept a job just like that?" she muttered. "I'm not *that* desperate."

"But you are desperate, no?" the man said. His mouth was set in a straight hard line.

Janna cursed herself internally. "How much do you know?"

"Enough." The man stood up abruptly, causing Janna to start. "We can talk more on the streets, away from prying ears. You'd be surprised how much a bartender can remember when he has a militia bayonet pointed at his throat."

He left no room for disagreement and Janna knew she had nowhere left to run. She stood reluctantly, dropping the newspaper on the seat and fished in her coat pocket for a couple decats, her last remaining cash save for some small change that wouldn't buy her a matchbook. Her knuckles banged against the little tin flask, empty now from this morning's binge. She wished it wasn't. She tossed the coins on the table and hitched her coat up higher on her taught shoulders.

The man's eyes lifted from the coins to her face and for the first time since he entered the room, the faintest hint of a smile passed over his lips. "Just how much did you drink?"

"The prices are exorbitant," Janna snapped as they made their way to the door. "And the beer is watered down!" she added loudly for the benefit of the bartender, who only waved a dismissive hand at her without a second glance.

The cobbled streets of lower Gorand were slick from the evening's acid rain. It was growing dark now, nearing curfew, and the windows of the brick buildings stood black against the night like sentinels. Janna followed close on the man's heels, dodging iridescent puddles. Her eyes roved nervously, watching for a flash of red or the glint of a bayonet.

"You'll want to watch out up here," she said as they neared the intersection of Pruit and St. Martin's. "There's a militia kiosk on the corner."

The man did not slow down, but turned sharply into an alley scarcely wide enough for the two of them. Janna followed, struggling to match his long strides. She wasn't short, but the top of her head came only to the man's collarbone. "So, you are on the run," the man said, glancing back at her mildly.

"Does it matter?" she snapped as she drew up beside him.

"You expected an inquiry."

Janna grimaced. "Fine, but let's keep walking. I don't know if you're from around here, but the rain could start again anytime and that stuff burns like bad bourbon."

The man nodded, his face unreadable in the gloom. "So why is the militia such bad news for you?"

"I got into a fight at work," she admitted after a moment. "Destruction of property, the like." It was almost not a lie.

"If it's anything like the skydocks back in Bolden, that's almost grounds for a promotion."

Janna bit back a laugh. "So what's the job?"

Instead of heading back to the main road, the man turned a corner and wound deeper into the labyrinthine alley system. Concerningly, Janna realized they were heading toward the shadows of the undercity.

The city of Gorand was split into three tiers, built one on top of the other, towering into the air on massive struts of metal and stone. It was usually simple to tell a man's class by which tier of the city he came from. The topmost layer was referred to as "the crown." Though perhaps not an affectionate title, it was true to the gold and marble palaces and mansions which gracefully adorned the upper heights of the city. The second layer, far larger, was home to the enviable middle class. The houses there were clean, the jobs paid well and weren't likely to break your back, and for the most part the crime wasn't too bad.

Of course, Janna never dreamed of living on either of those levels. For the better part of three years she had been bumming around in rented rooms of pubs and bars on the lowest layer until she got behind enough on rent to be kicked out. That was the nature of life in the lowest tier of Gorand. Where there weren't sleazy bars and dives, there were horrible factories and workhouses which used the blood, sweat, and tears of workers to grease their gears. The part of the lowest tier that lay directly beneath the middle layer was known quite infamously as "the undercity." The undercity lay in perpetual shadow beneath the upper platforms, festering in the dark and rarely spoken of without a curse. Though some innocents lived there in destitution, whether in slummy apartment houses or on the streets, most who ventured there were involved in some kind of crime or vice.

Janna had been to the undercity only a few times to visit some of the underground casinos. The men there were viperous and she found herself so afraid for her life and freedom that even the itch to blow her hard-earned money on a game of baccarat couldn't pull her back.

There were a few long moments of silence between Janna and the stranger, interrupted only by the low hum of machinery or the rattle of steam engines on the trestles above. Finally, Janna asked again. "What is the job?"

The man looked around, his eyes seeming to take in the entirety of the city as he made sure of their privacy. Curfew was fast approaching and there was no one on the block besides themselves. "It's something...illegal."

"No kidding," Janna laughed, a hoarse barking sound that was too loud in her ears. "Well, go on!"

The man kept walking, not even looking over his shoulder as he spoke. "In the morning, we are going to the skydocks. *Early* in the morning, before it's crawling with sailors. You're going to get me an airship."

"It got confiscated, didn't it?" Janna asked, rolling her eyes in disappointment. "That's going to be expensive." She had seen captains pay through the nose to get their ships out of the baron's clutches after some minor infraction. Sometimes the charges were trumped up. It was all part of doing business in Gorand, the domain of "Bloody" Baron Schulhard, who held ships hostage on a whim to fill his personal coffers. And he usually got the money, because most people weren't stupid enough to try and unlock the controls under the watchful eyes of the dock union guards.

"It isn't mine," the man said without missing a step. "You're going to steal one for me."

Janna stopped dead in her tracks. The man continued on ahead a few paces before coming to a halt. "Well? Aren't you coming along?"

She reached for the holster hidden beneath the hip pad of her corset and produced a pistol. It was small, delicate almost, and she'd never had need for it. Not with her father's men around. In Gorand, she kept it hidden at all times. Only the militia and soldiers were permitted to bear arms inside the city, but fortunately there was no man who wanted a black eye enough to check where she hid it. Her hand steady, she pulled the hammer back and aimed for the back of the man's head.

"Take one more step, rebel, and it's going to be a short night for you." Her voice was laden with contempt.

"I'm not a rebel," the man said sharply. "Only a man mad enough to say 'no.'" One hand went under his coat and he pulled out a pistol nearly three times the size of Janna's. It was beautifully engraved, with gilt along the handle, painted in red and blue. An officer's gun, intended for show rather than action. Janna had seen the like on the corpses of her father's enemies. But she wasn't going to test it, especially as he turned and pointed it right between her eyes.

"What are you talking about?" Janna asked, her hand beginning to tremble. All she could think to do now was stall for time.

"'At the heart of resistance is a man mad enough to say 'no', and he will be the eye of the storm which will topple nations and grind tyrants to dust.'" It was a recitation, a line borrowed from some book or play, and the man's voice was bitter as he spoke it. "I am that man, Janna Tulli, not one of Greyer's stooges. I work for myself."

Janna shook her head, unable to comprehend him. The revelation that he knew her full name was not unexpected, but hearing it from his lips sent a jolt of fear through her. She endeavored to remain calm, not taking her eyes off of him. As she stared, she thought his face seemed vaguely familiar. "That tells me nothing," she said at last, the words thick in the back of her mouth. "Who are you?"

"My name is Arthur Pendington. And you, Miss Tulli, are going to help me steal an airship or you'll never see the outside of this city."

"Arthur Pendington?" Janna spluttered. "Arthur Pendington died three years ago. His dreadnought malfunctioned and crashed in the desert. No survivors." She could see the paper in her mind's eye, the headline long forgotten, but his portrait stamped in black and white across the front, large as life. It had been the day she arrived in Bolden, Pendington's home city, only a few weeks after she'd left the rebellion for good. Flags flew at half mast on every government building, a tiny tribute to the great war hero who'd bombed her father's people into the earth. She remembered his face, all hard lines and angles, a grim expression and knit brows, strangely luminous eyes glaring up from beneath them. She tried to tell herself that this was not the same man. But deep in her gut she knew he was not lying.

Arthur Pendington barked a laugh. "You read the papers and you *believe* them?"

Janna hitched her shoulders in a shrug, allowing herself a wry smile as she remembered the headline on her table at the bar. "Guess I'd be a fool if I did." She did not lower the gun. "What are you going to do with this ship?"

Arthur's face was as impassive as stone. "I will strike at the empire's rancid heart. That's all you need to know. Come on. We have to go pick up my crew. You know I'm your only chance of getting out of this city alive."

Janna bit her lip, hesitating for only a moment, then stepped forward and ripped the ornate pistol out of Arthur's hand. Checking it, she clicked her tongue. It wasn't even loaded. "I won't kill you because I need out of this city," she said, shoving the gun into her belt and tapping her on pistol on his chest. "But you *can't* kill me, because without me you won't even see the outside of an airship. Or am I wrong?"

His grim smile told Janna everything she needed to know.

HOSPITALITY

The two unlikely companions crept through the back streets and alleys of lower Gorand, keeping their heads low and their collars turned up against the chilly damp wind. Janna held her pistol to Arthur's back, prodding him gently with it every now and then so he wouldn't forget who was in charge. She let him lead, running quiet calculations in the back of her mind as she scanned dark-windowed buildings around them. She was counting on the fact that his crew, whoever they were, wouldn't risk harming their captain. But dread crept up the back of her throat as they wound ever closer to the undercity. There was no telling what sort of people she was dealing with. Even still, she told herself that anything was better than being carted off to an imperial prison.

They finally halted beside the mesh staircase of a rickety fire escape. It belonged to one of the innumerable apartment buildings, built of crumbling plaster and sooty brick, the corroded tin roof perched uncertainly on top as though it could slide off at any moment. Janna gave Arthur another prod with the gun and with a grunt he started up the stairs. She kept close behind him, though for the moment she was more preoccupied with keeping her balance on the slick steps than with monitoring her hostage. They had nearly reached the top, swaying nine stories above the ground, when Arthur stopped on the landing in front of a battered wooden door. Janna angled herself so that he couldn't slip past her, and watched as he knocked rhythmically against the flimsy rotten wood. There was a moment of silence and then she heard an answer from inside; another series of rhythmic knocks.

"What'd you just signal?" she snapped.

"Only that it's me, not some agent of the empire." Arthur's voice was cool and collected. He did not seem at all phased by the fact that she had a gun to his back. He answered the signal in turn with a new pattern of knocks and Janna heard the sound of a bolt being shot back. She followed close on his heels as he pushed the door open and stepped inside.

"Paul, get Maria to-"

Arthur's stern voice was cut off by a knife, which whizzed past his shoulder and stuck in the doorframe, right beside Janna's head. She let out a strangled cry and stopped, nearly pulling the trigger out of fear. Two people stood in the center of a ratty one-room apartment with a look of murder in their eyes and weapons ready in their hands.

One of them was a stocky man with a pleasant if not handsome face. His bushy brows were forced together into a furrow, though it seemed an effort for him to express true anger. He had the look of a middle-class man, with well-groomed sideburns and a neat tweed waistcoat with a silver watch chain dangling from the pocket. He held an antiquated blunderbuss, pointed right at Janna.

The knife came from the hand of the other resident. It was a woman, and her anger seemed effortless. She was short and plump, but her strong arms showed that the had the muscle to match her physique. Her hair was mousy brown and perhaps her round face would have been agreeable if it hadn't been fixed in such a furious scowl. Her large dark eyes flashed fire in the dim light and she held another knife in her right hand, ready to throw. Janna was sure that the blade stuck in the wood next to her head was only a warning shot. The tiny pistol shook in her hand. She hadn't bargained for this.

"Paul, stand down," Arthur said calmly, "And tell Maria to as well."

"We didn't expect you to come back as her hostage!" Paul exclaimed. As he hefted the butt of the blunderbuss against his shoulder, he looked at the woman. She made a few signs with her free hand and Paul nodded in agreement. "Maria's right, how can we trust her to behave?"

"She's agreed to help us get the ship," Arthur said calmly. "Believe me, I have everything under control. Lower your weapons."

Paul slowly lowered the blunderbuss. As soon as he had set it on the ground, his hands began to fly in a pattern of signals like the ones Maria had made. Turning her head to face Paul, but still holding the knife ready, Maria began to signal in turn with her left hand. Janna recognized it as sign language and though she couldn't understand it, she could tell that they were having an argument. When Maria saw Janna withdraw her pistol from Arthur's back, that seemed to do the trick. She lowered her knife and tucked it neatly into her belt.

Paul regarded Janna with a bemused smile. "She says you're pretty brave to walk in here with a gun pointed at Arthur. You're lucky that she saw your face, otherwise she'd have turned you into a pincushion."

Janna shoved the gun back into its hidden holster, scoffing. "If this is how you greet your allies, I'd hate to see the greetings you give your enemies."

"Holding your allies' leader at gunpoint is hardly civil either," Arthur remarked. Straightening his coat, he turned to Janna and retrieved his ornate, but empty, pistol from her.

"Call it assurance," Janna said bluntly. "Can anyone be too careful in this rotten city? Speaking of which, how did you ferret me out anyways? I've been keeping my head down for over three years." As she spoke, she glanced around at the apartment. The flickering of a simple hearth was the only light, bathing the scant furnishings in an orange glow, partially obscured by the shadow of the pot that was boiling over it. A scratched oak dining table with three mismatched chairs filled most of the room. The "kitchen" consisted of a few mildew stained cabinets and a basin with a rusty water pump. Three tattered bed mats were rolled up in the corner, and there were a couple of tool boxes and foot lockers stacked opposite. The mean possessions almost made Janna feel fortunate.

Arthur shrugged as he sat in the most ornate of the chairs. "It's a long story. You know your way around an airship engine better than anyone this side of Odol; that much is public knowledge. I didn't ask for details, because we've already done some research, and beyond your identity and affiliation with Greyer, I don't care to know more. I assumed you weren't a shill for Odol at least."

"I work for my own benefit." Janna said. "Anything else can get dangerous. I'm only taking this job to get out of Gorand. May I sit?" Instead of waiting for a response, she threw herself down in one of the other chairs. Maria huffed and went over to tend the bubbling pot on the hearth, keeping her eyes on Paul.

Janna perked up. "Am I invited to dinner?"

There was a brief exchange in sign language. Paul turned to Janna after a moment, smirking. "Maria says you should have whatever's left at the end of the night as payback for bad manners. I've convinced her to let you have an even portion."

"Thanks," Janna crossed her arms and tried not to pout. "Very hospitable."

"Hospitality goes both ways. No use giving a dog your finest vintage." Arthur didn't even favor her with a glance as he spoke.

The comment made Janna's blood come to a quick boil. It was far too close to what she'd dealt with for so many years from her father. "Just because you think you have a noble cause or something doesn't give you the right to insult me like that!" She rounded on Paul, who seemed meek without his blunderbuss in hand. "Is this how he treats you?"

Paul raised his hands, abstaining from the conversation, but Janna took note of the bitter twist of his mouth. Turning back to Arthur, she put her elbows on the table and rested her chin on her knuckles. "You're right about not being a rebel. You couldn't have possibly worked for my father." Smugness tinged her voice and a smirk crept onto her face. "Because you're exactly like him. And there could only ever be one-"

"I am nothing like Greyer Tulli!" The raw fury in Arthur's tone and the sharpness of his glare made Janna flinch, but she held her ground with a certain dark glee.

"Yes, you are," she contended, "You pretend to have this noble cause, but really you're just a sad, bitter man. I guess being a fancy lord with a big house and a bigger ego wasn't enough power. You had to create a whole rebellion centered on your-"

She had begun to lose her train of thought when Paul interrupted with a polite cough. "I'm not sure how much the captain told you about the plan, Miss Tulli."

"Just Janna, please."

"Well, Janna," Paul continued sagely, "Maria has a point. If we want to get to the skydocks with the first shift we should get to bed sooner rather than later. We don't need to make things quite so...personal."

Janna glanced at Arthur, but he seemed to have moved past their conversation. Where a moment ago his face was seething with anger, he was now watching Maria intently as she portioned out savory vegetable stew from the bubbling pot. She divided it equally between one mug, two matching porcelain bowls with differing cracks, and a dented thermos lid.

The stew was delicious and the spices managed to hide the tinny flavor that the lid lent to Janna's portion. She wolfed it down as though she hadn't already eaten that evening. *And to think, I thought my last meal would be bad beer and stale chips!*

"So what are the terms?" Janna asked, looking up quickly from her empty thermos lid. "You said we'd discuss them when we got back to your apartment."

Arthur nodded but didn't take his attention off of his stew, which he was eating slowly and methodically. Paul, standing beside the table with bowl in hand, averted his eyes and began dutifully ignoring the conversation. Arthur finally finished his bite and looked at Janna with a sour expression.

"By terms you mean-"

"My pay."

"So passage to Bolden isn't enough?"

Janna bit her lip. She needed to get out of Gorand; that was the only reason she had followed Arthur into this place. But once she did get out, what then? And while Arthur's present circumstances were less than ideal, surely he had enough stowed away in Bolden to pay top dollar, especially in a tight corner.

"The rate for an engineer unlocking an impounded airship is one granz seven decat. It'll be about two and a half days to Bolden by air, so with wages, assuming I'm the one feeding the engine and maintaining it, that will be union rate at one sept a day. Plus the illegality adds a couple of premiums..." She pretended to do math in her head. "Ten talents. One upfront, as a retainer." She smiled sweetly at him. She would be talked down, of course, but even half of that fee would be enough for her to disappear and set herself up comfortably once again.

Paul gasped and when he had translated for Maria, she spat her soup out on the table and stared at Janna open mouthed. Arthur's face was so unmoving that at first Janna was unsure of if he'd even heard her. Then, he reached into the breast pocket of his coat and pulled out a coin purse. Fixing her with a level gaze, he produced a large, dingy gray coin. It was an inch around, stamped with the beneficent face of the late Empress Crysalia II, the previous ruler of Odol. Janna tried not to stare, but she could almost feel her mouth watering. It was more than she'd seen in months.

"The rest when we get out of Gorand," Arthur said harshly, tossing the coin across the table. It rolled, spun for a moment, and then struck Janna's tin lid with a clatter. Janna saw Paul's eyes go wide as he stared at Arthur.

"As soon as we're out of Gorand," she said shakily. "Deal?" Arthur nodded and Janna snatched the coin from the table. She ignored the whispered discussion that was beginning between Paul and Arthur, and examined the coin. It was a weeks pay and more, especially without the tax man to dock his share. Quickly, she stuffed it into the purse at her waist.

"Good," she said shortly, "What about the rest of the crew? And this plan of yours? I presume you have the right passes to get us onto the skydocks. I'll need one too, since I'm not about to go waving my current one around, under the circumstances..." She smiled wryly.

"We'll discuss the rest in the morning," Arthur said, returning to his stew with an air of finality. Janna sputtered her lips and tried a few more times to ply the man with questions, but he ignored her. Paul and Maria were already up and about, straightening the little room and beginning the washing up, so Janna sat at the table across from Arthur, feeling all the more alone. She fished in her pocket for the flask and brought it out, but remembered it was empty as soon as she began to unscrew the lid.

Arthur rose sharply, leaving his empty bowl behind, and strode over to the corner which contained the rolled mats. He selected one of them without much thought and tossed it at Janna. She narrowly caught it. "Get some sleep. We'll be getting up in a couple hours." As if to punctuate his words, foghorns wailed across the city outside, signaling that evening curfew had begun.

Looking around the room with renewed anxiety, Janna got slowly to her feet. She was trapped here with them now, unless she wanted to risk running into a patrol in the darkness outside. That would mean questions and rough handling and maybe marching her down to the office to have her papers examined properly, even if they didn't already know to be looking out for her. She glanced at Paul and Maria, who were huddled around the low fire, signing to one another between various tasks.

"Got anything to drink around here?" she asked a little too loudly as Paul went to fetch Arthur's bowl. He glanced at her with an inscrutable expression that she thought was a tad too close to pity.

"I've got a bottle I've been saving. I'm sure you could use something to settle your nerves; maybe we all could." He handed the bowl to Maria and crossed the room to one of the foot lockers, where he knelt and fetched out a bottle half full of amber liquid. Graciously, Paul passed it to her.

"Not too much now, we've got a long day ahead of us."

As Janna took a swig, she glanced over at Arthur, who had already curled up on one of the mats and was fast asleep. He had not removed his boots and overcoat, and the pistol rested beside his head. She wondered if he had loaded it while she wasn't looking. She looked back at Paul, but he was busy conversing with Maria over a basin of scummy water. Smiling, she filled her flask hastily from the bottle before recorking it and placing it gently in the locker.

Hospitality, she thought wryly.

THE BRIBE

Janna woke abruptly, heart pounding as she grasped for threads of a dream which had disintegrated like smoke. The skydocks were the first thing on her mind as she rubbed sleep from her eyes, feeling a dull ache beginning in the back of her head. Not very long now, and they would be sneaking in to steal a ship. She stared around, but it was impossible to tell what time it was now; the single gas lamp had been turned down low, throwing the windowless room into a guttering twilight that could have been any hour of day or night.

She sat up, rolling knots out of her shoulders from her uncomfortable sleep on the lumpy mat. Paul and Maria still lay on their shared mat, nestled against each other beneath a ratty comforter that had been patched beyond recognition. Arthur, however, was awake. He was kneeling in the corner, packing a few meager possessions into some of the toolboxes.

"What time is it?" she asked in a hoarse whisper, sliding gingerly off the bed mat and getting to her feet. Her throat was burning. The air in these apartments was hellish.

"I don't know," Arthur replied without looking up from his task. "Paul's the one with the watch."

"Shouldn't we get them up about now?"

"Paul's my navigator and we have a long flight ahead. He needs his rest. Don't worry about someone else's orders, Miss Tulli, worry about your own."

Janna huffed, causing Paul to stir gently in his sleep. With exaggerated care, she crossed the creaking floor to where Arthur knelt, dropping down beside him.

"Listen Arthur, if we are going to have any kind of partnership, then we are going to need to come to terms on a couple of points. First things first, Paul and Maria may be convinced you're some great lord they have to grovel to, but you're just a client to me. I'm not going to put up with you barking orders at me."

Arthur paused in his packing. "Miss Tulli-"

"Janna, please."

"Miss Tulli," Arthur repeated, "When we get aboard my ship, the *Heart of Resistance*, I will be the captain. My word aboard ship is law and any court would side with me on that."

Maybe after they got done hanging you for stealing said ship. Janna smiled grimly to herself at the thought and got up to rummage through the scant cabinetry, hoping for a quick breakfast. She was thoroughly disappointed; each shelf was somehow barer than the last.

"Another thing," she snapped over her shoulder, banging the cupboard closed in frustration, "I don't know how long you've been doing this, Arthur..."

"Captain will do."

"Arthur," Janna insisted, rounding on him, "You're not in the sky navy anymore. Respect is earned, not granted with a sealed letter from the emperor. You can't get respect by lording it over everyone from the cush lounge aboard the *Formidable*, you understand?"

"Is that what you think I did?" Arthur asked incredulously. He gazed at her with a look of utter contempt that shook Janna, though she continued on.

"In all my years with Greyer I never saw a hardworking naval captain," she insisted, crossing her arms as though to shield herself from his gaze. "Every one of them was an overfed, underprepared, spoiled, pompous-"

"Miss Tulli," Arthur said, his voice dangerously controlled, "Perhaps *you* do not understand. You think that the captains of His Majesty's Imperial Dreadnoughts lounge about in their cabins drinking champagne? Perhaps others did, but I spent my time on the bridge or the gun decks with my men. I rained death from afar on the empire's enemies and civilians alike. Every night I was forced to face that. And when the *Formidable* went down it was no mechanical failure. I destroyed it, before it destroyed me. That is what it is to be a captain, Miss Tulli."

With that, Arthur turned away and began packing again, as if there had been no exchange between them. Janna opened her mouth to ask one of the hundred questions buzzing in her head but then she heard the sound of someone stirring on the other mattress. She clamped her mouth shut as Paul and Maria began to rouse.

"I won't miss sleeping on that," Paul said bemusedly as he knuckled his spine and stretched. At a signed question from Maria, he pulled out his pocket watch. "It takes about ten minutes to get to the lift, and the lift opens in twenty."

"We should leave in five then," Janna said quickly. "The lines pile up pretty quickly, even with curfew."

"Hurry and get your things together, Miss Tulli," Arthur said sternly, rising to his feet and brushing off the knees of his threadbare trousers.

"All I have is what's already on me," Janna grumbled, thumbing the flask in her pocket. "I want to see these passes you've forged."

She looked to Paul and Maria. Maria slung a belt of throwing knives about her waist, which she quickly hid beneath a heavy knit shawl. Paul pulled on a brown wool overcoat that fell almost to his ankles. He slung the blunderbuss over his shoulder on its thick strap and tucked it beneath the coat, so that when it was closed the weapon was hidden. He looked for all the world like a respectable middle class gentleman, though when he walked his gait was somewhat stiffer and more awkward.

Arthur had removed his military coat and was buckling on a set of holsters over his shirt. It held six guns, three to each side, less auspiciously decorated than his captain's gun but still well made and clearly polished with care. He loaded the captain's pistol and tucked it into another holster at his hip. Then he pulled his faded coat back on and wrapped a heavy scarf around his neck, stuffing it down the front of the coat to help conceal the guns beneath.

Janna looked around at her new companions with distaste. "They'll have to be good. We look like everything *but* dockworkers."

Paul translated for Maria and she laughed, signing something back. "We've been in this business long enough and Maria is extremely handy; she can forge most Odolian documents," Paul said jovially. "The baron's own officials never churned out better." He took four slips of paper from Maria, who had produced them from a sewing case she was stowing in one of the toolboxes. "Here you go. Four tailormade work passes."

Janna snatched the papers from Paul and scanned them quickly. He wasn't wrong; they were perfect imitations of regular dock workers' passes, each matching their profiles precisely enough that no eyebrows should be raised. The names were fake, but plausible. Even her own description was spot on. "Brown hair, gray eyes, twenty-seven years old..." *Do I really look that old?* Then something occurred to her. The papers crumpled in her hand and she rounded on Arthur, who had begun to roll up the bedmats and stack them back in the corner. "This is me!" She waved the offending slip of paper. "How long have you had this? Maria wasn't scribbling these out last night. How long? How long have you known who I am?"

Arthur walked over and gently pried the permits out of Janna's grip. He studied them himself, stopping at Janna's. "Paul, tell Maria she forgot something on Miss Tulli's permit."

"What?" Paul said, bewildered and Janna echoed him.

"Under 'other distinguishing features' it should say 'ungrateful, difficult to work with, and refuses to acknowledge authority.'" His expression was infuriatingly blank. Janna snatched her permit back and stuffed it into the back pocket of her trousers, balling her hands into fists. If her own circumstances hadn't been so desperate, she would have punched him then and there.

"Listen," she snapped, "Enough with the 'Miss Tulli' stuff and we can call it even. And I still want to know when you started scoping me out."

Arthur glanced askance at Paul, who nodded, picking up the conversation without missing a beat as his captain went back to straightening up the apartment. "We really ran into you on accident. It was a while back, a couple of months I'd say. We were celebrating at a pub. Forget which one now...McMacy's? Gregor's...?" Paul trailed off, still signing his wandering thoughts until he was cut off by Maria, who elbowed him sharply in the ribs. "Sorry, we were celebrating the destruction of the undercity garrison, and saw you at the bar. Arthur pointed you out to us."

"And you've been stalking me ever since. What a comforting thought." Janna blinked in realization. "Wait. That was *you*? You were the rebels who- They arrested and executed ten men and two women for that attack, most of them from Karlsban..." *Like me.* "And they were innocent! But of course the baron needed his scapegoat."

Paul's face soured and he seemed to shrink in on himself, withdrawing from the conversation. Arthur, however, broke in angrily. "Not all of them were innocent. Besides, Commander Gracyn was responsible for countless abuses across the city. The people feared him and Baron Schulhard never held him accountable. We took it upon ourselves to correct his oversight."

Janna groaned. "No one liked him, including myself. But you know what people like less? Incendiary bastards like you causing innocent people to be sent to the gallows! I think I'm owed more of an explanation than what you gave me last night on the street. Just *what* are you planning to do with this ship?"

"I owe you less than you'll get at the end of this," Arthur barked. "You've made it clear that you're no member of my crew and our goals are privileged information. Be content with your fee and your freedom and leave well enough alone."

Janna scowled but said nothing.

Frowning pensively, Paul pulled out his watch again. "And now it's time we left. I'll-" He chuckled. "Ha, never mind, I don't think any of us will miss this old place." Maria gave a bark of laughter, too loud in the tense silence. Paul rubbed her shoulder affectionately.

Scowling, Janna checked her pistol and quickly hefted one of the toolboxes into her arms. "And I'll be twice as content if I never see any of you again after the job's done."

The undercity, subdued at night by curfew and patrols of militia, was just beginning to awaken as they stepped outside. The earliest workers collected rubbish from the streets and extinguished the gas lamps on street corners, flashing their permits to passersby as though to prove the legitimacy of their business. A few workers dared to break curfew five minutes early, hoping to get a good place on the lift. Unskilled jobs were first come, first serve, and in ten minutes the streets would be a bustling madhouse as laborers made their way to the docks or factories. The markets and shops still had another two hours until they would open to the public, and it was said that those in the upper city did not even stir until noon.

It had evidently rained again in the night; the cobblestone streets were pocked with oily puddles that shimmered in iridescent colors. Janna watched her feet, careful not to step in any of the small pools. They joined the flow of ragtag laborers straggling from their apartments and townhouses, all heading towards the nearest lift.

As she brought up the rear of the group, Janna noticed that Paul and Maria were constantly signing to one another, deep in some silent conversation. She watched bemusedly from behind, observing with interest that whenever Paul pointed out Arthur, Maria seemed to clench her fist angrily and swing it downward, as though she would have liked to punch him. When they reached a break in the conversation, Janna shuffled up beside Paul and nudged him in the shoulder.

"What were you two talking about?" she asked.

"Oh, Maria has some reservations about the plan," Paul said, doing his best to give her a friendly smile. "It isn't clear to me either, but I'm willing to go along with it. I trust Arthur's judgment."

Janna snorted. "I wish *someone* here knew what we're supposed to be doing," she commented, nervously stroking the end of her long dark braid. "Anyway, she seems more than a little reserved. She kept shaking her fist...why are you laughing?"

Paul quickly stifled a chuckle. "Oh, she's not angry...not necessarily. That's just what she calls him; it's a nickname, of sorts," he added, lowering his voice so Arthur, who walked confidently ahead of them, couldn't hear. Slowly, he repeated the sign for her: clenched fist, swung downward from the elbow.

"Oh? Does she have a nickname for you?" Janna inquired, natural curiosity getting the better of her studied indifference.

"Of course. It's..." He held his first two fingers to his heart. "A bit more affectionate than Arthur's."

"Does she have one for me?" Janna asked, almost eagerly. She felt all the thrill of being inducted into some fascinating secret society. This time, Paul really did struggle to contain his laughter, and if Maria hadn't been on the lookout, he would have splashed straight into a puddle. She barely steered him in the right direction and glared at Janna as though it was her fault. "What's so funny?" Janna snapped.

"Oh, it's just that I wouldn't like to sign yours in polite company," Paul said at last, finally getting a handle on himself. He tried to give her an empathetic smile but it was laced with suppressed mirth. Janna huffed in annoyance, falling back to the rear of the party without another word.

They were in the queue for the lift almost before Janna realized, and her stomach sank as she surveyed the rickety structure. The lift was a simple wooden platform encased by a metal cage, drawn up by a series of gears and chains to the middle level of the city. The seventy-five foot journey into the air made Janna uncomfortable every time she took it. The line to the booth in front of the lift gate was mercifully short, however. With only a handful of workers in front, Janna was sure they'd be able to take the first trip up and get comfortable spots on the carry trains to the skydocks. Better yet, the man at the booth seemed to be waving everyone by without so much as a second glance.

Janna looked behind her and desperately tried not to stare at the militia kiosk a hundred paces down the road. Two men in scarlet and blue uniforms were lounging against the wall with muskets slung over their shoulders, chatting and watching the swelling crowd of workers with languid gazes. She ducked her head as their eyes passed over her.

Arthur was the first of their party to reach the booth. He gave a stiff reply when the man in the booth asked a question, but Janna could not hear the words over the rumble of waking machinery. Scowling, Arthur indicated Paul, Maria, and Janna, stepping back so that the man could get a good look at them. The man in the booth was scrawny, with a bushy gray mustache that completely hid his upper lip. His narrow eyes scanned the group, and though his face at first appeared meek, there was a shrewd bent to his expression as he turned back to Arthur.

"Passes," Paul hissed, holding out his hand. Janna handed him the papers and hopped nervously from foot to foot as the man in the booth pulled out a pair of wire spectacles and placed them firmly on his thin little nose. He examined the passes with an austere eye, clearly expectant. Arthur reached into his pouch and pulled out a coin, sliding it onto the booth desk where it was quickly palmed by the man. Janna looked back at the kiosk. The men were still absorbed in their conversation. One of them had pulled out a pipe and was smoking serenely.

The man in the booth handed the passes back to Arthur with a weasley smile and waved them on. Arthur, Paul, and Maria passed by without issue, and Janna was about to do the same when the man caught sight of her.

This same man had been at the booth countless times before, Janna realized. Though she hadn't paid attention to him before, she saw by the expression on his face that the man *had* paid attention to *her*. Peering inside the booth, she saw a poster with the latest sketches from the garrison, showing a number of miscreants and villains not permitted under any circumstances to ride the lift. To her horror, Janna recognized her own face, grim and slightly smudgy, but undeniably hers, in the bottom left corner.

"I know you," the man said slowly. With the press of a button, the gate closed. The lift gears began to turn. Janna saw Paul begin to step toward her, but Arthur stuck out an arm in front of him, blocking his way. She watched as her companions were pulled up away from the ground, leaving her stranded.

"You were here yesterday too," the man in the booth said. He was leaning forward, almost out of the booth, his bony arms pressed flat against the desk as he peered at her.

"No, I think you're mistaken," Janna said stiffly. The lift seemed slower than normal. "It's my first day, and now you've separated me from my captain."

"Him? Captain?" The man scoffed. "No captain is ever up this time of morning. First ships don't leave for another couple hours."

Janna cringed. She had to keep talking. The lift was taking forever, though by the station clock she knew it had only been a minute. The men in the growing queue behind her were beginning to grumble and press forward. She kept her eyes fixed, knowing a guilty glance at the militia kiosk would add yet another piece of damning evidence to the pile.

"He will be very cross if I am kept from the first train," she said at last.

"And I'd be cross if I lost my position," the man in the booth said curtly. "Why don't I just wire down to headquarters and check your credentials." He pushed away from the desk at last and spun round in his chair to face the switchboard of a small telegraph machine. Pulling on a headset, he began to tap out a message.

As the lift began its slow return descent, empty now of passengers, Janna sucked in a deep breath and reached into her coin purse. The tapping of the telegraph ceased expectantly. She fumbled around for a second, her fingers finding only a few copper dul before they latched onto a coin that seemed big enough to make an impact on the man. She ripped it out and practically slammed it on the counter.

"Would this reimburse you for letting me through?" She pulled her hand back and saw the talent that Arthur had given her lying on the counter. The man in the booth gasped, as did the worker breathing down her neck.

The man in the booth made the talent disappear into his pocket with a single swift motion. "I've never seen you, and that's a fact," he said, looking up at her meekly over his wire-rimmed spectacles. The lift gate rolled back with a clatter and Janna stepped through, her hand going quickly to the flask in her pocket. As she took a hearty swig, she couldn't help but feel a little bitter about the loss of the talent and the fact that she'd drunk away the rest of her money the night before.

Laborers packed the lift like sardines, pressing in around her, and Janna grit her teeth, hoping they wouldn't exceed the weight limit. As the lift rose jerkily into the air on its chains and pulleys, she looked out at the booth. She could no longer see the little man from this angle, but as the ground beneath her sank away, she caught movement at the militia kiosk down the road. One of the guards was heading towards the booth, but before Janna could see what was happening, the lift shuddered to a halt and the second gate slid open behind her.

As workers swarmed out into the middle city, jostling her in their haste, she turned and couldn't help but smile with relief when she saw Paul, Maria, and Arthur himself standing on the platform waiting.

"What happened?" Arthur snapped, but Janna shook her head, passing them by without waiting to see if they would follow.

"Let's get a move on," was all she said.

The middle city was still fast asleep, save for the snake of workers winding their way through the streets, passing shops with carefully maintained displays showing goods none of them would ever be able to afford. Janna looked at them, as she had every day for the past three years, and felt a sudden strange melancholy wash over her. *I'll never see this place again, will I?*

She had wondered time and again if she would ever be able to go into one of the shops and simply buy something with her own hard earned money. Some of the stylish gloves and coats and hats were beautiful to look at, and though she didn't have much time for such things, Janna found herself envying those who did. Even if she ever made enough money, she would always have the fear of recognition dogging her every step, nipping at her heels. Perhaps now there was no longer a viable path to freedom open to her. Perhaps she had lost her chance.

They came to one of the rail depots which made a ring around the middle city, rails shooting out in all directions like an elaborate, elevated spiderweb encircling Gorand. Janna, Paul, Maria, and Arthur were herded into a boxcar with fifty or so other workers, where they stood crammed shoulder to shoulder as the train pulled slowly out of the depot.

Janna stood silently gazing out of the boxcar's open door as the train made its way over the trestle towards the skydocks. She saw the city expand under her feet, huge buildings and smokestacks reaching up out of the thick layer of smog. It was a city she hoped she would never have the misfortune of seeing again.

Stepping closer to Arthur, Janna crossed her arms, trying not to come into contact with any of the other occupants of the train. In the nearest corner, Paul and Maria huddled together, leaning against the grimy slats of the car, having one of their endless silent conversations. Paul smiled at something Maria said and signed something back, earning an equally warm response.

"So what's their deal?" Janna asked, nodding towards the couple. She kept her voice low so that it would not seem too loud and out of place in the crowded car. There were a few rowdy men in one corner, but most kept their heads down and their mouths shut, lost in their own troubles.

"How do you mean?" Arthur responded, seemingly shaken out of his own thoughts.

"I mean, are they courting, or what?"

Arthur smiled. It was a strange expression to see on his granite face, but Janna found it oddly comforting in their bleak surroundings. "I married them about five years back. One of the few joys I had as captain on the *Formidable*, performing marriages." As the train came to a halt at the skydock's station, Arthur's smile cooled, wryness replacing the warmth. "I'm sure Maria would rather tell you the details."

FIRST FLIGHT OF THE *HEART*

The skydocks of Gorand were unique; unlike other such structures across Odol, which were typically built a distance from the cities they served, they surrounded Gorand's central layer in an enormous ring. The outer edges were supported on massive towers of concrete and steel, while the inner portions were supported by a latticed network of trestles and scaffolding. The docks themselves were a maze of wooden walkways surrounding airship berths, not dissimilar to the seaport below, though these ships docked in the air rather than the water, resting in massive chain nets that cradled their hulls. In the spaces between piers, huge nets were suspended, intended to catch any falling airships or cargo and prevent them from raining upon the city below. The nets themselves were too open, however, to catch any unwary sailor or dockworker who might happen to fall.

Such incidents were rare, or so the officials said, but Janna had a healthy distrust of official statistics and minded her step as she paced the docks. She had positioned herself so that she could duck behind Paul or Arthur if any of the union guards happened to pass. It worked better in the predawn shadows left between the gas lamps that sporadically lit the walkways; in the pools of light she felt like a showgirl on stage with everyone's eyes on her. The workers were sparse at that time of day, but more were arriving on every train.

The task of finding an appropriate ship was not easy this day. Most of the ships docked were old stock, their hulls made of water stained wood which showed they'd originally been built for the sea and later upgraded for air travel. That's how it had begun: old ships of war were retrofitted with hot air balloons, engines, and propellors, and that had been enough to decimate the forces of Karlsban during the Twenty Years' War. Now, there were lighter, faster ships built expressly for flying, optimized for the job. Janna saw few such vessels today. Most of the stock was made up of old clippers and freight barges with patched balloons and scuffed sides.

"Do you see anything to my specifications?" Arthur murmured as they passed by a huge freighter, over a hundred feet long, which was already being loaded by a score of grim-faced laborers.

"Nothing which-" Janna began, and sucked in a breath as she saw two city militia marching down the docks towards them, their synchronized footfalls ringing loudly in her ears. Anxiously, Janna stepped forward into Arthur's shadow, putting him between her and the soldiers. Her eyes searched desperately for any unoccupied ship. The city militia never came to the skydocks unless there was trouble afoot; the dock union jealously guarded their jurisdiction. But it had been long enough since their departure from the lift that men could have been dispatched to follow them by one of the shuttle trains.

Janna's eyes snagged on a ship at the end of one of the docks. It was one of the smaller vessels, its half-inflated balloon draped heavily over the masts. It was a twenty-gunner, lean and narrow, with two decks, probably an old frigate from the war converted into a specialist merchant ship. The name emblazoned on the side in peeling paint was the *Worker's Chance*. It appeared inconspicuous among other much larger vessels, and unoccupied, which was even better.

"I think I just found one," she whispered to Arthur, jutting her chin to indicate the vessel. It took him a moment to spot it amongst the other ships and he turned back to give her an unconvinced grimace.

"Are you sure it's what we're looking for?"

"Positive," Janna lied. Though outwardly it appeared sound, she could not be sure of the state of the ship's mechanics from this vantage point. She'd worked on engines that could carry a ship stuffed stern to bow with lead and engines that could barely lift a bag of feathers.

Arthur signaled to Paul and Maria quietly, and the four of them wheeled towards the ship as though it had been their destination all along. The pier beside it was stacked with cargo crates as tall as Janna, and equally as wide. Janna noted the seals on the crates: Threadbury's Textiles. The work order tacked to the side was for a shipment of Odolian army uniforms. A small crane had been set up on the dock, but stood dormant without anyone to operate it.

"Start loading the ship," Janna hissed before starting up the gangplank. If they wanted to avoid the ire of the dock union, they would have to act the part of laborers. As she set foot on the deck, she became aware of the low grumble of the ship's water boiler somewhere beneath her and the soft hiss of hot air in the pipes. Staring upward, she realized that the balloon was now nearly inflated, spreading out in great folds of patchy white cloth as it slowly filled out the rigging. She turned around, mouth already open to warn the others, but Paul and Arthur were already half way up the gangplank with a crate between them.

"Hold on," she called, stepping forward, "There may be-"

Paul and Arthur dropped the crate on the deck with a loud *thud* and turned to face her, faces questioning.

"Why did you have to go and do that?" Janna snapped. "I was trying to tell you there may be someone aboard."

Arthur gave a start and for a single moment his self-assured demeanor dropped. "I thought you would choose an *unoccupied* ship!" His voice was carefully measured but Janna heard the hint of anger.

"I didn't... Well don't just stand there, let's-"

"Ay, what's goin' on here?" An unshaven man in overalls, a dock union emblem pinned proudly on one strap, came clambering up the steep stairs in the center of the deck. As soon as he saw the two men, he stepped back and wrested an unused belaying pin from a coil of rope lying over the bulwark, hefting it threateningly. "You ain't the lady's crew. They don't come on till later. That was agreed upon, an' I have my right to work..."

Arthur spread his hands in a soothing gesture, stepping closer to the man even as Janna backed away. "It's alright, you can stay down there and do your work while we load the crates up here."

The man shook his head, pointing the heavy wooden pin at Arthur. "If you don't stay off of this ship until nine of the a.m., I'll bash your heads, the lot of ya! Trying to steal my work. I have a contract ya know." He tapped the badge on his chest proudly.

"I'm sure you do," Arthur said calmly, even as he drew his hand back into a clenched fist and swiftly struck the man across the jaw. Pin and man went sprawling on the deck of the ship. Arthur stepped over the limp form of the worker and grabbed the pin, setting it back in place.

"There," he said, without a hint of feeling in his voice, "*Now* the ship is unoccupied. Paul, Maria, make ready for take off. I'll go down with Miss Tulli and see to the engine."

"No, you and Paul get to work loading the ship," Janna said stiffly, eyeing the unconscious man with distaste. "I'll do better unlocking the controls without you hovering over my shoulder, and they'll expect these boxes to be gone." She gestured broadly at the crates on the dock.

Arthur's mouth pressed together in a thin line and for a moment Janna thought he was going to yell at her, but he merely nodded stiffly. "As you will."

Not even pausing to acknowledge him, Janna scrambled down the steep staircase to the gundeck, noting that the wood was well worn, though polished. She tested the deck beneath her feet as she walked, pleased to find that the planks were solid. The engine room door at the stern was slightly ajar, and Janna slipped through, gasping when she saw the engine itself.

It was one of the most beautiful machines she had ever seen. A fine, polished furnace was glowing with a low orange fire, and two massive brass water tanks gleamed smartly in the light. The gauge on one indicated that steam pressure was rising rapidly. That tank was currently filling the balloon through a narrow lead pipe which snaked up into the ceiling overhead. The second tank, which drove the propellers, could not be heated unless the airship's main controls were unlocked. A key would do the trick, but without it, things would take a little more finesse. But the engine itself was a marvel, a twenty-four rate beauty, each piston and shaft oiled to perfection, each bolt torqued to just the right tension. It was in perfect condition and she couldn't remember when she'd seen an engine that looked faster. If the propellers were in good condition, they would have no trouble escaping.

"Is there a problem with the engine?"

Arthur's unexpected voice caused Janna to start.

"No, on the contrary-"

"Then get going on the controls. We haven't got all day." Arthur turned and made for the ship's ladder without so much as a glance at her.

Janna's mouth hung open and she stared in disbelief at his retreating back. "Well...well you're not loading the boxes either!" She huffed and stormed after him, climbing to the main deck, then making her way up the stairs to the helm, where she took a cursory look at the gearbox. It was just as good as the rest of the ship, and the levers seemed in working order. The locking mechanism was ingenious, though, installed by a master of the craft, with a hidden alarm system that would be devilish to avoid.

The merchants who owned most of the commercial ships on the dock were always careful with their control keys, but the captains who leased them out were, on many occasions, careless. Especially when they were drunk. Every couple of months, since she'd left the rebellion, she'd made it a habit to find such a captain who had lost their control key, and then charged an exorbitant amount of money to unlock the ship before the leaseholders found out. Sometimes they even came to *her*. Janna found it relatively easy, and since she took thrice the predicted time and made the job look twice as difficult as it really was, she could charge extra. Afterwards, she blew most of the money on booze or gambling. And then a few months later, when she got bored of working as a docks laborer, the cycle would repeat itself. It was risky, technically illegal, and, worse, frowned upon by the dock union. But those had been some of the few moments recently when she'd felt really alive.

She took a quick swig from her flask to steady her hands, watching bemusedly as Paul and Arthur struggled their way up the gangplank with another massive crate. *There's a crane right there*, she thought as she knelt down and began analyzing the maze of wafer-thin gears and delicate crankshafts. *But, of course, I doubt either of them know how to use one.* She slid her pick out of her boot and began the inexorable process of trying to open the various locks from the wrong angle and with the wrong tools. She only had one pick and that was typically enough. But this lady captain, whoever she was, kept her ship like no merchant Janna had ever met. *Probably a freelancer who owns her own ship...* A pang of guilt crept through Janna and she paused, though only for a moment as Arthur shouted up at her from the quarterdeck.

"It's been five minutes. How long, Miss Tulli?"

"You can't rush art, Pendington. This takes time!"

"Union," Paul said in a harsh whisper. Janna raised her head just enough to see a patrol of two union men pass by about fifty yards up the dock. The men never even glanced in their direction, but Paul and Arthur redoubled their efforts to load the ship. Maria had taken up a perch on a barrel in the middle of the deck and Janna was flabbergasted to see that she was knitting. The woman looked so purposefully unaware that she almost seemed part of the ship. But she caught Janna's eye and gave her a grim smile that told Janna that Maria was perfectly aware of everything going on around her.

Quickly, Janna wrenched her focus back to the task at hand. If she slipped up, the alarm system would alert the entire skydocks. Had that not been a concern, the task would have gone as quickly as Arthur demanded. As it was, she would have to take her time.

Ten minutes passed, then twenty. Janna was nearly finished with the fourth latch out of five when she felt a rapid tapping on her shoulder. Maria was standing over her, mouth set grimly, beckoning for Janna to follow.

"Not now," Janna grumbled, turning her attention back to her work. She had nearly slipped up and set off the alarm.

Again, Maria tugged on Janna's coat sleeve. Janna unhooked her pick from the latch and sat back, sinking four minutes of careful work in one movement. "Maria, I..." Janna groaned as she wracked her brain for some way to communicate with the woman across the language barrier, and finally stood up and shouted over the railing. "Paul! Could you get your wife to-"

It took her an instant to realize that the regular milling of workers and sailors on the dock had stopped. Men had clustered into small knots on either side of the boardwalk, making way for two squads of Gorand militia, led by a captain in a fine tricorn hat and a short, wiry man with a bushy gray mustache. Above the tramp of boots and the rumble of engines across the docks, Janna heard the nasally voice of the man from the booth: "There she is! The one at the controls. She's armed and dangerous..."

Cursing, Janna dropped back onto her knees to finish the job. There was no longer time for art; this was survival. She snapped the remaining latches in short order, destroying the lock and setting off every alarm in the machinery. Bells clanged from below and as if in response a shrill whistle rose from every dock union guard within earshot. Janna raised her head just enough to see the militia come to a halt beside the ship and begin readying their rifles. Paul dashed up the stairs and joined her and Maria on the deck.

"Stop what you're doing!" the militia captain barked. The man from the booth had vanished, though Janna was sure he must be hiding behind one of the many crates that remained stacked along the pier.

Arthur rushed up to join them at the helm, pistol in hand, placing himself between Janna and the soldiers below. He fired and his shot was returned at once with a volley from the muskets, splintering the railing of the deck. Paul, Maria, and Janna all fell prone, but Arthur stood proudly and pulled out another pistol from his holsters, firing it down into the squadron. A cry, the voice of the captain, rose above the din, as the second squadron fired off another round.

Janna watched in awe as Maria scrambled to her feet, drawing a pair of knives from her belt and rushing to stand beside Arthur. Paul crawled over to the controls and tapped her on the shoulder. "Is it unlocked?"

Janna nodded hastily, fumbling for her hidden pistol as Arthur fired again. They had only nine shots between them, and there were over a dozen men on the dock below, with more likely on the way. "The boiler has five minutes yet!" she whispered loudly as she rose into a crouch.

Paul's response was inaudible over another volley of musket shots.

"What?" Janna shouted, but Paul was already pulling at levers, checking gauges, and eyeing the sails on the side of the hull as they unfurled. The starboard sail opened fully with a crisp snap of canvas, but the portside sail stuck halfway.

"Miss Tulli, get that sail!" Arthur barked. Four smoking pistols lay at his feet and he was aiming carefully with a fifth. Six bodies, including the captain, lay strewn on the docks, and the remaining militia had taken cover behind the cargo crates on the boardwalk. Janna scrambled down the steps to the quarterdeck, nearly bent double in an effort to avoid becoming their next target. It was the most pressure she'd been under since her days in the rebellion and the sound of boots running up the boardwalk towards them did nothing to help. Reinforcements had arrived and if they weren't airborne soon, she didn't think there was much chance of them making it out alive.

Arthur fired again, scattering the score of newly-arrived militia across the dock as they sought cover. He still stood erect, completely unphased though he made a clear target.

"Haste, *haste* Miss Tulli! Get that sail or you'll get a fine beating once we're in the air."

Arthur's bellowing was met with a *snap* as the catch in the rigging came loose without so much as a touch from Janna. The sail unfurled and the ship quivered as it lifted slightly off the suspended chains. Paul was pouring hot air into the balloon at full throttle and it hung droopily over their heads, full enough now to give just enough lift. Rising to his feet, Paul pulled a lever with all his might. The engine roared, the propeller whirled, and the ship lurched forward towards the city.

Janna's heart leapt but her whoop of excitement was interrupted as the ship jerked to a halt, tethered to the pier by a single rope on the port bow. The entire deck tilted and as Janna clung to the railing she saw the form of the unconscious dock worker collapse forward onto the deck from behind one of the crates. He slid across the planks toward the gap in the railing where the gangplank had lain. In another moment, he was over the side.

"Cut that rope, dammit!" Arthur barked from his position on the steering deck.

Janna dragged herself across the tilted deck to the bow, pulled out her work knife, and began hacking at the thick hemp. It was pulled taught by the force of the ship's lift and the individual strands were parted easily enough by her blade, but the rope itself was nearly as thick as Janna's wrist. As she sawed desperately, the remaining soldiers began to regroup, drawing up in three rows so that they could fire on the ship in a continuous volley. She redoubled her efforts as the first row raised their muskets to fire, and was rewarded as the fraying rope finally snapped beneath her fingers. The ship whipped back, flinging her to her knees as it shot into the air.

Arthur fired his last gun as they soared away from the skydocks, though it was impossible to tell whether he hit anything. Janna's fingers found her own pistol tucked beneath the hip pad of her corset and she pulled it out, dragging herself upright against the railing and scanning the docks below. The remaining guards were firing wildly at them, their bullets striking the underside of the ship uselessly as it passed overhead.

Janna spotted the man from the booth as he scampered away down the boardwalk, his royal blue uniform standing out against the dull planks. She took aim carefully, gnawing her tongue as she steadied her hand. Arthur and Maria were not going to be the only ones who got a shot off.

It was new, killing. She hadn't done it before, not in all her time with her father. But in that moment the burning desire for revenge welled up in her gut, compelling her. She pulled the trigger, but a rattling from below shook the deck and she was jarred against the railing as the gun fired. Groaning, she righted herself again, but the dwindling docks obscured the fruit of her action.

Her hand shook and she tossed the pistol away in disgust. The burning hatred for the man who had singled her out, who had almost cost her her freedom, turned to hot shame in her stomach. She had hated him, but though she had stood by her father and seen men cruelly tortured and killed, she felt that this hatred was different. She wasn't sure she would ever want to hold a gun again.

The hull trembled once more, pulling Janna back into her dire situation. She raised her eyes and realized that their altitude had dropped significantly. The ship was careening straight for the lower city. She saw the flash of a sentry tower and felt the ship rock again as a cannonball struck the hull broadside. They were gaining speed as they dropped, passing in and out of the smog that choked the lower city. The sentry towers seemed to fire at random; she saw flashes here and there amidst the smoke but many of the shots went wide. Maria was busy stuffing a ramrod into one of the six-pound cannons on the quarterdeck as Paul stood grim-faced at the helm, his hands steady on the controls.

The roaring in her ears subsided and she realized that Arthur was screaming at her above the rush of the wind.

"Miss Tulli, get that rope. The balloon is loose!"

She saw at once that he was right; the starboard anchor point for the balloon rigging had been smashed by one of the cannonballs. Factory smokestacks and spires of buildings rose up around them as Paul navigated deftly despite their falling altitude, threading a difficult path as they passed into the shadow of the undercity. Janna crossed the deck and leapt for the rope, the weight of her body pulling it down just enough that she could wrap her legs around the railing below, anchoring her to the deck once again. The integrity of the bulwark had been compromised by a cannonball shot, and she hoped that her desperate ploy would not send her careening through. Though if she didn't manage to retie this tether, she wouldn't have to worry long about heights.

The sentry towers continued their volley, but at this altitude they had little hope of landing a shot. Instead of the sound of splintering wood, explosions of metal, brick, and concrete cut the dawn as the cannonballs struck the sides of factories and apartment buildings. Janna laughed in spite of herself. *They're firing on their own city!*

Struggling to get the right amount of tension, and fighting the ship itself, Janna managed to pull the rope in and tie it around a post on the railing, burning her fingers and blistering her palm. Cursing again, she spit on her hands in an attempt to relieve the rope burns.

Another blast, louder than any that had preceded it, shook Janna to her core, and she turned to see Maria and Arthur returning fire with the ship's cannons, though they had no chance of hitting a sentry tower at this distance.

"You're wasting your time, Arthur!" Janna shouted, starting up the deck towards him. She looked to Paul for help, but his gaze was fixed over the bow of the ship and she didn't know if he could even hear her above the cannon fire and the roar of the wind. Arthur ignored Janna entirely, rushing past her to reload the cannons that Maria had fired off. The ship lurched again as Paul swerved to avoid the smokestacks of a factory complex. Janna wrapped her arms desperately around a rail post, tightening her grip as the ship was rocked once more by a heavy cannonball strike. Once she was sure of her footing, she abandoned Arthur and Maria on the deck and climbed to join Paul at the helm.

"Paul!" she shouted desperately, "Are we going to make it out of here?"

"Almost there, we're gaining altitude," Paul said, and pulled a lever. Janna looked toward the bow of the ship as they picked up speed, breaking through the clouds of smog into the cold, still morning air. They were headed south, the sea a smear of hazy green to their left. Beyond the city wall, Janna could see the trash heaps spreading out ahead of them, ending abruptly in the flat expanse of the Wastes. The land was crisscrossed by a web of rails, including the massive Veturi line, which traced over the horizon and out of sight. In the early morning sun, beyond the fog of the city, the flat expanse seemed starkly beautiful, though it was mostly featureless but for a few dry riverbeds making seams in the gray earth. Janna felt something twist inside her chest. She was getting out, leaving Gorand at last. She was almost free.

There was an enormous, grating *crunch* of wood and metal, and the ship shuddered beneath Janna's feet as if in pain. Arthur stopped in his mad rush between cannons and swore. He turned around and scrambled below deck with Janna close behind, cursing under her breath all the way.

"I'm losing altitude," Paul called from above. "See what's loose!"

Janna threw open the door to the engine room and clapped a hand over her mouth. The final cannonball had struck the engine room directly, blowing most of the machinery out the opposite side. Mangled pieces of metal reached like grasping hands, all twisted towards the left side of the room, where the ball had exited, bearing the bulk of the engine with it. The water tanks were merely dented, but without an engine that point was moot. Wind gushed through the holes in the hull, sucking air from Janna's lungs. She turned to Arthur, tears stinging in her eyes, but his expression was as flat and stoic as it had ever been.

"See what you can do," he said in a much too calm voice. "I'm going to tell Paul to prepare for a crash landing." He ran back up the stairs, leaving her alone with the damage.

Speechless, she shook her head and meandered towards the center of the room, where she sat down amidst the metal carnage. The wind whipped her braid and stung her cheeks. There was nothing she could do now. The adrenaline which had kept her going drained out of her, leaving her limp and hopeless. Pain she hadn't noticed before wracked her body. The air streaming through the hull grew warmer as the ship plummeted toward the ground at a steady pace, though much slower than Janna would have expected. *Paul must be doing his utmost. Shame, we were nearly there...*

The ship jolted again, throwing Janna into the air. Her head slammed against the deck above and everything went black.

LOYALTY

Stiffly, Janna rolled over. Her head was cushioned on a wad of red cloth: the scarlet wool of an imperial uniform. Raising her eyes, she saw a bent piece of sheet metal hanging haphazardly over her head like a kind of awning. A tiny piece of yellow-gray sky was visible through a rust hole. Sitting up with a start, she looked around, her heart sinking as she took in her surroundings.

Heaps of junk, twice or three times as tall as a man, surrounded her on all sides; scraps of unwanted metal, leftover bricks, bits of machinery, and tattered cloth mortared together with rotting food and other refuse. She was in the Wreckage, the dumping ground immediately outside of Gorand, where only the city's rubbish collectors dared to venture. The sheer wastefulness of it crashed over Janna as she took in the heaps of unopened canned food, the piles of sound building materials, the lengths of fabric and sail cloth ruined by the wind and rain and filth of the place. She felt a rush of disgust, the same sort she'd felt as a partisan years ago, when her father had led her, scoffing, through the house of a rich man, ridiculing his wasteful self-indulgence. That had been before her father slit the man's throat and used his blood to paint rebellious slogans on the fine wallpaper.

Her lean-to had been set up intentionally, with two stacks of bricks supporting the bent and curling sheet metal roof. A bed of sorts had been made out of more imperial uniforms and her arms had been bandaged carefully with strips of the red cloth. A few feet from her, a small fire crackled on a circle of bare gray earth. The sun could not be seen from her vantage point, but it seemed to be setting, turning the clouds orange-red and making it look as though some of the mounds were glowing from the inside.

Maria sat near the fire with her back to Janna, stirring a pot. Janna's stomach growled when she caught its scent and she opened her mouth to speak, but the words caught in her throat. It would be foolish trying to talk to her out loud. She did one more scan of her limited vantage point but neither Paul nor Arthur were anywhere to be seen.

Janna sighed to herself and cast around for something to throw. Her eyes lighted upon a heap of small stones and she snatched them up, tossing them in Maria's direction. She hadn't meant to hit the woman, merely to get her attention, but one struck Maria in the back of the head. With a loud cry, Maria whipped around, scowling at Janna for a moment before her hands flew in a series of incomprehensible signs. Finally, she spread her hands and gestured firmly at Janna's legs.

"Look, I'm sorry, I don't even know..." Janna groaned. "Where's Paul? Or Arthur?" She tried making some vague descriptive motions, raising her hand above her head to indicate the taller men.

Maria stopped signing, though her glare did not abate. With a blunt move of her broad hand, she pointed behind Janna to a large mass about fifty yards away, which was difficult to distinguish in the dusking light. Turning her head, Janna squinted and realized that it was the hull of a ship, half buried in a heap, the deflated balloon draped over top and camouflaging it with the rest of the rubbish.

"Alright, that's the ship. Are the men there?" she asked. Maria only gave a loud puff and went back to tending her soup. *Fine,* Janna thought, *I'll just go get them myself. Maybe* they'll *tell me what happened.*

She got halfway to her feet before red hot pain lanced through her left calf, causing her to stagger. Clutching at her leg, she collapsed onto her side on the packed earth, groaning as spots blurred her vision. In all her years of dangerous work, whether as a partisan, rebel, or mechanic, she had never been in such pain as this. Inhaling sharply through gritted teeth, she looked down and saw that the leg of her trousers had been torn off below the knee. A bandage, red imperial cloth, had been wrapped tightly around her calf and bore stains of darker crimson on either side of her leg. The pain seemed to redouble as she pulled the cloth back, revealing the angry red wounds. A row of neat stitching had pulled out with her movement.

Looking helplessly toward the campfire, Janna was relieved to see that Maria was hurrying towards her, waving her hands for Janna to stay still. Maria knelt down by her and made a few sharp signs before one very emphatic sign when she saw the state of Janna's stitches. Scowling even deeper than before, Maria produced a needle and thread from a pouch at her belt. She licked the end of the thread and pushed it through the needle's eye in one deft, practiced movement. Unceremoniously grabbing Janna's leg, she began to sew the wound closed again.

Swearing, Janna clenched one fist and dug her other hand into her pockets, searching for her flask. She pulled it out and saw that a lead musket ball had embedded itself in the tin. She unscrewed the lid with her teeth and shook it, hoping there were even a few drops left, but nothing so much as wet her tongue. Seething, she threw the flask over Maria's shoulder into a pile of mangled cans, fighting the urge to cry out as the needle whipped in and out of her raw skin.

"Will you *please* be more caref-" Her words were cut off with an oath as Maria gave one last tug on the thread. Satisfied, she tied off the last stitch, snipping the remaining thread with a pair of tiny tailor's scissors. Gingerly, Janna pulled her leg away from the woman and propped herself up on one elbow, wiping sweat off her face with the back of her hand.

"Alright, now can you tell me where Paul is?" She tried to annunciate, hoping Maria could read her lips. Maria shrugged and pointed behind Janna in the direction of the crashed ship.

Janna rolled her eyes. "Well I can't get there now, seeing as I can't even move without those damn stitches coming undone. So can you go *get* Paul? Please?" Her voice rose to a shout, echoing off of the heaps that surrounded them.

Maria looked up over Janna's shoulder and began signing, her hands making each shape firmly and slowly, as though she was communicating with a small child.

"'If you'd have only looked behind you, I was trying to tell you that Paul is right there.'" Paul's mellow voice broke the silence, startling Janna. She turned her head in time to see him step into the glow of the campfire. The light was fading fast now, wrapping them in the chilly darkness of twilight. "She said some more, but I've told her that I won't use that kind of language, especially not with a lady." He came to Janna's side and crouched beside her. Maria crossed her arms in irritation.

Taking a few deep breaths, Janna managed to compose herself. "Sorry," she said, struggling to keep her tone even, "I just wanted to know what happened. I apologize if I'm a little tense, under the circumstances."

"Impatient, more like." Paul frowned. "If you wanted to know what happened, you could have waited. And, according to Maria, you threw something at her. It's unwise to bite the hand that stitches you up." He chuckled as though it was funny. "And just for future reference, she can read lips."

Janna closed her eyes and nodded, feeling her anger ebb, only to be replaced by exhaustion and the dull ache in her leg. Paul was a calming presence, soothing her frayed nerves. "What happened while I was out? I remember the engine being wrecked, but that's it."

Paul exchanged a few signs with Maria, who finally stood up and went back to tend to her pot. He turned to Janna and offered his hand. "Let me help you up."

Janna waved him away. "No thanks, I think I'll stay here a while." She shifted her leg and settled back against the ground, staring up at the dark hazy sky. "So what's the story?"

"Well, we were sitting ducks without the engine, so the captain told us to drop." Paul pulled up a rusty tin bucket, flipped it upside down, and settled himself. If he was sitting in an overstuffed armchair by the fireplace, he couldn't have looked more at home. "It was a bold move, but he was always one for the theatrical. I barely managed to crash us without killing everyone, but as soon as we hit the ground Arthur got down and started lugging a barrel of gunpowder south as fast as he could. I thought he was crazy, but I helped him rig up a good show. The patrol that flew over must have thought we had met a fiery death, which was his intention. They'll leave us alone now."

Maria, who had been observing Paul out of the corner of her eye, huffed and signed something at him. Paul laughed and shook his head. "No, we aren't better off dead! Arthur has things under control. Odol thinks we're dead—twice dead, in fact, so we don't have to worry about search parties."

"But we aren't dead," Janna observed, "which means you're a good pilot." She wanted to thank him, but pride, and guilt over her outburst, caught the words in her throat. She hoped that her admission of his skill was enough.

"Being good at what you do is necessary when Arthur Pendington is your captain." Paul beamed as he rose to his feet. "I'll help you walk. Maria says food is almost ready. I know from experience that getting shot is hungry work. I'm famished too." This time, Janna took his offered arm and got carefully to her feet.

Closer up, she saw that he looked pale, even in the orange firelight, and a few cuts and bruises marked his cheerful face.

Maria's expression was less pleasant, but she forced a smile and propped a sturdy length of pipe under Janna's other arm to serve as a crutch. With some effort, Janna made it over to the fire. More rolls of imperial uniforms were set around as cushions and Janna slumped down onto one gratefully.

"'It isn't that bad,'" Paul said, translating for Maria. "'Your leg, I mean. The bullet just passed through your skin. You should be thankful. It could have been far worse. If you keep off it for a few days, it should heal right up and I could get those stitches out.'"

"I'd be much better with a shot of something for the pain. Any of that bourbon left?" Janna asked hopefully. Paul shook his head as Maria ladled out three bowls of stewed vegetables and rice. "Damn," Janna grumbled. "Was the captain hiding anything in her cabin?"

Paul laughed. "She's probably a teetotaler by the look of things. Not a drop on the ship. Not even a bit of cider."

Janna mumbled a curse just as Maria pressed a bowl unceremoniously into her hands and sat down beside Paul. Janna's mouth began to water at once and she shoveled a spoonful into her mouth right away, wincing as it burned her tongue. Looking up, she saw that Paul and Maria had paused with their hands folded and their eyes closed. Maria's lips moved slightly as she bent her head, but she made no sound. After a moment, they opened their eyes and began to eat.

A stifling silence hung over the little campsite. Janna realized that she hadn't heard real silence in years, not since she'd lived in the city. Really, not since she'd lived in Odol. Now, it felt unsettling. She wracked her brains for something to strike up the conversation once more. "So, what's your story anyways?"

"What do you mean?" Paul asked absently between bites.

"I mean to say, how did two reasonable people like yourselves end up with, well, *him.*" She looked around nervously. Arthur was still nowhere to be seen.

"Oh that." Paul managed a smile while chewing. "Best finish eating first. Maria will want to participate in this conversation. I'm sure she has some thoughts on the subject."

When they'd all had their fill, Janna handed her bowl to Maria, who collected up all three and put them into a washbasin. Gray smoke from the campfire trailed up into the ochre sky. The glow of Gorand was visible in the north, blocking out the stars and lending the sky its hue. Janna stared up, her eyes searching hopelessly. She hadn't seen the stars since she'd moved to the city, and rarely a fitful, distant moon.

Paul and Maria tidied up the campsite, communicating silently with their quick hand gestures between tasks, their silent conversation punctuated now and then by soft chuckling from Paul or a short barking laugh from Maria. Janna had to guess from their mannerisms that they were flirting. Finally, the two finished their domestic duties and sat down with her around the campfire. It was growing colder and Paul warmed his hands briefly over the flames. Maria pulled out her bundle of knitting.

"Arthur said we shouldn't have a fire," Paul explained, signing the conversation for his wife's benefit. "I disagree, though. The benefits of a hot meal and some warmth are worth the risk of someone seeing the smoke, after what we've been through. And I doubt anyone could find us out here."

"Agreed," Janna said, shivering and shifting closer to the heat. "So, why did you join with Arthur?"

Maria, who had apparently been following Paul's translation even as she knitted, laughed loudly, startling Janna. She put down her needles and began signing. "'Oh, I was dragged along by this oaf.'" She pointed emphatically to Paul as he translated. "'He went willingly.' Which is true, I did," Paul added. "I've known Arthur for most of his life. In the navy, I served under Captain Lord Pendington, Arthur's father. I rose to the rank of quartermaster and when Lord Pendington retired he took me back to his estate as a servant. Arthur would have been just a lad then.

"I continued my nautical studies and kept up with the development of the new airships. Arthur came of age and was expected to take over for his father during the twenty-years war, after Lord Pendington died. When Arthur got his own ship, he took me on as quartermaster, but I proved myself to be a good helmsman, so I was moved there. I was good enough that when Arthur was made captain of the *Formidable*, I joined him on the bridge as chief navigator. I'd follow him anywhere."

"But he treats you so poorly!" Janna cried. "Why on earth do you put up with him? Call him captain and lord and all that nonsense?"

"It's what he is," Paul said, shrugging.

"Well, glad to see someone is keeping the feudal spirit alive," Janna mumbled sarcastically.

Paul gave a patient smile. "You don't understand, Miss Tulli. Despite himself he is my friend. For his sake I won't delve too deep. He may tell you someday, but he was a different person before what happened..."

"What happened with the *Formidable*? At this point, I just assumed he snapped under the pressure," Janna said bitingly. "I mean, firebombing civilians must have done a number on his psyche."

Paul sighed. "Again, I won't give you details; that is something for Arthur to give in his own time. But I will say that he stopped believing in *why* he was firebombing civilians. I was glad when he gave it up, but..." He hesitated and Maria gave a disdainful look. "After he crashed the *Formidable* and escaped, he became a vengeful man. There were about a dozen of us..." Maria signed something and Paul nodded. "Sorry, thirteen of us to be precise. Including Arthur."

"A nice baker's dozen. What happened to the rest of them?"

"Four starved. You know that the *Formidable* went down miles from civilization."

"That leaves six unaccounted for. Must have been miserable."

"It was. I think, more than anything, *that* put a massive chip on Arthur's shoulder. It gave him a pretty substantial vendetta against Odol." Paul sighed again. "One of them...Clemen. He left as soon as we got back to Bolden."

"Five more."

"We couldn't stay in Bolden. Arthur's estate had been confiscated by the crown and there was too great a chance he could be recognized. So we left two men there and went to Gorand. The other three got killed during one of our missions against Baron Schulhard. Of all the Odolian leadership, I think Arthur hates the baron the most."

"I can't blame him," Janna said. "I haven't had the misfortune of meeting the Bloody Baron in person, but I know even red-blooded Odolian patriots dislike him."

"He only got the barony because of the dreadnought he captains, the *Redoubtable*. Arthur has had a plan for a while to destroy it, and-"

Janna cut him off with a snort of derisive laughter. "That's madness. Unless you're in command of one of those monsters, I don't see a way to destroy them. The hulls are impenetrable and the guns would blast any meager opposition out of the sky. I was in Karlsban when they came. I know."

Paul shook his head. "I trust the captain has a plan."

"That makes one of us," Janna said sourly. "Two, if Maria joins in with you, which I doubt." For the first time since they'd met the night before, Maria gave Janna a knowing, appreciative nod after seeing Paul's translation.

Paul sighed. "Regardless, we won't do any good discussing it behind Arthur's back. It's getting late. Why don't you get some sleep and rest that leg of yours?"

Janna didn't want to admit that he was right. She wanted answers but her aching body said those could wait. Reluctantly, she let Paul help her over to her makeshift bed mat beneath the metal canopy. Shifting gingerly with her wounded leg, she made herself as comfortable as she could, pulling her coat up to her chin against the chill. *Whatever Arthur is planning doesn't concern me anyways. As soon as we reach Bolden, I'm gone.*

FALL OUT

Janna awoke to the smell of sizzling bacon and the greasy popping sound of frying eggs. As she blinked the sleep from her eyes, another harsher noise startled her. Maria was sharpening her throwing knives as she sat by the fire, filling the morning air with the rough scrape of metal on metal.

"Well, that's pleasant to wake up to," Janna grumbled, rubbing a sore spot on her back. Her entire body ached, her spine was stiff, and the wound on her leg throbbed with a dull pain. "It'd be nice if Paul were here, or even Arthur," she muttered to herself, glancing around the campsite and seeing no evidence of either. "Then I'd have someone to talk to."

Janna had never been one to move slowly or carefully but it was with great trepidation that she got to her feet and tested her weight on her bad leg. The pain was still jarring and she quickly snatched up the length of pipe that Maria had fetched her yesterday to serve as a crutch. With her weight off the leg, moving around was much easier.

She stumped awkwardly over to the fire. As she approached, Maria set the knife down and peered into the large cast iron skillet.

Eight eggs were frying nicely next to four thick slices of bacon, swimming together in sizzling grease. Janna's mouth watered. She considered the irony that she was eating better while marooned in the largest dumping ground in Odol than she had in recent memory. Maria pulled the skillet off the fire and tipped some of the grease over the side before she set the pan down on a makeshift table made of overturned shipping crates.

Janna's musings were interrupted by the return of Paul, followed closely by Arthur himself. The captain looked much the same as he had the last time Janna saw him, though his face was streaked with dirt and something that might have been engine grease.

"There's a derelict airship dumped not far from here," Arthur said, sitting down as Maria divided the breakfast onto dented tin trays. He took his curtly and began to eat, though without much apparent relish.

"What, you mean ours?" Janna quipped. Arthur just stared at her, so she relented after a moment. "Whatever. This is important because…?"

"This one has an intact engine," Arthur explained as though he was talking to a small child. "It's all Paul and I can do to move it and neither of us know the first thing about getting one installed. I'm sure that's something you're up to, though."

"Suppose I do help. What then?" Janna asked, sponging her egg around in the remaining bacon fat that clotted her tray. "Are we going to fly right back into cannon fire? Engines don't grow on trees and we can't count on getting airborne again if we go down a second time. It'll be a miracle if you can get off the ground as it is. The one you found may not even be compatible with the gearbox."

"The alternative is walking two hundred miles to Bolden," Arthur said slowly. "I doubt you'll get that far on your leg."

Janna sniffed derisively. "I'm not rejecting your plan, but we need to be realistic. This will take time and concentration."

Arthur shoved the last bits of egg into his mouth. "And you don't trust that I know how to get a ship off the ground."

"No," Janna said, "I don't. We'll be hiding out here for months while I work on getting it operational. Do we have food for that?"

Paul stood and began collecting the empty trays. "I took stock of what stores survived. Quite a bit, actually. Not all as entertaining as this…" He indicated the frying pan. "But food nonetheless. Months, perhaps not. But weeks, absolutely."

Janna sighed and turned back to Arthur. "Alright, *captain*, how long are you giving me?"

"Five days."

Janna choked on an indignant yell and gestured around at their surroundings. "If I were in a well equipped workshop with the finest tools and the best assistants, I couldn't do it in fewer than eight!"

"Three." Arthur gave no indication that he had heard her objections. "Three, and it gives us a window to prepare."

Janna scoffed. "You're mad. Why are you so stuck on this ship anyways? If we're going to Bolden, why don't we go by foot? There's a mining town a few days from here, and we could hitch a ride onboard Veturi…"

"This is not your plan, Miss Tulli," Arthur thundered. "If you are going to stay on, you will listen to orders."

"And you will listen to me, captain. If you want the ship to stay airborne, you need to give me time. If for whatever reason you can't give me that time, we should start heading south. I don't remember what day exactly, but Veturi will be travelling this way soon. The dockworkers have been abuzz just to see it." She closed her eyes. "And if you won't do either of those, I will take my leave."

Paul frowned. "Why? You have food here. Shelter." He looked to Maria, who was signing something quickly. "'And you won't get far on that leg.'"

Janna sighed and looked at Paul and Maria. "You two have been kind, but this isn't freedom. It's just another cell, like the one the baron probably spent all day preparing for me. What happens when an airship flies overhead? We'll all cower and hide hoping it isn't a patrol. And some of this is fresh." She indicated the surrounding refuse. "They're still dumping stuff out here. So we'll have to hide from them too. I've been hiding since I left my father. I want to be done hiding. If you give me a reasonable timeline I'll stay. If you decide to head south, I'll accompany you. If not, I'll have my severance now. Two talents, by my count." Janna held out her hand.

Arthur didn't move a muscle. Not a nerve in his face twitched. Without easing his expression, he spoke softly. Dangerously. "All the money is in Bolden. I set the timeline."

Janna dropped her hand with a sigh. "Fine, I'll make it without. If I may, I'll at least take some food with me."

She clambered to her feet and began to regret her big words. Walking was agony, but seeing the pity on Paul and Maria's faces, and the disdain on Arthur's, she forced herself to move, resting herself as much as she could on the makeshift crutch. Biting her tongue, she started towards the canopied shipwreck, expecting Arthur to run after her promising whatever she needed.

She stopped when she heard the unmistakable click of a pistol hammer being pulled back. She turned back towards the campsite. Arthur stood behind her, arm extended, holding the ornately decorated pistol aimed right at her head. Paul and Maria scrambled to their feet but Arthur bellowed, "Stay back!"

"What's this?" Janna asked, curling her lip in disdain. "Threats, now?" *The gun was empty last time. There's no way...*

"You are going to stay here, Miss Tulli," Arthur said evenly, his finger hovering on the trigger of the pistol. "I don't know exactly what trouble you got yourself into back in Gorand, but I got you out of it. You owe me-"

"Absolutely nothing!" Janna cried. "I got your ship. I followed orders. I offered terms I think are entirely reasonable, but you have refused out of hand. Why do you need to drag this poor wooden carcass to Bolden anyway? There are better ships there and the city isn't run like a prison! If you had just left quietly on a train, you wouldn't have had to drag me into this mess."

"Perhaps, but that would have left you in a very uncomfortable position, wouldn't it?" Arthur retorted.

"As opposed to this?" Janna stood, leaning on her makeshift crutch, staring down the barrel of Arthur's pistol, her mind racing. A silence deep enough to sail through grew between them.

"Both of you," Paul began, slowly stepping between Arthur's gun and Janna, "We aren't solving anything. I'm sure that we could wait just a few more days. Arthur..."

"We don't change a damn thing!" Arthur bellowed past Paul. "Certainly not for her. Deserters are basically traitors by naval law, right Paul?"

"We aren't in the navy!" Janna cried. "I'm not part of your crew. And I'm not going to stay one more minute than I must!" *I can't run on this leg...damn! And even if I could, would I make it?* The deadly calculus of whether or not the gun was loaded seemed to tip in Arthur's favor the longer she thought about it.

"Do you have any idea how hard it was to find you?" Arthur said bitterly. "And after all I did for you..." He trailed off for a second, the uncertain words not matching the conviction of his hand. Then, he seemed to regroup himself. "You're staying, or-"

"Or what, you'll kill me? I'm unarmed, you crazy bastard!"

Maria went to stand by Janna, staring into Arthur's eyes with a grim determination. Her hands flew in a flurry of signs to Paul.

"Maria is right," Paul said. "This isn't helping. If you can't see reason..."

In that moment, Janna was not sure if Paul was talking to her or Arthur. He took a carefully placed step toward the captain. "Arthur, this isn't what we are trying to do. What *you* are trying to do. If she wants to go, let her." She was sure now that Paul was talking to Arthur. Not as a crewman to a captain, or a servant to a master, but as a friend to a friend.

Paul reached Arthur's side and placed a hand on his shoulder. "Think of Helena. Could you face her, if you did this?" He motioned to Janna.

At the name "Helena" Arthur's face became suddenly blank, his eyes like blue glass reflecting the sun's watery light. For a moment Janna thought he was going to fire. She prepared herself for it. Instead, he lowered his gun.

For a moment, everything was completely still. Janna sighed out a long breath, feeling her shoulders drop as the tension dissipated. Paul stepped forward and gently took the gun from his captain's unresisting hand. Maria hurried from Janna's side to join him, casting a sympathetic glance at Janna before she buried her face in Paul's shoulder. Janna shifted on her crutch, incredibly relieved but uncertain of her next move.

"You'll be gone within the hour then?" Arthur's voice had all the emotion of a block of granite.

Janna swallowed the knot in her throat and nodded slowly. "I can't stay here any longer. I'm sorry," she said, turning to Paul and Maria, "But I'd rather take my chances out there than here with him." Maria's eyes hardened and Janna thought she gave the slightest of nods.

"I'll help you get some food," Arthur said in the same hollow voice. Pushing Paul aside, he stalked past Janna toward the hulking shape of the ship. He indicated for her to follow. Looking briefly at Paul and Maria, she limped after him, her length of pipe clicking against the ground.

The silence as they walked weighed on Janna's shoulders like lead. They reached the ship and immediately Arthur began opening barrels and crates of food that had been pulled up from the hold. "Do you have a sack?" he asked, not looking at her.

Janna gave a snort of laughter. "After all of that? That's what you have to say?"

"Fine, I'll make you one," Arthur said flatly, tying one of the uniform coats into a makeshift bundle.

"Why are you doing this?" Janna took a good armful of apples, half-loaves of hard bread, some cheese, and an assortment of machine-dried meats and wrapped them in the coat.

"You said you wanted to go. I'm helping you on your way."

"No, I mean this." She waved to the airship. Up close, it was almost miraculously intact. The masts stood straight, bearing the slouching weight of the deflated balloon overhead, and the hull, besides the great hole in the stern where the engine had smashed through, was still solid. One propellor was smashed but the other spun freely on its axle, not even bent. Janna felt the urge to pat the bulwark in some kind of sympathy. The ship had been through a lot and it was still kicking.

Arthur paused in what he was doing, his eyes staring at something she could not see. "In a week, Baron Schulhard is going to launch his dreadnought, the *Redoubtable*. I don't know why. An old friend telegrammed me about it. The dreadnoughts have been dormant since I killed your father and if they stayed that way, I could forget about them." He blinked and Janna felt a shudder run through her. Yes, it would have been him, up there in the dreadnought, raining fire from the sky on the town her father held hostage, slaying him and Odolian civilians alike. She tried to be angry, tried to conjure rage at her father's killer, but found nothing inside herself but weariness.

"I may not know his exact aims, but nothing they do is good," Arthur said, breaking into her thoughts, "Those machines can only kill or destroy. I want to stop the *Redoubtable* before it takes off. If I can, I will bring down every one of those machines."

"Stop it?" Janna was aghast. "How can you hope to stop even one of those things?" Even after what Paul had said, hearing it from Arthur's own lips did nothing to assure her of his so-called plan.

"The *Redoubtable* is docked in a pit in the mountains, only accessible by air. Its hull is so thick that a hundred pound shot from a cannon couldn't penetrate. But from above, if we could get a shot at the air tank, we could ground them for good. If the cannons don't do it, even the smallest sky-skiff, falling at a high enough speed..."

Arthur trailed off for a moment, deep in his own thoughts.

A sickening feeling collected in the pit of Janna's stomach. "You wouldn't do that though, would you?" she asked, already knowing the answer.

"If I don't have to. But the *Redoubtable* must never go airborne again. If I don't have to take that final measure, I'll have time to find a better way to destroy the others."

He would do it, Janna thought. Of course, it was madness. They'd be blown out of the sky by sentry towers as soon as they crossed the mountains. But a ship crashing into the air tank would be just as effective as a cannon shot, if not more so. Her father had suggested it in the last days, with the dreadnoughts bearing down on him. He had started getting a crew together to man the ship that would fly straight into the *Formidable*, the dreadnought which would be soon be his demise. The crew had included his daughter, the most capable mechanic in his entire gang. But even that desperate measure had come too late. And it had shown her exactly what sort of man her father was, if she had still doubted it.

She no longer had doubts about Arthur.

"Do they know?" was all she said, but in her head the sentence continued *that you're leading them to their deaths?* In her mind's eye she could see Paul's eager face and Maria's terse one looking at her across the flickering flames of the campfire. *Of course they don't know.*

Arthur shook his head, confirming her thoughts. "Not the whole of it. And nor will they. Some things are for only the captain to know. They follow hope, or at least Paul does. Hope that we can win. My only hope is to do as much as I can to strike at Odol's rancid heart before I die."

Janna lifted her head to look him in the eyes. Arthur's piercing blue eyes were tired. Sad. What he did, he was compelled to do, she thought, but that did nothing to absolve him. "I'm leaving now," she said quietly, dropping her gaze at last. "I'm not getting wrapped up in this again."

Janna limped back down the ramp, not bothering to hide her raw face from Paul and Maria, who were waiting on the ground beside the ship. She wished that the tears were from the pain in her leg, but she could barely feel that for the numbness that enveloped her body. She had a makeshift bag of food slung over her shoulder and a waterskin at her belt. She tried not to look at Paul and Maria as her makeshift crutch struck solid ground once more.

"Please," Paul said behind her. When Janna looked, she saw that he was translating for Maria. "'Please, you have to stay, at least for now. You don't have to help Arthur, but you'll die if you go out there on that leg.'"

Janna shook her head. Looking up, she saw Arthur standing at the top of the ramp, a grim expression on his face and hands clasped behind his back. Maria's eyes were rimmed with red and Paul looked near to tears himself.

"Tell Maria I'm sorry. I'm sorry for both of you." Janna took a deep breath and wiped her eyes on the sleeve of her coat. She made as if to go, but then turned back one last time. "Thanks," she told Paul softly. "Thank you for the meals. Thank you for the first real kindness I've seen in..." She trailed off, unsure of how to finish the statement. Sentiment was new to her. She wasn't quite sure she liked it. *Thank you for saving my life.* But she couldn't bring the thought to her lips.

She turned away and began to walk as quickly as she could, following a narrow gulley between two mounds of rubbish. She considered turning around, running back, telling Paul and Maria, begging them to come with her. To tell them that Arthur was willing to throw away not only his own life but theirs as well for his crusade against Odol's war machine. Her chest burned with shame for every step she took away from them. But she found she could not turn back.

Shoving the thoughts away, she recalled the end of the conversation, Arthur's final words to her. "Paul would gladly follow me to his death," he had said, "And Maria would always follow him. If you cannot follow me like that, then we have no more business together."

She shivered as she rounded the bend. The pipe she carried made walking easier, but every step still managed to be a chore. Blood thundered in her head, blocking out any sound. She thought she heard Paul's voice behind her but she couldn't be sure. No one came to stop her. She was glad of it. It made leaving slightly easier.

Janna made her way through the labyrinth of junk and debris, clambering awkwardly over drifts of scrap metal and machinery that blocked her southward path. There were no roads in the Wreckage, only random gullies and tracks between the heaps and mounds which ultimately lead nowhere. Occasionally, she was forced to dodge falling refuse or pieces of broken masonry that tumbled down at random.

Janna was glad, and lucky, that Paul had managed to glide so far away from Gorand. Otherwise, she might never have found her way out of the Wreckage. Getting out, however, proved far less encouraging than she'd thought. As she rounded a last bend, the ground opened up into endless miles of flat, empty nothingness. It was bare of any vegetation and in some places even of dirt. To the west, a dry riverbed cut starkly into the bare earth. The wind whipped across the plain, scouring the surface with dust and debris.

Throwing back her shoulders, Janna gave a deep sigh and stepped out into the frightening unknown. As she had told Arthur, there would be a mining town a day or two to the south, easy enough to reach if she could find the Veturi line. Perhaps there would be work aboard the train-city. *Not with my leg,* she thought bitterly, hitching the crutch more comfortably under her arm. If not, she would rest up and go south from there, she decided. It was freedom, and everything that came with it.

With one final look back, she began to limp southward.

PART 2:
THE ORPHAN

ELSIE

Elsie never knew her last name. She never had and never would. Her parents must have had one of course; she probably heard it once or twice in her childhood. But at the end of the day, she would never know it. The mistress at Threadbury's workhouse never told her, always admonishing that the last name of an orphan girl would never be important to anyone. It was important to Elsie, but the things that she valued seldom mattered to anyone else.

Growing up on the streets of Gorand, Elsie learned from her parents that the world was an unforgiving place. She watched her father struggle to get a good job to support the family, despite a bad leg. She helped her mother try to support herself and Elsie as a flower girl. When they clamped down on the poor and the homeless in the middle city, selling flowers did not make enough money to afford any kind of living. She was separated from her mother before she turned six and never saw her again. Now, she made a living, so to speak, working in Threadbury's, a textiles workhouse on the edge of the undercity.

While the older women spun out the cloth, cut it up, and stitched it together, it was Elsie and the younger girls who dyed the fabric. For ten to twelve exhausting hours, Elsie would stand with the other young women over the vats of acrid dyes. "Fifteen minutes in, then rinse," was the mantra that Madame Harban drilled into the girls as she stalked down the rows, yardstick in hand ready to strike any slouchers in the rear.

They typically made uniforms for the military which, except for special orders, were always red. The work had been worse ten years ago when Elsie had first joined; she hadn't understood until she was older, but the textile workhouses were instituted at the beginning of the Twenty Years' War to churn out uniforms for Odol's military, and demand surged again with the advent of Greyer's rebellion.

When she was about fourteen, the demand for uniforms slackened again and soon the workhouse was filled with other labor: creating cheap dresses and suits for the middle class. Elsie loved to admire the work done by the older women. Though the gowns were relatively inexpensive, they followed the latest fashions from Veturi and Odolia, and she sometimes daydreamed about wearing them herself. As the years wore on, however, such dreams seemed less and less likely to come true; now nearly seventeen, she was no closer to leaving Threadbury's than when she'd first been taken in.

Elsie lived in a cramped room with two other workhouse girls. She slept on the bottom of a bunk bed, with Cattia above her. Hanna, being the eldest of the three, got a cot to herself. The brick walls were an oven in the summer and an icebox in the winter. Though they worked in textiles at Threadbury's they were given none of their own stock to wear or to use as blankets, only drab, moth eaten dress uniforms and scratchy wool coverlets.

Often, she would sit on the edge of her bunk and stare out of the barred window at a slice of gray; gray streets, gray buildings, and gray skies. Her comfort was knowing that there was a rebellion out there—people trying to right things for those like her. She'd heard the women speak of it in hushed tones, fearful of retaliation from Harban's yardstick. She swore to herself if she ever got out of her situation, she would become a rebel and fight for people like herself and her friends.

On the day before Elsie's eleventh anniversary at Threadbury's, her mind drifted to the rebels again as she dipped long sheets of cloth into the noxious dyes. Red again. No doubt with the capacity they were pushing out, it was a military order: the first she'd seen in a long time. She started as she heard M. Harban's yardstick snap against the palm of her hand.

"Okay girls!" her shrill voice called out. "Big day ahead of us. We have an entire shipment of uniforms to complete by the end of the week! If it is completed ahead of time, the generous Mister Threadbury will give you all free dinner for a whole month!"

All the girls, including Elsie, began to clap. Free meals practically meant freedom. It meant, at least, a chance for freedom. All of the girls at Threadbury's were paid three kent-five dul a day, but it cost three kent for room and board and five dul for a single meal. A ticket out cost at least a sept, which would pay for a month's rent elsewhere. In recent memory, a few women had nearly starved themselves to death to try and escape, but in the end only found themselves in more trouble and at the mercy of Harban's yardstick.

Yet another reason to join a cause. Just thinking about the hopelessness of the situation churned Elsie's stomach, even as she clapped for the free meals. The stick snapped again and M. Harban looked more cross than ever.

"Get back to work! We don't pay you to stand around like you're in a playhouse!"

The clapping died and the women hastily began pushing and pulling the cloth to and from the dye vats. Elsie returned to work as well, but her gaze was drawn when the door opened behind Harban.

Threadbury came through and tapped Harban on the shoulder. She jolted and nearly slapped Threadbury. "Please," he said in a hurried whisper that was hardly subtle. "It's the client. They're here to inspect-"

Three figures filed into the large dyeworks behind Threadbury and Harban. One was a tall woman in a fine overcoat. She had a hat tucked under her arm which told Elsie she was a sailor. Her skirts billowed as she walked—she strode like a soldier, not a woman.

The second stranger was a man and Elsie did not like his look one bit. He had a hideous powdered wig on his head and wore a gaudy suit with a large collection of medals on the left breast. His stomach rolled and shook as he stamped into the room.

"Threadbury," the fat man said quietly, "This is my son Theodore. It's his first assignment for the emperor and I don't want you, or anyone, to mess it up for him. Theodore!" he shouted.

A third stranger entered the dyeworks. Elsie gasped. He was like a man out of one of her dreams. Though his face was slightly boyish, his long blonde hair, sharp green eyes, and slender figure were everything she hoped for. She clamped her mouth shut as she realized it had been hanging open.

"What's that girl there doing?" the fat man asked. "She's just standing there, staring at us."

At that point, Elsie came to the realization that she was staring rather than dutifully working. She turned quickly to push the cloth back into the dye vat. "Oh, that's Elsie," Harban said with contempt. "Just one of the girls. A daydreamer, really."

"Is that the one you told me about? Who talks in her sleep?" Threadbury asked.

"The one who fancies herself a rebel of sorts? Yes," Harban said harshly.

The tall sailor woman strode forward and stood behind where Elsie worked. "A rebel? Then you ought to deal with that as soon as possible. With our baron being so instrumental in eliminating the last of Greyer's men, we can't be conciliatory with the next generation." Her strident voice pierced the drone of the surrounding labor.

"Well spoken, Captain Marjen. You'll be a patriot yet," the fat man said and strode forward, squeezing Elsie's shoulder as he passed. "Make an example of her," he said and walked away. Elsie let the breath escape her chest. Her relief overwhelmed her dread of the punishment to follow.

"Of course, Baron," Threadbury said, and bowed.

"Now, make sure the color is perfect. Theodore is quite particular. Aren't you my boy?"

Theodore nodded slowly. "Not *that* particular. As long as they are identical on the field. Wouldn't want the enemy to think we are barbarians," he said with a small smile. His soft voice caused a strange warmth to rise in Elsie's chest.

The baron laughed dismissively and the group continued on through the dyeworks. As M. Harban passed, she swatted Elsie on the rear with the dreadful yardstick. It stung, but she knew all too well that it was merely a sample of what was to come.

The punishment itself was bad enough, but what bothered Elsie more was the follow up. Twenty strikes with the yardstick hurt, but sitting on a narrow stool in the mess hall during the twenty minute meal nearly brought her to tears. Her mind conjured all sorts of angry, hateful things to do to Harban, Threadbury, the baron, and even Captain Marjen. Only Theodore Schulhard, the baron's eldest son, escaped her mental wrath. When the twenty minutes of pain were done, she staggered back to work with the rest of the girls. With nothing for her mind to focus on, she entertained more of the unpleasant thoughts.

When the clock struck eight, it was finally time for the agonizing day of work to finish. Her narrow shoulders ached as she followed the other girls to their room on the highest floor of the workhouse. Once there, Cattia and Hanna hazarded to whisper to one another about the unusually eventful day. Elsie was quite sure that they tried to talk to her, but the aching in her bones and throbbing of her bruised skin pulled her into a uncomfortable sleep.

A Better Life

The next day was much the same—red cloth and tension from on high. Elsie worked as quickly as she could, handling swaths of dense wool being dyed the deep red of Odolian army uniforms. Red dyes were her least favorite; after hours of laboring over the vats, her hands would be stained scarlet for at least the next month, and it always made her feel self-conscious. Already splotchy red lines were forming in the wrinkles on her knuckles and around her fingernails, and they wouldn't come out no matter how hard she scrubbed.

That evening, after two hours of grueling overtime she'd thought would never end, Elsie sat in the dining hall with Catia and Hannah, listlessly stirring her watery potato soup. Usually oversalted, tonight the dish was tasteless, perhaps a sign of being stretched even thinner than normal.

"Do you really think we'll get free dinner? For a whole month?" Cattia said, squeezing her hands together in excitement.

"I doubt we'll make the shipment on time," Hanna said as she took another spoonful of soup. "What do you think, Els?"

Elsie chewed thoughtfully on an underdone potato, painfully aware of the ticking clock. The workhouse schedule allowed little time for considered conversation. Her friends waited eagerly for her response, hurrying down their own food.

Finally, she spoke. "I don't think it matters if we get the uniforms finished. After the month is done, it will be back to the usual routine." She looked ruefully at her pitiful bowl of soup. "Free dinner for a month won't mean enough savings to get out of here."

"Who'd want out of here?" Cattia laughed. "You know what goes on out there, Els. War, starvation, rebellion, people looking to hurt girls like us."

Elsie rolled her eyes. Cattia was probably a year older than herself, but she had been born within the workhouse. She never knew a day outside of Threadbury's, unlike Elsie, who still had vivid memories of life in an apartment, and later on the streets.

"Well, we should at least be able to get ourselves some-"

She was cut off by the yardstick slamming onto the table beside her bowl, which caused all three girls to jump. "I'll have no complaining from any of my girls," M. Harban said, slowly withdrawing the yardstick from the table as she glared at each of them in turn. "Either you stop complaining, or you stop eating. Is that clear?"

The question begged no answer and the three girls simply nodded. They resumed eating their soup, keeping their eyes on their bowls as M. Harban stalked past, glancing over her shoulder at them as if the moment she turned her back they would resume their wayward behavior. Once she was far enough away, Elsie glanced up quickly at Hanna and Cattia. They were both spooning away dutifully. But with four more minutes left until the bedtime bell, Elsie was going to enjoy eating as much as she possibly could.

❖◦❖ ◦ ❖◦❖

Every day of the week was as backbreaking as the first; Elsie worked over the vats for twelve hours every day, punctuated only by a brief respite for lunch, which made it that much harder to get back up and begin the exhausting work again. In the evenings, she was far too tired to socialize with her friends. She had to take extra care when she was working not to draw the ire of M. Harban, who was most emphatic that there be no "rebellious talk" on the job, or at any time. Another girl was thrashed for "rebel talk" after mentioning her dream of having a house with a garden on the middle level of the city. Elsie supposed that any talk of living outside of the workhouse was considered rebellious by M. Harban.

The crackdown might also have been due to Captain Marjen, who made an appearance every day to inspect their progress, albeit without the baron or his son. Twenty thousand uniforms had to be made, and, according to what Elsie had overheard, it was over a single lapel buttonhole that had been moved to a different point. She took a moment to look at one of the freshly made uniforms as she rinsed it out with clear water. It was nearly identical to previous uniforms she'd made, save that the button would be attached just two inches higher on the lapel. She fiddled with the closure absently. *What a lot of work for such a small change...*

"It's so that the collar will look neater when it's buttoned," Captain Marjen assured as she noticed Elsie examining the uniform. Hurriedly, Elsie turned it over her arm to take it to the drying racks.

"I'm terribly sorry, ma'am," she murmured, staring fixedly at the captain's polished black boots peeking out from beneath the hem of her dress. "I didn't mean to-"

"Nonsense, it's no crime for you to admire our imperial might. You're the one from the other day, aren't you? The day-dreamer? Talks in her sleep?"

Elsie nodded, keeping her eyes down. Moisture from the damp uniform was beginning to seep through her thin apron into her dress.

"Don't be afraid to dream," Marjen said. She reached out and took Elsie's chin in her hand. Elsie flinched involuntarily and found herself looking up into the captain's face. She was older, but not nearly as old as M. Harban, with ashy blonde hair and deep lines at the corners of her worn gray-green eyes. "I know how it feels, working here. But I can see you making yourself useful to our empire someday. Don't let the machine grind you down."

Elsie stared at the woman for a moment, then dipped her head in a quick nod. At the edge of her vision, she saw Harban approaching, a fake smile plastered on her sour face. "You are walking a dangerous line, filling that girl with such fancies," she commented, though maintaining a respectful tone. "She won't be as productive with her head in the clouds. Remember what you said about rebels?"

Elsie wasn't completely certain, but she thought she saw Marjen almost roll her eyes. "Would a rebel be admiring our handiwork?" she asked, her voice laden with sarcasm as she gave M. Harban a crisp, practiced smile. "Make sure you are nurturing a patriotic mind," she told Elsie, clasping a firm hand on her shoulder for a moment, before turning back to Harban. "You would be wise not to crush this girl's patriotic spirit with ill treatment, Madam. We need more like her in your fine city."

The captain turned on her heel and walked away down the rows of dye vats. Elsie stood for a moment, somewhat con-founded, the red uniform pressed against her skirt. It had begun to drip. Harban dismissed her with an angry wave of her hand, and she hurried to the drying racks, chewing over the strange interaction in her mind. She wondered if Marjen had been trying to apologize, in some way, for her hostility earlier in the week.

She was still thinking about it hours later at lunch, pushing her food around on her plate while Cattia and Hanna—but mostly Cattia—chattered away about some fresh piece of upstairs gossip. *How would she ever understand what I feel? Has she ever set foot in a workhouse except to berate girls about quotas and uniforms?*

"...and I don't care how much that silly captain fawns over you, you're still *my* worker, and I'll have none of your daydreams! Are you even listening to me girl?" Elsie looked up in shock and found that M. Harban was standing opposite her behind Hanna, glaring down her thin nose. Hanna stiffened and shrunk away from Harban, staring desperately across the table at Elsie. *Please*, she mouthed, her eyes darting up as if to check for the presence of the dreaded yardstick.

Elsie sat up straighter, keeping her eyes low and her demeanor submissive. "I'm sorry ma'am. It won't happen again," she murmured.

"Of course it won't," Harban snapped, turning sharply and continuing her rounds up and down the rows of cafeteria tables. "I'll have no slacking. Remember girls, free dinner for a whole month, if you finish on time. Why don't you mull that over, if you've a mind to think at all!"

By the end of the day, every one of the girls was aching from head to toe. But with only an hour of overtime, they managed to finish the uniforms, dry them, and pack them all into huge wooden crates. Thirty total, each of them stuffed with neatly folded uniforms and stamped with the Threadbury's seal, were now on their way to the skydocks. Mister Threadbury came down to the dining hall to congratulate the girls on their hard work and there were extra helpings of soup and bread all around. It was a nice gesture, but it didn't stop Elsie from collapsing onto her bed as soon as she made it up to her room. She kicked off her shoes, peeled off her wool stockings, and gave up on the rest of her uniform. She squirmed her way under the thin quilt and flung her arm over her tired eyes.

"That was tough, huh Els," Cattia said around a yawn as she pulled on her threadbare nightgown. "I can't believe they still have you working the dyes. Our hands are stabbed near to death with putting those uniforms together."

"Don't rub it in," Elsie said, not even shifting her arm. "My hands are as red as a beet, and more wrinkly than Harban's! I hope I never see another Odolian uniform again."

"Don't talk like that," Hanna said primly. "Our military protects us from threats to our peace and safety. You'd do well to thank a soldier anytime you see him."

"If I have to see him, it had better be without the uniform," Elsie mumbled.

Cattia gave a snort of laughter and Elsie opened her eyes a slit just in time to see Hanna give her a duly shocked look.

"Elsie, don't speak that way," she said, smoothing down the front of her nightgown as though to brush off Elsie's comment. "At least be grateful for the work that keeps you employed!"

"Yeah, we're getting free food out of this, remember?" Cattia piped up from the top bunk, as if that was the final word on the matter.

"What good is free food if we can't use the money we save?" Elsie asked, finally sitting up and crossing her arms on her knees. "You know it isn't enough to get us out of here."

"There's nothing out there," Hanna stated firmly, slipping into bed beneath the worn charity quilt. "You keep talking about 'out there.' Why don't you listen to the Madame? She knows better than you would; she's been out there."

"So was I, when I was younger," Elsie snapped. "Don't forget I used to live on the streets."

"And you still want to go back out there?" Hanna's voice was laden with exasperation.

"It would be better than being caged up in here," Elsie shot back. "And for your information, there are people out there who care about girls like us. People who have nothing to do with the empire or the workhouses."

"Suit yourself, I'd rather be comfortable in here than uncomfortable out..."

Hanna was interrupted by the clanging of the yardstick against the pipes in the hallway, followed by the voice of Madame Harban. "I did not give anyone permission to talk after lights out! Next voice I hear better be when you say 'thank you' for your meals, or you won't get any."

With that, the girls' conversation was over. Elsie sighed and rubbed her eyes, feeling her bitterness slowly drain away. Despite her aching body, she got up and went to the tiny window. There were patches of brown grass in the workhouse courtyard below, a couple of bushes, and an old, dead tree. It wasn't much to look at. *I can't believe that this is all life has for me. Not when there are rebels, people out there fighting to make it better. I can't believe that work and slop and bad sleep are all I deserve. I will find a way out, if I have to starve myself to death.*

Elsie turned her back on the window, climbed into the bed, and pulled the covers up to her chin. A new resolve was filling her. Tomorrow was another day and she would make the best of it.

9

FIRST GOODBYES

With a roaring crash, Elsie was jolted out of her daze. Cattia and Hanna were already up, looking out of the barred window. She sat up, clutching the blankets to her chest.

"You gotta come see this!" Cattia cried.

Elsie scrambled out of her bed, panic bubbling in her throat as she pushed her friends from the window. She pressed her face to the cold metal bars, trying to see what was going on in the city outside. *Rebels?* She thought almost hopefully. *Are we under attack?* She had heard explosions and gunfire in the city before, but never this close, and never this much. Silhouetted against the foggy dawn, Elsie saw the shape of a single airship soaring between the buildings. The orange flash of cannon fire illuminated it for a moment, but she couldn't catch sight of the standard it was flying. From that narrow angle she could see a single sentry tower, which returned fire with another flash.

She remained at the window as though transfixed. With a start, she realized that the airship was heading straight for Threadbury's workhouse.

"Come on Els!" Cattia whined. "Let me see, you've had your turn!"

"Get away!" Elsie stepped back. "Find somewhere to hide, quick." From where Elsie stood, it seemed that the ship was completely out of control.

"What's happening?" Hanna cried.

Just in time, Elsie pulled both Cattia and Hanna to the front of the room, away from the window. With an enormous crash, the entire building seemed to shake. Plaster fell from the ceiling and Elsie flung herself to the floor, dragging the other two with her. Hanna screamed. Looking up, Elsie saw that the wall in front of them had been hit. A gaping hole had appeared in the bricks a foot from the window where they were just standing.

Taking a moment to calm her nerves, Elsie staggered to her feet, disoriented from the noise. Lodged in Hanna's bed frame was a large, smoldering iron ball, stamped with the insignia of the empire. As the ringing in her ears subsided, she could hear hysterical screaming coming from the other rooms. All down the hallway, girls were banging on the doors, begging to be let out. But all Elsie could see was the hole in the wall.

She heard the roar of the ship pass overhead, trailed by the continued sounds of cannon fire. A chill wind blew through the hole, rustling the wrinkled skirt of her work dress and bearing the unfamiliar scent of gunpowder, and the oily smell of fresh fallen rain. It was a small hole, but large enough that she and the other girls could crawl through.

"Now's our chance!" she called out to the others. Shaking, she stumbled to the wall and poked her head out into the chill dawn air. She saw the flashes of cannon fire, followed by the delayed sounds of blasts and gunshots. Louder, however, was the sound of Madame Harban in the hallway, letting the girls out of the locked rooms.

"Come on girls!" the old hag shouted. "Get yourselves decent! It's safer in the cafeteria!"

Her shrill voice and the jingle of her key ring was coming closer with each passing second. "If we don't move, we'll be here forever. Cat, Hanna, come on!" Elsie was nearly crying from eagerness.

Hanna and Cattia both stared at her, dumbstruck. Elsie groaned and grabbed both of their right hands and pulled them to the hole in the wall. *Our escape,* Elsie thought with an eager smile on her face. That was, until she looked out of the hole. She hadn't considered how tall the workhouse was and it forced her to pause for one valuable second. She steeled herself, and without bothering to put on her stockings or shoes, she threw one leg out of the hole, then the other. Gingerly, she lowered herself onto a ledge, scraping her knees and shoulders against the jagged bricks. Clutching the lip of the opening, she turned and pressed herself against the grimy exterior of the workhouse.

Poking her head back up through the hole, she looked at her friends. They were getting their stockings and shoes on, and Hanna even pulled one of the thin wool blankets over her shoulder, clumsily tying it around her neck. "Hurry up!" Elsie urged. "Harban will get here soon."

"It's cold out there," Hanna warned. "I'm not about to catch my death."

"Yeah, what good is this so-called 'freedom' then?" Cattia teased.

Elsie groaned and looked to the left, and then to the right, shifting her weight awkwardly on the narrow ledge. She saw that there was no easy way for them to reach the ground. Their room was near the top of the workhouse, countless stories up. She breathed a sigh of relief when she saw that a huge metal pipe ran the entire height of the building, from the top to the courtyard below. Even in the dim light Elsie was sure that she could make it if she got to the end of the ledge.

Taking a deep breath and gripping the bricks as tightly as she could, Elsie stretched her free hand desperately toward the pipe. Her fingers grasped only air and she jerked her arm back at once, clinging to the ledge as she tried to steady herself. Her breaths came more rapidly, heart fluttering. Hanna clambered down out of the hole in the wall to join her, followed a few moments later by Cattia.

"Are you sure about this?" Hanna cried, her knuckles white from her vice-like grip on the ledge above. "We were safe in our room!"

"We were slaves in our room!" Elsie sniped back. Taking another breath, she let go of the ledge and leapt desperately for the pipe. All too quickly, Elsie realized that it was no water pipe, but rather a scalding hot pipe for funneling steam up from the dyeworks. She cried out in pain and bit her lip as her hands barely managed to cling to the rusted metal. After a couple of seconds, the pain subsided.

That was when she heard Madame Harban unlock the door to their room. The old woman almost passed by, but after a slight pause, Elsie heard the door slam open. The old hag rushed in.

"Good heavens. Elsie, Hanna, Cattia!" Harban began searching through the rubble in the room.

"You won't get another chance!" Elsie whispered harshly to Hanna and Cattia.

Hanna looked uncertain. "They won't be angry with us...we could say that we fell! They'll take us back in..."

"We have to go!" Elsie said, shifting down the pipe so that her friends would have a place to leap to.

A tear streaming down her face, Hanna nodded, and leapt to the pipe, but misjudged the distance and went too far. Time seemed to stop. Out of reflex alone, Elsie reached her hand out and grabbed for her falling friend, but only managed to grasp the blanket that she had on her shoulders. The knot came loose and Hanna would have continued falling if she hadn't grabbed the blanket as well. Both of Elsie's shoulders tore with pain as she desperately held onto the blanket.

"Take the pipe!" Elsie screamed. "Grab it, quickly, or we are both going to fall." Hanna's weight and the sweat from her hand meant that she was not going to hold for long.

Cattia deftly leapt over and grabbed the pipe above Elsie. Hanna whimpered, gripping the pipe below. The metal creaked uneasily and Elsie urged her friends to start moving down. Harban poked her haggard head out of the hole in the wall.

"And to think, I was worried about you three!" the woman snapped. "I should have known you would try something like this! No doubt you're the ringleader, Elsie. Now get back here this instant!"

"Elsie, maybe we should go back," Hanna cried.

"Never!" Elsie replied sharply. She glanced back at the shouting woman one last time, then began to climb down the remainder of the pipe.

"Do you hear me, you little wretch?" Harban shouted shrilly.

"Use the connectors with the rivets!" Elsie said, after her toes splayed out on one of them. "They're not as hot."

The other two must have gotten the message and ignoring Harban they gingerly made their way toward the courtyard below. The dawn became uncomfortably quiet when Harban's tirade came to a sudden end. The commotion from the city had died down, though Elsie thought she heard sirens wailing just on the edge of hearing.

"I think she's going to the bottom floor to meet us," Cattia exclaimed.

"Boy, that would be my luck," Elsie mumbled, "to get all the way to the bottom only to be caught again. Can you imagine the punishments we'd face?"

Hanna winced and began climbing faster.

Elsie's sore and scalded fingers became slick with sweat and she nearly lost her grip. Steadying herself, she got a chance to look more closely at the building she so desperately clung to. Beside her, rows of large, dirty glass windows cut through the monotony of the grimy bricks. Inside were the dyeworks. "We're never going to work there again," she said firmly. "Not if we have to starve."

"Are you sure about starving?" Cattia asked. "I'm getting hungry..."

Elsie rolled her eyes, unsure of whether Cattia was being serious or not.

They finally reached the bottom of the pipe and one by one dropped onto the paving stones of the front court. As soon as Elsie hit the ground, she frantically looked around to find an escape. Threadbury's workhouse was walled in completely by a black, wrought iron fence. Each fencepost was topped with a devilishly sharp point, and the gate, flanked by two brick columns, was locked.

"We'll want to climb the fence," Elsie announced. "It'll be easier than the gate or the columns."

"Ugh, would you look at our dresses?" Cattia groaned. She was right too, Elsie observed. They were scuffed and oily from their descent down the pipe.

"Now isn't the time, Cat," Elsie said, feigning patience. She could practically feel the yardstick slamming into her. *I'm never going back,* she reassured herself. Ignoring her scalded hands, she went to a nearby segment of the fence and used the horizontal braces to start climbing.

It wasn't easy, and Elsie discovered that Hanna knew a surprising number of ways to curse. However, it wasn't long before the girls scaled the inside of the fence. Hanna's skirt snagged on one of the points and she fell clumsily to the slick stone below. Elsie looked back at the doors of the workhouse. "Come on girls. They'll catch up soon and we'll be prisoners again."

"Would it be that bad?" Hanna whined as she nursed her ankle.

Elsie knelt to help her friend up, but there was a commotion behind her in the entry hall. "I'm going to drag those girls back in here by the scruffs of their necks if it's the last thing I do!" Harban cried in her shrill voice, her head visible through the dingy glass in the doors. Beside her, Threadbury struggled with the keys.

Elsie pulled Hanna to her feet and let her lean on her shoulder. Cattia in tow, they staggered forward as Harban rushed out of the doors, the skinny figure of Mister Threadbury scrambling close behind her.

"Threadbury, get the gate. Quick, they're getting away!" Harban was screeching. Threadbury obediently fumbled past, rifling through his key ring.

Elsie urged her friends on, running blindly with them into the first narrow alley that they could find. The buildings were pushed so close together that it was difficult for the girls to walk abreast, much less run. Oily rain barrels and heaps of refuse lined the narrow ways. They took turns heedlessly, hoping to throw off any pursuit, though none of them could see anyone following. At last, Elsie called for them to stop, struggling to catch her breath as she took a moment to survey their surroundings. She bemoaned that in her haste she hadn't put on any shoes or stockings. The thin layer of water that slicked the cobblestones stung her feet. The girls shivered in their torn dresses, staring up at the sheer faces of the buildings crowding all around them.

"Now you've done it," Hanna complained. "Where on earth are we going to go now?"

"Give me a moment to think," Elsie said, forcing herself to sound calm.

The bricks behind them were slick with grime and dirt, and the windows she could see high above were as narrow and wretched as the windows back in the workhouse. Elsie looked all around them desperately for a ground floor window, but the walls of the buildings on either side of the alley were bare and smooth, save for the occasional discoloration of a bricked-up doorway. Thinking back, she realized that Threadbury's had no ground floor windows either.

"Are we out of luck?" Cattia asked.

"Not if I have anything to say about it," Elsie huffed. She began to pick her way through the alley again, avoiding the puddles of iridescent water collecting on the worn cobbles. A moment later, she looked back and saw that though Cattia was following close behind, Hanna had not moved an inch. Sighing, Elsie went back to her. "Come on, I'll help you walk.

The whole way felt gross and the girls' eyes shifted from high window to high window. It felt like they were being watched, though they couldn't see a soul around them. One or two were lit faintly by gas lamps or flickering candlelight, but otherwise they seemed to be empty. The morning sun was completely blocked by the shadow of the city above, and the ambient light that was beginning to filter in did nothing to dispel the threatening darkness that filled the alley.

After a few more twists and turns, the three girls nearly stumbled into the middle of a broad street which was beginning to buzz with morning activity. People were making their way purposefully through the streets. It didn't look as though many of the men had washed their faces for some time. They wore dingy work uniforms which were patched or threadbare. Some of the women were similarly attired, with simple, serviceable skirts and plain blouses. But there were other women as well, lingering on the edge of the street and on corners. Those women had faces that were caked with powder and rouge and wore frilly petticoats under elaborately colored skirts.

"Who are they?" Cattia asked. "Rich ladies?"

Elsie looked at their surroundings. "Do you really think that rich ladies would be down here?"

"Could be. Maybe they'll help us out?"

Elsie shook her head, hiding a smirk. Cattia was never the brightest. She turned to Hanna to see what she thought of their position. Instead of sharing Cattia's awed expression, Hanna was slowly stepping backward, shaking her head, eyes wide with fear.

"Hanna? What's wrong?" Elsie turned and went to help her.

"I'm not going out there," she said in a hoarse whisper. "Threadbury's will take me back. Someone will. You should come too."

"We've come this far," Elsie reasoned. "We can't just go back."

"It's honest work," Hanna said. "Threadbury's, I mean. And it's a dignified life. Elsie, everything we've heard is true. It's just like I remember. You can come back too! They won't punish us too much."

"Hanna, get a hold of yourself! We'll be fine," Elsie pleaded and moved to take Hanna's hands. "Those workers, they look just like us. If nothing else, it can't be worse than the workhouse. I for one won't miss the twelve-hour shifts in the dye vats."

"Then you can go. I wish you luck out there. Cat, are you coming with me?" Hanna asked. A tear rolled down her smudged cheek.

Cattia paused for a moment and Elsie thought she was going to go with Hanna, but then Cattia shook her head. "We've come this far. I'm sorry Hanna," she said despondently. "Will you be alright on your own?"

Hanna frowned but nodded. "Goodbye, then. I hope you two do well."

"You too," Cattia said. Elsie simply huffed and turned to stare back out at the street. Her frustration subsided almost at once, but when she turned back she saw the alleyway empty, save for Cattia standing there dumbly.

"Come on, Cat," Elsie said softly, taking her hand. She blinked a stray tear away. A pang in her heart told her that she should have said goodbye.

10

RYE

Peering back into the street, Elsie was startled to hear a familiar voice rise above the growing commotion. "What the...what do you mean my ship?" The voice belonged to Captain Marjen and she did not sound happy. Ignoring the dull ache welling up in her throat, Elsie stepped into the street.

"What are you doing?" Cattia asked.

"I think that Captain Marjen is over there! She'd help us for sure." Elsie stood on her bare toes, trying to see over the crowd. Marjen had her hat on, which made her easier to spot. It was an elaborate, tri-cornered hat with a large red feather plume stuck in the brim. The tall woman was struggling to don her coat over a haphazard dress as she marched through the crowd. Even her grayish-blonde hair, usually neatly combed, was a frazzled mess.

"Are you saying that some criminal...Do you even know how complicated that lock is? And of all of the ships in the-" Language which Elsie had never heard spilled from Captain Marjen's mouth.

Elsie took Cattia's hand and began to push her way through the crowd. Nearby, a church bell began to toll the hour. "How is it so busy? It's just now eight o'clock!" Elsie gritted her teeth in frustration as she pushed her way toward Marjen's hastily retreating hat, which bobbed above the crowd. Without Hannah, she needed something familiar to grasp.

"Els, wait. You're not thinking clearly!" Cattia pulled Elsie to a halt. "What if she just sends us back?"

Elsie hesitated. A large man in denim overalls shoved himself between the two girls, knocking Elsie to the ground. "Watch where yer standin'!" the man growled as he stepped over Elsie's prone form.

Gritting her teeth, Elsie tried to stand up again. More people began to push past and step over her, obviously in a rush. Each of them muttered some rude remark as she was knocked this way and that. Finally, tripping a young man in the process, she staggered to her feet. Her dress was stained and filthy, grit and grime covering her scraped knees. She sniffed and wiped her nose with her sleeve, anxiously looking through the crowd.

She couldn't see Cattia.

Shoving through the crowd, she finally caught sight of Cattia wandering aimlessly through a gap between two parallel flows of people. Elsie had nearly made her way to the middle of the broad street when she heard a loud roar and the clanging of bells. From down the street, on Cattia's side, a large machine was being driven straight toward her.

"Out of the way!" a man on the four-wheeled machine called out to Cattia, but the girl seemed planted like a statue. *An automobile,* Elsie thought. She'd heard of them, but hardly believed something like that could be real. This one had a huge engine in the back of it, pouring putrid black smoke. Its metal-rimmed wheels scraped the cobbles. It also had a huge tank on the side, and there was a young man holding a long rubber hose with a metal end. People on the side of the street stopped to watch.

Elsie rushed over and shoved Cattia out of the path of the clattering auto, knocking them both to the ground. The driver swore and yelled at them as the vehicle drove past. "This is no place for games, urchins! Can't you see there's a fire?"

Behind the automobile, there was a platoon of uniformed men wearing dented metal helmets, each carrying buckets of water. Some sloshed onto the girls and Elsie bit off an oath as she began to stand up.

"Come on Cat, let's go."

Barely keeping her composure, Elsie dragged her friend to the nearest alleyway, dodging some garbage which floated in a puddle. They came to a halt, silent save for their ragged breathing. Closing her eyes, Elsie tried not to panic. Her heart was thudding in her ears and her body shook uncontrollably—whether from cold or fear, she couldn't tell.

"This is what you wanted?" Cattia asked, winded. "How are we going to-"

"Looking for somewhere to stay, girls?" A low, baritone drawl echoed through the alley. Elsie's heart leapt into her mouth. Sitting on the first landing of a fire escape, his long legs dangling precariously over the edge, was a tall and extraordinarily lanky young man. "I tell ya, you're looking in the wrong place. Folks around here, ya see, they ain't hospitable. Especially not to workhouse runaways."

Elsie stepped forward, shielding Cattia with her body as the man stood up. His clothes were worn and stained: a brown wool coat, an ill-fitting vest and rumpled shirt beneath, corduroy trousers which might once have been tan, but were past recognition of their original color. A flat cap rested on his shaggy brown hair. His bright eyes snapped cheekily at her as he perched nonchalantly on the fire escape. He appeared relaxed and made no move towards them, but Elsie was immediately on edge.

"How do you know we're from the workhouses?" she asked, jutting her chin forward defiantly. She felt Cattia lean forward, and glanced over to see her staring wide eyed at the stranger on the fire escape.

"Easy there, little lady," the man said in his soothing drawl. "Your dress couldn't be anything but a workhouse uniform. I know the type. Besides, you work textiles, right?"

That shook her. "How...how do you know?"

"Your hands," the man said with a smug grin.

Glancing down, Elsie saw that her red-stained hands were on full display. Scowling, she clasped them behind her back and edged in front of Cattia.

"You could do with some manners!" she said shrilly. "You haven't even told me your name. How do you expect me to trust you? The women in the workhouse told us about men like you. Warned us, more like. Why aren't you out there doing honest work with those other men?"

"Honest work? You think that I'm not doing honest work? I'm hurt," the man said, dramatically feigning an injury to the chest, which made Cattia giggle. "To think that I would be called a dishonest man." He recovered quickly, though, and the smug smile returned. "I'm a labor scout. And I know a better place for young ladies like you to work."

"You still haven't told us your name," Elsie said pointedly. Cattia had once more extracted herself from behind Elsie and was standing beside her, gawking at the man. Elsie was confounded for a second, but then a thought struck her like a punch to the gut. *Has she even talked with a man before, other than Mister Threadbury?*

"Ah, my mistake." The man laughed and took off his flat cap. "Name's Rye. What's yours, pretty lady?"

Elsie felt an involuntary blush streak across her face, but her mouth twisted crossly. As she started to reply, Cattia interrupted.

"I'm Cattia," she said breathlessly, "but my friends call me Cat, and you can too, if you like. This place you mentioned...what's it like?"

Rye twirled his cap on his finger. "Oh, just a little place where, for a bit of light work, young women can find a comfortable place to stay and get food in their bellies."

As he was speaking, the clocks of the city struck eight-thirty in the morning. As if on cue, Elsie's stomach growled like a starved animal. Cattia turned to look at her with pleading eyes and Elsie felt the rest of the fight go out of her. It wasn't wages, true, but the exchange of labor for food and shelter seemed reasonable.

"Alright, we'll try it," Elsie said stiffly, crossing her arms over her stomach as it began to cramp. "But if we don't like it, we're leaving, understand?"

"Of course, of course. Whatever you please." Rye hopped over the railing and landed gracefully on the cobbles ahead of the girls. "Why don't you come along and I'll get you a nice, warm meal first. Then I'll take you to meet my boss. I think you're just what she's after."

"She?" Images of working for another wretched woman like Harban flashed through Elsie's mind.

"Yes, she's a marvelous woman. I'm sure you'll love her and I'm equally sure she'll enjoy you. Now come along, it's a bit of a walk..." Rye began to saunter away down the alley.

Without a moment's hesitation, Cattia dashed after him, slowing down to walk shyly at his side. Swallowing her rising misgivings, Elsie started after them, her bare feet slapping against the cold paving stones of the alley, skipping over metal pipes and around puddles as they delved deeper into the undercity. Rye led them up a small stair, then looked back at Elsie as she clambered after, bringing up the rear of the little group.

"I just noticed; you don't have any shoes on, pretty lady. Run away in a hurry?"

"I...our escape was well timed," Elsie admitted, avoiding his impetuous gaze. "But yes, I forgot my shoes and stockings."

"Well, here." Gently pushing Cattia out of the way, Rye sat down on the concrete steps and pulled two handkerchiefs from his pocket. He grabbed Elsie's foot and wrapped it up, tying the fabric securely around her ankle. Elsie looked at Cattia helplessly, but the other girl's attention was still fixed on Rye. "Try not to step in any puddles, and this should do until we get to..." He trailed off as he began to wrap her other foot.

"Get to where?" Elsie asked.

"Oh, get to where we're going. There, you should be set." He gave her a grin and got to his feet once more.

Even the thin barrier of the handkerchiefs made Elsie's sore, dirty feet feel better, and she felt begrudgingly grateful to the man. Perhaps he was one of the rebels. That thought stemmed her lingering doubts, though she couldn't help but think that they were going deeper into the city's underbelly than they ought. The people they passed seemed to skulk through the streets, peering warily about without catching the girls' eyes. Many of them appeared to know Rye and nodded or touched their caps respectfully to him as he passed, but besides a wink or a nod in return, Rye took little notice of them. He stopped to speak to no one.

They crossed over a mesh catwalk above a deeper layer of Gorand than Elsie knew existed. Peering down nervously, she saw that the streets they were walking on had been built on top of another layer of dirty brick buildings, which spiraled down into the darkness below her feet.

After two long hours of walking, Cattia gave up and slumped onto a pile of damp, slimy bricks. Elsie stopped beside her, taking her friend's hand as she waited to see what Rye would do. He continued on for a few paces before he checked himself and looked back over his shoulder.

"We're nearly there girls, don't give up now."

"I've gotta rest," Cattia groaned. "I can't go on, not without anything to eat and not without a good sit-down..." She slumped back against the grimy wall. Elsie thought she caught a glimpse of Rye rolling his brown eyes. Her own stomach had long ceased cramping with hunger, but she could still feel the hollowness. The warm meal Rye promised had not yet materialized.

"C'mon, we're so close," Rye wheedled, turning back to face them, his hands shoved into the pockets of his worn coat. "If you girls can't handle a little brisk exercise, my boss..."

"If your boss is as hospitable as you made her sound, then she can wait five minutes for Cat and me to rest our legs," Elsie snapped. "Have you any idea of the day we've had?" She was nearly at the point of shouting, but Cat did not stir. She had fallen asleep in her uncomfortable seat. Elsie looked up, expecting to see Rye's face twist in anger at her response, but he just laughed.

"Okay, little lady, you and your pretty friend could use a break I'm sure. I'll just run ahead and let my boss know you're coming, eh?"

Elsie nodded mutely and watched as he disappeared down the dark alley. She sank down next to Cattia on the pile of bricks, cringing as she felt moisture soak through her thin skirt. Cattia was breathing evenly, her mouth slightly ajar, her dirty face glistening with sweat in the light of a solitary gas lamp. Elsie was dismayed as she saw how disheveled her friend looked and realized that she must look much the same. She could feel her damp hair clinging to the back of her neck. Cattia's blonde waves were frizzy from the humidity and already beginning to tangle.

Though she felt more comfortable in Rye's absence, Elsie realized with sickening clarity just how alone they were, lost in the depths of the undercity. She thought vaguely about waking Cattia and making a run for it, but she could not remember the route they had taken to reach this godforsaken place, and didn't want to trust their luck in the winding alleys without a guide. Reluctantly, she grabbed Cattia's arm and shook her gently. Rye had been gone for some time, though it was impossible in this sunless twilight to tell exactly how long. She was beginning to grow nervous.

"Cat, wake up, we should be moving."

Cattia mumbled something, shifting away from Elsie in her sleep. Elsie shook her again, harder.

"Cat, come on. Wake up."

Cattia yawned hugely and rubbed at her eyes, smudging a streak of greasy dirt across her cheek. "What is it Els?" she mumbled, her words slurring as she struggled awake. "What's the matter?"

"Rye's gone," Elsie said quickly, glancing over her shoulder. The alley he had taken was still empty. "Do you remember the turns we took to get here? I think we should leave…"

"Leave?" Cattia gasped. "What do you mean he's gone? We've got to find him!" She scrambled to her feet, staring wildly in all directions. "Which way did he go? Did you see?"

"Cattia, I really don't know about this," Elsie protested. "How do we know we can trust him?"

"Els, are you crazy?" Cattia turned back to her, her eyes wide with fear. "We can't make it on our own. We're totally lost, we'll never find our way without him. And he said he could get us good honest work. Isn't that what you wanted? Which way did he go, Els?"

Elsie bit her lip, then pointed up the alley into the gloom. Cattia took off without warning, pelting over the cobbles.

"Come on, Elsie!" she called over her shoulder. "We've got to find him."

"Cat, wait!"

Dodging under pipes that expelled hot steam, she hurried through the labyrinthine alleys after Cattia. Finally, she caught up and managed to grab her friend's arm. Cat tried to pull away, but Elsie just managed to keep a strong hold.

"Cattia, we must find our way out of here. I don't trust Rye. Not one bit. There's gotta be someone else who can help us."

"What if there isn't anyone else?" Cattia asked. "What if he doesn't come back?"

"We'll survive," Elsie reassured her.

Cattia frowned. "Survive? How? Elsie, the only thing we know is Threadbury's. I thought you wanted to get away from there. I thought you wanted to build a new life!"

She's right, Elsie thought, her heart dropping at the realization. "Okay, we'll see what's ahead. But if I don't like what I see, we're leaving and going somewhere else."

Cat nodded firmly, then braced her hands on her knees, ducking to catch her breath for a moment. Elsie's own mouth was dry after her sprint and she realized dully that she was thirsty. After a brief respite, they continued on, walking now, skirting around abandoned firepits, makeshift shelters, and the detritus of street life. Just as Elsie began to despair of ever getting out of the dreadful maze, a warm, reddish glow appeared ahead of them. Cat pointed with an eager cry and Elsie followed quickly on her heels as they bore toward it. They stumbled out into a bustling street, the first they'd seen in many hours. Cat looked around, drinking in every sight with enormous eyes, but Elsie grabbed her friend's wrist once again in caution. She did not like the look of this place one bit.

Men in fine tailcoats strolled up and down the street lethargically, absently gawking at what sights there were. Shops and restaurants, all shuttered with dark blinds or curtains, lined the damp pavement, many with red paper lanterns flickering on hooks by their open doors. She caught the mixed scent of perfume, incense, sweat, standing water, and coal smoke. The entire street was painted a dull crimson by the gas lamps, tinted by tissue pasted over the glass. Women stood silently on each corner or just outside of the doors of the shops, bedecked in gaudy, low-cut dresses, frilly hairdos, and far too much makeup. They reminded Elsie strongly of the "rich ladies" they'd seen on the street earlier that morning. Something curdled in the pit of her stomach and she gripped Cat's arm with renewed fear.

"You like what you see?"

Rye's unexpected drawl made Elsie start. He approached nonchalantly from across the street, hands shoved deep into his coat pockets. "Don't you want to be all dolled up like those pretty girls?" A grin crept onto the man's face and his eyes twinkled, but not with warm mirth as she'd thought before.

"Elsie..." Cat began, her blue eyes fixing on her friend's face. Her voice was laced with fear and confusion. Elsie squeezed her plump wrist so hard that her nails dug into the flesh.

"Come along, no need to worry," Rye interrupted. "The boss says she's eager to meet you pretty ladies." He took Cat's other arm firmly in his large, strong hand.

"Hey!" Cattia gasped, right as Elsie snapped, "Let go of my friend!"

"You know, I think I know why I recognized those uniforms of yours," Rye said, ignoring their protests and turning to drag them out into the street. "Another of the boss's girls was wearing one when she arrived. She started out underfed like you, but don't worry; when you grow up-" Rye let out a sharp cry, interrupting his absentminded monologue as Elsie jammed her fist into his gut as hard as she possibly could. Rye doubled over, releasing Cat's arm as he clutched at his stomach.

"Come on, Cat, let's go," Elsie shouted, causing passersby to stop in their tracks and stare at the two girls. She stumbled back towards the alley behind her, pulling Cat along, her eyes bouncing from face to face as a small commotion began in the street. One of the dolled-up women advanced towards Cat, reaching out a gloved hand.

"C'mon pet, it's alright..."

It was Cat's turn to shriek and in an instant she turned from a lead weight into a force of fury. She turned on her heel and darted back into the alley, picking up speed as the chatter of the crowd grew behind them. Elsie followed, calling her friend's name between gasping breaths as Cat pelted on ahead, never once glancing over her shoulder. Elsie ran faster than she had from Threadbury's, blood pounding so loud in her ears that she heard nothing else.

Cat did not slow down. Clutching her skirts, she took every turn and ducked into every back alley she could find, leading Elsie on a wild chase. Cat caught her breath and froze for an instant when they barged into an alcove where a ragged family sat huddled around a makeshift fire. Then, she spun back around and stumbled away, brushing past Elsie as though she hadn't seen her. All Elsie could do was follow mutely after her, hoping that soon exhaustion would overwhelm her fear and they could rest at last.

Finally, after what felt like ages, Cat collapsed on her hands and knees beside an overflowing bin of garbage behind another faceless brick building. As Elsie knelt beside her friend, Cat crumpled to the cobbles. She pressed her cheek against the moist stones, her golden hair flowing over her shoulders, heavy with grease and dirt. Elsie put her hand on the girl's back and Cat whimpered, squeezing her eyes shut. A few tears leaked across her face and collected in the corner of her mouth. Her lips were dry and cracked, her skin hot and flushed.

Elsie opened her mouth to say something, anything, but both her breath and her words were long lost. She sank back onto her heels, unable to hold herself upright any longer, and slowly slumped down until she was lying beside Cat. Her hand rested on her friend's back, which rose and fell unsteadily, shaken by sobs. She had no idea how long she lay there, watching Cat as their breathing began to even out into a more relaxed pace. Elsie was still tense, certain that at any moment Rye or someone else just as bad might come along and scoop them up, but she knew if they did, she would be unable to resist.

We never should have left. Those were the first words that surfaced clearly in her mind. She stared at Cat's face. The girl's eyes were shut and her jaw had relaxed, spilling the trapped tears across her chapped lips and onto the filthy cobbles. *We're going to die out here,* was the next coherent thought. Elsie groaned, swallowing as her tongue searched wearily for any remaining moisture in her dry mouth. *Yes, if we can't find anything to eat or drink, we will die out here. Cat will die...*

The thoughts mounted and then subsided in a wave, replaced by a growing awareness of something else. Faintly, through the stench of smoke and trash, Elsie realized she could smell a savory aroma, something she had not smelled in a long time. Sometimes, when the girls completed a large order, or did an especially good job, Threadbury's client would donate some spare food. It was usually better than the millet and gruel that the girls normally ate, and sometimes there was even something extra special like cheese, fruit juice, or fresh fish. And once, long ago, there had been crispy, crunchy, juicy, pan-fried bacon.

Elsie sat up, heart pounding with excitement as she hardly dared to hope. She got to her feet, legs threatening to buckle again, and peered over the edge of the rubbish bin. Her stomach cramped and her mouth began to water. An entire skillet's worth of bacon, twisted and blackened but still recognizable, lay in the trash.

"Cat!" she cried, shaking the girl with a little too much enthusiasm. "Cat, wake up! Cat, I've found our breakfast." Cat looked up groggily, sputtering something incoherent as snot dribbled down her upper lip. Elsie shook her again. "Cat, get up, there's something to eat."

"What is it?" Cat slurred, rolling over and sitting up slowly, scrubbing at her face with a filthy bare arm. Rather than answering, Elsie reached into the rubbish bin and drew out a handful of the burnt bacon. She tossed it into Cat's lap, then another handful, then stuffed some of the bitter, blackened meat into her own mouth. The salty charcoal taste exploded across her tongue and she found herself laughing even as fresh tears began to well in her eyes.

"What are you eating? Was that in the trash, Els? What are you doing?" Cattia was completely shocked, staring in disbelief as Elsie dove back into the bin and extracted another handful.

"It's bacon," Elsie said with her mouth full. "Eat; it doesn't matter where it's been. C'mon, you've got to eat!" Cat stared dubiously at the burnt and tangled strips spread out on the skirt of her dress.

"Els, that's disgusting..."

"What choice do we have?" Elsie asked, laughing again even though her heart was rapidly descending into her toes. *We never should have left. We were comfortable. We were fed and safe. Cat was safe...* The raw hunger, the deep bone-felt need for survival, overrode her regretful thoughts as she stuffed the last of the bacon into her mouth and sat down across from Cattia. Cattia herself had begun to eat reluctantly, one eye on Elsie and one on her dubious fare. As she ate, however, her own hunger seemed to get the better of her, and soon she was picking crumbs from her skirt and licking her fingers with relish.

"Come on," Elsie said, grinning through her last few bitter tears, "We never ate like that at the workhouse, did we?"

Cattia laughed in spite of herself and they were both overcome by a fit of something between sobs and giggles.

"Now what?" Cat finally asked, looking up at Elsie with her earnest blue eyes. Elsie looked around vacantly, struggling to think once more as exhaustion crested over her.

"We should find shelter," she said, mustering as much conviction as she could. Cattia nodded. Elsie helped her to her feet, shivering as a bitter wind blew through the undercity, cutting through her thin, damp dress. Turning, she saw the rusting wreck of an abandoned automobile at the end of the alley. Her heart gave a little leap when she realized that the canvas roof was still mostly intact. A quick glance around told her that no one else was about. Taking Cat's hand gently in hers, Elsie led her forward and crawled under the damaged canopy. They lay down in their clothes in the back seat of the auto, wrapping themselves in some rough canvas torn from the roof.

Cattia nestled herself into the crook of Elsie's body, stirring and shifting as she tried to find a comfortable position. Elsie stared up at the underside of the remaining canopy, her eyes picking out spots of damp and blooms of mildew that discolored the surface. Fatigue washed over her, followed by bitter disappointment. She had forgotten how dreadful the streets could be, how dark and desperate, and she knew now that she could no more protect Cattia than she could protect herself. They had escaped from Rye's clutches by the skin of their teeth, but nothing promised they would be that lucky again.

Cat was breathing quietly now beside her, her face half hidden beneath her arm as she slept. Elsie struggled to keep her own eyes open, to remain vigilant against the danger that crowded in from every corner.

BITTER FREEDOM

Elsie didn't remember falling asleep, but she must have, since she woke with a jolt as she felt herself tossed against Cattia's knee. She nursed a bruised temple as her eyes fluttered, vaguely registering the dim light that filtered into the interior of the rusty automobile.

There was a sound of groaning metal, and Elsie, still only half awake, was tossed again, more violently. A low snore from somewhere beneath her indicated that Cattia was, inexplicably, still fast asleep. Elsie became aware of several voices speaking close by, but it was only when the industrial noises lowered to a gritty hum that she was able to make out what they were saying.

"It's incredible," a man said in a thick, undercity accent, "The things people throw away. You'd think we was all kings 'round here."

"Oy you jus' stop complaining, Bert," a second, higher male voice said. "Jus' cause y'aint got any autos lyin' around to be thrown out."

"I knows it Tom, but think o' what Bill could do wi' this. 'E could 'ave built it inta a right nice ride. But noooo, we has to take it out to tha Wreckage."

"Ye want to be put up in prison? Ye'd be a theif if ye took this anywhere but outta the city."

"If the baron wants all this rubbish outta 'is city, 'e can come down and drag it out 'imself, I says," Bert said sullenly.

The conversation faded into the pounding sounds of a huge rumbling engine situated far too close for comfort. Somehow, Cattia remained asleep, but there was no way Elsie could close her eyes again. She lay, petrified with fear and exhaustion, as the automobile shuddered once more and then began to move.

Elsie drifted in and out of consciousness, lulled by the hum of the machine until it jolted or shuddered, seemingly at random. She knew that there was nothing she could do except wait for the journey to be over. Finally, after an interminable and uncomfortable trip, the auto was set down with a grinding jolt. Elsie lay still beneath the rough canvas, holding her breath as the two men continued in their leisurely discussion. Finally, their voices were overwhelmed by the sound of the huge engine, which faded away into the chill night. Elsie strained her ears, but she could hear nothing except the sound of the wind whistling.

She hardly dared to move even then, but she felt Cattia stir and wake beside her. Yawning, the girl sat up and stretched, inadvertently punching Elsie in the cheek. Elsie gave a sharp cry, causing Cattia herself to shriek in surprise, and several hurried apologies later they were both finally conscious enough to take in their surroundings.

"It smells horrible," Cattia complained, wrinkling up her unwashed face and covering her nose with one hand. "Where are we?"

"I don't know," Elsie admitted, beginning to extricate herself from the heap of fabric, "But wherever we are, it has to be better than being with Rye."

Cattia shivered and went to pull the cloth back over herself, but Elsie put a hand on her shoulder.

"Come on," she said. "We need to get out of here." She took a deep breath and pushed the rusted door of the automobile open. Half stepping, half sliding, she wriggled out into the cold night. Her feet, still wrapped in Rye's handkerchief, scrabbled for a moment in empty air and then landed in something sticky. She swayed for a moment, then caught her balance. Elsie grimaced, even as she took in their surroundings with uncomprehending eyes.

The automobile had been placed haphazardly at the top of a large pile of slag. All around them, similar hulking heaps of indiscriminate rubbish ranged off as far as the eye could see beneath rolling gray-orange clouds. Over her shoulder, Elsie saw the ambient glow of Gorand itself, the skydocks silhouetted in a great band against the night. They were so far away from the city that Elsie, used as she was to the confines of Threadbury's workhouse, could barely fathom the distance.

"This must be the Wreckage," she said, more to herself than to Cattia, who had scrambled out of the rusted vehicle herself and now stood shivering uncertainly beside her.

"I've heard the women talk about this place," Cattia said softly. "They said it's the biggest dumping ground in all of Odol, maybe even the world."

"Is there a world outside of Odol?" Elsie asked bitterly, kicking at the heap. A hunk of broken brickwork went skittering down into the darkness.

"What are we going to do now?" Cat asked.

"We're going to find our way out of here," Elsie said with forced resolve.

It was, however, easier said than done. The landscape was hardly hospitable for travel on foot; piles of discarded machinery sat next to stacks of unused bricks and scrap metal, all mortared with gunk and spoiled food. Shreds of fabric and rotten tarpaulin flapped against the sky in the cold night breeze. Elsie took one step forward, and then another, crouching low, trying to scale down the mound they had been set upon. Cattia began to follow, but almost immediately missed a footing and was sent tumbling down the slope. Elsie flung out her arm and grabbed the girl's hand, but the momentum of Cat's fall pulled her off her feet. They landed, groaning, in a pile of filthy burlap sacks.

Elsie staggered to her feet first and helped Cattia stand up. They were in a narrow ravine between the mounds of trash, which thrust up against the sky, blocking out what little light there had been to begin with.

"You hurt, Cat?" she asked, rubbing her own scraped arms and hoping desperately that she hadn't received any cuts on the way down. She had heard horror stories from the women of infections caused by rusty metal or broken glass, and now they were surrounded by heaps of it.

"No, fortunately. I slid into something...gooey." Cat let out a wry snort of laughter.

"We are a mess..."

"Yeah, we are." Cat paused for a moment. "Hey, Els?"

"Yeah?"

"Did we do the right thing?"

"What do you mean?" Elsie asked.

"Coming out here. Away from Threadbury's. This isn't freedom..."

"Cat, just imagine what Harban would say if she saw us now."

Cattia stopped and stared incredulously at Elsie for a moment, her eyes roving over her stained and torn dress, scuffed arms, and dirty face. Elsie stared mournfully back at her friend, observing the same, and both were quiet for a melancholy moment before suddenly Elsie laughed aloud. Cattia began to laugh as well.

"She'd make us wash for two days straight!" Cattia squealed, and the more she laughed, the more Elsie laughed. The more Elsie laughed, the more Cattia laughed, and for a moment, the Wreckage felt just that much brighter to Elsie. *I can't imagine what it'd be like without her.*

All too soon, the laughter subsided, and Elsie knew that it was time for them to move on. Watching carefully where they stepped, they began to follow the thin, winding gully that snaked between the heaps of refuse, keeping the hazy glow of Gorand at their backs. As they traveled deeper, Elsie thought she caught sight of a faint reddish light over one of the mounds. Squinting in the dim orange night, she saw that there were faint wisps of smoke rising against the dark sky. She grabbed Cat's arm and pointed.

"Is that a fire?" Cattia asked eagerly, once she had seen the dim point of light.

"I think so," Elsie replied. Taking Cat's hand, she began to lead them along more quickly through the Wreckage, keeping the fire in sight as much as she possibly could.

Despite the relative flatness of the gully, it was an unpleasant walk. The girls could hardly go ten feet without a cry or a groan as one of them stepped on something too hard, too soft, too wet, or too slippery for comfort. Elsie found herself wishing more than ever that she hadn't been so hasty in her escape as to forget her shoes and stockings. Not that those would have rendered the journey entirely comfortable; Cattia began to complain of how wet her feet were getting, and at one point took off her shoe to dump the liquid that had collected inside of it.

"Elsie, what are we doing?" she asked plaintively as she struggled to don the sopping shoe once more, balancing precariously on one leg; neither of them dared to sit down upon anything.

"Going to the light."

"But *why*? How do we know it'll be any better there?"

Elsie was silent for a moment, thinking hard. Cattia finally slipped the shoe back over her heel and gingerly lowered her foot back to the ground, testing for a firm footing.

"We are going to find freedom, Cat," Elsie said at last, imbuing her tired voice with all the conviction she could muster. "*Real* freedom. Not what *he* was promising."

"Are you sure those women weren't happy?" Cattia asked, looking up at Elsie with something like defiance, tired and tattered though it was. "How can you know? Maybe they found what we're looking for..."

"Does it matter?" Elsie said, tugging on her friend's hand. "We're out here now. We must keep moving."

"It does matter! Els, he said that a girl in a Threadbury's dress was working for his boss. Maybe it's not so bad..."

It took substantial will for Elsie not to shake the girl. *How could you say that? How could you even think that? We would be no freer there than if we were back at Threadbury's!* Taking a deep breath, she forced herself to conjure up some last reserve of patience. "Cat, we can't go back now. There's nothing we can do besides go on. We've got to make for that fire; maybe someone lives out here who will help us."

"Nobody lives out here," Cattia said dully, but she stumbled after Elsie all the same. Elsie frowned, knowing it was true. No one lived within a dozen miles of Gorand's city walls, and beyond that there were only small supply towns dotted periodically along the train lines. The women at Threadbury's had not spoken much about the world beyond Gorand and often only in passing. Too much of "that sort of talk" could lead to a reprimand from M. Harban. But Elsie had gleaned enough to know that they were completely alone.

Not much further along, the sad excuse for a path veered far to the left, taking them away from the light. Wordlessly, Elsie and Cattia decided that it would be better to climb the mound of decomposing paper and crushed upholstery in front of them, rather than diverting from their course. The yellow light seemed no nearer than when they first set out. Nonetheless, Elsie hoped that soon they would stumble into some kind of settlement, perhaps one of the mining towns, where kind people would offer two poor runaways shelter and food.

Lost in thought as she ascended the heap of refuse, Elsie felt a yank on her arm as Cattia froze in place behind her. Looking back,

Elsie opened her mouth to speak, but she immediately saw the girl's eyes fixed on something above them. Elsie whipped her head around and felt her heart seize in her chest.

A figure had appeared on top of the mound, facing away from the girls, silhouetted starkly against the rolling clouds. Its frame was thin and lanky, with long greasy hair hanging in scraggly curls over thin, bony shoulders. It was dressed in tattered scraps of various garments clumsily stitched together, with no discernible shape. As they watched, both petrified, the figure's head turned back to look at them. What little they could see of the face was gaunt, wrinkled and weatherbeaten, and the eyes were covered by makeshift leather goggles with mismatched lenses. The lower half of its face was covered with a grimy handkerchief, and it was impossible to tell whether it was male or female. One hand extended towards the girls, and it beckoned them nearer, its gloved finger creaking softly as it bent.

Cattia was the first to scream and Elsie found herself screaming as well. She lurched to the left, half scrambling and half sliding down the slope, and hit the path running. She barely registered the fact that she had let go of her friend's hand.

Only once she had left the figure far behind did she stop moving, and then she froze and held her breath, listening for any motion or sound of pursuit. It was then she realized Cattia was not behind her. She spun in a slow circle, straining eyes staring into the orange gloom, desperately searching for any sign of the other girl.

Throwing away all caution, she shouted Cat's name as loud as she could again and again, her voice swallowed up by the heaps all around her. *I can't go on without you, Cat! Please, please hear me.* She began to walk, then jog, uncertain of what direction she was heading, whether she was going away from where they'd seen the figure or towards it. She called again, and then again, her heart pounding with more vigor as the adrenaline surged, carrying her exhausted body through the desert of Gorand's excess. But soon enough, as Cat made no appearance and she grew more bewildered about where she was, she felt the energy draining. Finally, she came to a halt at a crossroads.

Vainly, she looked around again, as if she expected Cattia to appear around the next mound, but the girl was nowhere to be seen. Elsie felt a lump growing in her throat and she pushed back tears. She wasn't sure if they were for herself, or for Cattia. *No, they're for Hanna,* she thought, and then wondered what she meant by it. *I suppose she's in the best place after all. She knew better. We should have stayed with her at Threadbury's.* She began to walk sullenly along the path, barely caring to dodge acrid puddles and sickly-sweet smelling piles of food waste. The stench didn't make her gag anymore.

She reached a small clearing in the refuse and saw that a makeshift structure had been set up. Four tall beams and a rusted sheet of metal made a sorry home, but it was the first structure she had seen that looked intentionally built. She was bone tired, dragging her aching feet through the muck and rubbish, and she halfheartedly scrounged in a nearby pile, finding an old moth-eaten blanket that had only one wet corner. She ducked into the shelter, wrapping the blanket around her, and hunkered down beneath the shade of the bent metal.

Warily, she took stock of what she could see from the hut. Her vision was disturbingly limited. *This might be that...person's haunt,* she thought grimly. *But if it is, I'll never see them coming. What sort of person are they? Do they live out here in this awful place? What did they want from us?* She shuddered, vainly hoping that Cattia would find her soon.

The wind howled through the mounds, slicing through blanket, dress, and skin, cutting Elsie straight to the bone. Before, she had considered the winters at Threadbury's to be unbearable, but that had been a comforting spring breeze compared to the frigidity she experienced now. Maybe there wasn't anything to fight for in the world, she mused bitterly. Maybe Madame Harban was right after all. *And that Marjen woman was wrong about fighting. About dreaming.*

She shifted, laying her head down on her arm. From this angle, she could once again see the faint reddish light, flickering slightly as it reflected off the distant heaps. Before, it had seemed like a beacon of hope. Now, it seemed to taunt her.

12

A Chance Meeting

Elsie wandered aimlessly in the cool daylight beneath a gray sky, hoping against all common sense that she would stumble upon Cattia somewhere in the Wreckage. The cramps in her stomach were getting worse and the relentless wind chilled her to the bone. She knew she would need to find something to eat, and quickly. She felt a harsh pain in her stomach and clutched at her abdomen, stumbling to a halt and doubling over. Her hands were still scalded from the pipe outside of Threadbury's, her feet covered in cuts and barely covered by the handkerchiefs. Sighing, she leaned down and pulled the handkerchiefs away, tossing them into one of the heaps. They were indistinguishable from the other rubbish.

Elsie began to walk again, this time determined to stay on a single path. The worst thing she could do out here was to stray; then it was likely that she would only end up going in circles and never get anywhere. *I have to find that smoke,* she thought, a new determination filling her tired limbs. *If it is that stranger's camp, I'll just sneak some food. There's nothing good to eat out here.* The remnants and food waste she'd seen in the mounds were far worse than anything out of a bin in the city.

After another hour of winding through the Wreckage, she looked back to find that the vague haze of Gorand had lessened, and the skydocks had shrunk on the horizon. A strange mixture of excitement and fear filled her. She knew that the city was the only thing she had to use as a landmark, and though the fact that it was diminishing meant she was going in the right direction, once it was out of sight she had no idea what she was going to do.

Taking a deep breath, she turned and set off again, making towards an exceptionally high mound of rubbish. It appeared to consist mostly of machinery, skeletal automobile chassis, and engine parts, with some broken bricks and sheet metal mixed in. As she approached it, a rush of excitement filled her chest as she saw smoke rising above the pile. Her footsteps quickened, even as she began to hear voices echo off the surroundings.

"…just because…doesn't mean we won't fly again…" a calm, level voice was saying. It was a man's voice, obviously Odolian, but the accent reminded her of the women at the workhouse who came from the central region of Bolden.

Another male voice erupted into a string of curses that made her ears turn bright red. "…she just walks off like that. Limping away! You know she won't make it. Think of what she could have done for us, that-"

Elsie let out a squeak of embarrassment as the barrage of insults was taken up again. However, she couldn't help but be relieved; there were *people* out here, and though one of the men was clearly more civil than the other, she was desperate enough to put that aside, assuming they appeared friendly. Almost too eagerly, she began to climb the mound, finding footholds on sheet metal and bricks. If nothing else, perhaps they could help her find Cattia. Maybe they had seen her.

"I don't care about probabilities, Paul," the harsh voice shouted. "I care that we've been stranded here by a woman who can hardly walk! I can't believe I let you talk me into letting her go…"

"It was for the best," Paul intoned calmly. "She made it clear that she was unwilling to work with us any longer. Please understand, I am not trying to supersede your authority. Maria and I were trying to make amends."

"She was only ever loyal for the money. Damn!"

"Arthur," Paul said slowly, "Even if you could get the engine fixed, how would you get it into the ship?"

The argument erupted again as Elsie rounded the edge of the heap, peering over the top of a foul-smelling paper bag. Two men stood in a rough clearing with a large hunk of oily, rusted machinery between them. The taller of the two, younger and in better shape, was bent over, fiddling with something in the guts of the mechanism. He was the bad-tempered one; Arthur. He was fit and distinguished, with his head of fiery red hair, but disheveled and covered in black oil stains. Paul, the far more pleasant of the two, was shorter and stockier, with a round face and large, well-groomed sideburns. Elsie raised herself a little higher. They certainly *looked* civilized, but the fact that they were both men gave her pause.

"Arthur, please," Paul insisted, "Take a break. Maria's going to be making dinner soon. You need to-"

"*You* need to find me someone who can fix this ship!"

"Please, Arthur, can't you be reasonable?" Paul admonished.

"I will be when this engine is working!" Arthur shouted. He pulled on something, a wrench locked around a bolt on part of the machine, but it didn't budge. Muttering, Arthur pulled again, but the tool must have pinched his hand, because he let out a cry of pain, cursed, and spun around in a rage, throwing the wrench straight in Elsie's direction. Elsie barely had time to react before the tool struck her.

Perched on the bent rail of the *Heart of Resistance*, Maria watched Paul and Arthur with a grimly bemused look on her face. They were standing by the engine that Arthur had found, which the two had spent hours dragging all the way back to the remains of the ship. *Idiots*, she thought. *Why not just sneak back into the city and try again? I certainly cannot put that engine in, and watching those two try to figure out how the mechanics work is one of the most entertaining farces I've seen.*

The argument was heating up, though, and simple frustration had turned into real anger, at least on Arthur's part. His face was turning as red as his hair and the muscles in his neck bulged as he yelled at Paul. It was no longer an amusing sight and Maria could tell that Paul was just trying to keep Arthur from flying off the handle. She rose from her perch and climbed to the ground, momentarily losing sight of the conversation.

Paul, you know we can just get out of here anytime. Sneak back into the city, get some honest work and save up. She sighed and turned around in time to see Paul raise his hands defensively. Judging by what she could read of Arthur's lips, he was saying some unpleasant things about Janna. *At least they'd better be about her. If I find out he's talking about me, I'll...*

Her eyes were drawn by a flash of movement near the pile behind the two and her body tensed. Unnoticed by the two men, a small, disheveled figure was sneaking towards them. She started towards Paul and Arthur, thinking to warn them, but then she saw the state of the figure more closely. It was a skinny young girl in a tattered workhouse uniform. She looked dreadful, like she had slept in the Wreckage, and her hands were stained red, as though with blood.

Maria tried to make a noise to get Paul and Arthur's attention, but whether it was not loud enough or whether Arthur's shouting drowned her out, she could not tell. For the moment, Arthur was not paying her any mind, just continuing to rant about Janna. Then without any warning, Arthur turned around in a rage and threw the socket wrench in his hand right at the child. Maria gasped, pressing her hands over her mouth as the steel instrument struck the girl in the eye and she fell to the ground. Paul made a wild gesture and began shouting at Arthur as Maria ran up to his side. Catching sight of her, Paul quickly began to translate for Arthur.

'*I didn't even see her. Maria, bring her into the ship so we can...*'

'*Can what?*' Maria signed, glaring daggers at Arthur.

'*Can fix her up. I wasn't trying to hurt anyone.*'

'*Come on Paul,*' Maria said, ignoring Arthur and waving Paul over. '*I'll need your help. She's small, but she's still a lot for me to carry.*' They went to the limp figure of the girl, who was fortunately still breathing. She had scraggly cropped black hair, filthy and tangled. Maria put an ear to the girl's chest. Though her breathing was a little shallow, it could have been much worse after a hit like that.

'*Probably just concussed,*' Maria signed quickly as she got to her feet. Paul nodded and knelt, scooping the girl into his arms. The girl turned her head away from the light, burying her face in Paul's chest as he carried her toward the ship, Maria right beside him. All the while, Arthur stood rooted in the same spot, staring at them with the dumbest look Maria had ever seen on his face.

They took the girl into the captain's cabin, which had been set up in some semblance of repair and was more habitable than the rest of the ship. Paul laid the girl down and Maria tapped him on the shoulder to get his attention.

'*Bring me one of my dresses. I need to get those rags off her.* You need to talk some sense into that man."

Paul sighed and began signing back. '*Which dress?*'

'*The green one. And bring my sewing. It will look a little rough, but it'll be better than those rags.*'

Paul nodded and left her alone with the girl.

As her first order of business, Maria stripped the girl of her tattered dress and soiled petticoat, leaving her stays, chemise, and drawers, all of which were still intact. She dampened a rag and began to gently sponge away the filth that coated her skin. *Poor thing...Arthur owes you more than just an apology...* She paused to grab a painted folding screen from the corner, arranging it in front of the bed to give the girl a little more privacy, before continuing with her work. Once the girl was sufficiently clean, Maria covered her gently with the bedclothes and brushed the hair out of the child's face. *She can't have eaten a good meal in weeks,* she thought, caressing the girl's gaunt cheek. *When you wake up, child, I'm going to make you as plump as I am. You'll finally have someone to look after you.*

She was interrupted by a tap on her shoulder. Paul had come in, holding her green dress and small sewing kit. With a huff, Maria pushed him to the other side of the screen. *'Stupid! What do you think the screen is there for? Give the child a little privacy.'*

Paul shrugged apologetically and set his bundle down on a small side table. *'The covers are over her, dear. Besides, how was I supposed to get your attention?'*

'You could have left it on a chair, you oaf.' Maria gave another huff and crossed her arms sternly. Getting no response from Paul, she rolled her eyes. *'She looks horrible, you know. Gaunt and dirty. But her dress is a workhouse uniform. You know how runaways are treated in the best circumstances, right?'*

Paul nodded. *'Yes, I know. You're sure she's a runaway?'*

'Not entirely. But she doesn't look adept to the streets either. Her feet are covered in acid burns and her hands look badly stained with dye. I'd say she ran away from a textiles workhouse.'

'Poor girl. What should we do with her, then?'

Maria looked back at the screen longingly. *'We've always wanted a child, Paul. Don't give me that look. You do too, you just think you're sparing my feelings. Perhaps we could-'*

Paul took Maria's hands in his and shook his head. *'We can't possibly bring a child with us. You know the kind of danger we're going into. I was reluctant to bring Janna along, for her sake. I couldn't stand to take a child...'*

It was Maria's turn to shake her head. *'I'm not saying we take her with us! Well, save to take her back to the city. We could settle down there together. You could find a job, a real job Paul. Arthur can go mad on his own. We don't need to be dragged along!'*

'You know I can't leave him!'

'Why not?'

'Because he is my captain. Loyalty matters! Besides, I try to keep him in check. If I wasn't here, he would do far worse than he already has. Think of the people he could hurt.'

'I don't care about those people; I care about you and me and this poor little girl. Arthur can kill himself if he wants, but I don't want him getting you killed too!' Maria felt tears well up in her eyes, blurring the view of her husband. Paul began to sign something, but Maria just slapped his hands down. *Just go. I'll take care of the girl for now. You try to talk some sense into your captain.'* She turned on her heel, hoping that Paul hadn't seen the tears of anger that had begun to stream down her face.

Paul's strong arms wrapped around her shoulders. He planted a kiss on her cheek, then turned her around, putting his lips on hers and burying his hands in her mousy brown hair. Maria felt her cheeks flush in spite of herself and by the time they broke apart her mood was softened. *Silly man...always finding a way to get me off my high horse.*

Paul made a passionate sign to her. *'I love you, Maria.'* She thought she could see the glimmer of tears in his brown eyes.

Nodding, she signed, *'Same,'* before turning back around. Her anger had dissipated, leaving a hollow ache she knew all too well. She would never be able to convince Paul to leave Arthur and start a normal life.

She looked back over her shoulder and saw that Paul had gone. Resigning herself, she snatched up her dress and sewing kit, sat down, and began to sew, hoping that she could make her old dress fit the much smaller girl.

It was about an hour later that Paul interrupted her again, signing frantically, his eyes wide and a bemused grin on his face. *'Maria, there's another one! Another girl out there, only this one's conscious and she wants something to eat.'*

VANITY

Elsie gingerly touched the swelling around her eye and gasped when a sharp pain prickled at the spot. *What did you expect?* she thought ruefully. She was still disoriented from waking up in a strange bed, dressed only in her ragged slip, drawers, and stays, her head throbbing dully. She lay still for a while, her mind racing as she struggled to recollect how exactly she'd ended up here. Tattered scraps of the escape from Threadbury's surfaced slowly in her head. There was Harban screaming, Rye leering, the stark image of Captain Marjen's hat bobbing away through the crowd. Her lip curled in disgust at the memory of the burnt bacon and her stomach growled as she realized that was the last time she'd eaten.

She bolted upright when she remembered Cattia, ignoring the pain that spun her head. *Cattia! Where is she?* She looked around frantically. Taking a deep breath, she forced herself to calm down and take in her surroundings for a moment. The bed was large and comfortable, though rather disheveled; perhaps she had tossed and turned in her sleep. A painted screen divided the bed from the rest of the room and as Elsie studied it, she realized that it was leaning. Or maybe the entire room was leaning; the bed was certainly not level. *I wasn't hit in the head that hard, was I...?*

She froze momentarily when she heard movement coming from somewhere beyond the screen. Then, deciding it would be better to be on her feet than not, she threw her legs over the side of the bed and, with a struggle, planted her feet on the ground. They had been carefully bandaged by her unknown benefactor, but they hurt when they touched the rough wooden floorboards. Elsie struggled not to cry out as every blister, sore, and cut on her feet burned with pain. She hobbled to the screen and peered around the edge, unsure of what she would find.

A small yelp of pain from the room's other occupant startled her. A plump woman with brown hair was sitting in a comfortable-looking armchair in front of a small desk, sucking on her finger. A bundle of green fabric, profusely pinned, had been hastily tucked under her arm. Seeing that it was a woman, Elsie felt more at ease. Her fears about Cattia, however, still remained bubbling below the surface of her immediate thoughts.

"Ma'am?" Elsie began hesitantly. "Excuse me? I was wondering if you could tell me...well, where are we?"

The woman gave no response. In fact, she didn't even seem to have heard Elsie as she finished nursing her hurt finger and went back to her sewing. Her plump fingers moved nimbly over the fabric, whipping the needle in and out as quick as lightning. The woman paused again to study her handiwork, grunted in dismay, and undid a few stitches before resuming her progress. Elsie hovered for a moment, uncertain of what to do.

"Ma'am, no disrespect—I can see that you're busy—but I don't have anything decent to wear, and I don't know where I am or what has happened to me. Could you at least tell me where I am? Please?"

Still, the woman gave no response. Elsie began to worry she was getting off on the wrong foot. In these unfamiliar circumstances, it would do her no good to come off as rude. "Please, I'm scared," she said at last.

"She can't hear you," said a man's voice. "And she gets so invested in her work she probably hasn't seen you yet." Elsie hadn't heard him come in, but a man with thick brown sideburns, one of the ones who had been fighting in the clearing, was now standing in the room on the other side of the screen.

Even as he was speaking, the woman glanced up casually from her work and saw him. She set the fabric down in her lap and watched as the man performed a complex series of hand signals before pointing to Elsie. The woman started when she met Elsie's fascinated gaze and began signing hastily to the man. Elsie understood a couple of the signs; there had been an older deaf woman at Threadbury's who used signs exclusively to communicate before she passed away, and Elsie had picked up a few things from her. She caught the man signing "sorry" before hastily turning his back to her.

"Apologies. Maria reminded me you aren't fully dressed." He looked over at the woman who had risen to her feet and signed something to her, but Maria only rolled her eyes. Paul repeated the sign and Maria relented, beginning to sign something back. Paul began to speak on behalf of Maria. "'Since I need Paul to translate for me, I guess he has to stay. But he keeps his eyes on me, or he loses them.'" He signed an unspoken response, causing Maria to snort with laughter.

Elsie watched in fascination. *I should have learned more from that woman...* "Okay, that's fine," she said slowly. "Thank you very much for your hospitality. But, oh! Have you seen Cattia anywhere? My friend? She's about my age, lighter hair..."

"She's here," Paul reassured. "She's outside right now, talking to the captain. In a moment, I'll go get her for you."

Relief flooded Elsie's chest and she began to breathe easier. Cattia was safe, and she was here. Suddenly, things looked much less dire. "Thank you. Um, could I have something to wear first?" She bit her bottom lip remorsefully. *Manners.* "Please?"

This time Maria responded. "'Patience, child. You mustn't rush my handiwork. This dress was mine, but,'" she gestured to herself and sighed loudly. "'As you can see it needs a few adjust-ments.'" Elsie saw Paul and Maria make yet another untranslated exchange, which ended with Maria giggling and blushing.

Elsie shifted, pulling back further behind the screen. "When will it be done?"

"'Soon. You took quite a blow to the head, child,'" Maria said, "'You should lay back down until I'm finished. Maybe just rest until I have dinner ready.'" Paul added, "She's a great cook. And don't worry, the food comes from the ship's stores, not our... surroundings."

"Alright, but..." Elsie hesitated, then thought better of it. Questions could wait for later. The throbbing in her head was still quite intense and she knew the woman was right; she ought to lie down. "Never mind. Thank you, again. Um...I look forward to meeting you in a less..." she paused, "awkward situation."

"Nonsense," Paul laughed. "Don't mention it. And as for awkwardness, I'll head out before Maria kills me with her eyes." Maria guffawed again, putting a plump hand to her mouth.

"Okay, thank you. Just tell me when the dress is ready," Elsie said hurriedly before ducking behind the screen. For a moment, she stood still, expecting Paul and Maria to have some further conver-sation. But after a few minutes of uninterrupted silence, she heard Paul's leather shoes clump against the floorboards as he left the room.

Of course you can't hear a signed conversation, dummy, Elsie thought reproachfully as she climbed back into bed.

A pair of hands gripped Elsie's shoulders and shook her violently. She sat up, frightened and blinking, and saw Cattia's relieved face hovering over her. Elsie snapped her eyes shut as the dull pain in her head returned, laying back against the pillows in a vain attempt to alleviate it. That wasn't meant to be, however, for Cattia launched into a sort of tirade, as if all the words she would have said to Elsie while they were apart had been bottled up inside her.

"Elsie! Goodness, you had me worried there. There's just so much that's happened in just a couple of days and you don't know any of it yet! You know I met Captain Pendington? His first name is Arthur and you wouldn't believe, but he's the most handsome man I've ever seen. Were you hurt? How'd you get that bruise on your eye? Well anyways, I was running for a while and lost track of you after we saw that horrible man. He was really creepy don't you think? Besides, he could have been dangerous. Paul and Maria don't live out here, you know; their ship just crashed and that's why they're out here in the Wreckage with Mister, um, I mean *Captain* Pendington. He's *very* upset that the engine got destroyed and no one will tell me exactly why or what happened, but he found another one just sitting there but he has no way to get it into the ship and, according to Paul, has no idea how to fix it up into working order either, and are you going to put something on that eye? There's a vanity over there with some things in it, not that I know exactly what you're supposed to do. Anyways, do you like my dress? I know it's blue and I've always preferred red, but do you think it suits me? It was Maria's old one, but it didn't fit quite right and she had to sew it up; you've been out for more than a day. Breakfast is almost ready and you really need to fix yourself up before you go out there. Captain Pendington has the reddest hair I've ever seen, and great broad shoulders, and-"

"Cattia, please!" Elsie didn't mean to shout, but in her desperation the words came out at a higher volume and pitch than she'd intended. With an effort, she lowered her voice. "Please, hold on for just a moment. I need to get my dress. Maria was mending one for me, so let me find it and put it on..."

"But your face! Your eye...you look dreadful!"

"Thanks," Elsie muttered, clambering out of bed and onto the uneven wooden floor. "Just give me a moment to freshen up."

"Yes, let's see what's in the vanity!" Cattia said energetically, bounding to her feet and following Elsie out from behind the screen. Elsie sighed deeply, doing her best not to roll her eyes.

The green dress lay neatly folded on the chair at the little desk. It didn't fit quite right, even with Maria's alterations, but Elsie was glad to put it on. As soon as the last lace was tied in front, as was the older fashion, Cattia swooped in like a bird of prey and commandeered a makeup kit from the vanity. Elsie wasn't even given a chance to look at her own reflection as Cattia strung words together like a seamstress at Threadbury's, powdering Elsie's face with an enormous soft puff that threatened to smother her. Though she was rather uncomfortable, Elsie couldn't help but smile. She'd seen Cat in good spirits before, but never as happy as this, overjoyed by the simple act of living.

Finally, Cattia ushered Elsie to the vanity, where with one-and-a-half eyes, she was able to look at herself. It was the first time she had really seen herself this way; at Threadbury's, mirrors were forbidden, as the women "could not be afforded such vanities." Elsie had caught a few glimpses of herself in the dye vats, curious to know what she looked like to others, but the harsh, swirling colors of the dye kept her from getting a clear view. She knew a few things: the cropped black hair, how thin she was...

But she had never gotten a look like this. It was shocking. Elsie stared, feeling as though she might faint. She was thin, stringy. She had bony arms and a gaunt, haggard face, so unlike Cattia's shapely features and a far cry from Maria's plump silhouette. Elsie touched her pronounced cheekbones and looked sadly into her sunken eyes, one of which was bruised purple with a useless layer of powder barely covering it. Scrapes covered her arms and there were even a few on her face. The dress did her no favors either. The puffy sleeves, already many sizes too large for her slight frame, only accentuated how thin she was. Though the dress had certainly been altered to suit her better, the fit was still quite roomy at best.

Regardless, it was a nicer dress than she'd ever worn before, so she managed a grin before noticing her hands. She rubbed them nervously. They were still stained red, blistered and scraped from the escape, conspicuous against the fine green fabric. She tucked them behind her back at once; the crimson stains only served to remind her of Threadbury's.

Cattia was ecstatic. "Oh, you look marvelous, Els!" she cried gleefully. Elsie rolled her eyes, but a smile tugged the corner of her mouth. Cattia's happiness was contagious. Without warning, Cat grabbed Elsie's arm and practically shoved her down into a red cushioned chair, which was bolted to the floor. "Now I'm really going to do your makeup. They have everything in here: rouge, liner, lipstick. You'll look just like a real lady!"

"Cat...Cat, I'm not a doll," Elsie said, growing nervous as Cat approached with a small palette and a fist full of makeup brushes. It took far too long and Cattia seemed to forget Elsie's bruised eye in her eagerness to apply pigment to every conceivable portion of her face. She finally she finished and stepped back proudly to survey her handiwork.

Elsie didn't even get a chance to look at herself in the vanity before Cat scurried over to another corner of the room where an old phonograph player stood in stately elegance. Cat snatched up a pair of green shoes that matched the fabric of the dress. They fit Elsie competently, though they were perhaps a little wide.

"These were Maria's too," Cat said with a broad smile. "You know, I really like them."

"What? The shoes?"

"No! Paul and Maria...and Arthur too, but Paul and Maria are very nice."

"I thought you liked Arthur more," Elsie said, standing up.

"Oh, he's handsome, as men go," Cat giggled. "But he's also a bit... harsh? I guess that's the best way to say it."

Elsie was about to reply but her stomach growled, reminding her that she hadn't eaten in far too long. "Well, I think that it's about time we went and got some food."

"Oh yes!" Cattia exclaimed. "Maria's a wonderful cook, and she makes all sorts of meals that you've never even heard of, and..."

Elsie allowed herself to be led out of the room by the incessantly chattering Cattia and onto the creaking, canopied deck of a wooden ship. The ship was definitely tilted, which only became more obvious as they picked their way down a makeshift ramp and out into the midst of the Wreckage. Her eyes landed on Paul, who was sitting beside a small campfire minding a pot of some bubbling aromatic concoction, stirring it occasionally to prevent it from boiling over. He took a swig of dark coffee from a chipped mug before glancing up at Cattia and Elsie. He nearly choked with shock, spitting out the drink.

"Look at her!" Cattia said with a squeal. "Isn't she wonderful?"

Maria came from around the other side of the ship and looked just as delighted as Cat when she saw Elsie. She signed to Paul, who was still recovering, and clearly didn't see. Instead, his eyes, wide with horror, were drawn to Elsie once more.

"What on earth did you do to the poor girl?" He laughed through the question and Elsie felt her cheeks warm with embarrassment. Maria got his attention and signs started flying between the two, before finally being cut short as Paul raised a hesitant hand. "Elsie, I apologize for my rudeness," he said sincerely.

"Oh, you needn't mention it," Elsie said, rubbing her hands together anxiously. She was well aware that she looked horrendous.

"Nonsense," Paul laughed brightly. "We've already met Miss Cattia, but we haven't properly met you yet. Let me introduce us. I'm Paul, Paul Kauisol, and this is my wife, Maria."

"I'm Elsie," she said with all the dignity she could muster, wishing she had a surname of her own. "Pleased to meet you. And please thank Mar...Mrs. Kauisol for the dress."

"Yes, I'll tell her of course," Paul said, and did so, much to the delight of Maria. "But," he added aloud, "It's just Paul and Maria. No formalities."

Elsie frowned, remembering the last time someone told Cattia and her to be less formal. She crossed her arms, fortifying herself from any potential danger. Paul and Maria didn't look dangerous but a lack of caution had caused nothing but trouble since their escape.

"So...what are you going to do with us?" Elsie asked, her tone harsher than she intended.

Cattia put a hand on Elsie's shoulder. "Els, they're fine, they're not like..."

"Do with you?" Paul asked confusedly. "I don't rightly know..." He looked to Maria for advice, then added, "What do you mean?"

"Where are you going to take us? What's the end here? Are we going to do labor for you? Or something worse? Because I'm not going to do anything like that!" Elsie's words tumbled out sharply, despite Cattia's reassurance. She hadn't realized until that moment but her dignity was still injured from their encounter with Rye. Though she'd been suspicious of him from the beginning, she never truly thought that someone could be capable of such a thing.

Paul and Maria looked at each other with concern. Paul was about to say something, but he was interrupted by the voice of another man.

"She's awake?" The red-haired man, Arthur, the same man who had thrown the wrench at Elsie's face, strode out from behind a pile of rubble into the clearing. His face was set and stern, but spotted with black grease, which also stained his unkempt hair. Solidly built, he looked impressive, almost commanding, even dressed in clothes filthier than Elsie's workhouse dress. He wore a dark red overcoat over a baggy shirt which perhaps had once been white; now it was sodden with grease and soot. His piercing eyes studied Elsie intently. "Paul, what have you been doing to her? She looks horrendous!"

Paul stood up hastily. "Arthur, could I speak with you for a moment? I'm sorry girls. Please excuse us. Maria will entertain you while we talk."

Frowning, Arthur begrudgingly stalked over behind a nearby heap of rubbish and began to exchange heated words with Paul.

Elsie couldn't make out exactly what they were whispering about, but she heard her own name mentioned by Paul more than once. All of Arthur's responses were gruff monosyllables.

Maria had ambled over to the fire and was serving up three helpings of the bubbling, savory stew into wide-bottomed bowls. Despite her hunger, Elsie could only think of what Arthur and Paul were saying to one another. Cattia clearly shared her sentiment, staring fixedly at the pile that hid the two men.

"You think they'll let us stay?" she asked in a hoarse whisper, leaning close to Elsie.

Elsie shrugged. "They're at least going to give us food," she said. A sudden, sharp noise caused her to start. Turning, she saw that Maria had begun to sharpen a knife that did not appear to be designed for cooking. The scraping noise was jarring but neither Elsie nor Cattia were about to complain. Not only did the knife look quite dangerous, but Maria looked like she knew how to use it. And, Elsie reasoned, the woman probably had no idea that she was even making a sound.

As Elsie watched, Maria looked up and gestured for them to come over to the fire. Reluctantly, Elsie and Cattia obliged. There were cushions on the ground, made of rolled up red cloth. As Cattia sat down on one of them, Elsie's mouth dropped open in shock as she realized what she was looking at.

"Cat, these are..." She picked one up and unfurled it. It was an imperial uniform, with the new buttonhole. Maria gave Elsie a queer look as she set two of the bowls on an upturned crate. The box was stamped with the words "Threadbury's Textiles."

"We made these!"

Cat scrambled to her feet just as Arthur came striding into the campsite. "Food ready yet?" he asked curtly.

Elsie spun around, planting one hand on her hip and waving the uniform in front of her as Paul joined them. "These are from Threadbury's! We made these. That ship is Captain Marjen's, isn't it?" Elsie continued, staring around at their confused rescuers, "Just who are you people?"

As Paul translated for Maria, the woman stood up as well, a frown creasing her small mouth. Elsie stepped over to stand by her friend protectively. A tense silence hung over the camp.

"I can explain," Arthur said.

"Okay, you'd better!" Elsie exclaimed. She shook the coat again threateningly. "Start with who you are, who you *really* are."

"My name is Arthur," the man said, "Arthur Pendington." Stepping forward on his long legs, he snatched the uniform out of Elsie's hand, causing her to cringe away, shielding Cattia with her body. Arthur examined the coat in his hands. "Never could get the lapels right, huh." He looked up. "I used to be a soldier. I'm not now. In fact, you could say that I am working against the empire's interests."

"And that means we should trust you?" Elsie asked, incredulous. Cattia swallowed a hoarse sob. Elsie thought she heard the word "rebel" choked out amid the girl's whimpering.

"I am the captain of the *Heart of Resistance*," Arthur stated proudly, seeming to ignore the question. "Paul here is my navigator, my pilot. And Maria's his wife."

Elsie looked dubiously at Arthur. "That...ship. That's Captain Marjen's ship you destroyed. How are you going to repay her?"

"I'm not intending to repay the baron's lackey," Arthur said coldly. "You look like you're starving, kid." He squatted to meet Elsie's gaze. "Paul, what should we do with these two runaways?"

"I guess it depends on what they want," Paul said firmly, giving the girls a reassuring glance. "You're free to go if you'd like, or you can stay here with us. Maria and I won't let any harm come to you."

Elsie considered for a moment and looked at Cattia. She no longer looked afraid. Elsie refused to be afraid either. "What can we do to help?" she asked. "And what would we be helping you do?"

"First thing you can do is grab a bite to eat," Paul said with a smile. "I must agree with Arthur on this; you look starved."

"Oh, goody!" Cattia cried, clasping her hands together with joy. "It *does* smell amazing!"

14

GREYER'S REBELLION

Breakfast was wonderful, if a little unusual for that time of day. Cattia had not exaggerated when she said that Maria was an amazing cook. The stew was so good it made Elsie forget the sickly-sweet smell of the refuse around her, at least for a few moments. Then it was time to clean up and Cattia quickly volunteered to help with the dishes. Elsie was left standing awkwardly, unsure of what she ought to do. Between the two of them, Maria and Cattia had the domestic chores covered. Arthur had left them halfway through the meal, wolfing down his food so that he could get back to work as soon as possible. Paul was hovering around his wife and Cattia, playing interpreter; they seemed to be deeply involved in conversation as they did the washing up.

As she stood ruminating and watching the others, a shadow fell over Elsie's shoulder from behind, startling her. She turned to see that Arthur had appeared once more. He stood with his arms crossed and a sour expression on his face, staring past her at Paul.

"Paul, I could use some help over here. I've only got two hands and about a dozen tools to pick through for every new bolt."

Paul shook his head slowly. "Last time didn't go so well. I think we should leave it for now." He glanced over at his wife, who was frowning sullenly at Arthur.

Arthur groaned. "Fine. Kid, you help me out." His eyes flicked momentarily to Elsie, which was the only indication she got that he was speaking to her, but he turned and stalked off before she could respond. She glanced back at the others, before making up her mind and scurrying away through the piles of filth to catch up.

Arthur made his way to a small clearing not far from the campsite which was dominated by a piece of machinery nearly as tall as she was and equally wide. At first glance it, appeared to be a solid hunk of blackened metal, but upon closer inspection she saw it was composed of dozens of pieces of machinery, gears, and piping, which fit together to create an intricate mechanism. The closest reference Elsie had for such a machine was the furnace which heated the dye vats at Threadbury's, but even that had been smaller and less complicated than the engine before her.

Arthur motioned her over to a large, rusted toolbox which sat open at the edge of the clearing and immediately got back to work. For an uncomfortable amount of time, he did not speak at all, and Elsie found herself unable to break the silence. She cast her eyes about the clearing, sometimes watching Arthur, sometimes fixing on a particularly strange shape in the rubble, all the time turning her present situation over in her mind.

Finally, Arthur began demanding various tools. Elsie scrambled back and forth between the toolbox and the engine, fetching what he asked for, still unable to muster the courage to speak. Arthur's air of authority was oppressive, and though there were dozens of things she wanted to ask him, they all slipped from her mind as soon as she opened her mouth. The pale autumn sun provided no warmth and Elsie felt that she was underdressed for the occasion. She did her absolute best not to get anything on Maria's green gown.

"Calipers," Arthur called out. He was on his back, his top half situated beneath the engine's bulk, fiddling with something deep in its metal bowels. Elsie rooted around frustratedly in the toolbox. She recognized all the tools so far, but she hadn't heard of calipers before. She looked up, glad to have something to say. But even as she opened her mouth to speak, the man slid out from beneath the engine and without warning pulled the filthy shirt up over his head. He was sweating profusely, despite the cool overcast weather, and glared at Elsie expectantly. "Calipers," he said again before returning to the work on his back under the machine.

Elsie choked back an annoyed squeak. "You haven't apologized!" she blurted. It was the wrong thing to say but it was all she could think of in the moment.

Arthur jolted up, hitting his head on one of the engine cylinders. He swore and clapped a hand over his forehead as he got out from under the engine. "What?"

"What do you mean, 'What?'" Elsie said, regaining her confidence. Arthur's impenetrable air of authority had finally cracked. "You threw a wrench in my eye!"

Arthur paused the futile rubbing of his bruised forehead. He gave Elsie a level, contemplative look which was impossible for Elsie to read. Beneath his stare, she regretted speaking altogether, and returned to rummaging through the tools.

"How'd you escape anyway?" he asked abruptly.

Elsie stopped, looking up at him incredulously. "I'll have you know that a cannonball blew away half my bedroom wall! I bet you know something about why there was cannon fire in the city the other night."

"Six or twelve pound?" Arthur asked, stepping past Elsie to get to the tool chest. After a moment, he pulled out a sharp looking measuring device she'd never seen before.

"What?"

"The cannonball, was it a six or twelve pounder?"

"I...I don't know," Elsie said. "It was, say, so big." She extended her hands to the approximate measure of the iron ball.

"Twelve," Arthur said, giving a wry snort of laughter. "So, they did bomb their own city. The *Heart of Resistance* only has six-pound guns."

He returned to his work as abruptly as he'd broken off, measuring various parts of the engine with the calipers and noting down the numbers on a grubby scrap of paper.

"Why'd you want to know how I escaped?" Elsie asked after a few moments. She watched him, intrigued by his deft movements and pinpoint focus. Something told her, though, that he had little idea what he was doing.

"Could be useful."

"How?"

"In my line of work, these details are useful to know."

"You mean being a rebel?"

Arthur made a sort of growling noise in his throat and his scowl was fiery as he sat up and glared at Elsie. "I am not a rebel."

"Then what are you?" Elsie shot back. "You steal airships, you seem to have a vendetta against the empire...sounds like a rebel to me."

"I'm not a rebel," Arthur said, his voice simmering with barely contained anger. "Greyer's men are tyrants in their own right. I'd tread lightly in this territory, kid. Doesn't sound like you know what you're talking about."

"I'm not a kid!" Elsie shouted, rising to her feet. "And I know enough to know you're exactly the sort of person Captain Marjen was talking about: angry and dangerous. I don't know if I'm safe with you. Do you even know what you're doing with that thing? Isn't there anyone else you could ask for help besides a runaway workhouse girl who doesn't know a thing more than you do?"

Arthur's face was almost as red as his hair and he seemed about to erupt in rage. "Now listen here, kid, I..." he began, but broke off abruptly. Elsie could almost see the gears turning in his mind as a sly brightness filled his eyes. "I do know a man, actually," he said slowly, reaching down to snatch up his discarded shirt and coat. He turned away from the engine and began to stride purposefully toward the camp.

"Who...what? What are you talking about?" Elsie called, once again finding herself sprinting to keep up with the man's long strides. Arthur ignored her existence, instead honing in on Paul, who was talking silently with Maria as Cattia scrubbed the dishes in a tub of gray scummy water.

"Paul!" he shouted, "Come here a moment. You can flirt later."

Catching sight of the captain, Maria scowled and held up a large kitchen knife, waving it menacingly at Arthur. Paul restrained her, signing to her reassuringly, and stepped forward. Elsie stopped at the edge of the campsite, watching attentively.

"Paul," Arthur said sharply, "If we had an engineer, you think we could get the *Heart* back in the air?"

"Yes, I do," Paul said. "But-"

"Do you remember those rebels, Paul?"

"Which?"

"The ones that went to Veturi after the garrison incident."

"You mean the ones that fled because they lost three of their members to the noose?"

"Yeah, those ones. They had that one fellow...what was his name? Engineer, worked mostly on factory machines, but he was smart, and that's what we need."

Maria snorted, reading Paul's translations.

"Shanks?" Paul said uncertainly, spelling the name with his right hand and earning a nod from Maria.

"Yes!" Arthur said excitedly.

"Remember when they said they never wanted to see your face again?"

"That was, oh, half a year ago. They've probably warmed up by now."

Paul frowned but retained his respectful demeanor. "Even if that is the case, I would advise against it. And I wouldn't let Maria go on a mission like that either."

"That's probably for the best; they likely have posters with our faces on them plastered across half the continent by now." Arthur mused sullenly for a moment. "Yes, together we would make quite a recognizable bunch. I'll make my own preparations; perhaps I'll be safer alone." He stalked over to a heap of boxes and bags on the outer edge of the camp.

"Captain Pendington, where are you going?" Cattia asked eagerly, running up to stand by Paul. "You're not leaving, are you?"

Arthur didn't seem to hear her; he neither broke his stride nor glanced back. Cattia bounced up and down on her toes, staring expectantly at him as he knelt and began picking through several toolboxes, which were stuffed with clothes, shoes, and other paraphernalia. Elsie stepped into the camp at last and went to stand beside the girl, gently laying a hand on her arm. While she wasn't about to let Cattia go off on some dangerous mission, she was curious about Arthur's plan.

Arthur hunted around, tossing items left and right haphazardly before sighing in exasperation. "Paul?" he called.

Paul was at his side in a flash. "Yes?"

"You bring your tails?" Arthur asked.

"His what?" Cattia squeaked, looking incredulously at Elsie, who only shrugged.

"Of course. They're neatly folded in the bottom there. Didn't want to risk dirtying them. Will they fit, do you think?"

"They'll have to," Arthur said grimly, pulling out a bundle of deep green wool which unfurled into a fine-looking jacket with long tails, complete with cravat and shoes which looked far too small for Arthur's feet. "I should be a bit dandied up if I want to pass on the top level. That's where Greyer's folks will be, close to the buzzards."

"You're looking for Greyer's rebellion after all?" Elsie asked, tightening her grip on Cattia's arm as the other girl opened her mouth.

"Yes, as a matter of fact," Arthur said, giving her another contemplative stare. "I am not one of them, but I sometimes do business with them, if necessary. Not that I would expect you to understand."

Elsie puffed out her cheeks in frustration and was about to speak again when Arthur stepped forward and jabbed his finger right at Cattia, acknowledging her presence for the first time.

"On second thought, I'll take the girl," he said decisively. "I've never been seen with her and I doubt the authorities give one fig about who she is. She'll give me some good cover."

Elsie gripped Cattia's arm so tightly that the other girl squeaked in pain. She looked over and caught Cat's gaze, shaking her head *no*. No, Cattia was not cut out for this. She was no spy, no rebel. She was happy right here, with Paul and Maria, tending to the little campsite. Elsie was the one who wanted to know more about Greyer's rebels and their doings. Elsie opened her mouth to protest, but Paul beat her to it, his subservient behavior wavering.

"Arthur, I don't think... she's just a child. You can't ask that of her."

"I'll do it," Cattia said, shaking Elsie off and clasping her hands together. "Whatever it is, you can count me in!"

"No," Elsie cried, grabbing Cat's shoulders. "Cattia no, you don't understand. This is serious business, with dangerous people. You don't want to go..."

Cat frowned, shooting Elsie an annoyed glance. "What's wrong with you, Els? Trying to keep Arthur all to yourself? I don't recall you being put in charge of me."

"The girl's right," Arthur interjected. "She can make her own choices."

Paul shook his head. "Arthur, are you even sure this is the best way?"

"What do you mean?" Arthur fired back.

"This plan, to find Shanks on Veturi. You'd have to go there, disguised as a laborer, then disguise yourself again as middle class to get onto the wealthy levels, and *then* find a way to get to the hideout, which, with all due respect, you don't even know the exact location of."

"I know their watchdog," Arthur said imperiously. "I know where she's likely to be. And anyways, I know the code."

"Code?" Elsie asked, trying to get a word in edgewise. Cattia crossed her arms and was glowering, but Elsie ignored her for the moment.

"Yes, *what is the cloudy sky to the sunny day?*" Arthur recited.

"'Greyer,'" Paul told Elsie, "Will be the response if someone is in the network. Yes, Arthur, but even so..."

"You forget your place, Kauisol," Arthur said, "I am the captain of my ship. I decide what I do with my crew."

"We're not your crew," Elsie interjected at last, stepping sharply in front of Cattia and glaring at the two men, "And Cattia's not going with you. I am."

Arthur and Paul turned to stare at her. Cattia gawked openmouthed. Elsie felt her conviction waver, but she stuck to her guns. "I'll go with you," she said to Arthur, crossing her arms tightly. "I *want* to meet these rebels I've heard so much about. I'll do whatever I can to help you and you needn't worry about me getting in the way." Behind her, she heard Cattia suck in her breath as though offended. Elsie felt guilt pool in her stomach, but she neither backed down nor turned to look at the other girl. *I can't let her go. She'd never survive out there. And I've got to meet these rebels. I have nowhere else to go...*

Paul and Arthur looked at each other in confusion for a moment. Paul was still frowning, but Arthur seemed to be taking the statement in stride. "Very well," he said, handing the rumpled tailcoat to Paul and squatting down to root about once more in the boxes. "We must prepare at once. It will be several days journey to the nearest refueling town and we need to catch Veturi there before it continues on its way."

Cattia huffed. "I don't understand. How can you catch a city?"

Arthur stood once more, brushing off a dusty satchel he had retrieved from one of the toolboxes. "Veturi," he said slowly. "The city of light and splendor. The jewel of Odol's excess. The city that travels by rail."

Elsie's chest tightened for a moment. She had heard the women speak of Veturi in hushed voices; its lavish excess was legendary among the lower class in Gorand. When it docked at the middle city, it threw huge swaths of the slums below into shadow for days at a time. She'd never thought she would have a chance to see it for herself.

"You're joking," Cattia interjected, forcing her way forward to stand by Elsie, still clearly fuming. "You're going there? And you won't let me come with you?"

Arthur ignored her. "Collect your things," he told Elsie as he strode past, not even looking her in the face. "We leave in an hour. Paul, come with me. We need to plan."

Elsie turned to watch them go, her heart sinking slowly into the pit of her stomach. She was leaving Cat, going her own way, trying to forge her own path in a world that had long denied her any agency. Now that she had it, was she doing the right thing with it?

"What's wrong with you, Els?" Cattia asked in a low voice, causing Elsie to start. "I thought we were supposed to stick together."

"I'm trying to protect you," Elsie said firmly. "Do you really want to be out there, all alone, with a man you barely know and can't exactly trust, traveling to some train-city to meet a bunch of rebels?"

Cat laughed a little. "When you say it like that, no. But what about you, Els? Why would you do that? Why can't you just stay here with Paul and Maria and me?"

Elsie glanced over at the campsite and caught Maria's eye. The woman was sitting on one of the rolled-up uniforms knitting something, her brows drawn together in a thunderous expression. It brightened momentarily when she saw Elsie, but the woman neither slowed nor stopped her furious knitting. Elsie got the feeling that she was distracting herself to keep from punching someone.

"Because... because I don't belong here," Elsie said after a long pause. "This is not what I escaped for, Cattia. This..." she gestured at the strangely domestic scene: the piles of boxes and food stores, the cheerful campfire, Maria knitting beside a newly bubbling pot, all overshadowed by the piles of Gorand's refuse. "This can't be where I end up. I have to keep going."

Cat seized Elsie's skinny hands in her soft ones. "Let me come with you then! Don't leave me alone..."

"No," Elsie said, avoiding the other girl's eyes. "Not now. I'll be back, don't worry. We'll go get Arthur's engineer and get this hunk of scrap off the ground." Even as she said it, she wondered if it were true or if, assuming they ever found the rebels, she would join them instead. Out of Threadbury's and with the intense pressure of their escape seemingly miles behind, she suddenly found that things she had once taken for granted were quickly coming apart. Her friendship with Cattia, which she had once felt to be unshakeable, seemed suddenly tenuous within her new sense of freedom.

"Okay," Cat said dubiously, releasing her friend's hands and stepping back. "Well, you'd better."

Elsie only nodded, not trusting herself to speak.

THE LOTTERY

At Arthur's insistence, they left within the hour. Arthur left behind his burgundy overcoat and brace of flintlocks, stowed carefully on the ship for their return. He took with them the battered satchel, stowing the carefully folded green tailcoat at the bottom, and piling food and various supplies on top, stuffing it as full as he could without it bursting. This he slung across his body in place of his pistols, a poor defense against whatever dangers they were sure to meet on the mission. Elsie was given a pair of hastily constructed bedrolls, made up from some of the uniforms that had been stowed on the ship.

Farewells were said quickly; Arthur seemed to have little time for such things. Cattia gave Elsie an enormous hug, nearly squeezing the breath from her lungs. "You come back soon, promise?" she murmured against Elsie's shoulder. Elsie nodded mutely, but once again found herself unable to make a promise she was uncertain of. She did wish Cat farewell with sincere earnestness before she let go and turned to wave to Paul, Maria, and Cattia before they were out of sight. They waved back, even Maria, who was glaring daggers at Arthur's back as he departed without even looking over his shoulder.

Then the campsite vanished and Elsie found herself in the middle of the trackless Wreckage, alone with Arthur. Perhaps, after Rye, she ought to have been more wary, but Arthur did not frighten her, not in that way at least. Somehow, she knew that taking advantage of her was the furthest thing from his mind. He hardly seemed to take any notice of her at all except when she started to lag behind, and then his only words were some variation of "hurry up" or "keep with me."

The haze of clouds that had covered the sky was beginning to break up, tearing in places to reveal patches of watery blue. Elsie found herself surprised when, for a brief moment, the sun showed its face fully and flashed bright illumination over the heaps of rubbish. It was quickly overtaken once more by scudding gray clouds. She was so used to the dim, diffuse glow that the sudden burst of daylight seemed almost violent.

The Wreckage ended abruptly and rather unceremoniously. As they rounded a bend through the endless gullies of trash, Elsie found herself confronted with a vast emptiness. Miles of flat land stretched out before her eyes, crisscrossed by the vein-like spread of dry riverbeds. The unchecked wind blew the gray dust across the surface, exposing the bedrock beneath. The horizon was broken only by the distant lines of great train bridges looming above the flat expanse, supported on slender pillars of improbable height. One bridge was especially large, with two sets of rails running parallel. Arthur pointed to it.

"That's the Veturi rail. We follow that and we should be in Locend in two days. Let's be on our way; we have a little daylight left." He shaded his eyes as he surveyed the patchy sky. The sun was quickening in its descent towards the horizon. "The clouds don't look too ugly. I don't think it will rain. Not yet."

Elsie nodded dumbly, hitching the bedrolls up higher on her shoulder. She stared out at the gray wasteland ahead of them, trackless save for the glittering rails suspended so far away. Without another word, they set off again into the vast expanse.

The first night in the Wastes was restless for Elsie. The bedroll was thin and lumpy, exposing her to every stone on the uneven ground, and the thin material did nothing to protect her from the frigid wind that sprang up as soon as the sun went down. Arthur was sound asleep a few paces away. It seemed as though he had not moved a millimeter from the moment he lay down. Elsie wondered if he was even still breathing and felt a claw of panic stab her heart. She sat up and stared at his shape in the dark, trying to discern the rise and fall of his shoulders. Almost at once, he stirred slightly, and she lay back down, weak with relief and slightly embarrassed that she should have been so frightened.

Her restless eyes drifted up to the sky overhead. The orange glow of Gorand was barely visible on the north horizon. The clouds rolled overhead, pushed and torn by the wind, allowing for fitful glimpses of a crescent sliver of the moon. Elsie had little experience with the night; most of the time she was so exhausted that she slept the moment she fell into bed at the end of the day. Sometimes, when she was wakeful, she had gone to her little barred window and stared out at her meager slice of sky, looking for the moon. Rarely, if ever, had it appeared. Even more rare was a star or two peeking through a tear in the clouds.

None of that prepared her for the experience of sleeping, or at least trying to sleep, out in the open. As she watched, a great swath of clouds blew aside, exposing the sable blanket of the sky. Slowly, she found herself able to pick out bright pin-pricks of light, scattered haphazardly here and there like jewels on the velvet surface. She searched and searched for the patterns she'd heard were visible in the stars—warriors and animals and mythical beasts—but found only a jumble.

She must have fallen asleep, for the next thing she knew, Arthur was waking her and pressing a can of sailor's rations into her numb fingers. The food was not entertaining but she found it filling enough for the day's walk. They started off again almost as soon as she had slurped down the last of the rations, tossing the cans on the ground for the wind to bury at Arthur's insistence. Elsie found herself wishing once more that she had put on shoes before her escape from Threadbury's; Maria's dainty slippers, even if they had fit properly, were not designed for long hikes.

Just before noon the clouds grew angrier. The rain broke at dusk. Arthur and Elsie each hitched up an oversized uniform jacket over their heads to protect themselves from the heavy drops. A fine mist began to rise from the ground and within minutes their line of sight was completely obscured.

"I can't see a thing!" Elsie cried, leaping over a small, fast-flowing stream that had formed out of nowhere on the bare rock.

"Just keep going in this direction," Arthur called, beckoning her to follow him. He strode purposefully though the downpour, seemingly unbothered by the lashing rain. Thunder cracked and lightning spread across the sky, and Elsie caught a glimpse of movement somewhere to their right. "If you look there," Arthur said, coming to a halt and pointing to the rails, waiting for the lightning to flash again as the large shape drew closer, "That's Veturi. Probably several miles away, but it will be passing us within the hour. It's headed north to Gorand, so we will get on when it returns."

"How much further to the refueling town?" Elsie asked, shielding her eyes with her arm as she stared through the blinding rain. The tracks, though descending on a gradual slope towards the earth, were still high above them.

"About a day. You can almost see the lights there to the south," Arthur said, starting off again in that direction. As Elsie looked, she stepped into a puddle that splashed up, soaking her shoes and the hem of her dress. She was surprised to find that, unlike the acidic puddles in the city, this water was cool to the touch, though still unpleasant.

As they walked, a roaring sound began to be heard under, then over, the sound of the rain. The shape on the huge elevated rail came steadily closer and Elsie saw, as Arthur finally stopped to pitch camp, that the shape was glowing. Using a tarpaulin he'd collected in the Wreckage, Arthur made a sort of tent for Elsie to sleep in, while he braved the pouring rain under a double layer of imperial uniforms.

Once again, Elsie found that she couldn't sleep, not with the rain streaming all around her and leaking through the dirty canvas overhead. She stared out into the night, eyes straining, watching the double line of tracks, now not far off. Then all at once she saw the shapes and lights of a city moving past at an incredible speed. Buildings of all shapes and sizes, some six or seven stories high, a huge church, and manor houses, flew past, moving faster than she could process. She stared and stared, trying to understand what she was looking at, but as quickly as it had come the vision vanished, leaving only the empty tracks quivering in the endless downpour.

It was still storming the next morning, so Arthur and Elsie ate their rations under the makeshift tent. They didn't linger, breaking camp as soon as they were finished eating, resuming their course following the hazy outline of the tracks. It was miserable going and the constant deluge of rain seemed to never end. Where the dust was thick on the flat ground, it became impassibly muddy, and wherever the bedrock had been swept clean, swiftly moving water poured in torrents across the surface. Even so, Arthur insisted that they continue to follow the tracks at a distance where they could just barely see their outline.

At last, sometime around noon, the rain cleared up and Arthur moved even further from the rails, fearing that someone on the train would notice them. The sun began to shine orange through the pale gray cloud cover and a fresh round of hazy fog rose around them as the temperature dropped. Elsie shivered in her soaked dress but said nothing.

"We're nearly there," Arthur said unexpectedly, breaking into Elsie's thoughts as she trudged dully through the wasteland, keeping in his shadow. "Stay close to me. Do as I say and don't give the overseers any trouble."

"Yeah..." Elsie said, looking up and trying to catch the captain's eye; he kept his gaze fixed straight ahead, even when speaking to her. "Just how exactly does this plan work again?"

"Don't concern yourself with the details," Arthur told her firmly. "Leave that to me. All you need to know is that we will be boarding the train as common laborers and working our way up to the higher levels as quickly as possible. They're so desperate for men they'll let almost anyone on." This time he did look back at her. Elsie gave him a sour look but he didn't seem to notice.

At last, they spotted the first few buildings of Locend: large coal silos covered in black carbon stains. A haze of dark smoke hung over the little town and a large rusty building rose up right next to the elevated tracks of Veturi, providing access to the tracks via a narrow metal walkway. Elsie had never seen buildings standing in the middle of so much *nothingness* before, and the sight unsettled her. Even the worst parts of Gorand had not prepared her for this place. The buildings were unnaturally spread out, short and squat, rambling instead of confined to grid-like streets. And there was no wall to keep anyone out...or in.

As they entered the town, they gathered some odd looks. Elsie couldn't blame the townsfolk for their curiosity. She wore a hastily tailored dress that was decades out of style, covered in mud and grime, with two bedrolls strapped to her back and an oversized imperial uniform jacket over her shoulders. Beside her, Arthur didn't look too out of place in his filthy stained shirt and nondescript trousers. Elsie kept her head down and tried not to stare. Except for Arthur, these were the first people she had seen in several days.

Their first stop was a dusty old clothing shop. They needed to look the part if they were going to get onto Veturi the way Arthur planned. He was shocked, however, at the price of the simple working clothes they requested. "Two kent? To rent for a single round trip? I'll pay half that at most," Arthur protested.

"You'll pay four kent now or you'll miss this trip. Funny, men usually take this job so their little ones don't have to work. Never seen a real man make his daughter work before," the shabby shopkeeper mused as he eyed the odd pair.

"Times are hard. Her mother is real sick and the little ones are too young, but there's so many mouths to feed," Arthur lied. Elsie was not a fan of the milquetoast characterization and felt that she needed to add to the lie as the man took his time picking through the various sizes of work uniforms.

"He didn't make me. I'm here of my own free will," she said as Arthur dug four kent out of his pocket.

"Eh, have it your way," the shopkeep said, laying out two dingy uniforms on the counter. "I'd not recommend it myself. Lots of fathers don't come back to their families once they set foot there. All the coal towns like this one have fewer and fewer men to send every time Veturi stops by. I think somethin's happening to them. A lot of us who stay back do."

"I have a few ideas," Arthur said grimly as he took the uniforms and handed the smaller one to Elsie. "Is there a place we can change?"

"Changing rooms are around the corner. You doin' anything with that dress, girl?" the shopkeeper asked Elsie.

"What? Why?" Elsie asked, incredulous.

"Dress like that would be valuable in a town like this. I'd take two kent off your bill for it," the man said, but Arthur interjected before Elsie had a chance to respond.

"Not for sale," he said bluntly and without another word he took Elsie's arm and escorted her around the corner.

Elsie was unsure of how she looked but she was all too sure of how she smelled. The blue corduroy overalls stank of oil and grease, yet they smelled better than the light blue work shirt she wore underneath, which reeked of sweat. There was no mirror in the little curtained-off room, but then again she didn't care to know what she looked like. She was sure, however, that it couldn't be good, especially once she saw Arthur, who looked utterly ridiculous in the uniform. His overalls and shirt were rumpled, ill-fitting, and no cleaner than her own, but she gave him a brief half smile that was quickly wiped away by Arthur's attitude.

"Come on, we've got to get to the registry at once. We have to sign up for our names to be put into the drawing."

Elsie's face twisted in confusion. "Drawing?"

"There are more workers than there is work, according to the shopkeep," Arthur explained crisply as he ushered her out of the shabby building. "Apparently, they can't just take everyone on board. Well, they could. They need *more* workers there by all accounts. But the unions think it's better to squeeze as much labor out of as few workers as possible than to properly staff the place."

"You said they'd take anyone!"

"I guess things have changed." Arthur shrugged.

"Are you sure about this?" Elsie muttered as they made their way through the narrow streets towards the tall, rusty access tower next to the elevated train tracks. As they got closer, the street began to fill with dozens of men dressed in the same shabby blue as they were, and by the time they reached the building itself, they found themselves at the edge of a large crowd of workers. Elsie kept close to Arthur, terrified of losing him in the throng of sullen, unwashed men. A man stood over the crowd on a large platform at the front of the building, surveying them with an unpleasant expression on his face. Behind him, a large clock was set into the wall, a time marked on its face with a smudgy red dot.

"Fifteen minutes until the drawing. Please go about your business until then!" the man shouted, but the waiting laborers didn't seem to notice. They just shuffled aimlessly about in front of the spindly metal stairs that led up to the man's platform. Arthur and Elsie skirted around the crowd and went into another shabby building with a big painted sign above that said "Registration."

It was a rather dull conversation, handled by Arthur in much the same way as the clothing shop. Elsie was impressed with how easily lying came to Arthur. Apparently, his name was Andrew Callaghan, and she was Corina Callighan, his young daughter. She looked at the rapidly filling basket that held the names of all the registrants on small paper slips. Elsie noticed with concern that their fake names were put into the drawing separately.

As they left the registration office, Elsie looked at Arthur with a curious expression. "How do you know we'll get picked?"

"I don't," he replied bluntly.

"Okay, so what's the plan if we don't get picked?"

"There's another coal town about a hundred miles down the line. That or we wait here and work the mines until Veturi comes back."

Elsie's mouth hung open for a moment. From what the women at Threadbury's had said, the hard labor at the workhouse was nothing compared to the misery of the coal mines. But she was distracted from her shock as they rejoined the mass of milling workers in front of the platform. As she stared about her, she saw that some of them were young, much younger than Arthur, maybe even around her own age. Others were old, gray-haired and bearded underneath a layer of soot from the coal mines. There was a curious lack of men in their prime and middle years. Arthur himself, though she was not sure of his exact age, stood out like a sore thumb.

They waited in a stillness that was like the calm before the storm. No one seemed to even breathe as the clock's large hands ticked closer and closer to the red mark. As soon as it struck, the laboring men began to shout in a cacophony of eagerness, each trying to edge their way closer to the rickety steel stairs ahead of the others, as if their proximity to the entrance would increase their chances of being chosen. Elsie covered her ears, deafened by the shouting. She was sure that the cannon fire that had woken her that one fateful morning in the workhouse had been quieter. But over the chaos she heard one man shouting. An overseer stood on his platform in front of the door, gripping the railing with his dark-gloved hands, trying to quiet the crowd of eager men.

The futile attempts continued for a full minute, until the overseer pulled a pistol from his belt and fired it into the air. The crowd went deathly silent and the man tossed the spent flintlock aside, taking another pistol from one of his assistants. "Any man make another bloody sound and he gets shot. Is that clear?"

The silence was suffocating.

"Right. There is only room for five more laborers," the overseer began and the entire crowd, save for Arthur and Elsie, burst into uproar once more. From what Elsie could gather, this was far less than the usual number of workers that would be chosen, and it made her even more worried about their chances.

The overseer's attempts at quieting the crowd once more seemed quite futile, until he finally lowered the pistol and fired it at a man near the front of the crowd. Elsie shrieked and grabbed onto Arthur's sleeve, and the crowd went silent again, contracting away from the platform like a single organism. The injured man let out a groan and slumped to the ground, hidden behind the wall of laborers. Elsie twisted the fabric of Arthur's shirt sleeve tighter in her hand, feeling a wave of nausea well up in her stomach. She could feel the tears standing in her eyes, but she could not cry. She stood paralyzed, terrified that if she moved a muscle, she would be next. She had never seen a man killed before and she never thought that she would. But suddenly the threat of death seemed all too real.

"I mean it! Five names, and if you don't stay quiet, you can expect a bullet in the gut too. Is that clear?" The overseer reached into the basket of names and pulled one out.

"Ethon Charleson!"

A young man with a ruddy face stepped through the crowd and climbed the rickety staircase.

"Benedict Ryans!"

An older man, probably in his late fifties, stepped forward and went to safety behind the line of overseers on the platform.

"Edwin Phillips!"

A broad-shouldered man, one of the few who looked in the prime of his years, pushed past the jealous men and joined the other two.

"Andrew Callaghan!"

Arthur began to move but Elsie grabbed his arm.

"Wait, what happens if he doesn't call my name?" she gasped.

Arthur paused.

"Andrew Callaghan! Is there an Andrew Callaghan here?"

The men began to murmur among themselves in confusion.

"You'll find your way," Arthur said quietly, not even looking back at her as he pushed through the crowd and joined the others on the platform.

Elsie's mouth went dry and she felt the blood drain out of her face. She couldn't hear the final name called over the buzzing in her ears but she knew that it wasn't hers. Around her the crowd grew rowdy once more as the final man started towards the staircase. Barely knowing what she was doing, Elsie shoved forward to the platform.

"Wait! Please! You can't leave me here." Elsie ducked between the row of assistant overseers who were guarding the staircase. She made it halfway across the platform toward the door before a man grabbed her and began to drag her back. "Let me go! I've got to go with him. You have to let me go!"

She managed to catch Arthur's eye and cried out to him desperately. The rest of the chosen laborers had turned and entered through the rusty door but he was still standing behind the overseer and his assistant, his blue eyes fixed on her. For a moment, she thought that he was going to turn and walk away.

"Toss her back with the others," the head overseer snapped, pausing in his futile attempts to quiet the crowd below. "Knock her out if she causes too much trouble." Elsie only thrashed more against the restraining grip of the man.

"She comes with me. She'll work for free," Arthur said. He had marched smartly across the platform towards the small group of overseers. The man restraining Elsie paused in surprise, looking to his superior for instructions.

"That's hardly regulation. Union wouldn't like someone working for free," the head overseer snapped.

"I don't care. I'm all she's got out here. She comes with me," Arthur said a bit more firmly, walking up to the leader in a commanding manner. The other overseers drew their small flintlock pistols but Arthur didn't flinch.

"Sir, I understand your sentiment, but no one besides the five requested laborers are allowed on the train," the head overseer warned.

Arthur remained motionless, starting defiantly at the overseer, a grim smile tugging at the corner of his mouth. Elsie pulled vainly, trying to free herself from the assistant's grip. Behind them, the crowed simmered in confusion.

"If you fire on me you'll have to pick another man and explain why your system did not live up to its promises. Some would say that you are corrupt, no?" Arthur's smile spread, crinkling the corners of his eyes. The murmurs of the crowd boiled over into shouts and jeers, some calling for Arthur and Elsie to be taken down off the stand so another man could be chosen.

"Enough! The drawing is final, no exceptions," the overseer shouted, raising his gun. "If I have to report that one of the men died in transit, then so be it." He turned his head, shouting out over the crowd, and apparently that was the opening Arthur had been looking for. In a blink of Elsie's tear-blurred eyes, Arthur knocked the man's gun to the ground, setting the charge off with a flash and a bang.

Chaos erupted, and Elsie felt a surge of energy wash over her from below. The assistant holding her dropped her arm and turned around, cursing. His gunshot, fired from directly behind her head, could barely be heard over the enraged cries of the laborers rushing the stand.

Every second seemed to increase the intensity of the riot and Elsie realized she was moments from being caught up in the storm. Bodies surrounded her on all sides, overseers in gray uniforms pressing forward to quell the rising mob. Desperately, Elsie tried to orient herself as workers scrambled up the platform like ants, all lunging for the overseers in an attempt to get onto the train. Screams for Arthur were torn from her throat without her consent as she felt herself being ripped away from the stand by the men.

A strong arm caught hold of her and she was pulled back from the edge of the platform, and out into the clearing created by the overseers, who had drawn batons from their belts, which they wielded with great effectiveness against the rioters.

"Quick," was the only word which Arthur spoke as he pulled Elsie forward toward the access tower. The door was stuck for a second and a fist-sized rock smashed against the rusted sheet metal. Elsie cried out in shock and looked back to see that the overseers were being overrun. One was being beaten with his own baton by a group of men and another was being trampled. With only seconds before the mob reached them, Arthur unjammed the door, and Elsie didn't hesitate to rush inside.

Pulling a bar down, Arthur managed to barricade the door as men hurled themselves against it. He leaned back against it with a distant bemused look on his face, even as the door rattled in its frame. Elsie was lost for words.

"What was that?" she finally managed to sputter.

"Labor riot. Happens all the time," Arthur said as distant gunfire could be heard, echoing harshly through the steel shack. As round after round was fired, the commotion began to die down. Elsie hoped it was from fear and not the alternative.

"Can we not do that again?" she asked, rubbing her bruised arms gingerly. She was trembling and it took all the strength she had to swallow the bile that rose in her throat.

"Wasn't planning on it," Arthur said and brushed off his overalls. He leaned down and picked up their packs, which he had somehow managed to keep hold of in the chaos. "Let's join the lucky ones."

The building was hollow inside, with a rickety stair that wound up from landing to landing into the dimness above. It was somehow colder here than it had been outside, and the sheet metal walls were frigid to the touch when Elsie tried to balance herself against. She kept her eyes on Arthur's back the whole way, not daring to look down towards the door, which had ceased its rattling. A deathly silence permeated the air.

When they reached the final landing, they found the four men who had been picked standing in front of a small gate leading out to an open platform overlooking the tracks. A frigid wind whistled through the bars and into the tower, causing their breath to steam. The platform gate was guarded by another man in a dark gray overseer's uniform. He also carried a pistol displayed proudly on his hip and leveled a hardened glare at the five men and Elsie. Elsie noticed that the four other men seemed to have no regard for her, Arthur, or each other. She found it hard to believe that they had heard nothing of the riot below, but she had the uncomfortable feeling that they *had* heard, and didn't care.

She stood musing for a moment, catching her breath from the climb and waiting expectantly for something to happen. Her eyes wandered to a dim window that looked north over the tracks, but through it she could only see the vaguest shapes and outlines. Then she saw indistinct movement through the grimy frosted glass. She became aware of the rumbling vibrations of the train far before she heard them. By the time they were audible the entire tower was shaking as if it might fly apart at any moment. She wrapped her arms around herself and stepped closer to Arthur, squinting through the foggy window at the approaching shape. It grew steadily larger and larger until it filled the entire window, and then suddenly ,with a colossal screech of brakes and a whistle, Veturi was barreling past them.

Elsie stared in awe as the enormous engine, all screaming metal and smoke, roared past outside the tower, followed by a tender piled with mounds of coal that would have dwarfed the trash heaps of the Wreckage. And then the engine was gone, replaced by a wall of stark metal paneling, streaked with soot and stained with shiny oil spots. First one car, then another, and then another passed this way, stenciled with harsh white symbols that Elsie barely had time to study before they vanished, replaced by the next. It wasn't until Elsie looked up that she saw the true Veturi, in all its opulence, resting atop the metal bodies of the massive cars. Sparkling buildings of glass and marble streaked by, difficult to see at this angle. She found that her mouth was hanging open; the magnitude of the train-city was difficult to comprehend, even up close.

Finally, the train came to a shuddering stop and they were faced with the sheer metal side of one of the last cars, pierced only by a small service door directly in front of them. Somewhere, a bell clanged, and the overseer turned smartly on his heel to unlock the gate. He stepped out onto the platform ahead of the workers and kicked a rickety walkway down across the gap between the car and the platform. The workers filed dutifully through the gate and onto the car. Arthur and Elsie brought up the rear.

As Elsie stepped onto the platform, she glanced to the left and froze. Veturi, the train-city, the city of light and splendor, wound away into the distance. Far away she could see the enormous coal silo next to the tracks, where they must be refilling the tender for the rest of the journey. But between here and there, an entire glittering city straddled the narrow confines of the train: marble white towers, expensive-looking brick townhouses, shops with advertisements plastered on the outside walls, as though someone out in the vast emptiness of the Wastes might see and want to buy their wares. Chimneys and smokestacks jutted out of the sides of many of the buildings, pumping a steady stream of smoke into the air above, hazing the gray sky. As the train settled and the air stilled, flakes of ash and soot from the engine's great smokestack began to flutter down around them like gray snow.

Arthur put his hands on her shoulders gently, breaking the spell, and ushered her across the rickety bridge and onto the car. The glimmering grandeur of Veturi vanished and she found herself hustled along through narrow corridors into the interminable depths of the car.

"You'll be workin' in the canning rooms," the new overseer said somewhere ahead of them in the gaslit gloom. "Follow me, and keep sharp!"

Before they were swallowed up into its interior, Elsie took one last look back, hoping to catch a final glimpse of the glittering city as it wound away to the south. But it had vanished like a dream.

PART 3:
THE PRINCESS

16
COUNCIL AT ALDIA

The heavy mahogany doors of the council chamber opened wide and Princess Yvonnia, heir apparent to the Siali throne, entered gracefully to the tentative bows of the delegates. Built only a hundred years ago, the opulent palace in Aldia had smooth adobe walls that met the ceilings in a high vault. Each door was framed with a sweeping, brightly painted arch. Green banners bearing the emblem of the Holanites hung in the arches behind the royal seats, fluttering in the warm sea breeze that blew in from the open balconies. It helped clear the room of the strong tobacco smoke which would have otherwise hung stagnant in the air.

There were three tables in the room, two of which sat near the doors. The other stood at the rounded end of the chamber, in front of the windows and the royal banners. Behind it, the three great balconies stood open to the elements; they would be used for private negotiations later in the proceedings. Yvonnia was looking forward to conducting at least some of the days' business outdoors.

To the right was the table for the delegates of the Ryokans. *Traitors*, Yvonnia thought bitterly as she passed by. The three generals seated at the table had all joined in rebellion against her father, King Holan VI. Even General Pretav Ozerov, with a languid gaze and a hookah pipe sticking out of his mouth, looked like a predator lying in wait for her to make a mistake.

On her left were the Thunats, a monastic order whose influence her father blamed for the lack of patriotism and loyalty of his subjects in the civil war. The Lama, their leader, sat stoically in his seat with his hands folded and eyes half-lidded in a meditative state. A gentleman sat on the far left, wearing an Odolian suit, his dark hair slicked back and his face shaved in the imperial style. The only Thunat delegate who stood at her arrival was Prince Basra from the far east of Sial, and he had bowed reverently.

She paid him no mind, however. Her deep blue saree fluttered in the breeze as she rounded the table at the far end of the chamber. To her left, her father's bejeweled rosewood throne stood empty. The king was conspicuously absent from the proceedings. On the other side of the throne stood General Vasada, the only Siali general who hadn't rebelled against King Holan. He was quite tall, though about equally as wide, and his eyebrows nearly matched the bushiness of his beard.

Yvonnia was shadowed by her bodyguard, a tall, proud man in uniform, who stood silently behind her chair even when everyone else took their seats. Though the rest of the attendees had been disarmed before being allowed to enter the council chamber, he still had his sword, a falchion crafted by one of Sial's master weaponsmiths. It hung at his side in a decorative sheath, and his hand rested lightly on the hilt as he scanned the room, grim-faced.

For a moment, the only sound was General Ozerov puffing at his hookah as the attendees waited for the council to officially begin. The princess found it difficult not to roll her eyes at the disrespect the Ynarusan general showed. The other Ryokans and Thunat representatives all sat respectfully, making no sound as the doors were closed by the clerk who had been appointed as mediator. The clerk himself was a common man, chosen by the elders of the villages in contested territory as a neutral party. For the duration of the council, he would be treated with the utmost respect by royalty and delegates alike.

All rose as the clerk made his way to the ornate center of the chamber, where he began to read in a loud voice. Though his accent was of the common peasantry, everyone, even General Oserov, listened attentively.

"All present raise your right hand. Any who do not agree to uphold these solemn oaths are to be expelled from the proceedings of this high council. Objectors may speak now."

No one spoke an objection and everyone in the room raised their right hand, even Yvonnia.

"Do all here swear that on pain of death, no Holanite, Ryokan, or Thunat will be harmed during this council by the hand of any soldier, servant, serf, adept, or any other person under command?"

All, including Yvonnia, spoke in unison: "I swear it."

"Do all here swear that on pain of death, no Odolian colonist nor their families, lands, servants, or animals will be harmed during this council by any soldier, servant, serf, adept, or any other person under command?"

Again: "I swear it."

"Do all here swear, on the grave of your very ancestors, that this council is attended in good faith, and that peaceful resolution will be attempted by all, even if no mutual agreement is reached?"

This time, the response was staggered. Yvonnia said "I swear it," followed by General Vasada. The three representatives of the Thunats were next, having only been shocked at the breach of normal ceremony by an uncommon oath. The Ryokans paused the longest and the three generals all looked at one another in momentary confusion. Before the clerk could say another word, however, the de facto leader of the Ryokans nodded to the other two generals and they barked out "I swear it" in military unison.

Satisfied, the clerk sat down in his seat to the side of Yvonnia's table, and then Yvonnia herself sat, followed by the other seven delegates. The proceedings had finally begun. Yvonnia faintly heard Pretav Oserov ask, "Will there be food?" Glancing quickly at the Ryokans' table, Yvonnia held a frown as best she could, though the comedic sneer on the face of General Gera, their leader, threatened to make her laugh.

Ozerov had always been mercenary. Yvonnia remembered standing at her father's side when General Gera first announced his intent to revolt. Then, General Ozerov had stood staunchly against the revolution and was the loudest to shout against Gera's audacity. That was when King Holan had been paying him. Then somehow Ozerov had been paid just a little more to betray Holan. How it was done remained a mystery. It was not as though General Gera was poor, and neither was Silander Rhela, the other general now representing the Ryokans. But neither were wealthy enough to pay the steep price Ozerov charged for his service and his men, and then surpass it.

The clerk took a small bell and rang it once. All was quiet and after a moment, the bell was rung again. At the sound of the second bell, Yvonnia stood up, the rattling of her innumerable gold bracelets cutting through the taut silence. "It is time to go over the old business of the last council," she said, hoping her voice did not shake. The last council held in Aldia had been when the civil war started. Bringing up the old business now might dredge up wounds that had been nominally resolved with the end of the war.

"Does anyone have anything to discuss?" She looked at the two tables. The Thunats sat, peaceful and attentive, though there was something in Lama Fanq Nakazo's eyes when he looked at her that she did not like. No one spoke, but to her right General Vasada cleared his throat awkwardly. The moment passed and the bell was rung again. Yvonnia's shoulders dropped as her tension dissipated.

"With that out of the way, we are on to new business, and I think we should start with..."

General Gera shot to his feet. The other two Ryokan generals rose with him, creating an imposing wall of chests decorated with dozens of military medals. He spoke out of turn, but so forcefully that Yvonnia stuttered into silence.

"I speak on behalf of the people of Trelasi, Sial's heart and strength across the jungle. They have heard of the militarization of the Odolian settlers in Turalik." Despite his usually politic demeanor, his voice was harsh and filled with urgency. "We stand just across the great river from them, and I tell all of the delegates here that they have brought in *soldiers* to patrol their quarter of the town. I ask you, do they truly need that? Will we allow this? I have heard that these are brutish, violent men. They bring no worth to these settlers, and if all they wish is trade, then they should keep to it. We have guards for our cities' streets. But I say that they do not simply wish to trade. They wish to invade our land piece by piece, man by man. How long? How long will we wait for there to be an army on our coast, or in the heart of our country? How long until *you* let them plunder our cities and farms, kill our men, rape our women, enslave our children? How long, *princess*?"

The title dripped with contempt as he pointed a thick finger at Yvonnia. She stood still with her chin raised and her eyes fixed back at him, waiting until she was sure he had no more hyperbole to spout. Then she answered, "General Gera, your concerns are shared by us as well, and I may speak out of line, but I think that even the Thunats would be concerned by such a development. However, when we first received word of this, we sent representatives to their leader..."

"Emperor Cristol?" Lama Nakazo piped, transfixing her with a disapproving stare. Yvonnia was surprised that the vacant man should have strung together the association so quickly. It was the opinion of many who were not seduced by his charismatic teaching that the monk was no more than an opportunist who embezzled much of the money donated to his monastery by Prince Basra.

Tension filled the silent room once more. It was a tension which Yvonnia knew she must not break too soon, for fear that she would draw suspicion on herself and her father. The civil war had come to an end after the battle of Ryoka's Pass, when the Holanite army was slaughtered entirely at the command of General Rhela. Yvonnia shuddered at the thought of the battle that had killed her brothers, and the memory of her father's reaction. First he had wept, then he was filled with a dreadful rage that she never wished to see again. He ordered diplomats to fly one of Sial's few sky skiffs to Odol and seek the emperor's help in destroying the Ryokans, in exchange for half his kingdom. Knowing that they couldn't fight off the entire Odolian army, the Ryokans had rushed to a treaty of peace, one condition being that sending any delegate or official message to the emperor would be considered an act of war.

The Ryokans' faces twisted with anger, wondering if one of the solemn agreements of the treaty had been broken so soon. But after a moment had passed, Yvonnia calmly shook her head.

"No, Lama Nakazo. I wouldn't dare, nor would my father, to go back on the sacred agreement." She was looking at the Ryokans the entire time, keeping her eyes fixed on General Gera's black goatee to avoid his blazing eyes. "Now, as I was saying, we sent a delegation to their *local* leaders, and they agreed that their streets would be patrolled by both their soldiers and our guards. On top of that, their soldiers are limited to their quarter at all times. They would be fined for even setting foot outside of the Odolian quarter of Turalik."

The veins in Gera's neck bulged as he fumed at the response. General Rhela, on the other hand, stroked his bushy beard thoughtfully with eyes set humbly on the floor. "If we keep allocating our men to patrolling the streets of these colonists, then it would take away from our military force and our capacity to defend ourselves from invasion hailing from other places. Odol is not our only opponent." He spoke respectfully, far calmer than his colleague. *I've missed Rhela,* Yvonnia thought, recalling the old days when the general had acted as an uncle to her.

"Yes," Gera said, making an effort to compose himself, "If we take all of our men and set them to guarding these colonizers, or guard our people *from* them, what good would it do us if we were to be attacked from another side? We are left wide open for attack thanks to your policy of opening our borders to these Odolian invaders."

"If we were all at peace…" Prince Basra stood, taller and leaner than any of the generals. "Then we wouldn't have any need for guards on either side. I think that if we could avoid all conflict, then no military resources would be needed for either situation."

A brief smirk passed over Yvonnia's face as she studied the confounded looks that Basra received from the four generals. Had he any brains at all, Yvonnia would have thought him guilty of some kind of subterfuge. She was sure, however, that he was merely a doughy idealist, with nothing more than the teachings of Thun in his head. Thun mandated pacifism and harmony with others, and that end was to be achieved above anything else. Such a policy appealed to the exiled prince, since he survived only on the asylum that the monks provided. Being one of the last members of the Basra dynasty, which had been destroyed over a hundred years before by King Holan's grandfather, he would have otherwise been a target. Though some saw him as a buffoon, others still saw him as the rightful claimant to the throne of Sial, something Yvonnia was glad that he did not press.

"There would have been peace," General Vasada said, slamming his fist on the table and causing the prince to jump, "if you traitors hadn't started the war! Princess, I think-"

"We are out of order," the clerk said, getting to his feet and ringing the bell. "Princess, if we may return to the business of the militarization of the colonists in the city of Turalik, it would be for the best. I would remind everyone of the oath they took at the beginning of these proceedings. You are to discuss any issues put forth in good faith."

Everyone but Yvonnia sat down. Generals Gera, Rhela, and Vasada all had sour expressions on their faces. Basra had a resigned and pleasant smile on his. The Lama absently looked out through the open arches behind Yvonnia's table rather than at anything important. The bell was rung again and she began to speak. "I wish to call a vote, that the agreement made with the local colonial leaders be recognized by all members of this council."

"I second the motion," Vasada said, but the clerk rang the bell.

"General Vasada, motions may not be seconded by delegates of the same faction."

Vasada grumbled and resumed his seat. A moment of silence passed and the clerk asked, "Is there no one to second Princess Yvonnia's motion?"

Another moment passed, and the clerk reached for the bell once more. Yvonnia's heart sank, but at the last moment the man in the suit, sitting at the table of the Thunats, stood up. "I will second it for the sake of mutual peace between the two peoples."

It was Lord Resna Kaliman. He would have gone unnoticed by most of the high lords of Sial, were it not for the fact that he refused to wear any semblance of traditional Siali clothing. Instead, he chose to wear Odolian fashion, of a sort. His suit coat was of a strange cut and all black, though the buttoned shirt he wore underneath was ivory white. He wore trousers, also black, with sharp creases down the middle, and hard black shoes that squeaked on the tiled floors. Yvonnia wondered how he managed, in such heavy, dark clothing, to not even break a sweat. Of all the delegates, she disliked him the most. He had been at her father's side when the king decided to request Odol's help, and Resna, along with his cousin Manik, went over to Odol with the call for aid. Only Resna returned, and he had changed.

"Then a vote will be called. Who will agree that the militarization of the Odolian quarter of Turalik is acceptable, under the terms discussed between the Holanites and the local leaders? Make known now if you say 'yea.'"

Yvonnia still stood, as well as Kaliman. Vasada stood up as well, quite predictably. Yvonnia knew none of the Ryokans would stand for such a measure, and bit her lip nervously. It needed to pass, or Odol would start sending colonists to more cities, forcing their way into having their own quarter in each port town. Then militarization across the board would be unavoidable, and more uncomfortable.

Finally, as the clerk reached for the bell, Prince Basra, smiling at Yvonnia in an odd way, stood up. The vote was tied and when the bell was rung, the four sat down. The clerk then asked the others to make it known if they said 'nay.'

The three Ryokans stood up in military fashion, though Yvonnia noticed that while General Gera and General Rhela both stood straight up at once, General Ozerov seemed to hesitate slightly. The three generals all looked to the delegate who still did not stand. If the Lama did not make known his 'nay,' the motion would be passed by the council. Lama Nakazo, however, seemed entirely disinterested in the vote. In fact, Yvonnia thought she heard him snoring as he leaned his head back in the chair. No one was allowed to influence the vote, so the Lama slept right on until the bell was rung again by the clerk, who seemed to ring it more vigorously than before. Nakazo jolted awake, and the clerk spoke to the standing generals.

"The motion to allow the militarization of the Odolian quarter of Turalik, under the terms discussed between the Holanites and their local leaders, passes and will be written in the declaration." There was some grumbling on the part of the Ryokans as they sat back down. Fortunately, the council moved past that issue without another word about it. However, there was still time to discuss further issues before the financial matters were brought forth, so there was a chance yet that a fight between General Vasada and the Ryokans would break out. *Were father here, I would be more confident that this council could end peacefully,* Yvonnia thought.

She stood up again. "Is there anything further to address before we begin discussion of the levy and the toll rates and the distributions of funds to all parties?" The idea was to try to unite the Holanites, Ryokans, and Thunats under the same Siali banner once more with financial motivation. If only they could get there.

"I have something I wish to discuss." Lord Kaliman stood up. "It concerns the victims of the razing of Jentia."

Yvonnia's stomach dropped, and she saw a similar consternation bubbling among the Ryokans. Jentia was the first settlement that the Odolians had made. They had begun to employ

Siali workers, and had lived there nearly a generation, dating from the reign of her father's father. It was the suspected mistreatment of Siali natives which had ultimately sparked the civil war.

Feeling that their presence was disrupting the traditional Siali way of life that had existed for thousands of years, General Gera mustered his regiments without first appealing to the king or warning the Odolians. Instead, he launched a surprise attack which resulted in the total destruction of the town and the slaughter of an unknown number of Odolian civilians. King Holan tried to punish Gera for his misstep, and that was when the civil war began.

Despite her misgivings, Yvonnia gave Kaliman a tentative nod, and he began to speak in a rather stilted, scripted manner. "It has come to the attention of the nobility of Odol, and specifically that of the city of Gorand, that there remain in Trelasi hundreds of Odolian citizens taken at the razing of Jentia. Most are women and children, who are being forced to labor at many different tasks in the city, including hard labor in the mines. I would like to suggest a motion that, as a goodwill gesture to Odol, the Ryokans release all of the captives they are currently holding, and send them back overseas after these two years in prison."

"I will not hear a minute more of this!" General Gera shouted. "They are the price that Odol paid for their invasion. Negotiation with these monsters is an outrage, I mean..."

The bell rang, silencing Gera. "The Ryokan delegate is out of order. You must wait to respond until the Thunat delegate gives up the floor." The general sat down, teeth gritted, biting back the rest of his response.

"If I may speak, Lord Kaliman?" Yvonnia asked. Kaliman gave a wry smile and nodded to her. "I had not known until this moment that there were any survivors from Jentia," she said sincerely, addressing the room at large. "This was not made known at the signing of the treaty. I also think these people be returned to their homeland."

"And why should they be?" Gera asked, though he stayed seated, awaiting her recognition. Yvonnia nodded, and Gera stood up once more. "They were uninvited! We had traded with Odol for years by passage of the southern straits. We could have even traded by airship if they had been willing to assist us in building a sky-dock, or whatever they call it. But no, they found the need to *settle* our land, our great Sial. These are not simply prisoners of war, these are trespassers on our land! The penalty for trespassing is servitude, if you know your law, *princess*."

"I know the law, General Gera," Yvonnia said patiently. "They are not under our law, however. They are not Siali."

"So you, as your father, say that the Odolians may come here and do as they please? Do you not know what they are capable of, what they have done in their other colonies? The lands are destroyed, the cities pillaged, the people held as serfs in their home-land, the kings and queens overthrown and killed, the women-"

General Rhela stood up abruptly to cut off the other general. His round face, lined with kindly concern, gave credibility to his argument. "What my colleague is trying to say, is that these people were already guilty of crime by our law, law which we hope that the king and princess still follow! Dear princess, the council should allow us to remain as we were, especially if the new settlers at Turalik are to militarize."

"You *were* loyal to King Holan," General Vasada grumbled under his breath, "I would that you were still."

The discussion ceased, and Yvonnia saw the two generals lock eyes across the room in a deadly gaze, both heated with anger. After a moment, the clerk spoke. For the first time, his voice was uncertain. "General Rhela, do you wish to give the floor to General Vasada?"

Neither flinched.

"No. I know what he's going to say," Rhela said.

"Afraid of it, rather!" Vasada said with a deepening frown.

"Why would I be afraid of the same discussion we have had a dozen times?"

"You should be afraid. I seem to recall a law saying that traitors are to be executed."

"Now see here..." General Gera began, and the three generals began to bicker in a jumble of words that, when mixed in with the sound of the sea wind blowing into the chamber and the frantic ringing of the clerk's bell, was impossible for Yvonnia to understand. After minute or two, the three finally stopped to look at the clerk. The man coughed politely.

"Generals, you are all three out of order. Please understand that if you cannot conduct yourselves properly, you will be asked to leave these proceedings. As such, you will be counted as abstaining from voting on this issue. Is that understood?"

Vasada and the two Ryokans nodded reluctantly before sitting down again. Lord Kaliman had a smug smile on his face, while Prince Basra wore an anxious frown. Lama Nakazo was fast asleep once more. Since the floor had been Kaliman's to begin with, he now held it again. Yvonnia was afraid of what he was about to say.

"This is why the Thunats align themselves with neither party!" Kaliman said, his mouth cracking in a self-satisfied grin. "Both are too focused on their own pride, rather than on helping the civilians of the world in their plight. Princess, I would like to call for a vote on the release of the-"

"Pride? You have pride in only one thing, you bastard!" Gera leapt up again, his face crimson, neck bulging and spit flying from his mouth in anger. It was all General Rhela could do to hold him back from rushing at Kaliman. "You only have pride in yourself! Who made you king over us? I'd rather side with that milky soft Holan than with-"

"Milky soft? The man who you once called king? The man whose sons you slaughtered? How dare you!" Vasada was shouting now, on his feet as well and pointing with an angry finger. His anger seemed directed more at Rhela than at the spluttering Gera. If it would not have been considered both rude and improper for her status as a princess, Yvonnia would have covered her ears. "How dare you, you who helped raise the crown prince and train him for battle, how dare you stand against everything your king stood for?"

"I am not standing against Holan!" Rhela snapped, his countenance more sad than angry.

"Then stand *with* him and abandon this Ryokan nonsense!"

"Please, we need not shout," Prince Basra said as he too stood up, arms spread open in a conciliatory gesture. Somehow, Lama Nakazo stayed asleep.

"I am not shouting!" Gera snapped. "Nor would I, if that little whelp could keep his mouth shut when talking about his betters!" He glared across at Lord Kaliman, apparently ignoring the shouting match between Vasada and Rhela.

"Generals, please." Yvonnia stood up and raised her hand to interrupt the argument. Surprisingly, the three generals, Prince Basra, and Lord Kaliman all became attentive to her. "We cannot reach any decisions if we devolve into *this*. I would like a vote on this issue. Could I have a second to that-"

"We cannot make any decisions, *girl*, if the king's dog is not kept on a tight enough chain!" Gera's voice dripped with contempt as he stared at General Vasada, whose face soured at the insult. "We Ryokans are a proud lot, that is true. We are proud because unlike those who lick the boots of the oppressive Odolians or the slothful king, we follow the path of Ryoka. We have no need of a king when we have the strength to back up our proud words."

With no warning, Gera turned his back on the council, facing the door. Yvonnia took in a deep breath, shocked at the flagrant disrespect shown by the action. Shrugging, Ozerov set the hookah pipe down and faced away from the council as well. After a pained moment, Rhela took his gaze away from Vasada and also turned his back.

"Generals..." Yvonnia tried desperately to reason. She could not begin to unite the kingdom if the Ryokans left the council. She was cut off by General Gera.

"We will return, *girl*, when your general apologizes to us, as an example to those who think they can insult the great Ryokans. General Rhela, General Ozerov." He nodded to each, but as they began to move toward the door, it was flung wide with a *bang*.

A woman stood there, tall and stately and devastatingly beautiful, chest heaving like she was catching her breath, though she looked as effortless as if she had just stepped out of a royal litter. She wore a golden tiara similar to Yvonnia's, though instead of displaying deep sapphires, it was encrusted with fiery rubies. Her arms and neck were covered in jewelry, and she wore a long chain which connected her opulent nose ring to her earlobe, which dangled with strands of rubies and pearls. It was an insult to be so adorned in front of the princess, but that was not what shocked Yvonnia.

It was Princess Basra, Princess Menava Basra, the missing princess who had an even greater claim to the throne than her cousin. She had always been a threat whispered of by her father's advisors, but Yvonnia had never expected to see her in the flesh.

"Princess Menava!" Generals Gera and Rhela exclaimed, and the three Ryokans dropped to one knee.

"Rise, good generals," the princess said, her voice deep and sultry as she smiled appreciatively at the bowing men. "I think that you have done me enough honor already." She looked up and studied the council room. "I expect you have been busy defending this land from the invaders? Or has this pretender convinced you that the Odolians truly mean no harm?"

She strode into the room, her deep red saree fluttering along like a flame behind her. She did not go to the table where the Ryokans sat, but instead went straight to face Yvonnia.

"My dear princess, you look pale," Menava said and with a slender finger traced Yvonnia's jaw, ending with one painted nail pointed at her throat. Yvonnia heard a rustle behind her as her bodyguard loosened his sword in its sheath. "You ought to be resting in luxury. I don't think this life is really for you. Maybe something more relaxing would-"

The pitiful jingle of the bell cut her off, but the rival princess transfixed the clerk with a baleful gaze that, for the first time in the council, made him shrink back on himself. *Great, she's scared him stiff! What am I thinking? She scares me too.* Yvonnia thought bitterly to herself as she inched away from Menava's hand.

"Where is your father, dear girl?" Menava asked, swiveling back to face Yvonnia. "I would have thought after he made it clear I was not to attend his precious council, he himself would be officiating! Instead, I find the insult of some serf telling *my* generals how they need to act. Remove this...person at once!" She pulled her finger away from Yvonnia's throat and pointed instead at the cowering clerk. "And bring your father in here. Then we can begin to talk."

Turning around, Menava stormed from the room as fast as she had come in, the Ryokans all kneeling once more as she passed by. The generals then turned back to the council and gave a curt bow, before shuffling after her. Yvonnia stammered to get a final word in, voice trembling in spite of herself.

"We will recess for the rest of the morning. The council will meet again after the midday meal. Clerk..." Yvonnia looked to him, hoping for some kind of help. The plain-looking man, who had seemed so stalwart in the face of the oversized egos of the generals and delegates, now visibly trembled in the wake of Princess Menava. The door slammed behind the departing General Ozerov, jolting Lama Nakazo from his sleep.

"Those treacherous scum!" Vasada roared, shaking his fist at the door, "And the nerve of that woman, to insult our princess in such a manner! Even you, Prince Basra, have more respect for her than that..."

Yvonnia rounded the end of the table and snatched up the bell, ringing it loudly to cut off Vasada's fuming. "This council is now in recess. General Vasada, a word with you, please."

She strode out of the council chamber, deep blue saree and sky blue veil streaming behind her, with her loyal and silent bodyguard following at her heels. His hand had not moved from the hilt of his sword and his face was set in stone, betraying no emotion. *To think how nasty they would have been if Jacik hadn't been there,* Yvonnia thought. But even with him standing watch over her, the council had certainly not gone according to plan.

YVONNIA

Yvonnia pushed open the door of her chamber, inhaling the scent of burning incense from a stand in the corner. Finally alone, she relaxed enough to let her shoulders slump and stumbled through the doorway. The journey from the council chamber to her room, through the throngs of curious courtiers and nervous officials, had been a grueling one, even with Jacik there to clear a path.

Her semicircle chamber was built in the same orientation as the council chamber, with two large balconies. One looked out to the southwest over the docks and crystal blue waters. The other looked to the north, where she could see much of Aldia, and even the hazy impression of Turalik on the horizon. They were at the top of the tallest tower in the palace. The room had been chosen so that if the Ryokans attacked, Yvonnia could at least leap to her death with dignity, rather than suffer the humiliation of capture and imprisonment.

Neither balcony interested her now, though peaceful fresh air would have been welcome. What interested her most was the bed in the middle of the room. Airy, iridescent blue silk covered an overstuffed mattress on a beautifully carved wooden bedframe. She flung herself on it, buried her face in one of the tasseled pillows, and let out a scream of raw emotion into its depths. She'd been saving it up the entire time she'd been dealing with the delegates. In just a few moments, she would have to deal once again with General Vasada and his frustrating outbursts. Why her father couldn't reprimand the general himself was beyond her, but she knew what she needed to do, regardless of her father's inactivity.

Yvonnia screamed once more, then finally raised her head and looked back at the doorway. Jacik had entered, closing the door behind him, and had taken up his seat beside it. Yvonnia forced herself to smile at him. He was a blessing, she knew. He never talked back, never gave her a hard time, never tried to tell her to be anything she wasn't. He just listened.

"I don't know how I'm going to handle it when I get back, Jacik," she said, sitting up and pulling the pillow into her lap. "It's all so...volatile. My father wants to bring about an agreement. You saw them. Do you see them agreeing to anything? I'm shocked it didn't all collapse because they didn't like the assigned seating!"

Jacik just shook his head and said nothing.

"Exactly my point. Maybe if they saw my father, and not myself, they would have more respect..." She got up abruptly and went to her vanity. Peering into the polished silver mirror, she gave a deep sigh and glanced back at the makeup-stained pillow. "I am not made for this, Jacik. I can't even keep myself put together. How am I supposed to put a kingdom back together?"

Jacik gave no response, only the suggestion of a shrug. Yvonnia looked down at the gold bracelets that rattled on her wrist with every slight movement. "These don't make them respect me, nor does this." She took the tiara from her head and cast it onto the painted wooden vanity. "Nor does this." She tugged at her saree, which was dyed a rich, deep blue that no other lady in Sial could match. "I wish my father would just-"

"Mistress!"

The high pitched voice rang from the doorway to her private bath. Her maidservant Enya ducked out, tugging the sleeve of her blouse up over her shoulder, and quickly hid her soaking hair under a plain blue veil. "I thought you would be in council for another few hours! Oh, and look at yourself! I've got to put your makeup back on before you go anywhere else."

Yvonnia rolled her eyes. "So *this* is why I never seem to have enough soap for my baths. You know that stealing from your mistress is a punishable crime," she said, a smirk returning to her face, smudged as it was with powder and kohl.

"You'd not punish me," the young girl said brashly with a hand on her hip. "Where would you be without me?"

"In a quiet room. With more soap. What put such an idea into your head, Enya?"

"The bath? Don't you remember?" Enya bustled around behind Yvonnia, fetching her powder and brushes. "You let me use the bath a couple months back instead of going out with the rest of the servants."

"That was one time. Enya, please just ask me if you wish to use the bath. For you I'd be free with it! But if you tried that with another lady, she'd have given you a bath in boiling oil."

Enya paused for a moment and grimaced. "Yes, my lady. No go wash your face so I can put you back together. Is the council done for today?"

Yvonnia smiled tolerantly at her maidservant. If the council was over, that would mean that the princess would have her meal sent up to the bedchamber, a meal which could always serve two people instead of one. She would almost always split part of it with Enya and Jacik. *Of course, her mind goes straight to food.*

"No, I'm sorry, we will reconvene later. Plus in a few minutes I have to tell off General Vasada..."

"Why isn't your father reprimanding him? Wasn't he there?"

Yvonnia just shook her head as Enya came up behind her and removed the veil from her hair. Jacik had to look away at that point, instead focusing on the intricate patterns painted on the half-dome ceiling.

"Well, I say that he should have been there," Enya said pertly. She began to brush out the princess's long, dark hair and Yvonnia shut her eyes as she enjoyed the relaxing sensation. "You can't be expected to hold up an entire country on your own! He's been doing this more and more; just staying in his room, reading his poetry..."

"Enya, you can't say that," Yvonnia warned. "He is still your king."

"Why can't I say it? Everyone else is," Enya snapped as she draped the veil back over Yvonnia's head. "Why can't he act like a king for once instead of..."

Yvonnia's eyes flew open. "Enya, I cannot allow you to speak in such a way of your king. That is an order. I don't care who says what about him. I can command you, and I will." Yvonnia stood up. "You must follow this order, no matter how many baths I allow you to take in my private tub. Is that understood?"

The unaccustomed sternness in the princess's voice caught Enya off guard, and she nodded mutely, her eyes wide. Her hands trembled slightly as she took the earrings out of Yvonnia's ears and exchanged them for lighter ones: big golden hoops rather than the enormous gold emblems.

"Now Enya, I think I will change," Yvonnia said, more gently this time, looking down at the serene blue she wore. She had hoped that the color would signal her desire for peace to the other delegates. And perhaps it did, though the generals all ignored her in favor of further dividing the kingdom. "Bring the purple brocade. It will let the generals know who their leader is."

Jacik looked back at her, his eyes softening with compassion. She knew he saw that it was only an act, but even an act could help swing the tide of the collapsing council in her favor, or rather in her father's favor. Standing up, she went behind the decorated changing screen opposite where Jacik sat and shed every garment that had even a trace of blue on it. In the meantime, Enya rummaged through the cherrywood wardrobe, pulling out a lavender blouse, deep purple saree, and a veil which matched the mauve skirt. The dyes alone probably cost more than an average merchant's house.

The outfit had been a gift from the master tailors following the death of her brothers. The people were clearly ready for Yvonnia to replace her father on the throne, a fact that made her uneasy. But if her people were already preparing for a Queen Yvonnia, then a queen was what the unruly generals would get.

Yvonnia's head was visible above the top of the screen, and before she had a chance to put her veil on, General Vasada entered the chamber. In a flash of movement, Jacik had his sword drawn, the sharp tip poised against the general's throat. To see a woman, especially the princess, without her veil was to practically see her naked. Yvonnia did not have such a strict conception of modesty, though she quickly pinned the light purple veil to her hair, leaving just the front of her black-brown locks visible, as was the fashion.

"General, you should knock before entering my chamber—or any chamber, for that matter. Jacik, stand down." With precise, fluid movements, Jacik resumed his seat by the door. The general breathed a sigh of relief. "General Vasada, thank you for coming here," Yvonnia said as she slipped the golden tiara back into her hair. She sat down at the vanity once more. "We have little time until the council reconvenes, so I need to ask you a favor."

"Whatever you ask, I will try to accomplish," Vasada said, bowing so far at the waist that for a moment he was looking directly at the floor.

"You will not try, general, you will *succeed* in keeping quiet during the rest of the proceedings," the princess said as Enya, suddenly meek and humble in the general's presence, began to reapply Yvonnia's makeup. She was all politeness and downcast eyes, not a hint of sarcasm or back-talk in any of her mannerisms. *Why can't she be like this all the time?* "I will not allow you to endanger the people of Sial with your fiery temper anymore. I know you take issue with General Rhela," Yvonnia continued, though the mere mention of Rhela's name seemed to infuriate the man, "but I cannot allow you to continue in this way. General, you have been like another father to me for much of my life."

The warmth came back into Yvonnia's expression, and as Enya withdrew, her task finished for the moment, Yvonnia stood up once again. She took General Vasada's rough, bearded cheeks in her hands and lifted up his bowed form to his full height, a head taller than herself.

"You used to play with me when I was young. I used to ride on your shoulders, remember? You have also been my comfort in times of greatest need. You, not my father, were there when the battle happened, when the news arrived..." She shuddered to think of it. "Now I need you to put aside those emotions. You cannot explode in anger like that again. I know you are still angry over what happened to my brothers; I am too. It is something I find hard to forgive and something I may never forget. But for the moment, it will not avail us to bring up such old wounds. My brothers died in the hope of peace, not for the advancement of vain wars. Please, I do not begrudge you the freedom to speak your mind, but getting into mindless shouting matches will not help anything. Is that understood, Vasada?"

Despite his towering height, the general seemed to shrink in on himself. "Yes, my lady," he said in a meek voice, respect creasing the corners of his eyes. "Is there any other way your servant can be of service?"

Yvonnia smiled. "Yes, there is. Tell my father his presence is required at the reconvening of the council. Tell him that Princess Yvonnia requests his presence there. Tell him of the arrival of Princess Menava. He should come for that, if nothing else. Is that understood, General Vasada?"

"Yes, my lady," the general said with another low bow.

"Good. Go then and let me ready myself. I require nothing more of you."

The general bowed once more, and backed respectfully from the princess's bedchamber, closing the door softly behind him. As soon as he was gone, Yvonnia dropped back into the small chair at the vanity, deflating like a balloon. *I can't keep doing this...* She caught Jacik's worried glance from the corner of her eye but turned away and massaged her temples wearily with thumb and forefinger.

"Mistress, if you don't take a break, you'll wither away," Enya said, coming around beside her and taking her arm gently. Yvonnia allowed herself to be led over to the bed, where she collapsed back into the inviting pile of silk-covered pillows. "You've had some kind of meeting every day this whole season," Enya chided. "Since the war ended, you've been the one running the court, the council of advisors, and the entire Holanite nobility! I think even the greatest king would be eaten up inside."

The princess shook her head sullenly as she pulled a pillow to her stomach. "I'm the only reason we haven't been plunged into war again. If only there were some way for the Ryokans to see peace..."

"I have an idea." Enya grinned. "Send Jacik! I'm sure after he roughs them up a bit, they'll come to see reason. They'd say anything you wanted if you had his muscle to back it up."

"Enya, I don't..."

"I mean, look at him. I know I'd do anything he said," Enya said with a flirtatious smirk.

Jacik shifted uncomfortably. "Princess..." he rumbled in his deep voice. His eyes practically pleaded with Yvonnia, and she was more than happy to help him out.

"Enya, have you cleaned up my bath after your little escapade?"

The handmaid's cheeks flushed, and she took her skirts in her hand and ran to the other room to clean up the mess she had no doubt made. Smiling gently, Yvonnia propped herself up slightly and looked over at Jacik. "I've told you to pay her no mind. I think she acts that way with every man who hasn't seen forty harvests. Besides, it's nearly time for us to go back into that gauntlet..." She glanced towards the door, already feeling daunted by the thought of facing another session of the council.

"She does that to tease me, on purpose," Jacik said, clearly hurt.

"No, she doesn't. I think she genuinely likes you, Jacik. I also think that she does it because you are the only man around here who doesn't try to sweep her away into a secret romance."

Jacik just frowned and stood up. "It is time to go," he said with his normal sternness, gently moving away from the subject.

"Yes, I suppose it is," Yvonnia said, setting the pillow aside and getting to her feet. "I do hope that my father will be there this time."

Prince Basra sipped absently at his ornate goblet, tasting the hardness of the well-water. He waited patiently in the council chamber for the other delegates to return. Beside him, Lord Kaliman took a drink of his water. They had just shared a brief toast; a prayer for Siali peace. Per the tenants of Thun, they couldn't drink the wine that the rest of the delegates enjoyed.

Snoring softly in his chair, the Lama had just finished his third glass of medicinal liquor.

"I'm concerned about his holiness' health," Basra whispered.

"Why?" Kaliman said between sips.

"He has slept so much and taken so much medicine."

"Of course he's healthy," Kaliman reassured the young prince. "These tense political meetings simply take a toll on his stamina; that's all."

"These meetings take a toll on *my* stamina," Basra joked. Seeing no reaction from Kaliman, the prince ambled onward. "Holan's daughter certainly is something though."

"Put politely, yes." Kaliman stared at the empty Holanite table.

"What does that mean?"

"I mean to say," Resna said with a sneer, "that the princess is nothing more than a puppet for her father. Your cousin's entrance gave her quite the shock. Princess Menava is dangerous, but so is Holan's inability to be a strong leader."

"You know that I do not love Holan past his peaceful influence on our people." Basra hoped he did not sound too earnest in his denial. "But his daughter is clearly made of sterner stuff. If only those brutish Ryokans and General Vasada could come to terms."

"Don't be swayed too easily by her physical beauty. Remember that it is the beauty of the soul, of the peaceful spirit that is important in anyone," Kaliman said firmly.

"But I see her spiritual beauty as well. I think she desires for peace as much as-"

"You desire her. My prince, your infatuation with her is immoral. Right, your holiness?"

The Lama snorted and jolted awake, nodding absently to Basra and Kaliman. He took another sip of his medicine before closing his eyes again.

"It is best not to bother him," Kaliman said, and returned to his drink of water, leaving the prince to his own thoughts.

18
LEAVE TAKING

The mahogany doors opened, and Yvonnia stood up from her seat. The five minutes she had been waiting in the council room seemed to have lasted for hours. She had spent them studying the faces of the delegates as they sat patiently. The balance of the delegates was kept—three to each faction—though the composition of the Ryokans had changed. Princess Menava now took the leadership role, though she replaced the lowly mercenary General Ozerov.

Menava was a commanding presence in the room, seeming taller than she really was when seated next to the two generals. Menava thought she had a victory, and alarmingly, Yvonnia had no idea what that victory looked like.

Everyone else joined Yvonnia in standing as the king entered the room; even the Ryokans wouldn't dare to show their monarch open disrespect, at least not yet. Yvonnia's father was a tall, broad man, with darker skin than hers. His curly hair and beard were ghost white, and numerous wrinkles covered his age-worn face. He wore green and blue ceremonial robes that were strictly traditional, looking much more like the Ryokans than either General Vasada or Jacik, whose uniforms showed Odolian influence. The crown on his head was dense with emeralds, sapphires, turquoise, and dozens of other blue and green stones. He strode with purpose and had a broad scowl on his face which was directed at every delegate, including Yvonnia.

He went around to Yvonnia's side of the table and sat heavily upon the rosewood throne, grim determination on his face. Once he was seated, the other delegates followed in unison and looked to him, not the clerk, for the next move. It was the clerk, though, who rang the bell and began to speak.

"The council is now in ses-"

"With what devilry do you threaten my kingdom?" King Holan's booming voice interrupted the clerk, rolling through the room like thunder. Though no formal address was made, it was clear he was speaking to Princess Menava.

"Whatever do you mean, your majesty?" Menava said coyly. "I haven't threatened any..."

"Your very presence, Menava, threatens my kingdom and my daughter! You were told to stay where you were."

A confused murmur arose from the other delegates. Yvonnia looked desperately to Vasada to see if he was as baffled as she was. To her shock and discomfort, the general seemed just as confused as everyone else. She wrung the fabric of her saree in her hands as she looked at Princess Menava's face, which had slipped back into smug self-assurance at her father's words. Anything which brought a smile to Menava's face made Yvonnia nervous.

"Yes, King Holan, I do recall you sent me a letter. Among others. Remember, all those years ago? I still have them. In fact, I brought them with me." With a flourish, Menava plucked a couple of old, age-stained sheets of paper from the breast of her saree.

Yvonnia glanced at her father in time to see his scowl deepen as his fist slammed onto the table. "What could you possibly want, Menava? Is it not enough that you kill my children and fund this war? You were told not to come here, Menava! I will not have this..."

The clerk rang his bell, about to tell the king he was speaking out of turn, but the king marched over to the clerk, wrestled the bell out of his hand, and with a fluid, rage-filled motion, flung it over the balcony. Holan stalked back to his seat and glared furiously at the clerk.

"Interrupt me again and it will be you I throw."

Yvonnia thought her heart was going to stop.

"Father, I-" She tried to insert herself into the proceedings but was rolled over by a cacophony of shouts from every end of the chamber. Evan the Thunats, who had previously been silent, were trying to comprehend what had just happened. Only King Holan, Princess Menava, and the clerk, who looked as though he was about to die of panic, were silent. The king and Menava were locked in a deadly stare.

For Yvonnia, seeing her father like this shook her to the core. He always had a temper, but he usually vented it towards the servants, and he had never exploded at any important councils or in front of the nobility. She tried to raise her voice over the chaos of questions and demands from the other delegates, but the words caught in the back of her throat as she stared helplessly at the scene. Out of the corner of her eye, she saw Jacik tighten his grip on his sword.

When every line of questions and confused exclamations from the delegates had died down, the cacophony was replaced with a deafening silence as everyone looked to the king and Menava for answers. "Father," Yvonnia choked out, "What is she talking about?"

"I can answer that," Menava snapped, standing up and strutting over to the Holanite table. Jacik had his sword out in a sharp scrape of steel and pointed it at Menava. Ignoring him, she leaned in to whisper so softly Yvonnia could barely hear. The intoxicating, spicy-sweet scent of her perfume smothered the princess with Menava's every breath. "Years ago, when I was younger than you are now, child, your father came to me to propose marriage. I denied him. Ten years later, when your mother died, he came to me again, and again I told him no. His next wife produced no children before dying, and three years ago he wrote to me provocatively. I know that he is incapable of *real* love. He wanted only a united Sial. I made sure it united against him."

She began to raise her voice, letting the others hear what she was saying. "Of course, when Holan began to lick the colonizing boots of Odol's 'explorers,' I knew what had to be done. I thought our little conflict would convince him of our ways, or at least bring him to heel. But now, dear child, and the rest of you too," Menava looked around at the delegates, all of whom, even the Ryokan generals, looked confused and apprehensive of what she was about to say, "I think it is time that we have a new ruler in this kingdom. *I* would be firm with the invaders, unlike the soft King Holan. *I* would be a true Queen of Sial, not a slavering dog begging for scraps from the Odolian table. I put forward a motion for the deposition of King Holan, effective immediately." She raised her head and stared defiantly into the king's eyes without moving away from the edge of Jacik's sword. Then she turned, jewelry jingling on her throat and wrists, and walked back to her own table.

A stunned silence hung in the chamber for a moment, before an outraged growl came not from Yvonnia's father, but from General Vasada. "You can't just-"

"I second the motion," interrupted Lord Resna Kaliman, an unsavory expression twisting his face, "For peace in the land. If we were all on good terms, then war would not be necessary."

The clerk, now shaken and hesitant, stood up. "There will be a vote. This motion, seconded by a different faction, will now be decided: whether King Holan will be deposed as of this day, and Princess Menava enthroned in his place. Who here will agree..."

"I will not have this!"

King Holan's fist cracked the veneer on the table, and he glared now at Lord Kaliman. "This council was not convened to decide who would be king! *I* am king, and she, my daughter, will be queen when I cease to be!" He gestured violently in Yvonnia's direction, causing her to shrink away involuntarily. "It was my birthright, and it is now hers since *some* here had my sons murdered on the battlefield like common serfs. You will not do this. This council is over!"

"Cousin," Prince Basra interjected from his table, looking pleadingly at Menava, "This is completely improper. We came here for a peaceful resolution, and you are suggesting that we..."

"There is a reason you will always be lesser than I, *cousin*," Menava spat. "You have no goals, no ambition. I am trying to depose this lazy, unproductive, sad excuse for a king, who-"

"Enough! I have power yet," King Holan shouted. "You are hereby banished from the lands west of the jungle. Both parties, the Ryokans and the Thunats, are banished on pain of death. So I declare here in the presence of these witnesses. The word of the king of Sial is law!"

Yvonnia squeezed her eyes shut in defeat. She could not see the reactions of the others, but she heard Lama Nakazo gasp audibly. When she opened her eyes, she saw that the Ryokans, including Princess Menava, had turned and were marching out of the chamber in military fashion. Lord Kaliman was collecting his papers into a fine leather case imported from Odol. Prince Basra just looked around sadly as he went to help the Lama up from his chair. General Vasada seemed to boil with rage.

"Father, this doesn't help the kingdom," she entreated. "Please, call them back. This will only result in-"

"Yvonnia," King Holan said in a low voice, not taking his eyes off the backs of the retreating Ryokans, who were quickly followed by the Thunats, "You will go to Odol. You will be my ambassador. You are the only one I can trust with this message, since you are my daughter and my last remaining heir. They will listen to you."

He sat down, pulled a piece of paper into place in front of him, and began scribbling a message in the Odolian language. Though she was not fluent in it, Yvonnia could decipher enough. As her father's hand swooped across the page, scratching down the looping script, Vasada, who did not know the language at all, looked up concernedly at Yvonnia. Her own brow was furrowed with dismay as she read the message.

"What does it say?" the general asked quietly.

"It says he is willing to become a vassal of the Emperor of Odol, giving no less than half of our land for the empire's use as a sign of fealty, if they will use the...I'm not familiar with the word...to destroy the Ryokans." A tear slipped down her cheek, followed by another. "Father, everything that you fought for...you're only proving them right! I thought we did not want Odol to take over..."

Hastily, Holan sprinkled powder over the paper to dry the still gleaming ink, folded it in three neat parts, and struck a match to melt the green sealing wax. He spoke quietly as the flame in his eyes seemed to burn hotter than that of the match. "Princess Menava is the one person that I fear in all of these proceedings. If it were not for her-"

"If it were not for her, you would not have come from your room, my king." General Vasada raised his voice as he stood up straight, puffing his chest and folding his arms in military fashion. "I am loyal to you to the end. Whatever you say is my command. But I cannot advise you to go through with this madness. My king, what does that woman have that you would destroy your kingdom over? You cannot break from them. Look at the kingdom of Karlsban. They tried to fight off the Odolian invasion, and they were nearly destroyed in the war. And years of rebellion later, they are no closer to their freedom. If you do this, we shall never be a free kingdom again."

"If we are going to be under a tyrant, I would rather it be one of my choosing, general. You know as well as I that we do not have the might to stand up to Ozerov's men, Rhela's strategy, and Gera's charisma. Too many of my loyalists have gone over. But our entire kingdom united could not withstand the great ships of Odol."

He sighed as he stamped his seal onto the envelope, the wax cooling and darkening with a gust of the sea wind from outside.

"Now, daughter, you must go in the night. Take this to Baron Schulhard of Gorand. He is one of the six great nobles of Odol and has the ear of the emperor. He also commands one of the great ships. It is my purpose that he take this letter to the emperor himself. Is that understood, my daughter?"

Yvonnia's eyes were unwavering as she looked at her father. She took the letter in her hands. The thin, featherlight paper seemed to bear the weight of a millstone.

"Yes father, I shall do as you say," she said, keeping her voice even and calm.

Looking accomplished in what he had done, King Holan turned to Vasada. "General, you will go with her as a guard. You have this evening to say goodbye to your wife and children, but by midnight I want you on the nation's fastest ship with twenty of the royal guard. Tomorrow morning you are to be well on your way to Odol."

"Our fastest ships would be the sky-skiffs," Vasada said. Yvonnia's hands went cold and she felt the blood drain out of her face. He was right of course, though the very thought filled her with dread. But King Holan was shaking his head.

"You would be seen, and then it *would* be war. The Ryokans must not know that we are breaking the treaty." He looked at Yvonnia. "Take your bodyguard as well, and your handmaid," he said without even glancing at Jacik. "I will have your ship outfitted with enough to make your journey pleasant. I am sure you will be glad to travel by water rather than by air."

"Yes, thank you father," Yvonnia said dully. "I shall prepare as well. If I may be excused, my king." She turned away almost before her father nodded to give permission. She left the chamber in a daze, barely noticing Jacik as he followed her at an even pace, his footsteps falling in time with hers.

The corridors of the palace were in pandemonium. Whereas before the nobles had been polite and demure, currying for favors with flattery and faux humility, now they were lunging at her, begging for news about the council. The treasurer, a stout, bald man with an enormous beard, grabbed her arm, stopping her in her tracks.

"Is it true? Is the treaty over?" he asked in a panic, his eyes roving from side to side as if he expected Ryokans to leap out from behind the columns at any moment.

"Of course not! The council just..."

Jacik forcibly inserted himself between her and the crazed treasurer, batting away his arm, and guiding Yvonnia through the crowds. Overwhelmed by the panic all around her, Yvonnia took a deep breath and plunged onward, walking as fast as she could without breaking into a run. She felt the pressure of the crowd growing behind her as she walked and once she and Jacik had hurried past the guards at the base of her tower, the guards locked their spears together to fend off a crowd of lords and ladies who were all clamoring for comfort after the tumultuous exit of the Ryokans. Some were even begging for safety in her company, knowing that if war broke out, the princess would be strongly guarded, along with anyone in her entourage.

Saying a silent prayer, Yvonnia turned her back on the people, her purple garments, woven through with gold, shifting in a dazzling array. To those on the other side of the archway, it must have seemed that the princess was flaunting her privilege in front of them. To Yvonnia, it felt like she was abandoning them to their death. Even if war did not break out and everyone was not killed in a pointless conflict, Odol would still come and put the people of Sial—her people—beneath their iron boot, leaving them at the whim of an emperor who did not know their customs and heritage, who might never even visit their land.

She felt the salty tears stinging her cheeks as the weight of the awful reality settled into the pit of her stomach. The staircase, which always felt like it took ages to climb, now seemed to be endless. Round and round she went, her legs beginning to shake more with every step. The floor below grew more distant and the height became increasingly unnerving. When she reached a slit-like window facing out over Aldia, she looked out and saw that smoke was already rising from somewhere in the city. Shouting now came both from the palace below and from the city itself.

She didn't realize that she was falling, but fortunately Jacik was there to catch her as she nearly fainted. He carried her up the stairs in his strong arms, shouldering aside the bedroom door. Enya bolted up from where she'd been sitting on the side of Yvonnia's bed and immediately began pelting them with panicked questions.

"Do not pester her," Jacik said gruffly as he set the princess down onto her soft bed. Enya immediately swallowed back her words and began doting over Yvonnia. The princess clutched the silky coverlet in her hands, her painted nails digging through the fabric into her palms. The room was beginning to swim into focus, and she could feel herself returning to her own body as the buzzing in her ears subsided. She pitched onto her side, wracked with fresh sobs. Enya grabbed her hand, nearly in tears herself.

"Princess you can't...Mistress, you have to..." The servant girl struggled for words as she knelt beside the bed. "Oh, don't go to pieces like this, you're ruining the makeup!" She half laughed, half choked on a sob. Jacik said nothing, merely resuming his position beside the door, just out of Yvonnia's view. "Mistress," Enya said finally, tilting her head to look into Yvonnia's eyes, as if that was the only way she could be sure to get through to her, "Would it help if I drew you a bath?"

Wordlessly, Yvonnia nodded, and Enya scrambled up and scurried away. The clatter of the pipes, drawing water dozens of feet up from the castle well, began in the next room. In the absence of her maidservant, another swell of sobs shook Yvonnia's shoulders. Jacik just watched from his perch by the door, wordless and expressionless as Yvonnia let out all of her grief.

She did not have enough energy to keep crying, and her sobbing soon melted away into bitter silence as she lay, clutching her bedding close to her chest. Finally, she heard the unexpected sound of Jacik standing up, and she managed to sit up herself, still hugging a mound of bed coverings, sucking in deep breaths as she sought to regain her composure. Jacik's expression was difficult to read. He stood to military attention, with one hand ready on the hilt of his falchion and the other tucked behind his back, looking straight into her tear-reddened eyes.

"We must move tonight. You should collect your favored possessions to take with you."

When Yvonnia gave no response, he crossed the room and sat down on the edge of the bed beside her, an act which would have carried a death sentence for any man but him. She gladly accepted his company, but said nothing.

After a few moments of silence, Jacik spoke again. "My princess, we cannot always fight battles on our chosen ground. Sometimes the most important battle must be fought on ground that we do not choose." For a moment, Yvonnia stared at him, eyes wide in shock. It had been the longest sentence she could remember him ever saying.

"But I don't want to fight at all, Jacik," she said at last, her voice hitching in another sob.

"No matter what you do, princess, you are fighting," Jacik said, his gaze unwavering. "You can only decide whether to surrender, or not." Then he stood up and resumed his post by the door, as if nothing had happened.

Yvonnia let out a sigh and eased her grip on the tangled bedding. She stood up and began to strip off all of her jewelry, setting the golden bracelets, anklets, necklaces, earrings, nose ring, and tiara on the vanity. She wiped the sweat and tears from her face with a soft towel, dipped it into the polished water basin, and wiped off her face again, the cool wetness soothing her burning eyes. When she looked up and met her own eyes in the mirror, she thought that she looked quite plain now, despite the royal robes. Just a Siali girl, sad and tired, overdressed in glimmering silk that seemed out of place of on her slight, square frame. She was of two minds for a moment; she wanted desperately to be Princess Yvonnia no longer, but she also wished dearly to fight to the end.

And there was only one choice that she could make.

Nodding to Jacik as she turned, she strode purposefully towards the bathroom door. "Collect what you can before the servants come. We will leave before sunrise."

DUTY

Yvonnia glanced listlessly around the little room, formerly the captain's cabin, which Enya had hastily transformed into the princess's bedchamber. Since they'd left Sial, the servant had worked tirelessly at all her duties, especially when Yvonnia was seasick, which was often. Yvonnia shifted on the cot. *Just a few more hours,* she thought, pressing a hand to her unhappy stomach. *Just a few hours, and we'll be on solid ground at last...*

There was a sharp knock on the door. "Enter," Yvonnia called tiredly. Jacik stepped into the room and closed the door behind him. She saw concern for her sorry state written in his dark eyes, but all she could feel was shame. She hated to be weak in front of him, though she so often was. Alerted to attentiveness by the commotion at the door, Enya bustled up beside her, wringing her hands.

"Oh, princess, whatever is the matter with you? I got over my seasickness in a few days! I don't think you've had a moment of peace since we left Aldia."

"I don't know," Yvonnia murmured aloud. "Perhaps it is the sea, and I am simply more delicate than you. I wonder, though, if I don't want to arrive at all."

"Arrive where?" Enya asked, crossing the room to fetch the kettle and pour Yvonnia a cup of soothing ginger tea. It was the only thing the princess had been able to keep down.

"At Gorand. I can't help thinking that it would be better if the ship steered off course or struck a rock or something..."

"How would that help anything?" the maid servant inquired, kneeling beside her mistress's bed with the steaming cup of tea.

"This whole treaty makes me sick to my stomach," Yvonnia said miserably, taking the tea gratefully and cradling the warm mug in her hands for a moment. "Dragging in weapons from across the sea just to oppress my people..."

"So...don't." Enya shrugged. "Why don't you just not do that?"

Yvonnia sighed, propping herself up a bit higher on the stack of cushions. "Because I need to save my father. That woman, Menava...she has something on my father. Something he's done is so horrible that he would become everything the Ryokans accuse him of just to keep it a secret." She stood, setting the tea down on a rickety table beside the cot, clenching her fists as she fought to keep down the bile rising in her throat. "It isn't the sea that's the problem," she muttered through clenched teeth, "It's that letter."

In the corner of the room on a small writing desk, her father's letter lay with its bright wax seal reflecting the light that filtered in through the curtains. Within it were the words that would bring the power of Odol's military and their unstoppable airships down on her country. If it were to be destroyed...

As she reached for the letter, Jacik rose smoothly and stepped between her and the desk. "I cannot let you," he said firmly.

"Jacik, stand aside," Yvonnia snapped. "I am your princess."

"And your father is my king," Jacik said gently. "I follow his orders first."

"But I cannot go through with it!" Yvonnia cried. Hot tears stung her cheeks as she tried to press forward, but Jacik maneuvered to block her way. "I cannot bring my people under Odol's boot!"

"Jacik, why don't you just let her throw it away?" Enya huffed. "She's actually getting sick over it."

Jacik shook his head. He took the letter up from the desk and stuffed it into the blue sash about his waist.

Defeated, Yvonnia collapsed back on the bed, her momentary energy gone as suddenly as it arrived. She knew destroying the letter wasn't the correct thing to do. It was the *right* thing to do, she thought, but hardly the correct thing. She wished that the two could be the same.

Jacik said nothing, though he laid the letter back on the table and took up a defensive position beside it. His post, it seemed, had changed.

"I cannot support the king's actions!" Prince Basra said vehemently. "Bringing the Odolians here will only bring more war and violence to our land. If you truly follow the tenants of Thun, you should disagree as well!"

Lord Kaliman shrugged, reigning in his camel as it began to draw too far ahead of Basra's. "It is my opinion, and the opinion of many, that we cannot achieve peace from within Sial. My prince, right now our biggest enemy is your cousin, and that is something we cannot easily ignore."

Basra sighed, forced to nod in agreement. "I know that my cousin is of a violent mind; whatever she has to threaten the king with, it *must* be horrible..." He trailed off, the sound of the camels' hooves and the desert wind drowning out the words.

The desert was unforgiving. Though the train ran straight through it, connecting the verdant east with the lush western jungles, both Prince Basra and Lord Kaliman insisted on strictly following the tenants of Thun, which forbade the use of such luxuries. Lama Nakazo had gone forward on the train, however, on Basra's insistence. In his health, the prince said, the Lama would not make it to the Great Plateau monastery and his leadership there was sorely needed. Thun was not merciless.

"Whatever your cousin has on King Holan is unimportant now," Kaliman said. "Besides, those were only heated rumors. There is no proof that he is bringing the Odolians to Sial."

"It's what he would do," Basra said, pulling his scarf up higher over his mouth and nose as the wind whipped the sand into a fine mist.

"It is, but he would not break the treaty so boldly without first declaring open war against the Ryokans. He would need to arrange a significant financial transaction with Odol as well. It would be hard to convince the emperor since he went back on his word last time," Kaliman retorted.

"You're right; he would basically have to offer them the entire kingdom," Basra conceded. "But he still may bring them in. He could find a way." He spurred the animal below him onward over a large dune, leaving Kaliman's side. He wished more than anything for peace to remain intact.

The civil war had scarred him. Too many of his friends came back maimed, or not at all. At his cousin's command, men went and died for what was called "national integrity," a concept that Menava and her three generals had borrowed from the Odolians. It ironically encouraged them to reject anything which came from across the sea, including valuable medicines that could have saved many lives during the war.

He blinked as he looked out at the horizon, which seemed to barely rise above the endless dunes. Drawing his beast to a halt, he took a long swig from his water skin and sighed. The sun was as hot as ever and it would be many hours before night brought its cooling influence to the desert sands.

"Resna," Basra called, looking over at the man as he drew up beside him. "You go on ahead. Give his holiness my regards."

"What do you mean?" Kaliman asked, struggling to reign his camel to a complete stop beside the prince.

"I am going back north. I should have thought of it sooner. Peace cannot be achieved if I hide any longer." Basra took a deep breath, inhaling hot, dry desert air. "I shall write, if I am able."

"That's madness! You have the entire desert to cross over again. At least come back to the monastery to rest and get supplies for the trip."

Basra shook his head, a new determination filling his eyes. "No, if I go back I will want to stay. I have the fire of Thun within me, Resna. I shall help to maintain peace or I shall die trying!"

"What are you planning to do, my prince?" Kaliman asked, his mouth creased in an uneasy frown.

"I'm going to stop my cousin."

Theodore Schulhard sipped the fine port from a small glass, peering surreptitiously at the other men around the table. He was not officially supposed to take part in the meeting between his father and the other counselors, but the baron insisted on dragging his son to every function and state meeting he possibly could. Theodore knew that his father was preparing him to become baron one day, but he did not find that prospect particularly exciting.

"I still insist that we treat the delegation from Sial with respect," Lord Hastings Louis, Gorand's treasurer, said emphatically. "I believe that they are coming here to reopen negotiations with our esteemed emperor, and the least we can do is to treat them reasonably."

Baron Schulhard laughed hugely for a moment, his large stomach quivering, before becoming still and deadly serious. "You do not understand," he rumbled. "We are going to treat them to a feast of extravagance, worthy of our fine city. But no doubt the barbarians will still find some way to spoil it."

"Still, we should wait for the delegation," Louis said with a dissatisfied frown.

"Trust me, we will give them a welcome they'll not soon forget. In any event, we must still discuss the situation that unfolded last night." The baron turned his attention to Theodore, regarding him cooly with his small black eyes. "Theodore, would you please enlighten us regarding what you are planning to do about the new regimental uniforms? The ones you lost...?"

Theo almost choked on the sweet drink, coughing for a moment to clear his throat. The question caught him entirely off guard; he had thought that the discussion would be confined to the matter of the Siali delegation. But even worse than the subject at hand was the tone in which his father reprimanded him.

"It was a rebel attack, father. I could have never known that-"

"It could not have been a rebel attack, young Lord Schulhard," said a dry voice, crackling over the silence that suddenly filled the baron's small council chamber. "The rebellion is dead."

"It was a rebel attack!" Theo insisted, growing animated. "Our soldiers identified the tactics used to steal Lady Marjen's ship as exactly the kind that the rebels used in..." he stammered to a halt as his protest seemed to fall on deaf ears. Even Hastings looked at him with unsympathetic eyes.

"The rebellion is dead," the dry voice repeated. "This is more than a fact. The last stragglers were recently eradicated from Veturi. In fact, Lord Ulysses Cadbury has wired us ahead of his expected arrival. We should have a celebration for *him* when he does arrive. But it is not the boy's fault, my good baron," the man added, turning placatingly to Theo's father. It was Lord Oskar Hollis, a high-ranking bureaucrat sent directly from Odolia. He had a habit of cropping up whenever there was a certain sort of "trouble" in Gorand.

"He could have had better security there," the baron said sourly, taking his large cup of wine into his plump hand and bringing it to his lips.

"Not to be impertinent, good baron," Lord Hollis said, "But I am led to believe that the lord of a province is the master of the skydocks in its principal city, and therefore responsible for maintaining proper security."

The baron choked on his wine and red dribbled down his pale, round chin. "It was that woman captain's fault then!" he bellowed. "Why the emperor still allows her to work I have no idea. If it wasn't the damned rebels, then who was it?" It was more a demand than a question. Once Schulhard set his mind to something, that was that as far as he was concerned.

"I believe it to be agitators, lord baron," Hollis replied cooly.

"What kind of agitators?" Theodore's father grumbled, wiping the wine from his chin with a fine embroidered handkerchief.

"From Sial," Lord Hollis said, leaning forward on his thin elbows. "It is no secret that fine citizens of our nation are still held captive there even after Sial's foolish internal struggle ended. Though some of our nationals are trying to build a new colony in their lands, we are sure that King Holan is desperate to capture and enslave these as well and start a new war with our emperor."

A heavy silence followed Hollis's proclamation. Every one of the counselors and lords had their eyes fixed incredulously on him. Hollis looked to the baron and received a curt nod of approval to keep going.

"It is, my lord, expedient that war is declared swiftly. Since King Holan's betrayal, we are certain that he will not allow a peaceful resolution to the matter of our commercial needs in that region. Remember that their land holds resources which are invaluable to our emperor and our economy."

"That is well known," the baron said. "But why would this be their move? I can think of many things much more harmful to our city that they could have done."

"Those uniforms, or the lack thereof, could start a ripple effect of confusion in our great military," Hollis plied. "Of course, we will show them that we are made of sterner stuff. There is a delegation from King Holan, you say?"

The baron's round face broke into a smile that sent a shiver down Theo's spine. He knew exactly what sort of smile it was. His father was about to do something extraordinarily cruel. "My son," the baron announced, turning the full effect of the smile on the squirming Theo, "Go out and find your friend, Manik. I believe that is his name. Tell him that he is required in the council room. You, my son, are no longer required."

Theodore nodded and took the rest of his port in one quick swig. Once he left the chamber and closed the door behind him, he heard the beginnings of an uproarious argument. He could not stop himself from wondering what they could possibly be planning, and why his father saw fit to summon Manik and not him. Manik was only a friend—a Siali friend, yes, but nothing more.

Knocking, General Vasada cracked the door open and dipped his head respectfully. "Princess, we are close to the port guard," he said, straightening up and folding his hands behind his back. "I have the documents, but it would be best if they were given by you, I think."

Yvonnia made a sour face, but she knew he was right. She was the representative sent expressly by King Holan, and she must do her duty no matter how ill she felt. She stood and went to the door, stepping out onto the deck beside Vasada. Beyond the masts and the ropes and the sails and the scrambling men, she saw the city of Gorand for the first time, and she found herself open-mouthed in terrified awe.

20
COLD RECEPTION

A wide port, bristling with masts, filled the immediate horizon. Yvonnia had never in her life seen so many ships riding at anchor: brigs and schooners and cargo ships and huge warships with cannons gleaming in the weak sunlight. They crowded the ramshackle network of docks that crisscrossed the dark sea in every direction, thick with passengers, sailors, and soldiers in scarlet uniforms. The water itself was a brownish-green hue, smeared in some places with rainbow slicks of oil, and smelling sickly-sweet rather than bracingly salty.

Behind the maze of docks and forest of masts, the lower city was cloaked in a haze of smoke, though she could make out the shapes of warehouses and other buildings, built mostly of red-brown brick. Above it, the middle city was supported by columns and steel beams, rising above the thick smog of the lower city. Railroads pierced it like shining needles, many of them running out on trestle bridges to the immense skydocks that encircled the middle city in a great ring. Though they were still a significant distance from the wharf, Yvonnia saw that they had already passed beneath the point where the skydocks crossed over the bay, supported on towers of concrete and steel.

At the very top of the city, situated on fine, straight pillars, the palaces and manor houses of the wealthy glittered like crown jewels thrown on a heap of garbage. The whole structure, the three layers, formed a roughly conical shape, like a man-made mountain.

"How on earth is that even possible?" Enya asked breathlessly, startling Yvonnia with her sudden appearance. Yvonnia just shook her head. The mass of metal and brick boggled her mind. It was alien from anything she'd ever seen or dreamed of.

There was a shrill whistle from over the side of the ship, and Yvonnia heard the confused sounds of men speaking in Odolian. Vasada came up beside her and laid a hand on her shoulder. "Princess, I believe you are needed portside to give the papers to the guards," he said, handing her a crisp packet bearing the Odolian seal. Yvonnia nodded and took it in her trembling hands.

There were twelve uniformed Odolian marines in a rowboat, besides the port guard himself. He took the papers from her and explained tersely that because of some recent events in the city, the dock security had been heightened. The Siali ship was to receive an armed escort into the port. Yvonnia knew that although the city of Gorand had a foul reputation for crime and violence, at least the soldiers and leadership were considered respectable. She returned the port guard's salute as the rowboat pulled around in front of the ship.

When they finally arrived at the dock and disembarked, the dozen marines took up station on the boardwalk, muskets resting against their shoulders, facing outward in a protective circle. Enya was carrying four leather cases, one in each hand and two slung over her back. They contained all the possessions Yvonnia had brought with her to Odol.

Enya wasn't complaining about the arrangement and she was sure to mention it. The entire time she stood beside Yvonnia and

Jacik on the boardwalk, she made sure they knew that she was not complaining.

"Enya, just saying that you're not complaining doesn't make it true," Yvonnia said at last. "You have to actually *not complain*."

"But I'm not complaining, mistress," Enya protested, widening her big dark eyes in an attempt at innocence. "I'm merely pointing out that I am the only one of the entire entourage who is carrying possessions that are not their own."

"Yes, and you've been pointing that out for the last thirty minutes," Yvonnia said icily.

General Vasada was having a hard time keeping a straight face.

The sun was hiding behind orange-gray clouds, and though it was midday, the wind carried all the bite of winter as it knifed through their thin clothing. Yvonnia's own blue silk saree and blouse were nowhere near enough to keep out the chill and she could see Enya shivering as she shifted back and forth under the weight of the leather cases. General Vasada, Jacik, and the Siali soldiers bore the discomfort with an unblinking stoicism that Yvonnia did her best to emulate.

Enya, on the other hand, had some choice words about the situation. "Why in the name of...why do we need to stand here?" she demanded as another gust of wind tugged at her veil. "What are we waiting for? It's frigid! I've never felt cold this bad. When are we going to move?"

Yvonnia sighed. "We're waiting for authorization to move. Apparently Captain Haraz needed to move his ship to a different side of the docks."

"Cutting off our escape," Vasada growled under his breath. "We're caught like animals in a trap." He glanced darkly at the row of Odolian soldiers further down the boardwalk, blocking their way.

"As if having the ship here would do us any good," Yvonnia replied, struggling to keep her teeth from chattering. "We'd be dead before we reached the harbor mouth. But I think that we are just experiencing the warmth of Gorand's hospitality." She raised her eyes to the hulking city that loomed over them, gray and faceless behind its screen of smog.

There was some commotion at the other end of the boardwalk, and suddenly the soldiers parted and arrayed themselves in neat lines on either side of the dock, creating a passage. A man in a fine green suit, with a tweed waistcoat and maroon cravat, passed between the rows of soldiers. He was at the head of a column of three dozen more red-uniformed marines. These were decked in all their finery, with tall feather-plumed hats, shining brass buttons, and decorative swords at their waists. Three dozen muskets gleamed against three dozen epauletted shoulders. The uniformity was a contrast to the elite guard of Sial, each of whom wore a different crest on their hats and a different pattern woven into the sashes about their waists, representing their families and houses.

The man in green stopped in front of Yvonnia and turned to face her, hinging slightly at the waist in a controlled bow. Yvonnia hesitated only a moment before speaking. "I am Yvonnia, the Princess of Sial, daughter of King Holan VI. Greetings." They were the first words she had ever spoken to an Odolian in that tongue and she could tell she was not pronouncing all the words correctly. Still, she maintained a regal stance, shoulders back, head straight, chin slightly raised.

"Greetings," the man said, a smile stretching across his pale, thin lips. "Baron Schulhard apologizes for the wait, especially in this unfamiliar climate. Your guard must make its way through the city and up to the palace, accompanied by our soldiers. You, however, have been given special allowance to accompany me directly, along with your personal servant and your husband." His eyes flicked to Jacik, who stood immovably beside Yvonnia, hand resting on his sword.

"That is not my husband," Yvonnia said firmly, fixing the Odolian with an imperious stare.

"Apologies," the man said with another thin smile. "He is still welcome. There is a ferry we can take a few piers down that will convey you to the baron's palace. He will then greet you formally."

"A ferry to the palace? Do you mean an airship?" Yvonnia said, feeling her stomach tighten involuntarily.

"Yes. Apologies, I did not introduce myself." The man gave an elegant bow, rendering the balding spot on the back of his head temporarily visible. "I am Wilson Linworth, ferry captain. I convey personal guests of the baron from the lower city to the palace directly, so they don't have to bother with the street traffic."

"How can we trust you?" Vasada said impatiently in his thickly accented Odolian.

Linworth paused for a moment, then laughed. "You would not have made it to shore if we were here to kill you, good General," he said lightly, but Yvonnia heard the steel in every word. He was not jesting.

"General, please," she said gently, "I will meet you at the palace. Let us not be contentious guests."

Begrudgingly, Vasada nodded. "We agree to your terms."

"Very good. Two marines will come with me and the rest will accompany you to the palace on foot."

The landing party was split. General Vasada gave Yvonnia a parting glance before marching off with his men and the Odolians. Jacik, Enya, and two marines followed Yvonnia, who was escorted to the ferry by Linworth. The wooden piers creaked beneath their feet as they made their way through the maze of docks, passing sailors and workers who ambled here and there on their duties. Cranes and other large machines dotted the wharf, loading and unloading crates of goods from enormous cargo vessels. Yvonnia wondered why the Odolians had guided them to this area of the wharf. It seemed to her to be no place to receive a royal guest.

They reached the ferry at last, and just the sight of the small airship made Yvonnia queasy. It was no more than thirty feet long, suspended on chains above the water, two propellors bristling from the stern. The balloon, which was attached by thick hemp ropes to the four corners of the ship, was about twice its length and as big around as the ship itself. They were led aboard by the two marines, who climbed up after them and hauled in the gangplank.

The propellers whirred to life, and the little ferry shot skyward with a sickening lurch. Enya did not seem perturbed by their rapid ascent and, having set down her bags, ran to the thick wooden railing on the edge of the deck and stared out, gasping in awe and clapping her hands at the view. "Wow, princess, would you look at the city!" she cried. "Why don't we have ferries like these back in Aldia? I bet the palace would look amazing from the sky."

Yvonnia opened her mouth to answer but shut it again almost immediately and buried her face in Jacik's sleeve, unable to bear the sight of the earth scrolling beneath them as they flew. The wind whipped heavily at her hair and gossamer veil.

"Fear not, princess, Odolian airships are built to the highest standards of safety," Linworth shouted, as the ship turned towards the city, bucking in the turbulent wind. As their course evened out into a smooth upward spiral, Yvonnia finally raised her head and withdrew somewhat from Jacik, embarrassed by her lack of decorum.

She looked and saw people in miniature going about their business in the narrow streets, climbing rickety staircases on the sides of buildings, pulling carts or carrying parcels, going into and out of shops, playing out their lives as she watched from a birds' eye view.

At last, they drew level with the uppermost layer of the city, and the palace and manor houses spread out before them in a glittering array. A broad plaza lay before the palace, where several other small airships were docked. Linworth steered the ferry down in a smooth arc, descending gently until they came to a halt on the flagstones.

"We made it! Was that so bad?" Enya called teasingly, hefting up the burdensome bags.

Yvonnia finally withdrew her vice-like grip on Jacik's arm, feeling the support of solid ground beneath her feet once more. "It wasn't...*so* bad," she said stiffly as the drone of the engine finally sputtered out and became silent.

Linworth pulled a few final levers and gave Yvonnia a jovial smile. "It wasn't bad at all, I think. No one fell off, after all." He was joking, but the thought still made Yvonnia uncomfortable.

As soon as the propellers slowed to a stop and the balloon began to deflate slightly, two liveried servants stepped forward on the flagstones and set down the gangplank. With Jacik and Enya close on her heels, Yvonnia scrambled down the wobbly plank. The palace lay in front of them, glittering in white and gold, with an expansive lawn that was still green and well-trimmed, even in the depths of autumn. Yvonnia caught sight of a small entourage approaching them across the grass.

Baron Schulhard led the way. He was clearly a man who enjoyed his meals. He had a round face, with red cheeks drawn into a smile, though something about his cheer seemed wooden. His small eyes darted about incessantly and he wore a curly white wig that added a few inches to his diminutive height. His dark blue dress uniform was covered in medals and honors. He was accompanied by four guards, each outfitted in a white uniform with a blood-red sash and ceremonial sword. Their faces were as stern and grim as Jacik's, and their movements as mechanical as a wind-up toy.

Behind the five uniformed men, however, three more elegantly dressed figures approached. One was a tall young woman trying desperately to look older, her sour face caked with too much makeup. Her slender frame was engulfed by an elaborate lace-covered dress and her diamond and peridot jewelry sparkled ostentatiously at her ears, throat, and wrists. Her striking blonde hair gave her away as a relative of her two companions. One was a slight girl, no more than ten years old, dressed in a simple but pretty frock that fell to just below her knees. The other was a tall young man, smartly dressed in a black suit and gray waistcoat. His face, clean shaven like the other Odolians, was dusted with a smattering of freckles, and he wore his blond hair pulled back into a long ponytail. Yvonnia thought he was close to her own age.

"Well met," Yvonnia greeted them cautiously, drawing a grin from the baron and a giggle from the young girl as the party halted a short distance away.

"Welcome to Odol," Baron Schulhard said with a nod in her general direction. "It is a pleasure to entertain such distinguished guests as yourself. Please, make yourself at home. I am Baron Brandomir Schulhard. This is my eldest daughter Elaine..." The tall young woman curtseyed. "My youngest daughter Nan..." The little girl curtsied also. "And my son Theodore."

The young man gave a deep, sincere bow, and looked up with a genuine smile. "It is a great pleasure to meet you, Your Royal Highness," Theodore said in a clear, pleasant voice.

"It is a pleasure to meet you and your family," Yvonnia said courteously.

"It would be *our* pleasure, madame, if you would come inside," the baron said stiffly. "I am sure that it would be far more comfortable for you indoors; our state-of-the-art gas heating keeps the palace pleasant during the winter. Coming from the eastern jungles to our northern clime must be quite a shock for you."

Yvonnia smiled patiently, but a quick glance at Enya told the princess that the maidservant was not quite so tolerant. Enya was shaking, betraying Yvonnia's attempt at etiquette. Whether she shook with cold or anger at the slights the baron made toward Sial, Yvonnia could not tell.

Yvonnia, however, shook her head. "I am afraid that your wonderful palace must wait. My father, the great King Holan, sent General Vasada and twenty Ajaras, our elite guard, to accompany me wherever I go." With each word she spoke, she grew more and more aware of her strong accent. "I do not fear that any danger awaits me, but I should not like to disrespect my father's wishes. I am sure you understand." She thought she heard a faint squeak of rage from Enya's direction. *It's the cold after all.*

Baron Schulhard's wooden smile relaxed ever so slightly. "Of course," he said. "If you must stay here, we may sit and chat for a while. A while it will be too, since I am given to understand that it is a long walk from the docks to my palace. Why don't you send your servants ahead to ready your room? You will be well protected..."

"We stay with the princess," Jacik said sharply and tightened his grip on the hilt of his falchion. This time, Enya's groan of protest was audible.

The baron nodded stiffly and no further words were exchanged. They stood in the courtyard for a long while. Even Jacik's teeth began to quietly chatter. The young girl, Nan, yawned and kicked her feet as the minutes stretched on. Yvonnia kept her eyes on Baron Schulhard the entire time, not looking at his children nor his solemn guards. She resisted the urge to study the ornate architecture around her. It was so different from the other glimpses she'd caught of Gorand and a world apart from the smooth, clean lines of Aldia's palace. But she did not drop her gaze.

Finally, when she was beginning to think that they would be stuck standing there forever, she heard the sound of marching feet begin to rise over the ambient wind and city noises below. It quickly became a confused clatter; the Ajaras and the Odolians were marching in different rhythms, their steps only occasionally matching. The movements of the baron's men were uniform and precisely timed, whereas the pace of General Vasada's men was looser and more comfortable. But at last, all twenty of the Ajaras, Vasada, and the Odolian soldiers reached the palace courtyard and filed neatly to a halt.

Baron Schulhard's thin lips twisted in a smile of victory as he met Yvonnia's eyes. She shuddered involuntarily and looked away.

"Now that all are present and accounted for," the baron drawled, "Perhaps we can make our way into the palace? We are holding a feast for one of our national heroes tonight and of course you all shall be honored guests. I am sure you could use some time to rest and freshen up before the festivities."

❦❧

Yvonnia, Jacik, and Enya, separated once again from Vasada and his men, were led through the elaborate hallways of Gorand's grand palace by the butler. He was a distinguished looking man, clean shaven save for neatly trimmed sideburns, dressed in a fine black coat and stark white shirt that was so starched it might have stood up on its own.

The Odolian palace was strange to Yvonnia in its architecture, but perhaps most of all in its pragmatic design. The grand entry hall, though constructed of the finest materials and gorgeously formed with sweeping arcs and buttresses, was totally colorless save for the stained glass window and a few banners and tapestries that hung upon the white walls. This was true for the hallways as well; they were decorated with all kinds of armaments, tapestries, hunting trophies, banners, and insignia, but each item of decoration was something that could easily be replaced with any other item. Coming from a castle where every inch of the walls was decorated with rich colors and paints, Yvonnia found it striking that here every image was removable. Even the door to the guest chamber was plain. It was of fine wood, delicately stained and reinforced with polished metal, but it was no different than any of the other hundred doors they had passed along the way.

"Your room, Highness," the butler said in his deep drawl, giving a respectful bow. "If you ever need anything, you need only ask."

"Thank you," Yvonnia replied, and gave the man a small smile as she stepped through the door.

The room appeared comfortable enough, lushly carpeted and filled with beautiful, heavy oaken furniture that was elaborately carved. The bed was a massive four-poster, with heavy blue curtains draped over it for warmth and privacy. There were large cabinets for clothes, a mirrored vanity, and a small writing desk. A large, covered radiator pumped warmth into the room.

"Finally," Enya huffed, barely waiting for the butler to close the door before she tossed the luggage bags on the floor. "I never want to stand out in that miserable cold carrying stupid clothes again! I don't care if this *is* a death trap, I'm just glad to be inside."

"Enya, watch the way you speak," Yvonnia chided. "I can tolerate your outbursts when we are safe in Aldia, but here we must be on the alert for trouble from any quarter. I do not like the way that Baron Schulhard addressed me, or the tone he chose, nor how forced this all feels. I cannot have your complaints undermining my authority!"

"Yes, princess, I'm sorry," Enya said, though Yvonnia thought she caught a surreptitious eye roll from the maid. "At least its warm and comfortable in here. And they're far more hospitable than the nasty Ryokans! Tell her, Jacik. Tell her we have nothing to fear."

Jacik just shrugged as he fetched the chair from the writing desk and set it beside the door. He drew his sword and sat, resting the blade across his legs, his eyes fixed on the door, unmoving. He said nothing.

"I think he means, Enya, that we must still be on guard against our hosts," Yvonnia said slowly. "They have not yet given us much reason to trust them. I only hope that my message will be received by the emperor himself and not just the baron."

"Yes, I noticed that," Enya said, scrambling up onto the wooden radiator cover where she perched, basking in the warmth. "I thought the plan was to immediately deliver the message to the baron so that he could take you to the emperor. But you didn't mention it the entire time we were just standing there, staring at each other like idiots."

"That *was* the plan, yes," Yvonnia said, rubbing a hand across her forehead. She felt tired and travel weary, but she knew that there was not much time before the baron planned to give his banquet. *Another slight. The banquet ought to be in our honor, as a royal entourage from a friendly nation, but instead we are merely shoehorned in at the last moment to a banquet in honor of someone else!* She remembered the defiant look in his small, dark eyes, the slightly mocking smile that said *I have won this skirmish, no?*

She would not let him win the battle.

"Milord!"

Theo jolted as the guard scrambled through the double doors into the banquet hall. He and his father were overseeing preparations for the evening's celebration. Next to his father was the esteemed Ulysses Cadbury, a man now renowned for his elimination of Greyer's rebellion. The baron took only minor interest in the guard as he directed the servants who were moving tables about.

"What could be so important as to interrupt the preparations for tonight?" The baron's question left no room for argument: whatever it was could wait for later.

The guard persisted, bowing first to Theo's father, then to Theo himself. "Apologies milord, but you asked for any information about the stolen ship."

"Stolen shi-" Cadbury was about to comment, but Baron Schulhard waved him away nonchalantly.

"Nothing to worry about. Siali insurgents. The worst of it was the cargo. Uniforms," he said and glared at Theo. Theodore grimaced, remembering the firm tongue lashing he received at the meeting a few nights before.

"Sir, we have the descriptions of the thieves."

"Oh?" the baron said.

"Yes," the guard paused. "I have a man who talked with them. He was shot by them but took the long walk up here to tell you personally."

A wiry old man hobbled in, using a cane for support. His mustaches bristled as he began to speak. "My lord...s," he began and bowed clumsily. "My name is-"

"Unimportant. Just tell us what you saw," the baron said firmly.

"Well," the man flushed and cleared his throat, rising, yet still appearing small and crouched. "I work one of the lifts. Dawn shift. It was real early when this man, real tall like and broad. Red hair.

Looked too good for a dock worker. He came up to me, had the worst fake pass I've ever seen. Saw right through it when his friend, a lady who looked like she's from Karlsban, pointed a gun at my head! I didn't know what to say, and…and then they threatened my life! Said they'd kill me if I didn't-"

Ulysses Cadbury gave a slight grin, one which Theo wished he could understand.

"Dear baron," Lord Cadbury began smoothly, "I do think I recognize the man. I could give a name if-"

"So you know some Siali savages, eh?" Theo's father jeered. "Their descriptions-"

"Baron, not to be impertinent," Cadbury said, "but I don't recall ever seeing a red-haired Siali before. But I did once know a man like the one this fellow has described."

Theodore saw his father flash the soon-to-be guest of honor a hawkish stare before turning it into an ingratiating smile. Theo was always reminded by his father that it was better to act the fool and reveal your wisdom, than to act the wise man and be proven a fool. "Lord Cadbury," the baron said in polite but venomous tones. "These are Siali insurgents and nothing more."

"They spoke civilized to me m'lords," the man from the lift said in a meek tone. "No savage tongue on 'em. The man had a Bolden accent though. Real proper too, though he tried hiding it."

Cadbury laughed heartily. "So it is Pendington! That man never ceases to amaze me. I haven't seen him since our academy days."

Theo noticed a lack of amusement in his father's face. "He died three years ago. The last I saw him, I was giving him a medal for killing his own people."

"Who's to say he died?" Cadbury insisted, his face melting back into a pensive frown.

"There were no survivors of the crash of the *Formidable*," the baron said grimly. "And even if he did survive, the airship thieves all perished in the wreck. My scouts confirmed the crash site's location."

Cadbury nodded. "No man is that lucky twice, I suppose. It would have been interesting, though, to have found out *why* he did it."

"If you're after something interesting," the baron said as the wiry tollbooth man was escorted away, "then tonight's festivities will more than live up to your expectation."

"HOSPITALITY"

In an hour, Yvonnia managed to clean herself up almost as well as she would have in three hours back home. The gas heating extended to the plumbing; hot water came straight out of a tap and that cut the time down significantly. She wore her best green saree and adorned herself with every piece of gold jewelry Enya had managed to stuff into the packing case. Gold was preferred on occasions such as this, when she wished to appear in a position of authority. She had another set of silver reserved for when she would meet with the emperor and place herself in a position of humility, begging for his assistance in the coming civil war.

Still, she hoped that she could avert conflict altogether. If the threat of Odolian airpower were brought to bear upon the Ryokans quickly enough, it could mean that they would surrender before the war truly began. Then, not a single life would be lost.

Yvonnia made her way to the grand dining hall with Jacik at her side, dressed in a clean white uniform and green sash that matched her gown. As they passed one of the broad glass windows, she caught sight of the rolling desolation that stretched endlessly beyond the city walls below. Even from the palace it could not be hidden. *No, no lives would be lost. My people would not die. They would simply become slaves to Odolia masters across the sea. Gorand has laid waste to its own land... Will they not do the same to Sial? Flatten the mountains, raze the forests, level the hills, divert the rivers, and for what? To build this... enormity of a city once more?*

She began to catch unfamiliar smells of food on the air as they approached the great hall. The scents were savory, not the sweet and spicy smells she was used to at feasts in Aldia. As they entered, she saw that most of the guests were already seated, eating strange dishes that she did not recognize. When the baron saw her standing in the side entrance to the hall, he stood abruptly and raised his glass, which held a curious pale liquor.

"To that mystical land, Sial!" he shouted. The guests looked around for a moment in confusion, and then as one they rose from around the two long tables and repeated the baron's words, each raising their own glass to mimic him.

When the commotion had died down, the baron motioned for Yvonnia to come over and sit at the empty place beside him. His table was apart from the other two, with two seats of honor on either side of his own. The chair beside Yvonnia's was already occupied by General Vasada, who nodded his head to her respectfully as she took her seat. Jacik took up his accustomed position behind her, his hand resting on the hilt of his sword even though it was held in the scabbard by a ceremonial peace-string.

On the other side of the baron sat a man and a woman Yvonnia had not seen before. The man had an angular face, with dark hair and a pencil-thin mustache. The woman was slender and young, provocatively dressed in a black sleeveless gown. Baron Schulhard introduced them as Ulysses Cadbury and Lady Genevieve, though the names meant as little to her as their appearance. Apparently, this Cadbury was the original guest of honor.

Once the brief introductions were over, the baron rang his spoon against his glass for silence. Ulysses Cadbury stood up and treated the guests to a dull speech about his great cleverness in rooting out the last of the rebellion in the city of Veturi. He was the chief of security in the city, and when the last of Greyer's rebellion fled there, Cadbury had succeeded in finding and destroying them with help from Lady Genevieve. The words, spoken quickly in an unfamiliar accent and with many flowery turns of phrase, were sometimes difficult for Yvonnia to understand. When they talked about Veturi, it seemed to her as though the city itself was moving, sometimes being near to Bolden, other times near the capital Odolia, and at still other times right outside of Gorand itself. Yvonnia gave herself to pondering the mystery of this traveling city so much that she missed the latter half of the speech, though perhaps that was no great loss.

Once Cadbury had finished pontificating, Baron Schulhard rang his spoon against his glass once more. "Ladies and gentlemen! I would like to announce, for those who are unaware, that tonight we are going to have a grand ball in honor of our most impressive guests. One is a hero of Odol, whose brave exploits you have just heard. And the other is a princess from a great and exotic land!" He put his hand on Yvonnia's back and pressed her forwards. Reluctantly, she stood and smiled out at the cheering crowd of nobles, raising her ring-covered hand to wave in the Odolian fashion.

"Baron," she began as she sat back down, but startled as his attention snapped to her with hawklike intensity. "Apologies, but might I request that my Ajaras, my soldiers, be permitted to attend this ball, along with the general and myself? They are all younger sons of noble families in Sial and will not be out of place among your distinguished guests."

The baron stared at her for a moment, seemingly taken aback by her request. It was true enough that in Sial the Ajaras were often invited to grand events and celebrations out of courtesy. But she wanted them there for protection, her own and theirs also. She did not like them being quartered somewhere in the palace alone, unseen and unheard.

The baron leaned over and whispered something to Cadbury. Cadbury murmured a reply, and the baron nodded, leaning back in to speak to Yvonnia, a concerned look on his face. "Apologies for my ignorance, princess, but I remember hearing that your soldiers may not be the most...courtable men. The balls that we hold here are intended for socializing, above all else." He gave her an apologetic smile. Yvonnia returned it with an innocent look.

"I assure you, Baron, that your ladies will be more than satisfied with the dancing and socializing that my Ajaras are capable of. And better yet, I can assure you that your gentlemen need have no fear of their ladies being stolen away, save for a brief dance."

The baron's smile remained, but now it was the smile of a merchant caught making a bad deal. "Of course. The ball will be held two hours from..." He took a round golden watch from the pocket of his uniform and nodded. "Yes, two hours from this very moment. The...Ajaras are invited to the ball, but any who are not in clean uniforms will be turned away."

Yvonnia thanked him and turned at last to her food. There was no sauce to coat the savory chicken and the steamed green vegetables were soft and watery, in desperate need of salt. There was a roll of bread also, but it was dense and dry, with nothing to dip it in. Halfway through the tasteless meal, she looked back at Jacik. His usually stoic face had a look of concern so uncharacteristic that it felt like an avalanche of accusations. Yvonnia's heart sank into her stomach.

She leaned over to speak to General Vasada, who was eating more than was polite and, which was more concerning, drinking more wine than he ought. It was sweeter than the vintage in Sial and no doubt to Vasada's taste, given his affinity for fruits and dainties.

"General," Yvonnia whispered.

"Yes?" The general started as though he had been awoken from a daze.

"Make sure your men are ready for the ball. I shouldn't like to be without them. Though I don't think it would be polite to be

fully armed, I also wouldn't like to be without some protection."
She thought of Jacik, hand resting on his sword hilt.

Vasada nodded amicably. "It's not so bad as we always say in
Sial, you know. Gorand, I mean. Their city is not the loveliest, and
I would not like to be one of the poor inside its walls, but it is not
so bad, I think. And the food is wonderful." He grinned in appre-
ciation, reaching fumblingly for his glass. "Someday I shall have to
bring my wife back here. I'm sure that she would get along very well
with some of the ladies."

Yvonnia nodded silently, a sad smile creeping onto her face. *If
only you'd been this amiable at the council, we might not have had to
come here at all,* she thought.

The banquet seemed to drag on and Yvonnia was beginning
to worry that General Vasada would never stop his drinking to go
and prepare the Ajaras. However, as soon as the baron adjourned
the feast with half an hour until the ball, Vasada snapped to
attention, gave a gracious bow, and in his broken Odolian thanked
the baron and Ulysses Cadbury for their hospitality before heading
on his way.

Yvonnia got to her feet and stood beside Jacik, finding comfort in the shadow of the big man. "Jacik, would you be my escort
this evening?" she asked formally, keeping her eyes lowered. She
knew that he would prefer not to dance, and that it would not be
particularly proper, but she didn't necessarily trust any of the
suited Odolians in their cravats and tailcoats, nor the men in
Odolian dress uniforms, their chests blazoned with medals.

"If you wish, my lady," Jacik said stiffly, his face unchanging,
though she felt a hint of awkwardness in his voice. She smiled
apologetically and took his hand. Her tiny fingers were swallowed
up by his massive grip as they followed the lords and ladies into the
grand ballroom, which adjoined the banquet hall via a short

corridor. Holding Jacik's hand, as though he were a nobleman or even a suitor, felt foreign, but she knew she was much safer with him by her side.

When they entered the ballroom at last, filing in near the end of a long column of guests, Yvonnia found herself stunned. It was as though all the art in the palace in Aldia had been taken and crammed onto the walls of a single room. It made up for the starkness of the rest of the palace. Huge columns, decorated with gilt and intricately carved designs both geometric and floral, rose up to meet a great vaulted ceiling, where frescoes of beautiful figures dancing out scenes from a mythic past were painted in vivid color and, to Yvonnia's embarrassment, often in the nude.

When her eyes finally returned to ground level, she was at last able to take in the crowd of nobles in their strange fashions, spread out in the glimmering gaslight across the ballroom floor. The women had great skirts which hung from impossibly narrow waists and swayed with even the tiniest movement. The colors worn were varied and bright like jewels: greens, blues, reds, purples, and even a few multicolored. The gowns were finely embroidered and all made of rich, heavy materials, with lace decorating the collars and cuffs. None of the other women wore jewelry that was as heavy or conspicuous as hers. They all seemed to prefer either pearls or delicate chains with single stones at the throat, and stud earrings that hardly stood out in their ears. She saw no rings either, for every hand was gloved with satin or silk or lace. Even the men wore white gloves.

At the back of the room, a quartet of finely suited men were tuning stringed instruments of varying sizes in a pleasant cacophony of musical sounds. An austere man with a white beard sat at a grand wooden instrument the likes of which Yvonnia had never seen before. When the others had finished tuning, he put his hands to the keys of the instrument and began playing a slow tune. It was far tamer than typical Siali dance music, though it seemed to Yvonnia that the dancing here was much more recreational than ceremonial. Many of the nobles flocked to the edges of the room to chatter and laugh, rather than taking part in the first dance.

As Yvonnia stepped further in, a short man with a weasley face turned to the ballroom. "Princess Yvonnia of Sial!" he announced loudly, not giving Jacik the same courtesy even though she was on his arm. Jacik towered above most of the other guests and stood out in his stark white uniform. White did not seem to be a color worn by the Odolians, at least not in this formal setting.

Few people appeared to take notice of her entrance at first, but then Yvonnia saw three men approaching. She stiffened and gripped Jacik's arm urgently, but then she recognized one of them as Theodore Schulhard, and another as...

"Princess, it's such a pleasure to see you," Theodore said with a grin. "You put the best of our ladies to shame. I'm gratified you turned out for the ball."

"Thank you," Yvonnia said hesitantly and with only the slightest curtsy. "You have not introduced me to your friends, my lord."

"Oh of course, how dashed impolite of me," Theodore said, the same smile still on his face. Turning to his right, he introduced the man Yvonnia didn't recognize. "This is my best friend, Eugene." Eugene bowed politely and kissed Yvonnia's hand, a gesture which both surprised and displeased her. "And this is another good friend of mine," Theodore said, turning to the familiar man, "Manik..."

"We know one another," Yvonnia said sharply, and gave an even briefer curtsy to the cousin of Resna Kaliman. "Your cousin is doing well, Manik Kaliman. I can see where he gets his fashions. Is it hard to practice the tenants of Thun here?" She could barely keep the venom out of her voice.

"Well, I say," Theo said, his exuberance not dimming in the slightest. "This is a wonderful occasion. Nik, you never told me that the princess was this beautiful!"

Manik had not taken his eyes off Yvonnia, but his attention was not flattering. "My lord, it never came up," he said evenly, his expression as unreadable as Jacik's.

"Well see that something this obvious does come up in future!" Theodore exclaimed. "Your most Royal Highness, how has father treated you? Well I hope?"

Theodore's polite chatter was beginning to grate on Yvonnia's nerves and even Jacik wore a disapproving frown, which was equivalent to a raging rebuke under the circumstances. "Lord Schulhard," Yvonnia said, "Your father has treated me with respect and kindness thus far. I must apologize for my attitude on the lawn." It came out more bluntly than she intended, with her accent burying her attempt at niceties.

"Well I say, that's good to hear. I told you there was nothing to worry about, Eugene..."

Before Theodore's friend could respond, the band finished their song with a flourish and the dancing couples gave one another a final bow. Everyone clapped, including Theodore. Yvonnia gave only the slightest hint of polite applause before Theodore turned back to her.

"I say, princess, would you like to share the next dance with me?" he asked, taking her hand before Yvonnia could object.

"Theo, what will Cassandra think? Remember what your father said," Eugene warned.

"Dash it all, Gene, I think I must insist on this," Theodore retorted before looking Yvonnia right in the eyes with a boldness that shocked her. "Your Highness, would you please share the next dance?"

Yvonnia dropped her gaze, embarrassed and slightly bewildered. "I'm afraid not...I am unsure of how to dance here. I am considered somewhat good in my own country, but here your steps are far more deliberate and much less fluid than what I am used to. Thank you for the offer, but I must decline, to save us both the embarrassment."

Theodore was gracious in defeat. "Well, it was a noble try I think," he said, giving her a subdued smile. "Enjoy the music then. Would you like a drink?"

At that, Jacik finally spoke. "No, the princess will not have a drink."

His deep, powerful voice gave the two Odolian nobles a jolt, and they excused themselves politely but hastily before taking their leave to another part of the ballroom. Yvonnia huffed. "Jacik, there is no need to be rude. I am perfectly capable of turning down the young Lord Schulhard."

"You did not seem to appreciate his attentions," Jacik said defensively.

"I did not. But he was kind at least, and genuine, if rather forward. I wonder if all Odolian men are so forward as that."

"I'm afraid they are," said the silky voice of Manik in the Siali tongue. "Brutes, all of them." For all his talk, Manik had certainly adopted the fashions of the Odolians. His hair was slicked back, rather than left to curl out naturally. His facial hair too was groomed in an Odolian manner, with a thin mustache trimmed to perfection lining his upper lip, and his dark beard shaved entirely save for a thin patch on his chin. Overall, he looked rather comical and ever so slightly devious.

"Manik," Yvonnia began.

"Lord Kaliman, if you please," Manik corrected.

"Your cousin is Lord Kaliman, unless he has passed and you have inherited his title and his lands."

"We are both lords: he of the lands around Dusain, and I of a small mining town nearby called Ferram," Manik imparted with a proud, slimy smile.

Yvonnia's face twisted in disgust. "How on earth did you get a lordship here?"

"Oh, anyone can get a lordship if they have the right friends," Manik said, glancing languidly in Theodore's direction. "And if they offer an agreeable payment."

"I doubt that even your brother would empty his pockets to pay for a useless lordship in a foreign country," Yvonnia snapped, "Even if he is trying to curry favor with those he thinks will come out on top in the end."

"Sometimes the price is in deed, not in capital, princess," Manik said with a grin.

Yvonnia felt the blood drain from her face, but before she could open her mouth to question further, the short man at the door made another announcement.

"General Kachik Vasada and the Ajaras of Sial!"

Vasada marched in at the head of a column of Ajaras. From what Yvonnia could tell, all twenty of the men were present and accounted for, which brought her some comfort. There was polite applause at their entry, led by the baron himself, who walked briskly to the front of the room, apparently preparing to give yet another speech. Manik gave Yvonnia a polite nod and went to stand with Theo and his friends, rather than with his own princess.

"Good people of Gorand, good citizens of Odol, and all of our many esteemed friends," the baron began with a flourish, his voice carrying surprisingly well in the huge, vaulted room. "We are beyond honored to have such distinguished guests tonight for our ball. I hope you are treating them with the courtesy and respect that we give all our guests."

The baron first introduced Yvonnia, with a string of flowery Odolian adjectives describing her beauty that she only partially understood. All of the guests turned toward her and clapped loudly. She gave a polite curtsey, but as she rose, movement around the edges of the room caught her eye. Several dozen Odolian men in scarlet uniforms had begun to filter in through the side entrances unannounced, spreading out around the perimeter of the room.

As the baron then introduced the Ajaras, skipping over Jacik entirely, Yvonnia felt her stomach clench. She looked anxiously to Jacik, but his eyes were fixed straight ahead. She saw with great consternation that he had reached across and deftly undone the peace string that was meant to keep his falchion from being drawn.

"Finally, we have General Vasada," the baron said, continuing on smoothly even as Vasada took a bow, "The lackey of the dangerous and treacherous King Holan, who called off our most generous intervention, tying our military up for months! Now they have come here to beg. To beg, they say, for our assistance again in their petty internal struggles!" The baron's voice rose both in volume and in pitch, grating on Yvonnia's ears as she looked around desperately for some way of escape. "However, the astute observation of our good and honored friend, Ulysses Cadbury, has informed us that this is no olive branch they extend to us. It is a plot to disrupt our military and assassinate our glorious emperor! Men!"

The Odolian guests fled with shrieks and cries of fear to the perimeters of the room as through their ranks marched a line of Odolian soldiers, bayonets held ready in their white-gloved hands.

Yvonnia barely had time to react as Jacik shoved her to the floor and drew his sword in a singing arc, the silver blade flashing golden in the gaslight. He lunged in front of her, shielding her body with his own, the falchion's blade an extension of his arm as he disarmed and dispatched several Odolian soldiers with fluid, calculated movements. Having trained his entire life for conflict even before he had come into the princess's service, he was himself a weapon. The sword was a useful addition to his fighting capabilities, but Yvonnia was sure that he would have been just as deadly without it.

The Ajaras were not faring as well. As Yvonnia rose onto her hands and knees, and then into a crouch, legs coiled be-neath her like compressed springs, she found herself unable to tear her eyes away from the awful scene. Her father's elite unit had found themselves completely surrounded by Odolian musket men, and just as the Ajaras were drawing their curved knives, the Odolians fired upon them as one, filling the room with a deafening roar. About a dozen of the Ajaras dropped at once, but those who were left standing found themselves in the center of a rapidly tightening circle of sharp bayonets. Cries of pain filled the air as the men were mercilessly run through, and blood pooled on the hardwood where only a moment before the finest company of Yvonnia's countrymen had stood proud and ready to fight. To the horror of even the Baron's guests, the Odolian soldiers waded into the pile of bodies and stabbed each one in turn with another bayonet thrust, making sure they had indeed finished the job.

It was almost over, though Yvonnia saw that Jacik was still holding his own, his dance with the sword and the enemy as graceful as any the Odolian couples had cut upon the ballroom floor.

Suddenly, a form shot up from beneath the heap of slain Ajaras. It was General Vasada himself, gripping one of the curved blades of his fallen men.

"Princess! Run!" he shouted, and with a fluid motion surprising for one of his bulk, he sliced the throat of one of the Odolian soldiers and knocked the bayonet from the hands of another. In only a few seconds however, he had a perfect ring of soldiers surrounding him. None of them had had time to reload, and all they could do was to threaten with their bayonets, each seemingly unwilling to press forward and get within range of the wickedly sharp knife. Yvonnia staggered to her feet, and looked behind to see that Jacik was in a similar situation, surrounded by a ring of slightly fewer soldiers. Of the several dozen Odolian soldiers who had flooded the ballroom, only about half remained standing, but Yvonnia knew there would be more on their way.

Looking again at Vasada, she let out a scream of anguish. Baron Schulhard was approaching Vasada from behind, a golden pistol gripped in his hand. Vasada, who had been her father's right hand since the civil war began, who had been like an uncle to her, locked eyes with her. He understood that he was going to die. He had never known exactly how or when, but he knew that someday he would die fighting, die defending her and her father. That was Yvonnia's consolation. He knew. That was what kept her from screaming again when the baron pulled the trigger of his flintlock and a single puff of smoke signaled the death of Kachick Vasada. She did not even hear the blast.

By now, the guests were evacuating the room. Theodore was last to go, meeting her vacant gaze with a horrified expression as he surveyed the carnage. Then, he was gone. When all the doors had been shut, the baron stepped forward and kicked the general's body.

"Good work men," he said, and raised his eyes languidly to Yvonnia. "Oh, please, kill her guard too. I nearly forgot about him."

"No!" Yvonnia protested. She turned to grab one of the rifles littering the ground but recoiled when she saw that it was clutched by an arm which was not attached to a person. "No!" She took a moment to contain her stomach. "He is too...important to kill here."

"Who's to say I won't have you gunned down next, plotter?" the baron drawled, stepping over Vasada's body and approaching her with a broad grin. "I am sure that he was the weapon you were going to use to kill our most esteemed emperor." He jabbed the smoking pistol at Jacik, who was still locked in a fighting stance in the center of the soldiers.

"Don't you want the execution to be public?" Yvonnia said desperately. "The plotter and the tool she was using?"

"Princess, I would that I die here," Jacik said in broken Odolian, a despair she had never before heard lacing his voice. He would not take the humiliation of public execution well, Yvonnia knew. Like most soldiers, he likely imagined himself dying in battle with his comrades. But she needed him. She could not imagine living on without him to lean on, whether it were for a few months, days, or mere minutes.

The baron smiled at Jacik's words, seeming to relish the last desperate plea for an honorable death. "That settles it then. Bring them both. And have her servant put away. I have uses for her in my house." A soldier stepped up behind Jacik and cracked the butt of his weapon across the back of the big man's head. He dropped to the ground like a bag of rocks.

"She was part of the plot too," Yvonnia lied quickly. "Integral, in fact."

Baron Schulhard snorted. "As you wish. Guards, seize them. I must ready the *Redoubtable*."

22
REDOUBTABLE

Theodore knocked at the door to the council room. It took a moment for Lord Hollis to open it, and the spindly man looked annoyed at Theo's presence. After a moment, he bowed respectfully and opened the door the rest of the way. It was dark, with only a single gas lamp coloring the stark room a dim orange. Other than Hollis, the only person in the room was Theodore's father.

"Ah, son, come in. Come! We have much to discuss!"

To say that Theo was nervous was quite the understatement. It had only been three, maybe four sleepless hours since the festivities had ended so badly. To think that the princess had been plotting an assassination was, to say the least, unbelievable. And he hadn't been told a bit of it!

"What is it that you wanted to talk to me about?" Theo asked, rubbing his eyes.

"About your reign. I am taking the assassins to Odolia myself, where the emperor can award me..." A polite cough from Hollis momentarily interrupted the baron before he continued. "Where the emperor can award *us* as the execution takes place."

"Really, Schulhard," Hollis said disapprovingly, "this could be accomplished here, in your own city. It could be dangerous. At least kill the man first. I don't like his looks."

"You think they have a chance of escape? You think that the dreadnought, our might and strength, can be escaped like a simple prison cell? Even if they formed a plan, they'll be airborne until they reach the gallows. If they have hope, all the more satisfying to crush." The baron clenched his fist and slammed it on the table to illustrate.

Theo flinched, mustering the courage to ask the one question that had been bothering him. "Father," he began.

"Yes? What is it?" Schulhard's cheeks regained their normal pale complexion as he looked at his son.

"Why are we doing this? Is the princess really an assassin?"

"Of course n-", the baron began but was interrupted by Hollis again.

"Of course she is," Hollis said smoothly. "But we must handle her in a certain way to provoke the Sialis to a timely war with Odol."

"War? Why would we want that?"

"Theodore, my flesh and blood, there are hard realities I've sheltered you from," the baron said expansively. "The truth is that we simply require more resources to keep our civilized way of life running, and the Sialis refuse to do fair business with us, which jeopardizes the wellbeing of our race."

Hollis looked askance at the baron and turned quickly to Theo. "Just don't worry about it. You only need to manage the city for a few months."

Theodore sighed and nodded, feeling the weight of responsibility settle heavily on his shoulders.

Yvonnia woke in a dark, dank cell, illuminated only by a single guttering gas lamp high on the stone wall. She stared around, eyes straining in the dimness. Enya was beside her on the small, hard cot, her wrists shackled over her head and chained to the wall behind. Yvonnia had been bound in much the same way. Her shoulders and back ached as she shifted, trying to find a position of relative comfort. Besides the cot, the room was bare. A single metal door stood in the wall opposite, a tiny crack of light seeping through a viewing plate set at eye-level. Jacik was nowhere to be seen.

Holding her breath, Yvonnia listened for any sound of movement or life outside, but all she heard was Enya's even breathing beside her, and the faint clattering of the chains as they knocked together with every subtle movement. She did not remember falling asleep, nor being drugged or knocked out, but she had no idea how long it had been since the betrayal at the ball. Everything following Vasada's death was a formless smear in her mind. They must be in the depths of the palace now, imprisoned by the baron as he prepared to transport them to the emperor.

Beside her, Enya stirred, murmuring wordlessly in her sleep. Yvonnia thought about trying to jostle her awake, but then thought better of it. The last thing she needed was the servant's inane chatter wearing on her already fraught mind. She repented of the insult almost immediately and looked over at the girl. A few strands of black hair had crept from beneath her veil, but other than that it was still wrapped firmly about her head. Yvonnia's own veil was missing entirely, perhaps lost in whatever rough handling she'd received from the Odolian soldiers. Enya's face was peaceful in sleep, unaware as she was of their dire situation. Yvonnia decided, more lovingly this time, not to wake her.

Suddenly she heard the muffled clomping of boots through the heavy door. She turned, struggling to sit up straighter, squinting to see if she could catch sight of anything through the narrow slit. The noise grew louder until it came to a stop in front of the door, blocking the light. There was the sound of keys jingling, then a bolt shot back. An Odolian soldier shoved the door open and, with the help of a companion, tossed the limp and bloodied form of Jacik unceremoniously to the floor. The two stepped back, and the figure of another man replaced them in the doorway, casting a broad shadow over Jacik's prone body. Enya stirred and finally awoke, looking blearily up at the silhouetted officer.

"Here's your dog, *princess*," the Odolian said, spitting her title like an insult. "You should be proud. He didn't talk. If it weren't for Baron Schulhard's orders, I'd take your pretty servant next. But I'm sure you would talk before we had much fun with her. You're that kind."

"What kind?" Yvonnia asked, her voice rasping in her dry throat. "The kind who would betray her own people?" She raised her chin defiantly, though her eyes darted to Jacik for an instant, betraying her fear. "I'd never talk, even if I had anything to confess."

"You're lucky I'm chained up," Enya snapped, rattling her shackles beside Yvonnia. "I'd beat you senseless otherwise."

The officer barked a laugh. With the light streaming in from behind him, it was difficult to make out what he looked like, but Yvonnia thought she glimpsed a broad scar across his thickly bearded face.

"I'd love to see you try, little missy," he retorted, "You wouldn't even land a blow, but the effort would be entertaining." He was interrupted by a groan from Jacik, who shifted on the floor. The officer stepped back quickly. "Well, since your hound is awakening, I shall leave you to it. Don't get too comfortable though." He grinned mockingly. "We board the *Redoubtable* in less than an hour."

He vanished from the doorway and the soldiers slammed the door shut, leaving them in sudden darkness.

"Jacik?" Yvonnia said, straining forward as she struggled to make out his form in the dim gaslight. "Jacik? What did they do to you?"

Jacik struggled for a moment and then sat up. He was facing away from them, and Yvonnia saw that his hands were shackled behind his back. Then he looked at her, and she was shocked to find that he was smiling; not just the reserved, knowing smirk she sometimes saw out of the corner of her eye, but a full grin, his white teeth stark in the gloom. There was a smear of blood on his lip. Dark spatters splotched his white uniform.

"What did they do?" Yvonnia repeated, her stomach turning into a ball of lead within her.

"I didn't talk," Jacik said simply. He was swollen with pride, almost preening, flaunting his bloodied lip like a medal.

"I just hope you're this cheery when your neck is about to be stretched in front of a crowd of bloodthirsty Odolians," Enya snapped. Yvonnia looked at her askance.

"Enya!"

But the remark had already thrown a soaking wet blanket over the bodyguard's mood, and his face collapsed back into its usual stern expression. He shifted, pulling himself across the floor until he sat in his usual position, his back resting against the wall by the door. She caught his eyes for a single moment, glancing up from beneath grim hooded brows, and felt a sting of reproach far stronger than any that could have been delivered by mere words. He had not forgotten that she had robbed him of a heroic death, a death defending her and everything he was duty bound to protect.

They sank into a depressed silence. Not even Enya spoke. Moments passed like syrup on a cold morning, the passage of time unmarked by any measurable change. Enya shifted now and then beside her. Jacik stayed completely still at his post, his eyes fixed on some unseen point directly in front of him. Yvonnia sat on the cot and contemplated death. She could not bring herself to think of the past, and the present was void of much to think about. The future, however, offered many miserable possibilities to ponder.

Yvonnia was roused from her stupor by the tramp of boots in the corridor outside. She jolted up, eyes wide as the door was unlocked and unbolted. Several armed Odolians pushed their way into the room.

"Okay, ladies, let's get moving," the officer said, smirking from the doorway as the soldiers roughly unfastened Yvonnia and Enya's shackles from the wall and dragged Jacik to his feet. "It's time for you to meet the power of Odol face to face, something your backward little kingdom will soon become intimately acquainted with."

Yvonnia glared at him with all the fury she could muster. They were unceremoniously frog marched past the officer into a dank prison corridor, built of roughly hewn stone bricks that dripped with moss and grime. Naked gas lamps guttered every few feet as they passed door after door of a seemingly endless line of cells. At last, they emerged in the back of some sort of barracks, but Yvonnia had no time to note anything further, for they were swiftly marched out into the smoggy yellow light of day.

As her eyes adjusted from the gloom of the prison, Yvonnia realized with a chill of fear that they were in Gorand no longer.

They were standing on one side of a great ring of industrial structures, all brick buildings and towering smokestacks, surrounding an enormous concrete pit scraped into the earth. The building they had just come from appeared to be the oldest structure in sight, perhaps a converted castle, with round turrets and a slope-roofed keep. It contrasted strongly with the harsh right angles and bristling pipes, smokestacks, and catwalks of the newer industrial constructions. Beyond the ring of buildings, jagged cliffs of mountains surrounded them on all sides.

The pit below appeared to be at least a mile across and so deep that its bottom was hidden in haze. Within the pit, suspended on great metal struts which extended from all sides, Yvonnia saw at last one of the great dreadnoughts of Odol. It stretched nearly a quarter of the length of the pit, and beside it there appeared to be several more berths, empty and waiting for its brethren. But even in isolation, it was terrifying. Its great body was made of dark metal, constructed of heavy plates layered over each other to create a scale-like armor. The hull bristled with enormous cannons, the smallest of which dwarfed even the heaviest guns of the Ryokans. At the front of the ship, a single command tower rose into the hazy yellow sky, strung with ropes and cables. The top was flat, like the deck of a ship, and indeed she could see men swarming to and fro around a central mound, the great hot air tank which the ship was built around.

"Could man build that?" Jacik asked, a note of awestruck disbelief in his usually monotone voice.

"A thousand men, but yes." Yvonnia was startled by the voice of the officer, who was suddenly standing beside them at the top of the stairs, a smug smile on his face as he saw their undisguised awe at the scale of the great ship. "The dreadnoughts are the pride of Odol."

"We shall...ride on that ship?" Yvonnia asked, indicating the vessel weakly.

"Yes, for the next week as we fly to Odolia," the officer replied, "Where you will face the hangman's noose, pretty lady, if you're lucky. Our illustrious emperor, long may he reign, may have other, more creative ways of executing assassins." He gave her a devilish grin, and then spat at her feet.

Yvonnia jerked away, glaring at the bearded man. Jacik made a deep rumbling sound in his throat and stepped forward as if to take violent action against the officer, but two soldiers quickly grabbed his arms, and another stepped forward and struck him in the chest with the butt of his musket.

"And what good will that do?" Yvonnia snapped, her rising anger threatening to boil over. "There will be other assassins more subtle than I." Her words were laden with a sarcasm that she was sure the officer would never understand. "Surely you don't think that killing me will be without repercussions."

"I think that is rather the point, Highness."

Yvonnia turned to see Baron Schulhard, oily as ever, arms folded behind his back and a look of smug assurance on his face. His broad chest was puffed out, straining against the buttons of his decorated uniform. His curly white wig, a foolish and ugly Odolian fashion, was perched precariously on his round head.

"The next stop of the *Redoubtable*—once we deliver you to his illustrious majesty, of course—is your own kingdom," the baron said crisply. "If they do not submit to the will of the great Empire of Odol, then they will face the wrath of not only *my* dreadnought, but of four others like it."

"You can't do that!" Yvonnia cried.

"And why not, my dear, if there are more assassins to come?" the baron asked innocently. Yvonnia felt her chest tighten. Her bluffing, a mere moment of anger, had lent credence to his lie. Enya gave her a level look but was wise enough to keep her own mouth shut.

"Yes, I think we have found out just who those so-called rebels really were," said a dry, raspy voice. Beside the baron was a tall, thin man with slicked-back white hair. He was so slight, almost wispy, that Yvonnia's eyes had passed over him at first. His voice sounded like cracked paint flaking off a dry wall. "Emperor Cristole will be glad to hear that all of this has been put to rest. Allow me to introduce myself," the man added, seeing Yvonnia's questioning eyes. "I am Hollis. I was just visiting Gorand for the celebration which your insurrection so rudely interrupted. I am coming alongside Baron Schulhard to maintain the emperor's wishes. I am glad to say that the Siali spies who stole Lady Marjen's ship were shot down by our brave men."

Yvonnia's brow buckled in confusion. She was not sure what he could be referring to. He seemed to be blaming some theft or attack she'd never heard of on Sial. *Are my people mere scapegoats? Is that all we are to you?*

"Thank you, Lord Hollis," the baron said dismissively. "I think it is impolite to treat our royal guest like a common criminal." His beady black eyes looked Yvonnia up and down in a way that made her shift uncomfortably. Jacik clearly noticed, for he started forward again and received another whack from the musket for his trouble. The baron held out a thick hand to her, his smile dripping venom.

"Princess Yvonnia," he said, carefully mispronouncing her name, "Will you join me for dinner in the captain's lounge? I would be delighted by your company, and I am sure you will not find me so disagreeable." Hollis gave a disapproving cough, but the baron only chuckled. "She will be no threat; she knows what will happen to her companions should she make any hostile moves upon the *Redoubtable*."

Hopelessness washed over Yvonnia as the officer stepped forward and unlocked her heavy iron shackles. Her wrists were raw underneath, and the cold air stung her angry flesh. She gritted her teeth for only a moment before regaining her composure. Enya and Jacik were already being marched away by half a dozen soldiers. Yvonnia turned to the baron and met his glance with what she hoped were eyes of steel.

"Sir," she said icily, and took his stubby hand with only the tips of her fingers. The baron enfolded her hand in an iron grip and escorted her down towards the *Redoubtable*.

PART 4:
THE CITY OF LIGHT AND SPLENDOR

23
VETURI

Three miserable days passed in the factories at the bottom of Veturi. The work was not quite so bad as Threadbury's, or so Elsie thought. Certainly, it was not as physically taxing; the factory specialized in packing canned goods and Elsie's job was to neatly paste the paper labels onto each can. But Elsie promised herself to never eat any food from a can again, given all that she saw going on within the factory lines. She was impressed to see that Arthur took the manual labor in stride, neither complaining nor showing a hint of displeasure on his face as he worked.

The nights were worse than the days. She was forced to bunk with about twenty other men besides Arthur in a cramped, dirty room filled with narrow, lumpy cots. She tried her best to ignore the stench of unwashed bodies and the snoring, but it was hard to pretend that she was comfortable being crammed in with a bunch of strange men. They all had the same sullen, occasionally angry expressions on their faces as they worked. She spent most of her nights tossing and turning, wrapped in a thin ratty blanket, trying to shut out the offenses to her senses.

Unlike at Threadbury's, the workers here were paid daily, so Arthur had acquired a decat and three kent over the past few days. But she had 'volunteered' to do free labor. As predicted, this was not objectionable to the overseers who gave out the money, though it meant she still had nothing to show for all her toil.

On the fourth day, she confronted Arthur during their brief lunch break, whispering since there was no other chatter to cover her words.

"When are we going to get out of here?" she murmured, stirring her spoon around so it would look like she was dutifully eating the slop they gave the workers. Their packs sat on the floor under the table by their feet; Arthur insisted on bringing them to every meal.

"We leave when I find the right opportunity," Arthur said, glancing around. "If I try to leave now, the guards will have a nice time putting a bullet in my back. Patience. We have a week till we get to Bolden and there we can hitch a ride back to Gorand."

"And what happens if we don't find a way out by then?" Elsie asked, looking up at him from beneath furrowed brows.

"It's not like our band of merry rebels will have moved on by then, so Shanks will still be around. A challenge like the *Heart* is something I think he will enjoy."

Elsie wasn't satisfied with his answers, but she resumed eating all the same. Over Arthur's shoulder, she saw two men step into the dining hall and order a young man to his feet. Arthur noticed, but didn't make any movements. The men were soldiers, of that Elsie was sure. *They have the wrong lapel button,* she thought as she studied their simple scarlet uniforms. She looked down uncomfortably at her hands and was thankful that she had been given a pair of work gloves to hide the red stains.

"What are they doing?" she asked, watching as the soldiers stood another young man up and sent him to the door of the dining hall.

"Press gang. I figured that's what was happening to the men who disappeared from here," Arthur said. "We should leave now. I know what I just said," he added, seeing Elsie's befuddled expression, "but I am among the most likely in this crowd to be sent off to fight in Odol's stupid wars. And you'd likely get nabbed to do their laundry or something."

Elsie's heart began to pound and her eyes darted to the soldiers. "But how are we going to get out?"

"Just watch," Arthur said calmly.

As the soldiers continued their circuit of the mess hall, choosing the youngest and fittest looking men from the laborers, Arthur went on eating as though nothing was happening. Elsie stirred her food without eating, her mouth dry and her heart pounding in her chest as the soldiers drew closer.

Suddenly, Arthur cried out and clutched at his stomach, groaning in agony. He pitched backwards off the bench and onto the floor, rolling around and crying as if he was in the worst pain imaginable. The sudden commotion caused several workers to get to their feet and crowd around Arthur, interrupting the soldiers' methodical progression through the tables. Elsie sat in amazement, unsure if this was part of the plan, or merely a cruel interruption of fate.

Benedict Ryans, the older man from Locend, pushed his way to the front and knelt to see if Arthur was alright. "What's wrong son?" he asked gently, offering his hand.

Elsie blinked and nearly missed what happened. Arthur grabbed Benedict by the overalls, threw him to the ground, and scrambled to his feet. Another man Elsie didn't know tried to intervene, and Elsie watched transfixed as Arthur drew back and punched the man square in the face. The man staggered back, tripped, and fell backwards into the crowd, accidentally catching another worker's face with the back of his hand.

Within seconds, a chain reaction had erupted through the room, and every man was fighting every other man. The two soldiers rushed over to the brawl, allowing the pressed men to make a run for it. As soon as the soldiers noticed, they broke from the fray and gave chase to the escaping men. It was pandemonium and

Elsie couldn't even tell where Arthur had gone. Then someone grabbed her wrist and dragged her to her feet. She let out a scream, which was drowned out by the commotion, and Arthur clapped a hand over her mouth to silence her.

"We've got to go. Now."

Elsie raised no objection, and they made their way to the door marked 'Kitchen' and bolted through. The two-man cooking staff began to shout at them, but Arthur ran straight past them, dragging Elsie at his heels, and burst through another door into a corridor. He spun around and slammed the door shut, then braced himself against it.

"Quick!" He motioned to a steel rubbish barrel that was moldering nearby. "Push that over here."

Elsie darted into position at once, though when she tried to push the barrel, she found that it was incredibly heavy and scraped horribly on the cement floor. With a burst of adrenaline spurred on by renewed pounding on the door from the inside, she gritted her teeth and strained every muscle to move the barrel into place.

"There, thanks kid," Arthur said with a sly grin. His ugly clothes were in worse shape than ever, his hair was mussed every which way, and he had a cut on his lip, but he seemed to be in the best mood she'd ever seen. "Now we need to find an access staircase and get to the surface."

They were in a long, dark hallway, with steam leaking from pipes winding along the walls and the ceiling. There was yet another steel door at the opposite end, about a hundred yards away.

They ran to it and Arthur peered out through the foggy glass. Elsie had to stand on her tiptoes to see what lay beyond. A set of metal stairs lead down to an open doorway, beyond which she thought she could see daylight. Arthur shoved the door, but it was locked fast. Grumbling something unintelligible, he unshouldered his pack and began to root around in its depths. Elsie stayed on her tiptoes, staring longingly at the tantalizing doorway. She heard the muffled crack of a gunshot from somewhere behind them. It sounded far away, but even that was too close for comfort.

"This is crazy," she murmured, then turned to glare at Arthur. "Why don't you ever tell me the plan beforehand? Why won't you tell me what's going on?"

"If you remember correctly," Arthur said with a curt smile, pulling out a small lockpick and a hairpin. "I made sure that we brought our packs to lunch breaks. Most men do, for fear that the overseers will rob them of their few belongings. You didn't ever wonder what precious belongings I might have in my pack?"

"I hoped it would be something useful!" Elsie snapped, "What good are those? Are you nuts?"

Arthur ignored her and stepped to the door, crouching down and peering into the lock. "Move aside," he said after a moment. "You're standing in my light."

Begrudgingly, Elsie complied, watching him nervously even as she tried to keep one eye on the blocked door behind them. Indistinct voices and shuffling could be heard over the sound of the train. The roar of the tracks was much louder here in the corridor than it had been inside the factory rooms. She had yet to hear another gunshot, which she found reassuring. After about five minutes, she glanced back at Arthur, who was muttering under his breath.

"Are you going to pick that lock or not?" she asked impatiently, nerves adding a harsh edge to her voice.

"I'm getting there, it's just that these locks are much better than the scrap they make in Gorand."

"Have you ever even picked a lock?"

"I know my way around," Arthur said, and the pick snagged, causing him to curse in frustration.

"Yes, but have you actually picked a lock?"

Arthur sighed. "No, but I've seen it done before."

Elsie groaned, bouncing on the balls of her feet with anxious energy. The walls of the corridor felt like a vice slowly closing in around her. She looked back at the door, still blocked by the overflowing rubbish barrel. As she watched, the door shook in its frame. She heard men grunting and shouting behind it.

"Arthur!" she shrieked.

"Quiet," Arthur snapped. "I'll get us there. Just keep watch."

Elsie stood helpless as the door shuddered again, pushing outward by a few centimeters.

"Got it!" Arthur shot to his feet, slipping the lockpick neatly into his pocket. "See, kid, what did I tell you?" He put his shoulder against the door and shoved it open. A blast of freezing, smoke-tinged air funneled into the corridor, momentarily knocking the breath out of Elsie's lungs. She dashed forward as Arthur held the door open for her against the howling gale. He paused for only a moment to snatch up the packs. Behind them, there was a horrible scraping, and then a *crash* as the barrel pitched forward onto its side, spilling its contents into the corridor.

"There they are!" a man shouted. There was a scuffling noise as their pursuers stumbled over the fallen barrel.

Arthur slammed the door shut behind Elsie, nearly catching the hem of her coveralls, and slid the bolt home. Gasping for breath, Elsie shielded her eyes against the diffuse light of the sun. They were standing on a flimsy catwalk that spanned the width of the train, all hundred feet of it. The next car lay directly in front of them, across a gap of open air through which Elsie could see train tracks racing by below them, suspended on trestles dozens of stories above the ground. She stepped away from the edge, pressing her back against the freezing metal side of the car.

"Come on kid, we've got to go," Arthur said, making for a gate in the catwalk railing. "They're not going to give up that easily."

"There's no way across," Elsie stammered. "What are we going to do?"

"There is a way across," Arthur said, pointing to the other side of the gap. A metal drawbridge, similar to the one they had boarded Veturi by several days ago, was pulled up on the other side of the gap, opposite the gate. Arthur pushed the gate open and stood poised for a moment.

"Wait," Elsie gasped, "What-"

Arthur jumped.

Elsie let out a cry as he grasped onto the railing on the other side and pulled himself swiftly over onto the catwalk with fluid, confident movements. He went quickly to a wheel on the side of the car, gripped it, and strained with a grunt. Neither the wheel nor the drawbridge budged.

"Damn," Arthur said, turning back towards Elsie. "Sorry kid, you'll have to jump." Elsie stared at him wide-eyed and shook her head once. Arthur scowled. "Come on, kid, we don't have all day. You've made it this far." She saw his eyes stray to the open doorway just to his right.

"Okay," Elsie said. Sucking in a deep breath, she shifted her feet on the mesh beneath her. Behind her lay misery and soldiers and factories crawling with sour-faced men. Ahead of her lay the gap, the hundred foot drop, or maybe, if she was lucky and hit the rails on her way down, the wheels of Veturi that would crush her on the tracks. All things considered, even the dingy catwalk looked better to her than the factory behind. Steadying herself, she closed her eyes and took a leap of faith.

For a moment, she seemed to be suspended in the air, a million thoughts flashing through her mind all at once. She was falling. She misjudged her trajectory. Her eyes shot open just in time to see Arthur reaching out to grab her.

He pulled her onto the platform with ease, hitching her legs up over the railing. "I told you, kid. You're fine," Arthur said, setting her carefully on the catwalk before letting go of her and turning away unceremoniously. "Now let's get in before..."

Even as he spoke, the door on the other side of the gap slammed open and two guards emerged, muskets ready in their hands. They shouted a vain warning and leveled their guns. Arthur dragged Elsie through the doorway and up the stairs as two musket balls slammed into the bottom step where they'd been standing just a moment before.

"In here," Arthur whispered harshly, pulling her back into a hidden alcove behind a rickety metal staircase. He dragged the sliding door shut, then hunkered down so that his form would not be visible through the frosted glass. Elsie dropped to her knees beside him. She heard the footsteps and muted shouts of the guards as they rushed past. Then, at last, silence, save for the muffled rumble of the train. Arthur stood slowly, keeping a wary eye on the door.

"That went smoothly," Elsie said sarcastically, twisting her hands together to stop them from trembling.

"We aren't dead, are we?" Arthur retorted.

"I suppose not," Elsie muttered as she glanced around the room. It was filled with all sorts of cleaning implements, barrels, sacks, boxes, and other paraphernalia, lit by an amber gas lamp over the door. Without warning, Arthur tossed his pack onto a box and began struggling out of his dingy work shirt.

"Get changed. They'll be looking for people in these uniforms."

Elsie coughed annoyedly and spun around, a flush rising in her cheeks. *He could at least pretend to be decent!*

The rustling of clothes finally stopped, and Elsie jumped when a hand was laid on her shoulder. Arthur was now dressed in a fine-looking—albeit wrinkled—tailcoat and knee breeches. He still looked a bit of a mess. She could hardly judge him though, as she likely looked no better.

"I'll scout ahead," he said. "You stay in here and get changed, quickly." With that, he unbolted the door, stepped through, and was gone.

"That man is going to be the death of me," Elsie muttered to herself as she changed hastily into Maria's green dress.

When she rejoined Arthur, Elsie found that they fit in quite well with that level of Veturi. Crowded slum apartments lined the windowless metal corridors, their contents—humans, objects, and even household animals—spilling out beyond the flimsy numbered doors. Elsie felt sick to her stomach as she passed through the narrow, never-ending walkways, dodging piles of detritus, angry cats, and the occasional slumped passenger resting against a door-post. It was worse than even the depths of Gorand's undercity. There was no light, no air, and precious little space. The gas lamps all along the corridor guttered in unison with the hollow rumbling of the train's great wheels.

Arthur came to an unexpected halt in front of a doorway where a woman, huddled in a ragged shawl and cradling a young baby in her arms, sat just inside. She looked up blearily at Arthur, and started, clutching the baby to her chest defensively. "What do you want?" she snapped.

"We need directions to the nearest stairwell leading to the upper levels," Arthur said briskly.

The woman shook her head, tucking the shawl tighter around her and covering the baby's small pink face beneath a corner. "Why don't you just take the lift?" she asked bitterly. "You look rich enough."

The corner of Arthur's lip curled into a frown. "The reason is not important. I just need to know." His hand flashed into his pocket and withdrew a coin, which glimmered even in the dull gaslight. Elsie could not tell which coin it was, but it was on the larger side. "Here, I'll give you this for your trouble."

The woman shook her head again, eyes widening with fear. "I can't take that. My husband...he'll wonder where I-" Her words were cut off by Arthur's strident tones.

"Just take it and save it for when you reach Karlsban. Apartments are cheaper there, and there's plenty of work since the war. Get off Veturi and stay off. Don't listen to their propaganda about some 'city of opportunity.'" He gestured at the filthy corridor.

The woman rose to her feet slowly, laying the baby back against her shoulder.

"But my husband...he'll think I...he's always so suspicious of charity anyways..."

"Tell him some rich fool was down here distributing to the poor and needed directions to the nearest lift. He pressed money upon you in return. Or don't tell him anything. But get yourself, your child, and your husband off this train." Before she could object further, Arthur pressed the coin into her curled fingers. The woman's mouth worked open and shut for a moment, then she swallowed and quickly tucked the coin into her skirt pocket.

"Yes, right. Look for the maintenance corridor with the amber light," she said. "It's about three blocks down. Follow that to the end and you'll find the stairwell. They're supposed to lock the door, but my husband says they rarely do."

Arthur nodded and, without another word, turned away and began to stride down the corridor once again. Elsie followed on his heels, not wishing to be left behind, though she did cast a backward glance over her shoulder just in time to see the woman step back into the room and quickly shut the door.

"This is awful," Elsie said after a moment, desperate to break the heavy silence.

"You'll see far worse," Arthur muttered so quietly that she barely heard him. "Come on, kid. We've got to go buy a hat."

24

A Visit from Lord
Callighan

Alven Tulain kissed his wife goodbye, clutching the satchel which contained his lunch in his hand. "I'm always safe dear," he said gently, putting on his top hat. "You just make sure Roland stays focused on his studies when he gets home."

Bettie was not impressed. "I mean it, Al. You've got to be careful. Didn't you hear about the rebel attack in Gorand? It isn't safe anymore, I tell you."

"I doubt that the rebels would have much use for my shop. I don't keep much cash in the store, and their taste is far too primitive to appreciate my gowns," Alven said, fondly reassuring his wife with another kiss. "I must go, my dear. The streets are already opening up and I am sure that it will be a fine day for business."

Bettie made no more objections. Alven, taking his umbrella, began his morning walk down the central avenue of Veturi. His apartment was two cars away from his shop. It was enviably short compared to the walk some of his friends had to make every day to the businesses they owned. He tipped his hat to all the regulars: the man who managed the fruit stand, Karl the fish merchant, the soup stand owner, the two men who petitioned for donations to help the poor. He always gave them a few loose dul from his coat pocket, and he repeated the ritual to a rehearsed "thank you very much sir" from the two men.

At last, he reached the shop and found that Teddy, his young apprentice, was already waiting there.

"Took ya long enough, old man," Teddy teased. His thick Gorandi undercity accent was always a little rough on Alven's ears.

"I just had to get my lunch," Alven replied with a smile. "Did you finish the dress I told you to make?"

"Yessir!" Teddy said eagerly, his brown eyes brimming with excitement.

"Well, let's get inside and see how you did," Alven said. He unlocked the shop's door and dutifully turned the small wooden sign to the side that said "open."

It was, in fact, going to be a slow day. Since Veturi had left Gorand, tensions were running high. Though just over a week ago the papers had proclaimed Greyer's rebellion exterminated at last from Veturi, now rumors circulated about an airship stolen from the skydocks at Gorand, right under the nose of the baron. Even with the news that the attack had been perpetrated by Siali insurrectionists, any rumors of rebellious activity were sure to put a damper on business in the city of light and splendor.

As Teddy pulled the dress out of his pack and unfurled it, Alven's unhappy thoughts dissipated at once. The dress was a fine dark blue satin, cut in the modern fashion, beaded with shimmering pearls so that it looked like a night sky. The dressmaker examined his apprentice's work in more detail: the stitching, the cutting, the finishing. Overall, Teddy had done an excellent job. He could still use some improvement, but Alven knew that even he himself could always use help here and there.

"It's fine work, Teddy. I'll put it in the window. You can start on another project now I think."

"What project, sir?" Teddy asked.

"Go ahead and clean up the storage room. I purchased a new broom just for the job." Alven's devilish smile was met by an equally disappointed look from Teddy, but he handed over the dress dutifully and made his way to the storage room in the back.

It was a dull day. The fourth day of the week was incredibly dull on the best of occasions, and when it happened that there was unrest on Veturi, it was bound to be even worse. Of the many pedestrians who passed by the shop window, only a few stopped to glance at the wares, and even fewer came inside the shop at all. None bought.

Alven could hear Teddy grumbling in the back as he faced the less fashionable part of being an apprentice, though he did accomplish the task. He would go places, or so Alven Tulain thought. He just had to get over these teenage years of his life—oh-so-eager to leave childhood behind without meeting the responsibilities of adulthood face-to-face.

The incessant dullness was finally interrupted by a girl outside of the window with an excited look on her face. She was wearing the worst dress imaginable. It was green, and not a nice deep emerald green, but a rather pale, sickly color. The shaping was all wrong, the sleeves were far too puffy, and the waist raised to make a silhouette that might have been in style about twenty years ago. The gangly girl who wore it also had a filthy face and unkempt black hair that was unfashionably cropped short.

From behind her came a tall, red-haired man who looked a tad more respectable, though Alvin thought he had the *seeming* of someone who was rich instead of actually *being* rich. He had on a dusty and slightly wrinkled green tailcoat, and carried a fine new cane that Alven recognized from one of the shops further down Veturi, as well as a fine silk top hat. The young girl seemed especially interested in Teddy's new dress, which was displayed proudly in the front window.

After a moment of discussion between the two, the tall man relented, and they entered Alven's shop. The man pointed at the blue dress. "I would like my cousin to have that dress there in the window. The blue one."

"Well, that is a fine piece. It'll run you a granz and two sept," Alven said with a proud and somewhat smug grin. There wasn't any way this faux dandy would be able to afford it.

"Sold. I'll have my valet send you a check," the man said, and went to fetch the dress off the mannequin.

"Well, sir, we don't accept-"

"Nonsense," the tall man said, patting Alven on the shoulder in a patronizing manner, "I'm sure the word of Lord Callaghan of Bolden is enough here."

It made some sense. His accent did wax a little more from Bolden than from Gorand, even the upper city. Not to mention his demeanor was that of a lord; Alven had met many in his day buying a new gown for his cousin or daughter or lady friend. "I shall need it written in full..." Alven was cut off once more by the girl practically squealing in delight as Callaghan put the dress into her hands.

"Well, try it on, Corina," Lord Callaghan said. "I need to discuss the exact details of our transaction with this fine gentleman."

With a nod, Corina headed straight for the changing rooms. Inquisitively, Alven turned his gaze to Callaghan. "How do I know that you're good for the money? That's quite a lot of money to be putting on hold. People usually carry cash on Veturi."

"With all those nasty rebels running about?" Callaghan scoffed.

"I...well, I will need to check with some banking authorities before I can let you have-"

"Sir, I see that you run an honest establishment," Callaghan said, leaning in to whisper. "Could you honestly allow that poor girl to go around in that abysmal dress? It was made by her aunt, and I can't take her to see Napolientti's opera wearing that thing. Your dress is far superior. And in fashion as well. Her aunt seems to think it's still wartime."

Confused thoughts were spinning through Alven's head, and he glanced at the piece of cloth draped over the door of the changing stall, the *thing* he refused to call a dress. "If you can-"

He was cut off again.

"I'll write you a notice. You can take it up with my estate in Bolden. Midland Union is where my finances are held, so you can speak with one of their representatives. With interest, you should be owed a talent."

A talent? "Of...of course sir, but you see, I don't take cr-"

"Of course you do. And for such a fine, modern dress, I will give you this as a tip. Or a downpayment perhaps." Callaghan pulled a kent out of his pouch and placed it in Alven's sweating palm. "That should cover the trouble we caused you."

"Ah, it's no trouble," Alven said, doing his best to smile warmly. "It's just that-"

Yet again, Alven was cut off, this time by the young Corina. She burst out of the changing stall wearing the blue dress and beamed. "I love it! It looks amazing, don't you think, Ar...er, Andrew?"

"Of course," Andrew Callaghan said as he placed a freshly signed piece of paper onto the counter. "Come along, Corina, we don't want to be late and the theater is still three cars up the tracks." He extended a hand to the girl and before Alven could object, they were gone. Befuddled, Alven slumped back into a chair behind the desk. Teddy came out from the recesses of the storage room and looked at the empty mannequin.

"Who was that?" he asked.

"Customers. Your dress was a hit," Alven replied.

Elsie settled the hat on her head and studied herself in the mirror. It was a simple brown felt, but it had a couple of blue cloth flowers sewn onto the band, which complimented her dress. She was beginning to think that this whole adventure was too good to be true. Arthur gave a different story every time, but every time the result was the same: the shopkeeper, baffled, would not be given the chance to object to the expensive "purchase" Arthur made. They were asking exorbitant amounts for every piece of clothing that the two obtained, which Arthur talked down to petty change and promises. She thought that her own acting, the part of the overexcited young cousin, didn't hurt either.

In fact, even Arthur seemed to be having fun, something Elsie found hard to square with the normal attitude he had towards, well, existence in general. As they hurried out of the hat shop, he gave Elsie a genuine smile. "I think we've got enough to get us into the wealthiest cars of Veturi," he said quietly as they slumped down onto a public bench to rest. "That is where our *friends* will be."

Elsie surveyed what she had gained from their adventures around the shops: sparkling new shoes that actually fit, new underclothes in the latest style with all the correct padding and shaping, a dazzling new dress, a fashionable hat, not to mention a warm bath. It was already late in the afternoon, but she was still full from the lunch they had procured for free, save for the tip Arthur gave the waiter. She had a parasol she carried on her arm, which beautifully matched the dress. He had gained new shoes himself, as well as a fine black umbrella and top hat, and traded in his green tailcoat for a shiny black one. They looked a match for any of the travelers making their way up and down the promenade.

The ridiculousness of it nearly made Elsie laugh. She had taken what had been denied her all her life. For so long, she'd seen beautiful gowns made at Threadbury's, but now she was dressed more beautifully than anything she had seen before. She had fresh makeup which hid the faint bruising that still remained on her face, and she was no longer afraid to look at her reflection. Yet, something about it made her stomach churn uneasily.

"Arthur?"

"Yes?"

"Are we doing the right thing?" she asked warily.

"What do you mean?" he asked.

"I mean stealing all of this from those shops. The people working in them seem, well, they don't seem bad. I understand the rebellion. I understand that the empire has done horrible things and needs to be stopped. But did the dressmaker do anything wrong? Or the owner of that shop you got your cane from?"

"What does it matter?" Arthur said nonchalantly.

"Aren't you fighting for the greater good? A better life for everyone crushed under the empire?"

"What gave you that idea?" Arthur suddenly turned his gaze on her, his brows knit together. "What I do, I do for my own reasons. Odol has a price to pay, and these trinkets are only a means to achieve that end. I thought you would be happy to make them pay!"

"But we didn't steal from the empire's warehouses, Arthur! These were innocent people..."

"Is anyone in the empire innocent?" Arthur snapped, before breaking off suddenly. He took a deep breath, gripping the lion's head cane forcefully. There was a look in his face that Elsie could only describe as *pained*.

Elsie was unsure of how to react. She hadn't realized that Arthur could be hurt. Not in this way at least. But it seemed she had found a tender spot in his seemingly impenetrable armor.

Silently, Arthur stood and beckoned absently to Elsie. He began in his long, purposeful strides up the lane, hands shoved deep into his pockets. She scampered after him, hiking up her cumbersome skirts, not wanting to be left behind.

FAIR TRIAL

The pair continued down the train, and Elsie observed for the first time how elaborate Veturi truly was. The shops they had visited were finer than anything that she had seen in Gorand, and yet they paled in comparison to the well-ordered townhomes that lined lanes planted with beautiful, red-leafed oaks. There were even stables on the ends of each car which held both carriages and horses, which Elsie saw carrying passengers to and fro.

Arthur had been silent since their discussion earlier, leaving Elsie to feel more alone, even amid the bustling streets. She occupied herself by looking back and forth at the people all about, many shuffling back to their homes after long days of work. Men in top hats greeted beautiful wives at the door with a kiss before being hustled inside for supper. A noticeable number of carriages were heading in the same direction as Arthur and Elsie.

"Where are they going?" Elsie asked.

"Where we're going," Arthur replied, finally breaking his silence.

"And where is that?" Elsie asked after receiving no further explanation.

"To see Napolientti."

"Arthur, you say that as if I know what you're talking about."

"He's a tenor. There's an opera tonight and he's the main attraction. It was on a poster I saw at the dress shop."

"So we're going to the opera? I didn't think the rebels would be there..."

"Oh, they won't be," Arthur scoffed. "They are crazed idealists. But they'll be on that car. The crown jewel of Veturi. That's where we'll find their watchdog."

Slightly disappointed, Elsie shrugged. "I guess they wouldn't have any use for the opera. That singer must be good though, to cause all this fuss." She gestured to the growing crowds which gathered as they crossed lane after lane and car after car. The townhomes got taller and wider and soon they were walking between towering manors which nearly swallowed the entire lane.

The car ahead of them was bisected by an enormous ornate building which ran the full width of the train. It was passible via an arched tunnel, which ran through the brick foundation of the building, flanked by alcoves containing sculptures the likes of which she had never seen. Angels, saints, and heroes were depicted larger than life in white marble alongside colorful murals. Above its decorated foundations, the building loomed, buttressed with carved stone and glittering with a thousand twinkling lights. Elsie gaped, barely hearing Arthur as he casually identified it as the Veturi Theater. Part of her wished that they could enter and perhaps catch some of the opera.

Arthur guided them straight toward the tunnel. The carriages parked, releasing a mass of pedestrians which shuffled their way through the tunnel. All these people looked rich. Incredibly rich. Glancing down at her dress in the dim gaslight, Elsie was glad that they had gotten the nice clothes before coming here. Even the tunnel was clean, dry, and ornately decorated. Elsie reached out to touch the wall with her gloved hand, marveling at the smooth surface.

It took her a moment to realize that Arthur was beckoning to her. She had stopped without knowing it, admiring the beauty of the man-made structure around her. The tunnel was punctuated with alcoves containing even more of the lovely white statues. Hurriedly, she gathered her skirts and joined Arthur.

"We're almost there," he said as he took her arm and escorted her along like a lady. The gesture made Elsie flush. Not from him, goodness knows, but for her sake. She *felt* like a lady.

As they neared the dim evening light at the end of the tunnel, air that was filled with a strange new freshness entered Elsie's lungs. Her eyes widened to take in the sights as they stepped out from beneath the building. The theater extended in wings on both sides of an enormous plaza, blocking the view of the Wastes entirely, creating its own little world. The walls were lined with intricate pillars and more amazing statuary, as well as banks of flowers that burst in colorful array from stone planters. The stones beneath her feet were not the rough cobbles of Gorand. Rather, each flagstone was a smooth, polished hexagon, placed in an intricately designed pattern. In the center stood a massive fountain, which sprayed a delicate sculpture of water into the air that fell again like rain into the stone pool below.

On the other side of the plaza, she saw a building made entirely of glass, glittering and full of green. It was lit by strange bulbs that lined every intricate arc of glass that made up the grand conservatory. Beyond, the steeple of a cathedral rose into the night, blocking Elsie's view of the rest of the train beyond.

The plaza was crowded with people of wealthy means. Elsie stared at all the amazing dresses the ladies were wearing. Madam Harban had been right; the dresses the workhouse made, even at their best, couldn't compare to the gorgeous gowns all around her. She looked down at her own dress again. It fit in well enough, but all the same she felt inadequate—thin, wan, and gangly as she was. The gloves were a blessing, covering the burn scars and red stains on her hands. She was certain that all the rich women around her had flawless hands. Indeed, some of the younger ones didn't even wear gloves, showing off painted fingernails in all colors.

Arthur looked around the plaza, seemingly unimpressed. "Their watchdog will be here somewhere, hiding in plain sight."

"Okay..." Elsie said, her eyes straining to take in the mass of people. "What does he look like?"

"*She* is young, dark haired..." Arthur made a grumbling noise in his throat as though trying to remember. "She'll probably be dressed quite elaborately in order to blend in. But I'll know her when I see her."

"That's a big help," Elsie muttered as the pair absently walked toward the fountain. Elsie stared into the water where the wealthy youth had tossed coins, some of which were more valuable than an entire month's wages at Threadbury's.

"Maybe she'd be in the conservatory," Elsie suggested, raising her eyes to the astonishing glass building.

"Perhaps," Arthur said absently, staring about as the crowd began to shift in uncanny unison toward the elaborate doors to the theater.

"We could still try out here. I'll ask around, using the code along the way," Elsie offered.

"You're just a kid. They'll think you're a trap. *I'll* ask around."

Elsie huffed and walked by Arthur's side as he moved deftly through the crowd, accosting various women who vaguely fit the description and asking them the code: "*What is the cloudy sky to the sunny day?*" Every time, it was met with similarly confused looks. One woman's husband seemed convinced that Arthur was drunk. Out of embarrassment, Elsie kept her gaze on the artistry displayed around the plaza.

Having no luck, they finally found themselves standing before the conservatory in its polished, crystalline glory. It was an ethereal palace of glass, all sweeping arches and vaulted ceilings, glowing softly with pink and purple light that was unlike anything Elsie had ever seen. Its huge gate stood open at the front, facing the plaza, and on either side two tunnels sloped down beneath the foundations so that pedestrians could reach the other side of the building. Inside, Elsie could see exotic trees, ferns, and flowers of all colors. Deep purples, bright reds, pure whites, brilliant yellows, and all manner of blues and oranges dotted the narrow paths that wound around the conservatory.

Elsie ran from Arthur's side through the gate past two guards. They were dressed in pale orange uniforms, rather than the rich scarlet ones Elsie had made en masse in Threadbury's. Just inside the gates, she was met with a wall of humidity, a striking contrast to the chill air outside. The second thing that struck her was the light; she had never seen anything like it. It was so clear and brilliant, and there was none of the flickering or smoky ambiance of gas light.

But her attention was immediately recaptured by the plants: the big, leafy plants that spread their fronds over the railings and onto the path; the strange, pointy-needled trees that reached to the ceiling; the overflowing flowerbeds knee-deep with blooms; the hedges trimmed into impossible shapes; and an assortment of other strange plants she had no words to describe. Elsie was enamored with them all. She wanted to reach out and touch each one in turn, to discover every texture and scent.

She tore her gaze away for a moment to see if Arthur had followed her inside and found, to her chagrin, that he was regarding everything with the same bland stoicism as ever. She wandered in aimless awe, not much caring whether Arthur followed her or not. He kept close to her anyway, peering down paths and into nooks as he searched for someone else to pester with the code. She broke from him momentarily, running over to a large rose bush that was taller than she was and twice as wide, trimmed into a perfectly round shape. She leaned in to smell the full, red blossoms. It was intoxicating. She was about to touch one of the petals when she heard Arthur mumble something to himself, breaking the silence.

"What?" she asked, standing up straight, afraid that something was wrong.

"Nothing," Arthur stated blandly. He was standing with his back towards her, staring out over a section of the conservatory.

"Is something the matter?"

"I've just been reminded of my home, that's all." Arthur's hand brushed a few wide-leafed hostas as he walked through the hushed conservatory, every sound muffled by the dense foliage.

"Home? I didn't think you had a home," Elsie said carefully, concealing her curiosity.

"I *had* a home. A while back. It had a garden, somewhat like this—maybe less exotic, but just as green." He took a flower in his hand and smelled it, closing his eyes for a moment.

"What happened? I thought...well, I've heard that all rebels were vagabonds and paupers out for revenge for not being..." She shut up, trying to rationalize all that she'd been told at Threadbury's about the rebellion. According to the older women, especially Madame Harban, every rebel was a poor drunkard for whom a swift death would be a mercy. Yet Arthur seemed to be a man of means.

"Kid, you have a lot to learn about the world," was what he said, and was about to add something more when he spotted another couple on the path not far away. He beckoned Elsie over and motioned for her to be silent. The pair consisted of a charming young man with fashionably slicked-back hair and a young, beautiful woman. Unlike Elsie, the woman had a perfect figure, and her hair was swept into an elaborate updo, with braids and a few loose chocolate brown curls artistically framing her delicate face. Elsie caught her breath and looked expectantly up at Arthur.

Arthur had returned to his businesslike demeanor and watched the couple intently. They seemed to be heading away from Arthur and Elsie. Undeterred, Arthur walked briskly over to meet them and addressed the woman without a moment's delay.

"Excuse me," he said abruptly, "But *what is the cloudy sky to the sunny day?*" The man gave Arthur the same baffled look as everyone else. Elsie caught herself rolling her eyes and flushing as she tried to hide behind a well-trimmed hedge.

"Well, the sky would be *Greyer*, wouldn't it?" the woman said lightly, giving Arthur a slow smile. She turned to the man she was with, who now wore an even more baffled expression. "Raoul, darling, would you be ever so kind as to take a wander down by the koi pond for a few? I've business to discuss."

"Can't it wait, Genevieve?" Raoul said, somewhat desperately.

"No, darling," Geneieve said. "Don't you worry, I'll be back within the hour." She gave him a kiss on the jaw that left a bright red mark from her lipstick and smiled seductively over her shoulder at him as she took Arthur's arm. Something about it, about her, the way she moved and looked and spoke, made Elsie uncomfortable.

Arthur said nothing but allowed himself to be led away from the befuddled Raoul towards the entrance of the conservatory. Elsie fell into step beside them in awkward silence, glancing at the woman again and again, trying to size her up. Genevieve molded seamlessly to Arthur's side, as though she was a piece of clay that had been pressed against him. As they passed the guards and exited into the now quiet plaza, she leaned her head against his shoulder and giggled like he'd said something funny.

"Awfully brave, waving our old code around like that," the woman said under her breath as they began to wander across the plaza. "Is she safe to talk around?" She jerked her head in Elsie's direction, separating subtly from Arthur's side as they drew further away from the conservatory.

"She's with me," Arthur said. "What can I call you?"

"Friends call me Genny."

"I hope that we can see eye to eye on this, Genevieve. I know I'm an outsider here. Andrew Callaghan." He extended his hand. Genevieve just gave a gracious nod.

"Pleasure, Ar...Andrew. If that's the name you choose to go by, it's no skin off my nose. You're supposed to be dead, twice in fact, so I imagine you'd prefer not to go blabbing your name everywhere."

"How did you know he was…?" Elsie interjected.

"Oh, we know about him," Genny said airily. "Heard nothing about you though. How did you come to be in the company of one of the most hated men in Odol?"

"Hated?" Elsie raised an eyebrow and looked to Arthur, who ignored her. "What makes him so hated?"

They stopped right in front of the fountain, their words drowned to any outsider by its steady low roar of streaming water. It was night now and the orange glow from the streetlamps made the water appear like golden mist as it struck the bottom of the pool.

"You mean you don't know?" Genevieve laughed. "He was one of the worst Odolian dogs there was. Ruthless. Captain Pendington here, he would root out Greyer's most secretive hide-outs and firebomb them till there was nothing left but ash. Then he went mad. Crashed his ship and became hated by the Odolians too. Seems to return the favor, or am I wrong?"

Arthur was bristling visibly, but Elsie failed to notice much more than that. She was too busy keeping her jaw from hanging open.

"You see," Genevieve continued smoothly, "This rat left some of our best men to the noose in a stunt that destroyed Gorand's garrison."

"I'm not here to be put on trial for that, Genevieve." Arthur's face was red with anger, and the veins in his neck had begun to bulge slightly. "Will you just tell me if Shanks is still here?"

Genevieve waved a gloved hand dismissively in Arthur's direction. "I'm not in contact with the group directly. I can tell you where to find them, though."

"How do we know we can trust you?" Elsie demanded, before being shushed by Arthur. He seemed about to speak, but he was interrupted by Genevieve once again.

"What *I* want to know is what the great scourge wants here," she said, tilting her head in Arthur's direction and looking up at him through long, dark lashes.

"We need Shanks' expertise. We have an airship, but it's down an engine. Need to get it fixed."

"Ah, now the pieces fall into place." Genevieve's face split in a sly grin. "That was you, wasn't it? In Gorand? Not Siali insurgents then. I'm sure that such an audacious display of anti-imperial sentiment will make you more than welcome among what's left of Gr...the men. *Shanks*, I'm sure, would be more than happy to help you."

Arthur seemed satisfied. Elsie wasn't. Something about the way the woman spoke, the way she said the name *Shanks*, the way she spoke of Arthur's past, seemed to suggest some great double entendre of which Elsie was unaware.

"So where are they?" Arthur asked.

"The theater. Box four. Good luck getting in. Napolientti is singing and he always fills up the seats."

Arthur nodded. "Don't worry, Genevieve. I'm sure we'll be able to find what we're looking for."

"I wish you luck," Genevieve said, giving them another coy smile. "Now, if you'll excuse me, I have a lovely young man to spend the evening with. Farewell, Lord Pendington," she said mockingly, then curtseyed, turned, and headed back towards the conservatory. Arthur clearly did not appreciate being called that, and the encounter left a sour taste in Elsie's mouth as well.

"I don't like her," she said finally.

"It's hard to like Greyer's people," Arthur said, turning his back on Genevieve's retreating form without a second glance, "Especially when they run around in fine clothes like that. Seems a little contrary."

"Yes, I agree. But I also think...oughtn't she to come with us?"

"She's just the watchdog," Arthur said, offering his arm to Elsie distractedly. "She doesn't want to be linked with the rest, nor they with her, in case the militia comes sniffing around."

They began to make their way towards the theater. It was even more beautiful from this angle. A huge frieze was set upon the lintel of the double oak doors, depicting a battle between ancient kingdoms, each face and body carved to painstaking realism. She could see the agony in the faces of the wounded men, and the triumph on the faces of the victorious. Perhaps it was some part of a myth or of Odol's history which she knew nothing about, and she wasn't sure if she wanted to. Men riding horses were impaling men on foot with spears or hacking others to bits with swords, but it was clearly meant to be a glorious thing, given its high place above the very doors of the theater.

When they reached the bottom of the staircase that led up to the door, they were accosted by another orange-uniformed guard, who stepped forward smartly and clicked his heels. "I'm sorry sir, ma'am. I cannot allow anyone inside once the performance has started."

"I think I could change that," Arthur said smoothly, reaching into his pocket.

"I'm sorry sir, no amount of money could..." The young guard launched into a long-winded explanation to which Elsie paid no attention. She had begun to hear from within the theater a beautiful sound. A great orchestra was playing an ethereal tune that drifted in and out of hearing as she strained her ears to catch it. There were songs and rhymes that some of the older women at Threadbury's used to sing or hum. They were all quick, jovial tunes that made it easy to find the beat and clap along. Singing was one of the few ways that the girls and women at Threadbury's had been allowed to have fun. But it had never sounded anything like this. What she heard reminded her of lullabies from when she was young, before the workhouse, even before she was on the streets. It was calm, lilting, like a warm summer breeze that stirred something deep in her chest. And she could barely hear it through the thick stone walls.

Interrupting the conversation, Elsie seized Arthur's arm. "Oh, you promised I could see him!" She knew she was acting, at least in part. But only in part, for she now desperately longed to hear the music in full, and the singing which accompanied it.

"See? My cousin was promised," Arthur said, but the guard seemed undeterred.

"I cannot cause any interruption to the music, sir. Lady Eritula would have my head if I allowed anything to disrupt the performance."

"But you see, my good sir, we *are* expected. Box two, right side," Arthur said, pulling a slip of paper from his pocket. He squinted at it, as if studying it. "Yes, this invitation is quite clear."

"Let me see that," the guard said, but Arthur snatched the note back and stuffed it into his breast pocket. Elsie saw for a split second that the paper was blank.

"Sir, with all due respect to your position, the lady gave me this *intimate* letter to invite me personally. My cousin is merely tagging along. I do not think that it was intended to be shown to every man I come across. I'm sure you have respect for a lady's dignity."

"But that's Lady Triasamai's box. She's..." The guard lowered his voice. "Pretty old, don't you think?"

To Elsie's surprise, Arthur unceremoniously stripped off one of his gloves and slapped the guard across the face with it. "Shame on you, sir. If I told her what you just said, I'm sure you would find yourself a few cars back that way. As a fireman. You *must* know she has the ear and heart of Lady Eritula. Now, if you would be so kind as to let us in? I give you my word we won't cause any disruptions."

Flushed and stunned, the guard nodded. "Of course...but I don't know you. Never saw you in my life. You don't know me either, understood?"

Arthur smiled pleasantly. "I knew we would see eye-to-eye. Thank you," he said and, taking Elsie's arm once more, guided her up the stairs and through the grand double doors into the theater.

The entrance hall was surprisingly unimpressive; a wide, blank white room with some simple columns built into the walls, and a few comfortable chairs and end tables. Perhaps it would have seemed statelier were it filled with the hustle and bustle of wealthy patrons sipping cocktails and socializing before the main event.

Now, however, it was completely empty, and they passed through quickly, their steps echoing on the polished floors. The music was growing louder, and Elsie could now clearly hear that someone, a man, was singing a melody over the accompaniment of the orchestra.

"We ought to find them quickly," Arthur said in a nearly inaudible whisper.

"Box four, right?" Elsie asked.

"Yes, but is it right, or left?"

Elsie looked both ways. "Why didn't you ask?" she said, irritated. "And why pick on an old lady like that?"

"It got us in. Besides, it doesn't hurt anyone."

"It hurts her reputation," Elsie mumbled, kicking her feet impatiently as they pondered which side to take. "And rumors can start very quickly."

"I think getting a man like me would improve her reputation substantially," Arthur said flatly. "And hopefully we'll be off of Veturi by then." Arthur picked up his pace and without so much as a glance over his shoulder, he continued down the hallway.

Elsie picked up her skirts and jogged to catch up to him. He was no longer acting the nobleman; in fact, he seemed almost animalian as he stalked down the entry hall, his knees slightly bent and his broad shoulders taut beneath his tailcoat, ready to spring at any moment. When they reached the staircase at the end, he simply hustled down the steps. Elsie, however, couldn't help but stop and stare.

The marble stairs swept down into a great vaulted room. Every square inch of flat space on the walls and ceiling was covered in brilliantly colored murals accented with gilt that glimmered in the light of an enormous glass chandelier. Each of the columns lining the walls spread at the top like a great tree, and each of the doors was decorated with intricate carvings of flowers and ivy. Slowly, she descended the steps into the cavernous gallery, hardly knowing where to rest her eyes in the opulent display.

When she finally made it to the bottom, Arthur frowned at her. "We can't just linger around," he said firmly. "We need to get to their box and find out where Shanks is. I *know* he wouldn't be caught dead in a place like this," he said as he began to head for the left side of the gallery, which housed yet another impressive staircase that led up to the theater boxes. "It's pretty smart to have their rendezvous here. The empire would never suspect..." It seemed to Elsie as though he was trying to convince himself.

There were about a dozen boxes on that side, each screened by a thick velvet curtain. As they drew closer, the beautiful song that entranced Elsie ended, and the theater just on the other side of the wall broke into polite, uniform applause. In a strange way, it seemed as though the audience itself was a part of the performance. Elsie longed for them to finish their polite clapping so that the beautiful music could start again.

They came to the box marked "4" and Arthur paused for a moment to listen. The applause ended as smoothly as it had begun, and the music picked up again, this time with fewer instruments and a pair of singers accompanying what Elsie thought was a far less beautiful melody. She wished hopelessly for the other song to play again.

Satisfied by the resumption of the performance, Arthur opened the curtain and they both looked out into the box. Elsie saw four people in the comfortable seats: two men and two women. The men were dressed in breeches and coats like Arthur's, though they were clearly pressed and tailor made, as opposed to Arthur's borrowed finery. One man was young and looked much like Raoul, the man Genevieve had been with. The other was old, with a bushy mustache and goatee, his silver hair combed back in elegant waves. The women were dressed in gorgeous gowns trimmed with lace and bedecked with pearls and gemstones. The first lady seemed even younger than the young man, and Elsie thought that she was very beautiful, with her blonde hair done up in bright curls and something like a tiara set upon her head. The other woman was older, with streaks of gray in her hair, though she still appeared strikingly like the younger girl.

Elsie tugged on Arthur's sleeve and whispered to get his attention. "This looks like a family. Are you sure we're in the right one?"

"No, but if the rebels are intelligent, they would make sure that their connections appeared inconspicuous," Arthur replied quietly, but his voice caught the attention of the older man, who turned around in his seat to face them.

"Can we help you?" the man demanded in a low, rather posh voice, giving Arthur a look of resigned annoyance.

"Oh, I was just wondering," Arthur began, undeterred, "What is the cloudy sky to the sunny day?"

"What?" the man spluttered.

"I mean that, well, where is Shanks?"

By now, Arthur and Elsie were being stared down by four important-looking rich people, each with an equally annoyed expression on their face. "Of all the nerve," the older woman exclaimed.

"My apologies," Arthur began, raising his hands defensively.

"Excuse me," the older man said sharply, "I would like you to know, *sir*, that this is a private booth, and if you do not leave this instant, we will have no choice but to call the guards on you. Not that Henri and I couldn't take you ourselves."

Elsie was never sure how exactly they ended up back in the hallway without coming to blows; she was more or less carried along by adrenaline than by any conscious thought. "That went well," she snarked at Arthur.

"You said left. We went left. At least they didn't suspect anything more than us being disorderly."

"Still," Elsie said as they descended the stairs to the gallery once more, "How do we know that Genevieve wasn't just wasting your time? She seemed like she might not be trustworthy."

Arthur sighed. "Kid, you have to understand that in this trade we are going to deal with people who don't seem trustworthy. If you weren't working with me, would you trust me?"

"I don't know," Elsie said curtly. Arthur didn't seem to notice that she had spoken and continued on his way.

That was when the most beautiful song that Elsie had ever heard began. She stopped dead on the staircase, legs melting as the violins soared in sweet harmony. Rich, lyrical notes were plucked out on a harp, and a cymbal, or perhaps a gong, reverberated along a crescendo. A man, the same one as before, started to sing sadly in a foreign language, reaching high notes that Elsie was scarcely sure were possible. She forced herself to continue up the stairs with Arthur as the man sang through two melodic stanzas. Then the music swelled and somehow became even sadder. All her life, she would wish to know the meaning of the words that he sang, because they moved her to tears. She was filled with a warm, aching, bittersweet gladness as she wiped her eyes with the blue gloves, staining them with tears that she did not understand.

They reached the box marked with the number 4 and this time Arthur and Elsie were both more confident going in. They paused only for a moment, glancing at each other. Arthur did not comment on Elsie's damp cheeks. Taking a deep breath, he opened the curtain slowly and quietly as the last strains of the beautiful song faded away and the theater erupted into wild applause.

This time, the people in the booth were all men. *A good sign,* Elsie thought. Arthur went to one of the five and whispered in his ear. Elsie couldn't make out what he said, but it was no doubt that silly code. The man's lips curled into a smile as he turned to look at them, but it was not a smile that Elsie cared for.

Each man was neatly dressed in a smart tailcoat, waistcoat, and trousers, with silk cravats at their necks. They did not look at all like rebels to Elsie. Her vague uneasiness turned into a mounting dread as the men rested their hands on the holsters at their belts, and she grabbed Arthur's arm.

"So, the lady has brought more flies into her spider's nest," the man said. "Keep track, private. We will need to pay her extra for this pretty insect."

Arthur reached for his own holster as if out of instinct, but his hand found nothing. "So, the code's been found out?" he said, masking a hint of panic that Elsie could detect behind his eyes.

"Few months back," the leader drawled, and in an instant the four other men had flintlock pistols drawn and pointed at Arthur and Elsie. "That's what brought Lady Genevieve to such a noble position. She is shameless, giving her old man and her husband to the noose. An invaluable resource."

Elsie clenched her fist in anger, incensed that the slimy woman had so easily led them into a trap.

"I take it that..." Arthur began, and his statement was fluidly continued by the leader.

"Greyer's rebellion on Veturi has been eradicated. Don't you read the papers? The empire is now focused on the new threats from Sial. In fact, just recently Baron Schulhard captured the King's daughter and is taking her to trial for espionage," the leader said slowly, savoring his victory. "But I never put much stock in that. I knew it had to be your work, Pendington.

"Now don't make a struggle," he said, smiling coldly. "Odol's constitution guarantees that even traitors like you will be given a fair trial. As long as you don't resist."

26
DWELLERS

Maria awoke slowly, surfacing from her deep sleep with a yawn and a luxurious stretch. She glanced over and saw Paul's face buried in his pillow, his shoulders rising and falling gently with each breath. No doubt he'd sleep for another couple of hours if she didn't intervene. She gave him a small kiss on his cheek and frowned as he didn't seem to stir. She gave him yet another, and a smile betrayed him.

Annoyed, Maria slapped him gently on the back. *'How long have you been awake?'* she asked as soon as he opened his eyes. He blinked and responded lethargically.

'About an hour. Thought you could use the sleep.'

'You wonderful idiot,' Maria said and ruffled his thinning brown hair. *'How about you go check on Cattia and I'll start breakfast.'*

Paul nodded, and they both stretched and got themselves dressed, Paul in his tweed waistcoat and corduroy trousers, Maria in a mahogany skirt and billowy white blouse. As Maria went to start the food, she considered how blessed she was to finally have time with Paul without Arthur involved. It had been three days so far and there was no end in sight. Without Arthur underfoot it had been the nicest, quietest time since before she and Paul had been married. Cattia behaved well, giving the two privacy at night and company during the day. The only thing that troubled her was Elsie. The poor girl, led on by the illusion of rebellion and entrapped by Arthur's force of personality.

Sighing, she pushed the bitter thoughts aside. She pulled her hair up and put on the stained white apron before reaching into the straw-packed egg crate. There were only about half a dozen left, and the generous slab of cured bacon was dwindling rapidly. She'd have to start cutting into the oats and molasses-sugar to supplement their diet. She hefted the ingredients up the stairs and smiled as she thought of Cattia enjoying the meal. *She's much more satisfying to cook for than Arthur.*

She got to work at the campsite, silently bemoaning the fact that she had to cook over a fire. The stove on the ship had been busted beyond repair in the crash, and while cooking over a fire had a rustic charm, it lacked versatility. As she prepared, she felt a hand close over her shoulder. Startled, she whipped around, only to melt back into ease as she saw Cattia standing there in the blue dress, an eager smile on her face.

'*Anything I can do?*' Cat asked, signing crudely with what Maria and Paul had been able to teach her.

Maria nodded with a warm smile and handed her a steel pail. '*Water,*' she said, and indicated the direction of the small pond they had been using to gather water. Of course, they hadn't drunk from it directly—it would be boiled, strained, and boiled again just for safety. '*And hurry back! We don't want you wandering off!*'

Cattia nodded, beaming happily as she scurried off to fetch the water. Maria mused and watched as Paul got to work patching up one of the sails on the side of the airship. She cut a slice of bacon, placing it in the hot skillet and watching the fat begin to sizzle off.

As Maria began to cook the eggs in the bacon grease, she looked impatiently for Cattia to bring the water. *We'll have no oatmeal at this point.* She turned to Paul and hit the metal spoon against the pan as hard as she could to get his attention.

When he turned around, his eyes went wide, and to Maria's shock, he scrambled up the gangplank. *What on earth is he doing?* When he returned in a flash, Maria stood up abruptly. He was carrying his blunderbuss and she flinched when she saw the flash and smoke. *A warning shot?* She turned around as he was reloading his weapon and saw a figure holding Cattia by the waist, a dingy, gloved hand over her mouth.

The figure was thin. Wiry. It had a jacket of patched tweed and wool, haphazardly sewn together, and goggles covering its eyes. Its face was covered by a faded handkerchief, and its mouth was moving under the mask, but she couldn't tell what the figure was saying. Maria turned back to Paul, who ran quickly up to the campsite and began to sign with one hand as he cradled the musket in his arm.

'Let us see your face!' Paul demanded.

'Don't shoot!' the figure responded. Maria could barely take her eyes off Cattia's fearful face long enough to see what Paul was translating.

Paul shook his head. *'Hand us the girl. Then we can talk like civilized people.'*

The figure glanced at Paul and then at Maria, who had just pulled out a throwing-knife. He loosened his grip on Cattia, who bolted over to Maria and threw her arms around the woman, burying her face in her shoulder.

'Alright, let us see your face,' Paul said again.

'The air is unhealthy,' the figure said. *'Doesn't it offend your nose? Doesn't it sting your skin and burn your eyes?'*

'Regardless, we need to talk like civilized people, not thieves and vagabonds,' Paul responded.

The figure hesitated, then began to remove the coverings from his face. First came the goggles, which he pulled up onto his forehead, revealing sharp gray eyes surrounded by a circle of clean skin, which was rimmed with dirt and grime. Then he slowly lowered the cloth until it hung round his neck, revealing a sharp, bent nose, salt and pepper stubble, thin cracked lips, and pocked and dirty skin that had its share of sores. *'Are you happy now?'* he said. Maria could at last read his lips well enough, though she could tell he was speaking in a thick accent.

'*Yes,'* Paul said simply.

'Since we are acting civilized, could you drop your weapons? We Dwellers are never armed.'

Paul nodded and set the musket on the ground. Maria looked to Cattia, who was trembling with fear and shock. She reluctantly shoved the knife into a sheath hidden beneath her skirt. *'He could be dangerous!'* she commented furiously, glaring daggers at Paul. *'At best, he's a thief!*

'You can't judge a man as quickly as that. He hasn't hurt us yet.'

'Yet!' Maria emphasized.

Paul sighed. *'What do you mean, "Dwellers"? Are there more of you in this horrible land? What are you doing?'*

'We could ask you the same. This 'horrible land' is the land above our home. It is plenteous in resources, both mechanical and, with enough skill, edible.' The strange accent forced Maria to keep her attention on Paul's translation, rather than relying on lip reading.

'What is your name?' Paul asked calmly.

'Clemen. And you are Paul and Maria Kauisol, though I don't know the girl.'

Maria's arms trembled, threatening to go limp. She searched the gaunt face for any trace of familiarity. *Yes, his eyes.* His eyes— the same piercing gray eyes she had once fallen in love with. But the rest of him was a man Maria did not know. Paul frowned but nodded slowly. *'Yes, I know you. We left you at Bolden. In fact, you left us at Bolden. What are you doing here?'*

'You only left me behind and turned Captain Pendington against me because you were afraid of me being close to your wife.'

'*That is beside the point!*' Paul roared, so loudly that Cattia clasped her hands over her ears. He began to speak rapidly, forgetting to sign what he was saying.

In the absence of Paul's translations, Maria's attention wandered and fixed on Clemen. His haggard shape was far from the broad, strong features she remembered. His gray streaked hair, tousled in a greasy, stringy mess had once been the softest, cleanest-cut dark hair. He was always clean shaven before, but now he had the ugliest excuse for stubble she had ever seen. He hadn't been bad to look at, and before Paul, Arthur's former quartermaster had caught her eye with how handsome he was. But now...

From what she could tell, the argument was only growing more heated. She hoped that it was not over her, especially in front of the young girl. Finally, Maria saw Paul say something so horrible it made her gasp. Cattia broke from her side and ran back to the ship in tears. Clemen rushed forward, snatching a toasting fork from the cooking fire where the forgotten breakfast had burned to ashes.

Maria snatched the knife from beneath her skirts and instinctively raised it to throw. Paul grabbed her arm and forced it back down as several other scraggly figures scrambled down the nearest mound to restrain Clemen.

Frustrated, Maria dropped the knife and shoved Paul away. '*Civility, remember? I know, easy for me to say, but at least I didn't go and say* that *to him!*' She thought of another stinger, though she immediately regretted saying it. '*If you'd shown this much backbone with Arthur, we wouldn't be in this mess.*'

Paul's face crumpled, and Maria felt as though she'd driven one of her knives into his heart, and hers as well. She was glad the others around them couldn't understand what she had said. '*Forgive me, my love. You're only standing up for me...*'

Her words were lost to the air, since he stopped paying attention to her, his face sullen. After a few moments of talking with the newcomers, however, she saw his face light up and he began signing excitedly. She could barely follow until he said, '*Give them food!*'

'*I'm not cooking for all of them, if that's what you mean,*' she replied.

Paul gave a brief laugh, and a reserved smile replaced his previously hurt expression. '*Not quite. They've offered us a trade. In exchange for our food stores—well, most of it— they'll fix our ship!*'

Maria frowned as she stared at the three, or perhaps four, dozen men who had gathered over the camp clearing, all wearing either goggles or spectacles, and coverings over their noses and mouths. Somehow, each looked ganglier than the last, with greasy, stringy hair, patched threadbare clothes, and shoddy gloves. Some had tools jammed into belts or strapped like a brace of pistols over their chests, but none carried weapons.

'*What choice do we have?*' Maria said, somewhat deflated.

Paul nodded to the Dwellers and turned back to put his hand on her shoulder reassuringly. '*We'll be okay. We'll keep enough food to get to Bolden. There's enough stored on the ship for months. They've not seen real food in a while.*' He sighed and seemed to do the same thing that Maria was doing: scanning the crowd for Clemen. He pointed the man out to her, and with some difficulty she spotted him. Clemen had put the mask and goggles back on and was nearly indistinguishable from the rest. He was one of them now, no longer of the Odolian world.

'*I'll go check on Cattia,*' Paul began, but Maria shook her head.

'*The way you were talking? What you said? No, you keep an eye these people. Make sure they stay off the ship until we're ready. I'll go check on Cattia.*'

Giving him a peck on the cheek, she ran to the shipwreck and looked out over the gathering at the campsite. Then, movement caught her eye that made her look past the nearby heaps of rubbish. There were more people than she could count: women, children, and elderly as well. All were dressed in bizarre patchwork clothing with covered faces. They flowed through the Wreckage and into the clearing in a steady stream, moving easily through the heaps of refuse.

Sighing, Maria admitted defeat. Their time of relaxation was over.

Maria stirred the huge cauldron of stew alongside another woman, Carla. The two had developed a friendly acquaintance over the past two days. Since she couldn't see their faces, it was difficult for Maria to gain any sort of relationship with the Dwellers. Cattia, on the other hand, began to wear a cloth mask and a veil within the first day, and was socializing with the Dwellers more than with Paul and Maria. *Paul really shook her up with that outburst*, she thought regretfully.

She glanced at where the men were. The airship was now upright and the propellers were completely repaired. The engine had been installed at last, and the only thing left was to finish patching the hull. Paul had been working nonstop, directing the men and supervising every sprocket, bolt, and pulley. Maria hadn't been expecting a tent city to be set up at their small resting place in the Wreckage, and yet there they were: about a hundred Dwellers with their weathered canopies set up over shabby bed rolls. She never saw any of their eyes, either. They feared the Wreckage, Paul said. Some even preferred to blindfold themselves than to go about with exposed eyes, and they only ever removed their masks to eat.

Some of them were children, many of them were women, but most were men, and often fairly old men. They were not expressive at all, and even the children were reserved and slow in movement. When Maria asked more about them, where they came from and who they were, Paul's explanation had been difficult for her to grasp.

'They live underground, far away from here. This is only a small group; they estimate twenty thousand total, though no one has

counted. Apparently, they've lived out here for many years. Some of the kids around Elsie's age were born out here. They live off what is thrown away by Gorand, though apparently they grow roots and mushrooms and small vegetables in their underground city as well.'

Maria had accepted the explanation, though it did not answer the questions swimming about in her mind. Where had they come from, originally? Out of the city? From the north? Most of them seemed to be native Odolians, but it was difficult for her to tell when they spent so much time swathed in their strange garments. They brought odd bits to add to the stews she helped cook for the group: strange roots and mushrooms and battered canned goods rescued from the trash. She could hardly fathom that the entire community's existence could have remained secret for so long, especially when they lived just outside the baron's own city. Yet it did not seem so strange, considering how little attention was paid to the Wreckage.

Maria's attention had wandered, allowing Paul to sneak up on her. Of course, he wasn't intending to, but the unexpected hand on her shoulder still made her start and whirl around, fist raised instinctively to strike. When she saw it was Paul, she rolled her eyes at him, and was about to turn back to her work, but he caught her arm, signing urgently.

'Maria, we need to leave now.'

Maria's eyes narrowed in confusion and she shook her head. *'What are you talking about? We can't leave now. The ship's not even half done! It has more holes than a block of cheese.'*

Paul's expression was grim and determined. *'I was just speaking to Clemen and some of the newer Dwellers about what Arthur and Elsie are doing. I tried to be circumspect, but Clemen guessed they were looking for the rebels, and told me that they heard Greyer's rebellion had been eliminated from Veturi!'*

'So what?' Maria scoffed. *'That just means they won't find any rebels and Arthur's cracked plan will fail.'*

'No, they won't find any rebels. They'll find Cadbury instead!' Paul looked over at a small group of Dwellers, who had gathered

expectantly near the cook fires. *'With your permission, I'll tell them to unload any food they need.'*

'No, you will not!' Maria signed sharply, feeling tears well up in her eyes. *'We are not going to fly half a ship for hundreds of miles across the Wastes, not even to rescue your beloved captain. We can wait here until Arthur gets back.'*

'If we don't go now, he may never come back.' Paul's hand motions were slow, deliberate, and there was a determined glint in his eyes that Maria knew she would have trouble standing up to. *'I'm bound to him, Maria. I promised his father before he died that I would look after him. And Elsie is out there with him. The sooner we get back to him, the less chance anything bad happens to them, and the less chance he has to leave her behind. I doubt he'd do it out of malice, but you know how he can treat people.'*

'Yes, it's how he treats you too! And what about Cattia? Are we just going to leave her?'

Paul looked at where Cattia was seated, talking to a young man with wavy dark hair. Cattia was smiling behind her cloth mask, her blue eyes glittering.

'I'm sorry I exploded like that the other day,' Paul said solemnly.

'Don't be sorry to me, be sorry to her!'

'I've tried, but she doesn't even like to be near me at this point.'

'Have you told her?' Maria said. *'Is she coming with us?'*

Paul shook his head, his mouth set in a firm line, his eyes tired. *'She says she hopes Elsie will visit her. Maybe come stay with her, away from danger.'*

Maria huffed in frustration and looked back at Carla and the other women cooking the midday meal. *'She's made up her mind, then. Let's leave after lunch. I can't imagine an hour will make much of a difference. It will give an hour more to patch up the ship, too. Besides, we need our strength, and you need to eat something. I'm not going to let you destroy yourself for his sake.'*

Paul frowned for a moment, but relented almost at once and went to inform Clemen and the other Dwellers of their decision.

He argued with Clemen and a few others for nearly half an hour, trying to convince them to come with the pair, but no one wanted to get near society of any kind. Maria felt she couldn't blame them. Perhaps it would be better out here, in a literal wasteland, than anywhere with Arthur. Certainly, it would have been more peaceful.

By evening, the *Heart of Resistance* was in the air once more, its name emblazoned on the side of the ship in bold red paint by Paul himself. Looking back at their campsite in the Wreckage as it dwindled away into the distance, Maria couldn't help but tear up once more. How long would it be until their lives stopped revolving around Arthur Pendington? How long until she and Paul could once more be at peace?

DREADFUL CIRCUMSTANCES

I've seen Odol's trials firsthand. I wouldn't like our chances," Arthur said with a grim smile. His eyes darted around the cramped opera box, searching for an out. Velvet covered chairs sat vacant, as the men who had occupied them were now on their feet, pistols drawn and leveled at the two intruders. Arthur and Elsie were motioned to stand by the railing of the booth, as far from the door as possible. The men lined up opposite them, blocking any hope of escape. One of them was sent for backup, but three loaded pistols still remained between them and safety.

"I said fair, Mister Pendington," the leader said. "Guilty men do get hanged, you know. That is what we consider fair. What you once considered justice." He was a tall, lanky man, with slicked back hair and thin black mustaches.

"Ulysses Cadbury," Arthur said, looking the man up and down with kindling recognition in his eyes. "Just as I remember. You always did prefer the law with only letters and no heart."

"Heart or no," Cadbury replied smoothly, "I doubt that you could defend yourself for stealing a ship, killing seven Gorand militia men, and wounding one innocent toll booth worker. In the best of times, you still hang."

"Well, she had nothing to do with it," Arthur said, nodding in Elsie's direction. "Let her go."

"No," Elsie said, sticking her chin out defiantly at the man, though she was trembling with fear. "I'm not so cowardly as that. I'm as guilty as he is. If you take him, you'll have to take me too."

What she saw Arthur do next at first confused her, then gave her a small spark of hope. He turned to face her, but his hand went over the edge of the railing behind them subtly, and he tugged on the banner looped over the front of the box, as though to test its strength. Elsie had no idea what he was doing, but she sensed that he had a plan.

"I can't let you do that, kid," he said, giving her a half smile before turning back to Cadbury. "You know, this opera is pretty good. What's it called?"

"Never knew you were one for the arts, Pendington. It's called *Fine del Mondo*. It's Arberitti's newest work. Good, don't you think?"

"Alright I suppose. I just think it could use a little more..." Arthur trailed off, searching for the right word. "Excitement."

"Yes, that's the Arthur I remember. Always the brute, eh? Surprised Helena put up with you for so long." Cadbury smiled wolfishly, showing brilliant white teeth. Elsie glanced at Arthur, but his face did not change. "Anyway," Cadbury continued, when it was clear that his barb hadn't baited Arthur, "I'm glad that you aren't in charge of writing the operas."

"Oh, I don't know. I may think about getting involved," Arthur said with a strange determination in his voice. His arm shot out and he seized the wrist of the man who was pointing the gun at Elsie, pulling him sharply towards himself. The man staggered, and Arthur wrestled the gun from his hand and flipped him bodily over the railing of the balcony just as the music swelled up in another crescendo. The man landed with a thud in the middle of the crowd, causing several women to scream and others to scramble to their feet. Arthur moved quickly, turning to shield Elsie with his body as the other two thugs fired their pistols in confusion. Elsie shrieked, squeezing her eyes shut, clutching desperately at Arthur's lapels.

"Hold on, kid," Arthur whispered, wrapping an arm around her. Elsie held on as tight as she could, eyes still shut and face pressed against the front of his jacket, arms thrown around his shoulders. He hoisted them both over the railing.

"Don't let them get away!" Cadbury roared, but they were already over the edge of the booth. For one desperate moment, they clung to the decorative banner that hung across the railing, feet dangling over the crowd below. Elsie opened her eyes just long enough to see Arthur aim his stolen pistol and shoot. Ears ringing, she clung to Arthur as the long stretch of banners came loose and swung them down onto the stage below. She landed badly, feeling her ankle roll beneath her, but Arthur landed like a cat and was back on his feet in an instant. The actors, actresses, and orchestra members in the pit below were already scattering with cries of fear.

Arthur snatched up a prop sword from the stage and grabbed Elsie's arm, pulling her stage right. "Ah! I can't, my ankle..." she choked out, limping desperately along with him, past tables of props, racks of costumes, and bits of painted wooden scenery. "Where are we going?"

"We have to get to the tunnels," Arthur said calmly, keeping his eyes fixed straight ahead even as they heard the clomp of boots and the shouts of guards rushing up the stairs to the stage.

"Arthur, I can't walk!" Elsie cried, trying to free herself from his vice-like grip. "Please, I can't keep up..."

Arthur paid no attention to her complaint, changing direction sharply to head down a corridor lined with doors. Extras and stagehands scattered as they approached, ducking through doorways into dressing rooms and powder rooms. When Elsie finally collapsed from pain, Arthur didn't miss a beat. He swooped down and scooped her up into his arms, still clutching the prop sword, as though that would help him. He carried her like a child, as if she weighed nothing, despite her encumbering dress. Over his shoulder, Elsie could see the dimly lit underbelly of the theater receding behind them.

They reached the end of the corridor, which terminated in a T-junction. To the left, rickety backstage stairs climbed into the darkness. To the right, the corridor continued, faintly lit by flickering gas lamps, into the interminable distance. Arthur took neither option, however, and instead forced open a concealed door in the tunnel wall, which at first glance appeared to be merely another part of the brick in front of them. They stepped out into a gloomy tunnel and Arthur kicked the door shut behind them and began to run once more.

"Thank you for helping me," Elsie gasped, squinting ahead into the darkness as she tried to figure out where they were. "I don't think I would have made it otherwise." She tried to laugh, but it was hollow in the gloom.

"If I didn't help you, you would have been tortured for information that you don't have," Arthur replied coolly. They reached the end of the tunnel and emerged into the shadow of the towering theater. The plaza stretched out before them, unnervingly empty and silent.

"We should make our way back to the shops," Arthur said. "I'm sure there's somewhere we can hide."

Elsie nodded and Arthur shifted her weight in his arms in preparation to start off again. As he broke into run, she caught a glimpse over his shoulder of shapes moving towards them in the dark of the tunnel. Before she could cry out, the muzzle flash of a musket revealed a score of men running towards them, each dressed in Veturi uniform.

Elsie screamed and Arthur flung them both to the cobbles as a full volley of musket shots thundered overhead. The dim coolness of the night was torn by the clamor of alarm bells, further deafening Elsie as Arthur hoisted her up and scrambled forward.

Behind them, the guards paused to reload, buying them a few precious moments. But Arthur made it only halfway across the bridge to the next car before another shot rang out. He cried out, stumbling forward, his neck and jaw clenched in pain as he righted himself and crossed the last few feet of bridge to the car beyond.

"Arthur! Are you hurt?" Elsie gasped.

"Only...grazed me," he said as he began to run once more, though this time his gait was much less certain.

Over his shoulder, Elsie saw that the rest of the guards were lining up behind them for another volley. As they leveled their muskets in a grim line, she cried out, tugging on Arthur's lapel. "They're about to fire—ah!" With a grunt, Arthur practically tackled her to the ground once more, finally dropping the useless wooden sword with a clatter. Bullets streaked overhead. She heard the explosion of the round after they fired, the sound reaching them a split second later across the gap between cars.

She lay on her back for a moment, petrified, the cold cobbles pressing through the satin gown into her spine. As soon as the volley was over, Arthur picked her up and, at a slower pace this time, began to sprint down the lane. Unfortunately, there were no turns, no obstacles, and nowhere to hide that wasn't barred by tall wrought iron fences. From what she could see in the dimness of the night, the detachment of guards had stopped to argue their course of action. It seemed that the guards were unable to decide whether to continue pursuing them or stop and reload their weapons. They were interrupted a minute later by the voice of Cadbury shouting from behind them, only barely heard by Elsie over the rumble of the tracks below.

They reached the next car with no further hindrance. Uniform townhouses lined the paved street. "We need to go further," Arthur said in a strained voice, slowing down for only a moment to catch his breath. "All these doors will be locked for the night, and I doubt we would get a warm reception."

"Arthur, you're hurt. We need to stop," Elsie said half-heartedly.

"I'm not hurt," Arthur lied through clenched teeth, continuing to lumber forward.

"Well, as soon as we get to-" She was cut off once more by a shot from behind them, and one of the gas streetlamps shattered with a *pop*. Behind them, the small force of guards was gaining ground. It appeared their numbers had grown.

To her dismay, Elsie saw that the townhouses on each side of the street had no alleys to duck into. Arthur was not daunted however and leapt over a flight of front steps to crouch behind a metal grating. The gambit appeared to work, and as the volley fired off, bullets ricocheted off the metal and struck the concrete steps. Only one whistled through the grating, striking the brick facade of the house behind them. In a moment Arthur was on his feet once more and took off like a shot down the street, endeavoring to beat their reload time.

That was when the real volley began. One smaller group of guards fell back to reload as another stepped up to take their place. Fresh muskets trained on Arthur and Elsie as they fled away through the broad, open street. Stones cracked and exploded near his feet as Arthur ran with a newfound burst of speed. One bullet struck home, causing him to jolt forward once more with a groan, though this time he did not slow down.

As the volley continued, Elsie saw lights coming on in the darkened windows overhead. Some people even threw open the panes, sticking their heads out to see what the commotion was. The alarm bells followed them down the train, as Cadbury and his men alerted more and more guards. *We'll have an army on us by the end of the night*, Elsie thought dully.

Injured though he was, Arthur ran doggedly on until they crossed over to the next car. Here, a combination of fine townhouses and expensive shops lined the street, this time separated by narrow alleyways. But Arthur ignored the alleys. Instead, he made for one of the stables which Elsie had noticed earlier that evening. Kicking in the door, he ran inside, setting her down wordlessly on a bale of hay. The unfamiliar stable smell filled Elsie's nose, the feed, the straw, and the fouler smells mixing to create a surprisingly comforting aroma. She stared in awe at the four horses that were housed inside. For a moment, she almost forgot the dreadful circumstances of her arrival here.

Arthur yanked open one of the stall doors and began to untie the horse inside, a gray spotted one with a white mane and tail. "Get the door open!" he shouted at her, then clicked his tongue and whistled gently to the horse, which was snorting nervously as Arthur bustled around it. Elsie saw dull crimson puddling beneath Arthur's feet.

Shaking herself from her reverie, she found the latch to the large front door of the stable, which was big enough to let an entire cart through. The moment she opened it, she saw Cadbury out front, ordering his men to surround the building. She grabbed the handle and tried to pull the door back shut with all her might.

"Arthur, they're..."

But Arthur was beside her, riding bareback on the big gray horse, and without heeding her warning he swept her off her feet, up onto the horse's back in front of him. She clung, terrified, to the horse's neck. Arthur dug his heels into the horse's flanks and they bolted forward through the half-open stable door, scattering unprepared guards left and right. A few wild shots were fired, clattering off the cobbles or the buildings around them, but they were off at speed, and Elsie only just caught the look of shock on Cadbury's face as they galloped away down the street.

PRONE

Elsie was sure that she had never traveled as fast as she did that night on horseback. The buildings blurred by, and instead of crossing the bridge to the next car, the horse simply leapt straight over the gap. Elsie shrieked, though this time it wasn't out of fear, but excitement. She clung to the neck of the gray horse tightly, staring out over its bouncing head and feeling its powerful muscles ripple beneath its coat as it ran. She knew little of animals and had only rarely seen horses pulling carts from her window at Threadbury's. All she knew now was that if she ever had another chance to ride one, hopefully under better circumstances, she would absolutely take it.

Finally, they were far enough ahead that they couldn't even hear the shouts of Cadbury and his men over the rumble of the tracks and the clatter of hooves against the paving stones.

"Have we lost them?" Elsie gasped, glancing over her shoulder into the gloom behind.

"A little longer," Arthur said gruffly. "Then we'll have to leave the horse and proceed on foot."

Grimacing, Elsie buried her hands in the horse's mane and held on a little longer. They finally reached the last of the town-homes and Arthur eased the beast to a halt.

"I think here is as good a place as any to stop," he said quietly.

She perched on the horse as Arthur climbed off, somewhat clumsily. He reached up to help Elsie down. It had begun to rain, a thin, misty drizzle that made everything a little hazy and chilled Elsie to the bone. Arthur limped as they crossed over to the next car. Elsie, walking carefully on her rolled ankle, looked up at him with concern.

She looped her arm through Arthur's in a vain hope that he could lean on her for strength. His face was growing paler by the second in the dull glow of the gas lamps and a steady dribble of blood marked their trail every few steps before being washed away by the rain. She had thought that seeing blood would be more shocking, even disgusting, but already she was numb to it.

"We should find somewhere to rest," she murmured.

To her surprise, Arthur agreed. "Yes. We should try to find an apothecary."

He was quite pleased with himself when, not a hundred yards down the street, they came across a shabby physician's shop on the right hand side, something Elsie had completely missed during their "shopping trip" the day before. As they stood before the shuttered shop, Arthur considering how best to get inside, Elsie reached up and felt the top of her head. As she had surmised, her hat had long ago blown off. On top of that, the skirt of her beautiful blue dress was torn and filthy from the multiple times they'd dropped down to avoid gunfire.

They circled around through a nearby alley, and without a second's warning, Arthur kicked in the back door of the apothecary. It caused an awful racket and within seconds a small man in a nightshirt and cap came down the back stairs, brandishing a golf club.

"What're you doin' in my shop?" he hollered. "Help! Robbers!" He was a wiry fellow, with a crop of unkempt white hair, a shabby white beard, and battered pince-nez. Arthur had a resigned expression in his eyes as he approached the man, hands spread disarmingly.

"Sir, we simply needed some supplies to tend to our wounds, and I'm sure that is something you'll be able to help us with..." As he spoke, Arthur edged nearer to the man, who continued to wave the club threateningly. Upon reaching striking distance, he punched the man sharply across the chin. Elsie gasped. The man groaned and collapsed to the ground, his club clattering on the floorboards beside him.

"What did you have to go and do that for!" Elsie cried as Arthur stepped over the man's prone form to get behind the counter.

"Can't have him going to the guards. He'll be okay. Just a bit of a headache when he wakes up."

Groaning, Elsie followed Arthur into the storefront, where they could see clearly out of the big glass windowpanes into the empty street. Rummaging through the shelves behind the counter, Arthur collected a few bandages, salves, and some pills, which he scooped unceremoniously into his arms before ducking back into the storeroom with Elsie. Arthur knelt, spilling the supplies into a heap on the dusty floor. He snatched up a roll of bandages and tore off a strip. "Let me see your ankle. Is it broken?"

"You've been shot," Elsie hedged. "You need it more than I do!"

"Sit down. You probably just need something to splint your ankle."

"I'm not going to-"

"Sit!" Arthur snapped, but she didn't think it was anger in his voice. Elsie relented and sat down.

Crouching in front of her, his brows knit in concentration, Arthur slipped the battered shoe off her swollen foot. "Not too bad. Just needs a bit of support," he mumbled to himself as he began to wrap the bandages tightly around her ankle. He hardly seemed to notice her, instead appearing lost in his work. Somehow, Elsie found his inattention comforting. Though the binding hurt quite badly, she could tell that it would make walking a great deal easier. Arthur seemed to know what he was about.

"Okay," she said as Arthur finished his work, "Now tell me where you've been shot so I can help you."

Arthur sat back on his heels, his face slack and dull in the dim light. "Well, three times at least. I think the ones on my shoulder and side were only grazes. The big problem is the one in my thigh." He winced, repositioning himself so he could straighten his legs. "And unless you've been trained in surgery like Maria, I'm not sure I'd trust you to get a musket ball out."

"It's...inside you?" Elsie asked, feeling bile rise in her throat as she looked apprehensively at his wounded leg.

"Yeah, solid lead. Can't be good for me." He laughed humorlessly. "Don't think it hit anything important, or I wouldn't be here. Worst that'll happen is I have to lose the leg. And I know Maria hates amputations."

"You will not," Elsie said firmly, scrambling off her seat and dropping to her knees beside Arthur. "Let me see it." She pawed over the torn cloth of his trouser leg. "The bullet went through. You're bleeding on the other side too. Give me those bandages." She moved swiftly, applying a healing salve, wrapping both sides of the wound with cloths and bandages and more cloths, applying as much pressure as she could.

For once, she was grateful for the strenuous work over the dye vats which had strengthened her scrawny arms and for the grandmotherly wisdom of the older women, who had taken care of any "little" injuries caused by the machinery. Of course, she knew she wasn't doing everything right. She was no doctor, but she wasn't about to let Arthur bleed out.

"Okay, where else were you hurt?" she asked at last, wiping her hands on an alcohol-soaked rag. She was flushed, and she eyed her handiwork nervously, expecting every moment to see a telltale flash of red seeping through the bandages.

Arthur wriggled out of the torn and bloodied tailcoat, discarding it on the floor behind him. His white shirt was filthy with blood and sweat and he unbuttoned it as well, gingerly peeling it off his wounded shoulder. As he had implied, these wounds were superficial, though still ugly. Elsie shifted closer to him on her knees, sucking in a deep breath as she prepared herself for the task ahead.

The wound on his side was barely more than a nasty scratch, potentially caused by some ricochet of shrapnel. His shoulder, however, was marked with a deep furrow, the sight of which threatened to turn Elsie's stomach. Nevertheless, she cleaned both wounds, applied the waxy salve, and bandaged them in silence. No doubt they would join the network of other pale scars that crisscrossed Arthur's arms and torso. She hadn't noticed them before, out in the Wreckage, but it was hard not to up close. Twice, she opened her mouth to ask him where they had come from, what on earth he'd done to end up with so many, but each time she bit back the words. She was beginning to realize that she still knew next to nothing about Arthur and his life.

Elsie and Arthur sat in the back of the apothecary for an hour, resting themselves. Arthur even dozed a little, resting his head back on a sack of beeswax pellets and drifting off as if it were the best bed in the world. Elsie remained awake, glancing nervously back and forth between Arthur and the storeroom doorway. He awoke abruptly and got to his feet with a groan and a wince, favoring his injured leg.

"We should get moving," he said, struggling back into the filthy white shirt. Every time he moved his injured shoulder, he winced sharply, and though he did his best to hide it, he limped when he crossed the storeroom to the back door.

"Where will we go?" Elsie asked, shivering as they went back out into the dank alley. Despite the splint, her ankle still throbbed with every step, and she found herself limping a little too.

"To the top of the tallest building."

"Why not find a nice corner to hide in?" Elsie asked, feeling her ankle ache in anticipation.

"That would be the first place they'd look. No one would expect us to be up there."

"Why not?"

"You'll see," Arthur said curtly. "When I say duck, you must do *exactly* as I say. Understood?"

Elsie nodded, though she did not understand what he meant. She found she was too tired to inquire. They walked the length of the alley, which ended in a brick wall. The only thing back here was an overflowing trash barrel and a rickety fire escape, which climbed the side of the building into the darkness above.

"This will do, I think," Arthur said, rattling the railing of the structure gently, as though to test its strength. "When I get to the second floor, you need to follow. Until then, keep an eye out and warn me if the goons catch up." Elsie nodded again, squinting up at the building with apprehension.

Despite his limp, Arthur began to climb nimbly up the fire escape, the wire mesh flexing alarmingly under his weight. At the bottom of the steep metal steps, Elsie balanced nervously on her heels, her mouth dry. The structure seemed unsturdy, and her hands quickly became stained with rust as she gripped the railing tightly, trying to calm her racing heartbeat.

As she expected, Arthur didn't even pause for her to catch up when he reached the second story, so she started up behind him. The rusty steel creaked under her, and she stopped, glancing over her shoulder to check the street. Somehow, her hesitation and carefulness seemed to amplify every tiny noise as she shifted on the creaking staircase. That was when she saw a guard pass.

For one fascinating moment, Elsie could see the face of the guard quite plainly in the warm yellow gaslight of the street. He was a young man, probably four or five years older than her at the most, and not unkind looking. His chin was rather scruffy, and he had auburn hair that seemed to blend in with the peach-orange uniform that he wore. He seemed about to pass by the narrow alleyway altogether, when Elsie saw his eyes flick to the side and meet her gaze for a split second.

Through the thrum of blood in her ears, she couldn't hear exactly what he shouted, but she saw him level his musket right at her, and that was enough for her to turn and run, scrambling up the fire escape as quickly as she could. She cursed under her breath, and nearly bit her tongue when she realized what she'd said. *Madam Harban would have had a field day with me,* she thought sardonically as she continued to scramble up the stairs, practically crawling at times in the effort to move faster.

She felt the fire escape shake beneath her. The men had begun filing up the metal stairs one by one. Elsie forced her legs to move. She ran even faster, dashing up the last few flights. She reached the last step and was by lifted by the strong hands of Arthur, over a concrete ledge and onto the roof of the building. Her knees wobbled with exhaustion as she stood there, looking back at the trembling fire escape. In a moment, they would reach the roof.

"You're doing great, kid. Now help me topple the stairs," Arthur said, rushing back to the edge of the building.

Elsie's mouth dropped open. "What?"

"Quick, before they get up here!" He dropped to his knees where the steel posts were bolted into the grimy bricks, and the muscles in his shoulders flexed as he tried to pry the two apart, fresh blood staining his shirt. He grunted in pain, and Elsie finally knelt to help him.

It was the hardest she had ever strained herself, and it almost felt as if her arms were going to break, but at last she heard a *pop.* The strain became less and Elsie pushed with a renewed burst of strength as she saw the first soldier drawing near. *Pop, pop,* and the *creak* of screaming steel echoed across the rooftops as the flimsy fire escape began to tilt backward into the alley. Elsie heard the guards below cry out in shock, followed by the *crash* of the metal structure as it collapsed to the ground. From below she heard loud cursing and shouting echoing up as the men endeavored to extricate themselves from the tangled remains of the fire escape.

"Come on, kid," Arthur said, clambering awkwardly to his feet and heading for the other end of the flat rectangular roof. "They'll find a way to get up here eventually. I won't feel comfortable till we're a couple buildings down the line."

Elsie turned to follow and stopped, gaping in awe. Looming in the distance past the wasteland was a tall, jagged mass, black against the cloudy night sky. *Mountains!* She'd never seen anything like it. The rolling cliffs ate up the sky as Veturi barreled onward, growing closer and closer with every second. Shaking herself, Elsie jogged after Arthur, though her eyes strayed to the mountains every now and then.

The buildings on this car were crammed close together, with only the narrowest of alleys between. Even still, when they came to the next gap between buildings, Elsie began to feel a little light-headed. The next roof over was about three feet below them, and covered with large chimneys which were, thankfully, unlit at this time of night. Narrow walkways ran between the chimneys, allowing utilitarian access for sweeps or maintenance men. Gritting his teeth, Arthur leapt down, landing in a crouch with a little gasp of pain only faintly audible above the wind and the rumbling of the rails. He straightened slowly, turned around, and held out his arms.

Elsie jumped, her numb legs barely propelling her over the gap. Arthur caught her heavily, biting back a curse when her hand reflexively gripped his injured shoulder. "Come off it, kid," he whispered, unceremoniously dropping her onto the walkway before striding across the roof once more. Elsie followed him silently.

The next several buildings were joined by walkways, which were much easier to cross. Then they reached another tall building, taller than any she'd yet seen, which was shoved so close to the next one that there was barely a gap. After a few attempts, Arthur scrambled up over the wide parapet and vanished over the side.

After a moment, his head appeared over the wall once more. He wore a grim smile.

"Come on up, kid, we're at the end of the line."

Reaching up, Elsie took his hands and scrambled over the parapet with the last of her strength. On the other side, she dropped a couple feet into a thick layer of gravel. The parapet was about knee high and the surface of the roof was low enough that if Elsie laid down, she would be completely concealed by the wall around her.

Arthur stood proudly, hands on his hips, surveying his surroundings. "We're on top of the guardhouse. I can't imagine they'd think we would stop here. They'll assume we've moved on a lot further, or even gotten off the roofs by now. Plus, this will be perfect..."

"Are you sure, Arthur?" Elsie asked softly, looking around.

"The other roofs along this way are sloped, and I don't like our chances with that." His eyes flicked to her.

"Alright, I'm good," she said with a nervous laugh, and sat down on the gravel with her back against the parapet.

Arthur did the same and for a moment they rested, despite the fact that she could hear alarm bells going off further down the train. *Maybe we will be safe here. Maybe we can just wait here until...until what?* They had no hope of being rescued. Elsie twisted the smooth skirt of her dress in her hands, which had begun to sweat. *We're going to die out here. I'll never see Cattia again...*

"You okay kid? What's wrong?" Arthur asked, startling Elsie. Elsie reflexively wiped a tear from her cheek. She hadn't realized she'd been crying.

"I'm alright," Elsie muttered, rubbing her nose. "I'm just a little worried."

"So am I, kid," Arthur admitted. He did not look at her face, but rather stared off into the distance. Elsie noticed that the sky was beginning to lighten. "It wasn't supposed to go this way. When Paul, Maria, and I first entered Gorand, it was different. Odol refused to admit that any form of rebellion still existed. Greyer was dead, and so the emperor decided to pretend that the silly rebellion died with him. But it didn't."

"What does that have to do with you though?" Elsie murmured. "You weren't one of Greyer's men. I thought you hated them."

"So I do. But a broken clock is right twice a day. There is evil in Odol. I wanted to stop a bit of it. When Greyer died, the big nobles, like Schulhard, stopped funding a lot of the home front military activities, which left an opening for fellows like me, and our friends on Veturi. We had a few operations. Some went better than others, but all were at least somewhat successful. Even procuring an airship was successful," he mused, "and I never thought that it would actually work."

Elsie barely had the energy to scrunch up her face. "But what did you accomplish? It seems to me that Odol doesn't care what you do, or the messages you're trying to send. All it cares about is money. I know that firsthand. I worked for them for ten long years of my life, just so that Threadbury could make more money off the empire—or rather so that the empire could get a cheaper price from Threadbury. They didn't care about *us*." Her voice gained conviction as she spoke, as she finally realized what she'd been thinking all along. "They *never* cared about the poor and destitute or the homeless. Arthur, they *don't care* if you live or die either. I'm sure that if they could use you to make them money, they'd gladly help you tear things down and steal airships!"

"Then I'd do something else," Arthur said sternly, finally leveling his stoney gaze at her. "Because I can't live my life letting them win. I've lived too much of my life doing that already. I ordered the death of thousands of civilians. Innocents. I can't let that happen again. For three years the dreadnoughts have been dormant, but now they are waking. I wanted to stop them before they could embark on another reign of terror. But now..." He trailed off, his gaze traveling once more to the mountains ahead.

Elsie wasn't sure she understood. At Threadbury's, things like politics and war were not discussed, at least not openly or often. It was hard to connect what he was saying with the actual meaning behind it. She felt she was missing some larger piece of the puzzle, of his past. She still knew so little about this man. Even after all of their escapades and daring escapes, he had hardly dropped the wall between them one inch.

She opened her mouth to speak, but found she had nothing to say. Arthur also seemed at a loss for words, and once again he was staring out at the rapidly brightening horizon with a vacant expression on his face.

Absently, she looked back at the front of the train and was shocked to see how close the mountains had become. She could finally see what they were heading for: cut into the mountains was an enormous tunnel, illuminated faintly by gas lamps, that was nearly twice as wide as Veturi and just barely taller than the train. She saw the engine miles in front of her pass underneath the low lip, smoke billowing out to the side for lack of anywhere else to go. She pulled herself up higher against the parapet, leaning over and squinting ahead, trying to see into the tunnel.

"Up there!"

Elsie heard the shouts from the street below. Arthur was on his feet in an instant, heading for the edge of the roof. They saw Cadbury and eight guards racing around to the other side of the building where there was an alley, and, to Elsie's dismay, a metal ladder that stopped just shy of the parapet. Arthur tried in vain to break the riveting as he had with the fire escape. But this ladder was far sturdier and he couldn't get much leverage in his awkward position above it.

"What are we going to do?" Elsie gasped as she looked over the ledge. The building was tall, but the men were climbing rapidly.

Arthur looked over his shoulder toward the front of the train and took a deep breath. "We wait here," he said softly.

"What? Are you crazy? They'll be up here any second!"

"Just do as I say," Arthur instructed, ignoring Elsie's panicked words.

Biting her lip, she clutched the skirt of her dress and moved away from the ladder. Arthur gripped her shoulder and dragged her further back, until they were both standing in the center of the rooftop. Within minutes, the first guard hoisted himself over the edge and stood on the gravel. He was followed by another, and another, each with a musket strapped over their shoulder, which they unslung quickly and leveled at the two fugitives, fanning out to surround them. Arthur stood, gripping Elsie's shoulder so tight that it hurt. Five more came up, and then Cadbury appeared at last, holding a pistol. The sky was beginning to turn pink behind them as the sun rose sleepily over the horizon.

What shocked Elsie most was how tired the guards looked. After hours of pursuit, even Cadbury had developed dark eye bags and a shadow of scruff on his clean-shaven cheeks. Pulling the hammer back on the pistol he held, he began to speak hoarsely.

"It's over, Pendington. You haven't anywhere else to run. I have mobilized every guard aboard Veturi. It's over, you hear?" A hint of desperation gnawed at the edge of his voice and his hand trembled visibly. "We are going to walk politely over to you and put you and the girl in handcuffs, understand? If you move, we blow more holes in you than we already have."

Arthur gave no response, not even in movement. He looked more akin to a statue than a man, motionless as the wind whipped his hair and his filthy white shirt. "Follow my lead," Elsie heard him mumble, his lips barely moving, "But only after I move first. You'll know what to do." She stood rooted to the spot, mouth dry and blood thundering in her ears. It was over. They had run out of options.

The guards closed in on them one step at a time, holding their muskets in front of them menacingly. Each gun had a sharp, wicked-looking blade affixed to the end of it. When they got within only a few paces, Arthur made his first movement since Cadbury had reached the rooftop: a simple nod. Then, in a blur of motion, he ducked and sprinted through a gap between the guards. Four guns went off in an instant, one jammed, and two men wheeled around, searching for Arthur. Elsie did not entirely understand what was going on, but she knew that she also had to move. Jumping forward, she ran between the disoriented guards to Arthur's side where he stood at the edge of the building.

Red began to pool in the gravel beneath Arthur; he appeared to have been sliced across the arm by one of the bayonets. But in the struggle, he had wrested a gun away from one of the guards, and he now held it pointed at Cadbury, who had aimed his own pistol directly at Elsie.

The guards began to reload their weapons but paused when Arthur shouted: "Everyone stops what he's doing, or I'll fire!" He shook the gun in Cadbury's direction.

Cadbury laughed bitterly. "If you do, I will shoot your little girl."

"You may, but are you willing to risk your own life on that?"

"To kill a rebel? Of course."

"If you kill her, I will kill you, and if I kill you, your men will kill me, and all that we will have accomplished is that a measly two rebels out of the whole network will have been dealt with." A tear of pain rolled down Arthur's cheek as he spoke. "And Odol's finest officer will also be dead. Hardly a win for your emperor, is it?"

"He's your emperor too," Cadbury growled.

"Is he? I...Elsie, duck!"

Elsie stared for a split second and then saw what Arthur meant. She dropped face down onto the rough gravel, scraping her face, knees, and elbows yet again. And Veturi went under the tunnel.

29

SPORT FOR MEN

Paul worked the levers of the *Heart*, trying in vain to pour more steam into the engine. It could travel only so fast, and after almost an entire day of following the Veturi rail line, they seemed no closer to catching sight of the train. Maria was perched at the bow of the ship, peering ahead, ready to wave to Paul at the first sight of their quarry. By now, they were probably being pursued, but with Elsie likely in grave danger, neither Paul nor Maria really cared. All that mattered now was getting her to safety.

Maria stood up from her perch. The night sky was giving way to dawn, and she felt it was unlikely that they were close to the train-city. She turned to look up at Paul. He had the same determined expression on his face that she'd fallen in love with so many years ago aboard the *Formidable*.

'*Aren't you tired, my dear?*' she signed, hoping she would get his attention even from across the ship. Paul didn't seem to notice, so she asked him again, and the only response she got was a slight shake of the head. She wanted to stop and rest, but she knew Paul would stop for nothing. In her heart of hearts, Maria knew she would keep going too, if only for Elsie. They didn't have much of a plan once they caught up to Veturi, though knowing Arthur, he would have blown half of it up by the time they got there.

She caught sight of a shape out of the corner of her eye. Obscured as they were by the clouds, the forms of the mountains were unmistakable. They had finally reached the end of the Gorand Wastes and it was an abrupt end. But a foggy dawn was a poor time to discover that.

Thousands of feet high, the mountains rose at first in a sheer cliff a hundred or so feet off the ground, carved into by Gorand's greed for natural resources. Then, the remaining natural form of the mountains swept higher still, rising into snowy autumnal peaks. The tracks they were following vanished into a large tunnel, still billowing smoke from the train's passage, though Veturi itself was nowhere to be seen.

Panicking, Maria ran up the stairs to Paul and began signing warnings to him, trying to alert him to the fact that they were headed straight for the cliff. Paul simply nodded. *Of course he must have seen it already,* Maria thought, *but...* She went to the bow again, staring out at the impending cliff face. *He had better do something quick!* Trying to fly through that tunnel in the dark would be suicide at best.

Maria was thrown onto her back, jarred her from her thoughts as she clutched at the railing for safety. She staggered to her feet, clinging onto the wooden banister at the bow. Her mouth hung open in shock as she saw the cliff face turn underneath the battered hull. The ship was almost perpendicular to the ground. There was no way that the ship could do this, no way it would survive this. *He's completely insane! We're both going to die...*

Mere seconds later, the ship leveled out as it surpassed the top of the cliff, swooping through the vales and gullies like a bird on the wing under Paul's expert hand. If she hadn't been so frightened, Maria would have appreciated the stark beauty of the mountains and their hidden craigs, streams, and valleys, which Paul passed through as quickly as if he'd been flying this route all his life. But as it was, she was scared to death, nauseous, and barely able to stand. Clambering up to Paul's side during a brief respite from the constant jarring of the ship, she signed frantically at him.

'We need to land! We're not going to survive these mountains, Paul. We're too high up for a ship in this state, and you know it. We need to better assess the situation. We didn't expect to get this far, or at least I didn't!'

Paul just shook his head, not lifting a hand from the steering lever. Maria was frightened, but she knew if there was one person who could get them out of this alive, it was him. She wondered what was going through his head, but each bob and weave through the steep slopes made her own head spin.

It is beautiful up here, she thought as she slumped down against the railing at the stern of the ship, watching in awe as they sailed past a half-frozen waterfall that glittered in the rising sun. *If only we could stop and rest for a while...* But it was cold up here too, and Paul looked as determined as ever to see them safely to Arthur's rescue.

At last, with dawn nearly upon them in the east, they finally caught sight of Veturi. Through the high peaks, crested with the pink-gold glimmer of the morning sun, they saw the engine pouring more billowing black smoke into the air than dozens of factories in Gorand. When they passed the last ridge, the land flattened beneath them into rolling brown hills, fields, and the occasional patch of red and gold trees, still showing signs of the waning autumn. The train-city was travelling far slower than the fast clip of the *Heart*, and many of the cars were still in the tunnel. They would have to circle overhead until they found any sign of Arthur and Elsie.

Elsie couldn't hear her own screaming. She hadn't seen what had happened to the others when they went under the tunnel. The cries of the men were quickly drowned out by the shrieking of the air and the rumble of the train. She could have lifted her head a little, but the rough underside of the tunnel was so close overhead that she didn't dare move a muscle. She lay prone for what felt like an eternity, hands clamped so hard over her ears that her fingers began to ache, eyes clenched shut.

A familiar rough hand grabbed her arm and her eyes flew open. Arthur had managed to belly-crawl over to her, having kept his wits about him slightly better than she did. His blue eyes were set with determination, and his mouth was moving, though she could not hear his voice. With some effort, Arthur pulled her hands away from her ears. She had stopped screaming and the sound of the tunnel no longer seemed so deafening. He began to speak again, still shouting over the rumble and squeal of the tracks below.

"As soon as we're out of this tunnel, we need to get off this roof. I mean it! No dawdling. And take this." He pushed a flintlock pistol into Elsie's hand. "It's loaded. All you need to do is pull the hammer back, aim it at your target, and pull the trigger. Run, kid, run as fast as you can and don't look back. I'll keep them busy."

Elsie stared at Arthur, his red hair flying wildly in the rush of air which was no longer so dark and smoky. No doubt the engine had left the tunnel far behind and soon their part of the train would be out in the fresh air. Hope and fear flooded her body with adrenaline. The pistol felt strange in her hand and the thought of actually killing someone with it made her fingers tremble as she clutched it. As she felt the rush of cool dawn air on her face, she knew they were getting close to the end of the tunnel. Soon, very soon, she would need to move.

Her heart was beating rapidly in her throat and then the roar of the tunnel ended as suddenly as it began. She leapt to her feet. Arthur was shouting, as were the guards and Cadbury. What they were saying, Elsie couldn't tell to save her life. All she knew was that she was walking unsteadily across the rooftop towards the metal ladder.

"Get back!" Arthur shouted. "All of you!" He had retrieved a musket during the confusion and was brandishing it once more at the disheveled men. Looking back at Cadbury and his men, Elsie noticed that, hauntingly, there were about half as many guards on the rooftop as there had been before the tunnel. The gravel was smeared here and there with blood. A pit of nausea welled up in her stomach and she bolted the rest of the way to the ladder.

For an uncertain moment, she hovered at the edge of the roof. Cadbury and the guards were distracted by Arthur and if she went now she could make a clean escape. But she couldn't leave Arthur alone, hopelessly outnumbered, with no chance of making it out alive. No matter who he was and what he'd done, she owed him her life now. She had a debt to pay.

Her mouth was dry and her heart was pounding, but she turned around and awkwardly raised her pistol, pointing it at Cadbury's chest. The surviving guards had scattered their weapons across the rooftop when they dropped to their stomachs. Held at gunpoint by Arthur, none of them dared make a move, even to grab for a bayonet. Elsie saw defeat in their exhausted eyes. Slowly, one by one, they raised their hands in surrender. Only Cadbury seemed determined to hold Arthur to the end.

"We can rush him. He only has one gun!" Cadbury shouted, brandishing his own pistol as he tried vainly to rally his men.

Elsie stepped forward in front of Arthur. "And I have one too. Don't move!"

She saw Arthur's eyes go wide in the corner of her vision, and he shook his head. "Kid, what are you doing? I told you to run!"

"I'm not going to let you stay here and die," she said as firmly as she could. "We are going to get out of here together, or not at all."

An unpleasant smirk crawled onto Cadbury's face. "I still have enough men to take you both into custody. I think you won't make it that far though, Pendington. I'd like to kill you myself. Slowly. No trial necessary, I've seen enough." His arm was steady as he aimed the pistol at Arthur's head. "The emperor himself will *thank* me for doing such a service..."

The tension was cut by Elsie's shrill voice. "Arthur, look! Up there. It's the ship! It's Paul and Maria!"

It was Arthur's turn to smile now, his chapped lips curling into an almost smug expression as he aimed the musket upwards, directly at the ship, which was circling above Veturi. Clearly leading the shot, he fired, apparently hoping to get the attention of the ship.

"That wasn't very smart." Cadbury grinned. "Now you only have a little girl to protect you. Men, put your hands down. I don't think she's dangerous. Now would be a good time to say your prayers, Pendington."

Arthur gave Cadbury a conceited smile and nodded to Elsie, the apparent next step in a spur-of-the-moment plan already figured out in his head. He shifted his grip on the musket, holding it almost like a staff, and then threw it right at Cadbury, knocking off his aim as he fired the pistol.

Maria leapt back when part of the railing she was leaning on exploded into splinters as a musket ball flew by, far too close for her comfort. She peered down at where it had come from and saw several tiny figures moving about on a tall rooftop. Turning back, she ran up to where Paul was still at the controls.

'I found them, I found them! They're on that roof down there!' She signed frantically as Paul turned the ship, circling back towards where she'd seen the movement.

As they got closer, she clearly saw Arthur, dressed in his usual white shirt and black trousers, fighting at least four men in a brawl, though surprisingly he seemed to be getting the better of them. What alarmed Maria was when she caught sight of Elsie. The girl stood alone in a tattered blue gown, holding a pistol in both hands, pointing it at a man who was standing off to the side out of the way of the altercation. *Ulysses Cadbury! Arthur, you idiot. How on earth did you get him on your tail?* Worse than that, the man was clearly inching toward a gun which had been discarded on the ground.

As the ship approached, Maria had only one course of action in mind. She had no intention of helping Arthur out; if he got beaten to a pulp by those guards, all the better. It would serve him right for putting Elsie in that situation, especially if she had been hurt. Her priority was keeping Cadbury from getting the upper hand and getting him away from Elsie.

The ship was now flying parallel with Veturi, struggling to keep pace without either shooting forward or dropping behind. She saw Arthur shouting at them. She didn't bother looking to Paul for an interpretation. He would be far too busy fighting the controls. Maria ran and grabbed Paul's blunderbuss from the stockade in the captain's cabin. She preferred to use knives for her kills, but at this distance a gun would be far better. She closed one eye, losing sight of Arthur amidst the chaos, steadied her hand, and hoped that her aim was sure.

"Now girl, you're not going to use that gun on me," Cadbury said smugly. "I know you won't. You don't have it in you."

Elsie had seen the vague shape of the ship off to her right, but she stopped herself from looking. The longer Cadbury was focused on her, ignoring the rest of the situation, the better. She also saw him edging toward where a musket lay. Perhaps he thought his maneuvering went unnoticed, but currently her mind was working at insane speed, picking up every sound, sight, and detail. Only a couple of minutes had elapsed since Veturi had escaped the tunnel, but to Elsie it felt like the longest stretch of time in her life.

"If you make one move toward me, I'll...I'm going to..." She wished her hands would stop trembling.

"You'll what, shoot me? If you even managed to pull that trigger, I'm sure you'd miss anyway. Killing is a sport for men, little girl."

A tear streaked down Elsie's face, and she shook it away. She almost managed to pull the trigger then. She *wanted* to pull the trigger, to kill another person. But she didn't, not really. She wanted to, but she knew she couldn't.

Trembling and letting out a soft cry, she felt the gun slip from her hand. It turned over as it fell and landed on the hammer, setting the charge off with a *bang*.

Several things happened all at once. As the gun went off, Cadbury scrambled for the musket on the ground and snatched it up. There was another gunshot, this time from the ship, and Cadbury clutched his shoulder, doubling over as blood sprayed across his face. Arthur broke free of the distracted guards and bolted to the edge of the roof. He leapt onto the airship, leaving Elsie alone on the rooftop.

She followed immediately on his heels but stopped short at the edge. It was one thing to look over the edge of a building to the roof of another building, solid and stable a few feet away. Looking over the edge of a building at the ground rushing by below was quite another. Worse, the ship was not a still target for her next jump. It bobbed in the air as it sped alongside the train, drawing further away, then closer again, then further away as Paul furiously worked the controls, desperate to keep the ship level with the rooftop. The ship itself, a shabby thing really, and somehow even shabbier now that it was in the air, rattled as though it was about to fly apart under the strain.

"Jump!" Arthur roared, while at the same time Cadbury shouted for his men to "Get her!" She stood rooted to the spot for a moment more, until she heard the crunch of gravel beneath the boots of the guards behind her and, emptying her mind of any reservation, she leapt forward as the airborne vessel swayed back closer to the rooftop.

The second she was in the air seemed to last forever. Her arms flailed wildly, and Arthur reached out to pull her to safety. But other hands grabbed her instead. A guard wrapped his arms around her and pulled her back onto the rooftop, where two other men took her roughly by the arms and dragged her away from the ship. Cadbury got unsteadily to his feet, leaning on the musket as though it were a crutch, clutching his bleeding right shoulder. The side of his face was spattered with red droplets.

"Girl, you are under arrest." With effort, he lifted the musket and pressed the barrel against Elsie's forehead. The hot metal burned her skin, making her cry out. "If any of your friends want to stop me, they know what will happen." He pulled the hammer of the musket back slowly and locked it into place with a deafening *click*. Elsie trembled. "Though I would prefer they didn't, as I would dearly love to squeeze you for as much information on your rebel friends as I can. They can leave, I'll find them eventually. Did you hear that?" He yelled in the direction of the hovering ship, spittle and blood flying from his mouth. "You can go your own way and live a while longer, Pendington!"

Suspended between two soldiers and with a gun to her head, Elsie knew she was helpless. She let herself go limp, giving up on any hope of struggling free. It was over.

Hardly daring to move under the threat of instant death, she glanced to the right just in time to see Arthur leap from the ship back onto the rooftop. He was saying something, but Elsie could not hear over the men's cursing.

Cadbury pulled the trigger and Elsie's heart stopped.

The gun made a snapping noise, but nothing more. Elsie flinched and the guards let go of her, almost out of shock. Whether it was a lucky misfire or the gun was not loaded at all, she could not tell. But she took the chance she was given and ran full tilt toward the ship.

Cadbury would have tried to stop her, but Arthur burst forward through the guards and punched their leader square in the face. Staggering back, Cadbury let the musket fall from his hands, and Arthur snatched it up, wielding the weapon as a bludgeon to hold off the guards as they flocked around Cadbury.

"Go on kid! I can't hold them off much longer," Arthur shouted, backing towards the ship as he fended off the guards with the heavy wooden butt of the gun.

Elsie didn't need to be told again. She ran toward the edge, still feeling the fear but pushing through with all her strength, and leapt across the gap. She was caught and embraced by the warm figure of Maria, who gently lowered Elsie to the deck as the adrenaline drained from her limbs.

"Come on! Arthur, you need to get on board. We won't leave without-" Paul was interrupted by another gunshot. Maria had gotten back into position and fired another round just past Arthur's head, hitting Cadbury yet again in the right arm. Cadbury cried out and crumpled to the rooftop. The guards no longer wanted to fight. Only two were left standing, and they were not eager to end up like their leader. As they backed away, hands spread in surrender, Arthur turned to the ship once more, grinning in triumph. He leapt over the gap, grabbing onto part of the rigging.

"Arthur, let's not do this again!" Paul admonished as he shifted the levers into gear. The ship drew away from Veturi, circling due south as the train-city grew smaller on the horizon.

Elsie wished she heard what Arthur said in retort as he climbed down onto the deck, but in the next moment she had passed out completely.

PART 5:
THE STORM

30

THE BARON'S CLUTCHES

Champaign, princess?" the baron asked smoothly, the bottle in his hand hovering over her empty glass. Yvonnia looked up at him, keeping her face carefully neutral.

"And what is the occasion, my lord?"

"To my victory," Schulhard said, pouring the sparkling liquid liberally and without her consent. They were sitting in the captain's lounge, an elegantly decorated room with oak paneled walls, thick carpeting, comfortable chairs, and enough alcohol burdening the decorative sideboard to kill an elephant. There was an oil portrait of the baron himself, excessively flattering, on the mantel above the small fireplace. Yvonnia could have almost believed that they were still in the baron's palace back on solid ground, if it wasn't for the constant low thrum of the dreadnought's massive engines. The steady vibration made her sick to her stomach. She had barely touched the delicacies that the ship's cook had personally set before her.

"Oh? And what victory might that be, my lord?" she asked, taking the overfull glass in her hand, though she did not raise it to her lips. The baron had started on his without the clink of glasses she understood was Odolian custom when making a toast.

"Ah, that would be telling, now wouldn't it?" the baron said, refilling his glass as soon as it was empty.

"A secret victory?" Yvonnia smiled in spite of herself. "Surely that is no victory at all, with no one to share it."

The baron laughed and pushed back his chair, his stomach shaking as he stood up. "I thought I would be celebrating with you, princess, but you've barely touched your steak tartare." He rounded the table towards her. Yvonnia stiffened as he drew near, and made to rise, but he stood behind her chair and put one heavy hand on her shoulder. The hairs prickled on the back of her neck as she sat straight and stiff, hands folded on the table, staring straight ahead as he ducked his head toward her ear.

"Why these coy games, princess?" Schulhard murmured, stroking the side of her neck with his rough thumb. "Please. I don't frighten you, do I?"

"I am not frightened of you, my lord," Yvonnia said. "In fact, if you must know, I am ill. I am stifled here, with no air, no light. I would beg leave to walk about the ship, perhaps upon the deck, until I have regained my composure."

The baron straightened, laughing once more. "What, the deck? With all the machinery and soldiers and sailors stripped to the waist? Hardly a place for a lady..."

There was a sudden knock at the door, and it opened at once. The baron hastily withdrew his hand from Yvonnia's shoulder, turning to see who was intruding upon them. Yvonnia's entire body relaxed as he stepped away, and she stood up at once.

"What in blazes do you want, Hollis?" the baron barked. The thin man stood in the doorway, an unamused look on his dry face. "Can't you see I'm trying to entertain our royal guest?"

"I see that, my lord, but I'm here to remind you to make your regular inspections," Hollis said. Yvonnia sidled out from behind her chair and took a few steps away from the baron, glad that he was distracted by the other man.

The baron groaned. "And who, pray tell, is to entertain our guest now? I can't very well go marching her all over this bloody ship, and I'm sure she would hardly find your company amusing." He sneered at the man. Hollis's expression remained unchanged.

"My lord," Yvonnia interrupted, "You are wrong in your surmise. I would not mind the company of Lord Hollis at all. Pray, give me leave to walk about the ship with him, belowdecks, and see if that would calm my nerves."

The baron swiveled his beady black eyes towards her, his thick brows knotted. "Yes, why shouldn't you amuse yourself, if it would please you," he drawled. "You can rejoin me for dinner once your nerves have acclimated to our more advanced ways of travel. Yes, go on." He waved a hand at her as though he were shooing a small child.

"My lord, is that wise?" Hollis cautioned, stepping aside as the baron pushed through the doorway, turning slightly sideways so that it would accommodate his bulk. "She is a spy, as *you* have said, and we do not want her learning the secrets of our great military..."

"She will be dead within two weeks, Hollis," the baron said sourly. "Let her amuse herself while she lives. Nothing she learns can hurt us now." He lumbered off down the corridor, his heavy steps echoing off the metal walls.

Hollis turned to look at Yvonnia with an expression of distaste curling his thin lip. "Princess," he said laconically, offering his stiff, bony arm. Yvonnia took it gratefully. *Not the rescuer I had in mind,* she thought wryly as they stepped out into the cold metal corridor.

"Well princess, where to?" Hollis asked, his thin lips barely concealing his sneer. "Your wish is my command."

Yvonnia glanced at him shrewdly out of the corner of her eye. "Where are they keeping my maidservant?"

Enya and Jacik were being held in a dismal little cell at the very bottom of the great dreadnought. Though not as grimy nor as dim as their cell at the airship docks, it was still cramped and uncomfortable. The only furniture consisted of two bunks built directly into the walls and a meager washbasin. There was nowhere for Yvonnia to sit, so she stood awkwardly, despite Enya's insistence that she sit down on the lower bunk. Jacik stood also, out of respect, while Enya sat cross legged on the upper bunk, chin in her hands, staring vacantly out into space. Hollis remained out in the corridor.

Jacik and Enya were unchained, but thick steel collars had been welded closed around their necks, marking them as prisoners. Yvonnia wished she had one of her own. She felt ashamed that the baron should treat her so well when she was just as much a prisoner as her companions.

"Find a way off this deathtrap yet, princess?" Enya asked, forcing a wry smile. Somewhere on the way to the cell she must have had her veil torn off; her dark hair, cropped short, hung around her face in soft curves. Yvonnia had offered her sash as a replacement, but Enya had refused, despite seeming uncomfortable without her head covering.

"Not yet," Yvonnia said. "I've only just been granted liberty aboard the ship, and what little I've seen of it has been a maze." She tried hard to believe that she would find a way out eventually.

"That man...did he hurt you?" Jacik intoned, his dark eyes fixing Yvonnia with a somber look. His sword was gone, and without it his arms hung loose at his sides, fists clenched and ready as any weapon.

"No," Yvonnia said, swallowing the coil of dread that tried to slither up her throat. "I am sure he expects me to throw myself at him in exchange for my life, but I know what a futile bargain that would be. Perhaps if Lord Hollis had not been there, he would have..." She stopped, shuddered, swallowed, and started again. "I doubt he will do anything if I stay in the company of others. I will keep myself safe, Jacik. You know that. I won't be foolish."

Jacik's only reply was a dissatisfied grunt. Yvonnia knew he was berating himself for not being there to protect her, but there was nothing either of them could do about it.

"Hollis?" Enya scoffed. "You think highly of a man sowing lie after lie about your country? Our country?"

"I don't think highly of him at all," Yvonnia explained patiently. "But he is clearly here on *business*. I don't know if Schulhard knows the meaning of the word." She dropped her eyes.

"Then why not stay as far away from him as you can get on this metal trap?" Enya asked, lifting her face from her hands. "Why go back out there at all? We're all going to die anyway."

Yvonnia flinched. She'd never heard the girl express so much despair. Even Jacik turned to look at Enya with mild surprise. Yvonnia rubbed her palms, clammy with cold sweat, on the skirt of her saree.

"Because..." she said at length, almost choking on the words, "Because we need a way out. We need to have hope. And I want to stay informed, no matter how this ends. Besides, drunk and happy men tend to make mistakes..." She thought mournfully of Vasada, unseeing eyes staring up at the beautiful ceiling of the ballroom as he bled out. She saw the baron again, standing behind him, smoking gun in hand. She had been willing to die honorably and peacefully when the ambush was sprung. It would have been the right thing to do. Now, she was going to die simply so that Odol could provoke her country into war.

"Then why not send me?" Enya asked, eyes wide and earnest. "I'm pretty enough, and younger than you. I'd get that fat monster to spill everything he knows without lifting a finger." She flipped her dark hair and made a simpering face, but her eyes were serious. "And I don't have nearly as far to fall as you do, if it goes badly."

Something broke inside Yvonnia. Enya had always been flirtatious, provocative even, but with a girlish innocence that was more heartwarming than concerning. But now, hearing her offer, with all the earnestness of her sixteen years, to give herself away in exchange for the hope of some kind of clue or information... It made Yvonnia want to weep in despair. The girl didn't deserve this. Enya was not royal or important or anything other than stubbornly loyal and a little too headstrong. But she could not weep. She had to be strong, to pull herself together, for Enya's sake if not her own.

"You don't have liberty about the ship," she replied straightforwardly, swallowing back the lump that rose in her throat. "And besides, I think the baron is more interested in the power I hold than my appearance."

"Then what can I do?" Enya asked desperately, dropping her hands into her lap and tossing herself back upon the bed with a groan. "Besides lie here being useless baggage, I mean."

"You can be patient and...and trust me," Yvonnia said, the words tasting like sawdust in her dry mouth. She shut her eyes and took a moment, steeling herself. She had to believe that there was some hope left. She needed to get off this metal hulk and warn her father that a threat greater than Menava was facing their country. She turned to Jacik. "I am going out again. I want to see if I can find the command bridge and get a lay of the land. Perhaps if I can find a map of the ship, it will show me where the...how would you say? The ship's boats? I am sure they must have smaller vessels on board for escape in an emergency. If we can escape on one of those..."

"When we escape," Jacik corrected, meeting her gaze directly in a rare show of firmness. Yvonnia raised an eyebrow; he had never interrupted her before. Jacik saw her expression and bowed his head. "Princess, I have vowed with more than just my life to protect you. To go to an execution that will incite our people to a war they cannot win...this is something I must not do."

"I know, Jacik," Yvonnia said bitterly. "What are you saying that I myself have not already said?"

"I am saying that we *must* get off this ship on our terms, whether we do so alive or dead." Jacik paused, pressing his full lips together. He was visibly struggling with his emotions and words. "I wish I could have died fighting in Gorand, rather than waiting here," he finished. He did not meet her eyes again, and clearly the conversation was over.

Enya had not risen from the cot, and Yvonnia decided it was time to take her leave. She turned to the door, casting one last glance over her shoulder, and knocked on the steel. After a moment, a slot shot back and one of the guards peered through.

"My business is finished," Yvonnia said primly, unflinching beneath his curious stare. "May I come out now?"

The eyes vanished for a moment, and there was some muttering. Then the bolt was shot back and the door opened. Yvonnia saw Jacik stiffen for a moment, as though he meant to leap for the opening, but he made no move as she stepped out into the narrow corridor. Everything on the dreadnought, every room and passageway, was narrow, as though it had been squeezed down to fit within the great steel hull. Yvonnia felt the thrum of the engines beneath her feet, louder now that she was out of the tight cell, and remembered once more that they were in flight. Her stomach turned and she staggered for a moment. Hollis caught her arm, appearing suddenly at her side.

"Princess, are you ill?" he asked, though his grip on her arm was more clawlike than comforting. Yvonnia leaned on him, only slightly exaggerating her need for support. The two guards watched her with wolfish grins on their lean, hungry faces.

"I cannot breathe in this steel trap," she complained. "The walls are so close...I fear I will faint if I cannot get some air." Hollis made a sort of grumble of complaint in his throat.

"Princess, the upper decks are no place for you," he said, his dry voice grating on her ears. "Let me take you up to your room so you can lie down."

"No," Yvonnia said, "The baron gave me liberty aboard this entire ship, save for the ammunition stores and the engine room. Take me to the upper deck at once—or do you wish me to tell him that you do not respect his authority?"

Hollis's fingers spasmed, digging into her arm for a fraction of a second. And then he was all cordiality again. "Of course, your majesty," he muttered. "Forgive my insolence. Come this way." Still clutching her arm, he led her back down the corridor the way they had come. Yvonnia was instantly on high alert, her eyes scanning about for landmarks, trying to memorize the twists and turns they took so that she could repeat them to Jacik and Enya later. But the narrow, winding corridors and steep mesh stairs were so repetitive that she quickly lost track. She wondered if Hollis was deliberately leading her on an indirect route, meant to bewilder her and keep her from finding her own way. But then again, this metal monstrosity seemed not to be designed for human beings at all.

At last, they came to a narrow stair which spiraled up around a thin steel pillar, disappearing into the ceiling. It was barely wide enough for them to walk in single file, and Hollis beckoned for her to go up first. As she climbed, Yvonnia found herself thankful for her narrow skirt and close-cut sleeves. She tried to imagine one of the Odolian ladies making her way up these stairs in a great frothy ballgown with bell sleeves, and the idea was so ludicrous that she might have laughed aloud under different circumstances. As it was, she was relieved to finally reach the top of the staircase.

The first gust of wind nearly knocked Yvonnia off her feet. She was standing on the measureless deck of the massive ship, staring out over great banks of clouds as they swept past. It was evening, and the sun was about level with them on the horizon, throwing yellow and orange light across the dull metal plates, catching in the rigging and glinting off the rows of polished cannons that lined the deck. Beside her, in the center of the ship, the mound of the great air tank dwarfed her, protected by a shield of tarps and sheet metal, blocking her view of the other side of the dreadnought. Ahead, she could just see the command tower at the front of the ship, strung with cables, glass windows glowing in the fading light.

Hollis coughed behind her, and Yvonnia stepped forward, clinging to the railing that ringed the central tank. The lord stepped out onto the deck beside her and looked around, a frown creasing his thin lips.

"Does this suit your majesty?" he asked cooly. Yvonnia felt sicker than ever, but she steadied herself and forced a grateful smile.

"Yes, very much. Thank you."

The wind, though strong, was certainly refreshing after hours below in the stale metal deathtrap. To her dismay, however, Yvonnia saw no sign of ship's boats, or their airborne equivalents, on the upper deck. There were, however, plenty of sailors scrambling up and down the rigging, swabbing the deck, and standing ready beside the massive cannons, as though waiting for trouble to begin. As Yvonnia started down the deck, leaning on Hollis's arm once more, she gathered some looks, a few crude shouts, and a handful of whistles from the men. Her heart grew cold as she wondered if she and Enya were the only women on board. They might not fare well in the event of an escape attempt, if one was even possible.

They rounded the tip of the air tank, coming within sight of the base of the command tower. Some of the ropes and cables that festooned it like cobwebs were part of the rigging, but Yvonnia recognized many as telegraph lines. The big metal door was guarded by two Odolian marines in crimson uniforms with blue sashes. Their eyes flicked from her to Hollis, and they stood up a little straighter. One man even puffed out his chest. Yvonnia suppressed a smile.

"Can we go up there?" she pointed at the command tower. Hollis shook his head firmly.

"Your majesty, I cannot allow a foreign national to go traipsing all over a military ship without restriction, and I'm sure you can understand why. Besides, there is hardly anything up there that would interest you."

Yvonnia was about to press the point when the metal door opened, pushed outward on groaning hinges. She bit back her retort when she saw the baron himself ease his bulk through the door and out onto the deck. The two marines saluted in unison as he turned to face her and Hollis. If he was surprised to see her on the upper deck, he did not show it in his jovial face.

"Ah, princess, fancy meeting you up here," he bellowed, closing the gap between them and holding out a cordial hand. "I suppose Hollis has been giving you the grand tour?" There was a barb hidden somewhere in that question, and she saw his eyes linger on Hollis's face for a moment. No, the baron was not at all pleased to find her here. Yvonnia felt her chest tighten. It seemed this avenue of opportunity was about to be cut off.

The baron pressed forward, guiding them back towards the staircase that led below. He put one hand on Yvonnia's back and the other on Hollis's shoulder as he walked, speaking genial nonsense about the weather and the grandness of the Odolian dreadnought. Yvonnia glanced over her shoulder and caught sight of a young boy, no more than fifteen years of age, running up behind them waving a piece of crumpled paper.

"My lord!" he shouted, gasping for breath, "A telegram for you. It's from Lady Eritula, governor of Veturi! Urgent, sir."

"What, who?" The baron seemed befuddled. He turned around. "Well, read it boy! We haven't got all day."

The boy gasped in a great breath of air and began to read. "Urgent message for Brandomir–stop. Rebels led by Pendington attacked Veturi and killed many men–stop. Escaped on stolen airship *Worker's Chance*–stop. If you are in region northeast of Bolden hunt them down."

"Brandomir?" Lord Hollis's voice was dryer and more caustic than ever. "Since when are you and the Lady of Veturi on a first name basis?"

The baron coughed loudly and gave Yvonnia a smile that did not reach his eyes. "I assure you, Lord Hollis, the lady does not hold a candle to my esteem for our beautiful princess here." He suddenly drew himself up and assumed a military dignity that Yvonnia had never seen on him before. "Yes, we shall hunt these...*Siali rebels* down." Another barb at Hollis, who did not seem to notice. "Come, we must make ready at once."

He started down the deck towards the command tower once more, shouting orders at the lolling sailors, who began to scramble over themselves to obey. As Yvonnia made to follow the baron, Hollis seized her arm. "Dear lady," he said firmly, "If we are to go on a military assignment, then it would be best for you to avoid danger and go to the lower decks at once."

Yvonnia tried in vain to wrench her arm out of his clawlike grasp. "And why should I seek to avoid danger, when I am to die at the end of this voyage?"

"I never said it was for your sake," Hollis snapped, dropping his feigned politeness once and for all. "Now get below!" He began to drag her back toward the stairs. A sailor darted in front of them, nearly colliding with her as she struggled against Hollis's surprisingly strong grip.

"Hollis!" the baron shouted. "Aren't you coming to help?" She caught sight of him at the base of the command tower, arms crossed, scowling in their direction.

"I shall, once I return the princess to her quarters," Hollis replied, pausing only a moment to answer before redoubling his efforts. Yvonnia shrieked as he twisted her arm in his grasp.

"Forget such nonsense, Hollis," the baron barked. "We must take up arms at once! Bring her to the bridge where we can keep an eye on her. If she's troublesome, we will deal with her."

The baron had completely shed the facade of the buffoonish politician Yvonnia had met in Gorand. No longer was he caught up in his own vices and desires. Now, he was acting as the captain of the Imperial Dreadnought *Redoubtable*, and his men came crawling up stairs and ladders and rigging onto the deck like ants from an anthill, swarming in organized chaos as he shouted orders. Sailors in baggy tunics and loose-fitting breeches, with a club or hatchet tucked into their belt for defense. Officers in fine Odolian uniforms of black and red, with plumbed hats and polished buttons, equipped with both pistol and sword. Marines gathered on the deck in tight formation, loading their muskets with practiced precision as the officers shouted commands. The dreadnought was coming alive for war, and at the center of it all stood Baron Schulhard.

By the time Hollis led her back to the command tower, the baron had already disappeared inside. One of the marines held the door open for them, and they stepped into the hollow metal box. Another spiraling staircase rose into the gaslit gloom above, and Yvonnia caught sight of the hefty figure of the baron charging up the stairs to the bridge.

The bridge stood high above the deck of the ship, and was walled completely by huge panes of glass, larger than any she'd seen in her life. Yvonnia found herself staring in awe, even as she despised the workings of the Odolian war machine. The room was filled with the constant *clack clack clack* of the telegraph operators, who sat ranged around the room at cramped desks, headsets pressed to their ears as they listened for codes over the wires. At the center of the room, a huge table held a sprawling map of the world, with small metal figures scattered over it to represent ships and armies. The baron stood beside it, next to a couple of proudly uniformed officers in high crested hats and medal-decorated coats. They were pointing at the map and speaking rapidly, and their backs were to Yvonnia and Hollis. In the noise and confusion, she found it difficult to understand what was said. Many of the words, Odolian military and naval terminology, were completely unknown to her. Her heart hammered in her throat as a wave of overwhelm swept through her.

Hollis finally released his grip on her arm and stepped forward to join the baron and the other officers. She stepped after him, and heard murmured words that were surely not meant for her ears.

"Kill the other prisoners. We only need the princess."

The baron looked up and met her gaze. Yvonnia started, trying to keep her eyes from going wide, but she feared her expression had already given her away. Schulhard murmured something else to one of the officers, who saluted and stepped aside. The baron then approached her, smiling his usual guileless smile. She knew now that it was merely a facade.

"My dear, what seems to be the matter?" He raised his hand to her face, clumsily caressing her cheek with a thick finger.

Yvonnia suppressed the urge to flinch away. "It is only a small rebel ship. My *Redoubtable* has faced far worse and come through unscathed."

"Siali," Hollis corrected. "Remember, Baron, Greyer's rebellion is dead. It was Siali insurgents who stole that ship."

"You bloody fool," Schulhard growled, "You heard the message! It was Pendington. Cadbury was right: he's still alive after all. You can drop the damn charade." He withdrew his hand from Yvonnia's face and returned to the war table to discuss plans with the remaining officers. The man he had whispered to was nowhere to be seen. Yvonnia's heart sank.

She coughed loudly, fanning her face with her hand in an exaggerated fashion. No one paid her any attention, so she tried again, louder this time. The baron looked up at her with a barely disguised scowl. "Is something wrong?"

"I apologize my lord," she said desperately, coughing again and fanning at her face. "It is so stuffy in this room...might I go down and get some fresh air?" The baron rolled his eyes and turned away.

"I wouldn't recommend that, princess," Hollis said with a lizard-like smile on his pale face. He had resumed his accustomed false politeness.

"Why not?" Yvonnia asked innocently, tugging at the jewels about her neck as though they were a collar. The baron grunted at the interruption, though he did not look at her again.

"We have a report here," Hollis said, holding up a machine-cut piece of paper with harsh black letters stamped across it. Yvonnia could not read what it said. "We're heading into a storm. Looks like a bad one. You'd best stay indoors." His smile grew and his words seemed to tremble with sadistic joy. Yvonnia felt the last flare of hope stamped out. She was trapped, unable to get the attention of the baron as he shouted orders, and unable to fool Hollis any longer. The officer was on his way to execute her companions, and she could do nothing to prevent it. All she could do now was pray.

31

Tender Respite

Elsie gazed ruefully at herself in the mirror. She was beyond tattered; the beautiful blue dress was coming apart at the shoulder seams, her face was covered in scabs and bruises from the fight, and her forehead was marked by a red circle where the hot musket barrel had burned her skin. *Arthur has a lot to answer for,* Elsie thought as she tried her best to make herself look somewhat presentable. She raked her fingers through her matted hair and brushed down the dusty skirt of the gown. She was still groggy, her limbs heavy and yearning for the soft bed behind her, but she knew that she shouldn't sleep any longer.

She went to the door of the cabin, feeling the faint rumbling beneath her feet that reminded her that the *Heart of Resistance* was in flight, hundreds of feet in the air. The thought made her feel woozy, and she leaned on the vanity table to steady herself as she eased the door open quietly. The rush of outside air immediately chilled her skin, cutting through the tattered dress. The vague shape of the sun could not be seen through the thin, gray clouds at either end of the horizon, so it must have been close to midday. No one was visible on the deck, and she knew that if she wanted to get any answers, she would have to venture out onto the airborne ship. She had no idea where Arthur and Maria were, but she knew that Paul would be above her on the steering deck, tirelessly navigating the ship towards their unknown destination. She hadn't yet seen any sign of Cattia.

The deck creaked beneath Elsie's feet as she stumbled out onto the planks, crouching slightly as though she might be blown over the side at any moment. Above her, the patched cloth balloon bulged with hot air, looking like it was about to come apart at the seams under the pressure from within and the harsh wind from without. Elsie turned so that her back was to the wind and gazed up at the stern of the ship and the steering deck, where Paul was seated at a stool in front of the controls. His eyes brightened when they locked onto Elsie, and he gave a cheery smile, waving her up.

Elsie climbed the narrow stairs, holding onto the railing, and joined Paul at the helm.

"Mister Kauisol?" she gasped, barely able to hear her words over the wind and the roaring of the engine.

"Yes, Elsie? What is it?" Paul asked, inclining his head towards her, though keeping his eyes fixed on the bow of the ship. "Speak up a little, dear, I can barely hear you!"

"Yes, sorry, I was just wondering…" She had to shout to be heard. "Where is Mrs. Kauisol? And where is Arthur?"

Paul laughed. "Arthur is getting chewed out at the moment. If I wasn't too busy flying this old girl, I'd be there to translate for Maria. As it stands, she's writing her tirade on some loose scraps of paper."

"Then could we talk for a minute, Mister Kauisol?"

"Of course. And please, call me Paul."

"Okay, well, Paul," Elsie said, "How long was I asleep?"

"Not too long, though frankly, I'm jealous." Paul chuckled. "I could use a little rest myself."

Elsie cocked an eyebrow, hoping that Paul wouldn't fall asleep at the helm. "Where is Cattia?"

Paul sighed gravely, his demeanor slipping into a stony chill. "She stayed back."

"What?"

"I lost my cool...she stayed back."

"What?" Elsie stammered, unbelieving. "How could you let her stay back? She'll never survive out there!"

Paul shook his head. "You'd be shocked to know, but there are people living out in the Wreckage. They call themselves the Dwellers. Cattia chose to stay with them, rather than continue on with us. She told me to tell you that you should come and visit her sometime."

Elsie frowned, feeling her heart sink. "But...why would she stay with them? Are they good people? How do you know they won't hurt her..."

"They are a peaceful people; they carry no weapons. And they assisted us in fixing the ship. The engine might not be pretty, but at least she manages."

Elsie nodded absently, but her mind was still on Cattia. *So she's gone her own way, and I've gone mine... But I suppose that is what we wanted, leaving Threadbury's. We wouldn't have stuck together forever, surely.*

"That was fortunate," she said at last. "And they just helped you repair everything for free? That was kind of them."

"Oh, not for free." Paul chuckled. "Though fortunately for us they don't use money in the Wreckage. We traded them most of our remaining food supplies and the rest of those uniforms. They are a strange people, I'll tell you that."

"Why didn't Arthur just go to them?" Elsie asked, brow furrowing in confusion and annoyance as she thought of the pointless endeavor they'd undergone on Veturi.

"We didn't know anyone was out there until Clem...until the Dwellers came to us. I think if Maria'd had her way she might have stayed with them too, if it weren't for the fact that you were with Arthur," Paul said.

"What do you mean by that?" Elsie asked sharply.

"He means they'd have gladly left *me* to the wolves, if I'd been alone," Arthur said as he climbed up the steep stairs to the steering deck, leveling a hard-to-read expression at Paul and Elsie.

The sight of him in the broad daylight jarred Elsie. He was shirtless, though most of his torso and left shoulder were heavily wrapped in bandages, which were speckled here and there with blots of scarlet. His blue eyes were as piercing as ever, though she sensed something tired and resigned behind them. Perhaps it was merely the dark circles which gave her that impression. His burgundy coat was draped over his bare shoulder.

"I don't think Mister Kauisol meant it like that, Arthur," she said pointedly.

Arthur chuckled sardonically, drawing a deadly glare from Maria as she climbed up onto the deck beside him. "Oh, he meant it alright," Arthur said, running a hand through his limp red hair in an effort to slick it back out of his eyes. "Maria did, at least. I always have to wonder where she picked up *that* sort of language..."

Elsie coughed, interrupting him, and crossed her arms, giving him her best glare.

"Well since we're all here, I have a few questions for you, Arthur," she said with a huff. "First, why did you jump when I had a *gun* pointed right at my head? I could have been killed if it was loaded!"

"I knew it wasn't loaded," Arthur said flatly. He limped past her on his way to the railing to survey their surroundings, and Elsie noticed for the first time that the railing around the steering deck had not been repaired at all. If anything, it looked worse than when she'd first seen the ship crashed in the Wreckage. "The barrel wouldn't have burned your skin unless it had just been fired off," Arthur said, glancing back at her over his shoulder. "I can still see the mark on your forehead."

Elsie's hand flew unconsciously to her forehead, and she began to feel the ring of blisters absentmindedly with her thumb.

"But he could have reloaded when you weren't looking!"

Arthur shrugged. "He didn't."

"I don't care! Don't gamble with my life like that again."

Arthur kept his eyes fixed out over the rolling brown land below. "The alternative was that you would have been dragged off to prison, or worse: taken to Baron Schulhard's palace, where you would have been tortured for information you don't have and then executed." His firm tone left no room for dissent.

Elsie tried another tack. "Alright, then, who on earth was this Cadbury fellow? He seemed to know you personally."

There was a pregnant pause, broken only when Paul cleared his throat awkwardly from his perch at the controls of the airship. Maria climbed up to where her husband was sitting and began interrogating him in sign about the conversation. Arthur just continued to stare out over the wild landscape as it blurred past. Elsie followed his gaze, trying to take in the tangle of brown-and-gold-leafed trees and wind-torn shrubbery. It was unlike anything she'd ever seen, but somehow, though it differed greatly from the endless awful sprawl of the Wastes, it was no less lonely and miserable. Here and there, where the sun peeked through the gray haze, she saw it glint off streams and rivulets that coiled between exposed roots and heaps of disturbed soil.

Finally, Arthur spoke.

"He's just an old friend."

Elsie huffed, folding her arms over her chest. "That's not going to cut it! We were chased—*I* was chased all night by this man, shot at by soldiers under his command, and almost killed, all by someone *you* seem to have more than a passing acquaintance with. I think I deserve a bit more of an explanation."

Paul cleared his throat again, more pointedly this time. "Elsie, dear, some things are better left alone. I'm sure Arthur will explain in due time."

"We'll I'm not sure he will," Elsie snapped. She puffed out her chest and tried to stand up as tall as possible, though she only reached Arthur's collarbone in height, even as he leaned on the unstable railing. "Arthur, I want you to tell me everything. After what I've been through, which was apparently pointless, I think I deserve to know."

"Everything's a lot to know, kid," Arthur said softly. "I think there are some things you need to experience on your own before I tell you *everything*."

"Then just tell me this: who is Cadbury? Why does he dislike you so much that he *personally* chased both of us across the entirety of Veturi?"

Arthur exhaled heavily and straightened up, crossing his arms as he towered over Elsie once again. "Ulysses Cadbury is the chief elected officer of security on Veturi. He makes sure that everything runs smoothly, and more to the point he makes sure no one gets on or off the train who isn't supposed to."

"He clearly did a great job with us," Elsie muttered.

"Actually, I'm surprised that we got as far as we did with him in charge of that circus," Arthur interjected.

"But why was he after you specifically?"

Arthur sighed. "Again, kid, he was an old friend. His family were retainers for my parents. Took care of managing the land, and such. We went to the same naval academy." His eyes grew distant once again, and Elsie felt an enormous gulf open between them. "But we both sought to court the same woman, and that sort of thing can break even the firmest friendship apart. You'll understand more when you're older."

"Older? How much older do you think I need to be?" Elsie exclaimed, mouth agape. "I'm not a child, Arthur Pendington! As far as I can figure, I'm seventeen years old, and I can think and act for myself."

She looked to Arthur for any sign of emotion, any sign that she'd shaken his conception of her even an inch, but he merely returned a dull, faraway gaze that did not seem to ever truly meet her eyes. Instead, it seemed more as if she had shaken Paul and Maria. The two of them exchanged guilt-ridden glances and then a quick flurry of unknown signs before Maria clambered down from beside Paul and crossed to take Elsie's arm.

"Elsie, why don't you go down to the cabin with Maria," Paul said nonchalantly, glancing over his shoulder at Arthur, who had turned his back to them once more, "And have a nice chat."

Elsie was about to argue that she *couldn't* chat with Maria, not without Paul present at least, but Maria's insistent tug on her arm allowed no room for discussion. She followed the stout woman down the stairs and back into the captain's cabin, ears pricking as she strained to catch whatever Paul and Arthur might be saying behind their backs. Then the door clicked shut behind them, and she was alone with Maria in the dim, cold room.

The windows at the back of the cabin had been shattered, and the gaping hole left behind covered with the heavy damask curtains, haphazardly tied shut with twine to keep the wind out. The result was simultaneously stuffy and frigid, and the furniture had been so upturned and bounced about during the crash and subsequent flight that the air was now thick with dust. Elsie sneezed when they entered, scrubbing at her nose with a tattered sleeve as Maria fetched a crumpled piece of paper and an elaborate fountain pen. With some help from Elsie, she turned the little writing desk right side up and spread the paper out with a neat gesture. The little stool had been lost or broken in the chaos, so Maria was forced to stand as she wrote upon the paper.

"*Can you read?*" She scribbled the words down in a wiry script with thin, delicate letters that looped into one another. Elsie nodded, though it took her a moment to understand what had been written. Clearly expecting a longer response, Maria held out the fountain pen.

In big, clumsy letters, Elsie printed her words: "*I can, though I'm not great.*" She had been taught just enough when she was younger so that Threadbury's would meet its quotas and continue to receive funding from Gorand's provincial government for the "betterment of the poor." It had been a sad excuse for a school, or so some of the older, better educated women said. Basic reading, writing, and arithmetic were the only academic subjects taught. The science of the dyeworks, needlework, and the process of garment making had been drilled into the girls with much more gusto.

She looked back at what Maria was writing. "*Understand, dear child, that Arthur is a boar of a man. You cannot reason with him. He lost his humanity years ago, and only my fool husband believes that it still lies somewhere inside him.*" She stopped and looked up at Elsie.

Elsie shook her head, her face crumpling into a sad expression. She took the pen from Maria's hand again. "*Don't say that,*" she wrote carefully, embarrassed at her childishly blocky letters. "*He is a strange man. I don't understand him, but he isn't a monster.*"

Maria frowned. "*I think he is,*" she replied in her beautiful script. "*He is taking my Paul away from me. I hated to let you go alone to Veturi, but I also wanted to spend time alone with Paul, without that man always looking over our shoulders. We've never truly been able to have much of a marriage together, you understand.*" She sighed and laid down the pen, rubbing her temples, waiting for Elsie to write her response. Elsie herself waited, not knowing what to say, curious if Maria would reveal more. Finally, Maria began to write again.

"*You will understand when you are older,*" she wrote, and then scratched that out and began to scrawl the script again. "*When you find someone you love as much as I love my Paul, you will understand what I am talking about. You wouldn't want to be dogged by Athur, no matter how much you think he isn't a monster. He would never stop—he would persist, forever, and you would find yourself unable to have a life outside of Arthur Pendington.*" The period at the end of the sentence was more of a blot, and Maria's hand trembled as she dipped the pen back into the inkwell.

Thoughtfully, Elsie reached for the pen, unsure of exactly how she was going to respond. She would never know, however, because at that moment she heard footsteps descending the stairs outside of the cabin door, and the doorknob began to turn slowly. She tapped Maria on the shoulder, and the woman looked up. She reached to cover the paper but stopped when she saw who was opening the door.

Paul stepped in and flashed a tired smile. Able once again to sign freely, he began talking to Maria in a flurry of hands that was impossible for Elsie to keep track of. Finally, he spoke aloud. "I'm on my break, I suppose. It should be pretty smooth sailing for the rest of the night." He looked at Elsie. "Could we...have a moment here?"

"Yes, of course," Elsie stammered, skirting around him towards the door.

"No need to scramble, I just need a little rest," Paul said kindly. "I'm sorry to send you out to Arthur like this..."

"No, you've more than earned your rest, Mister Kauisol. I'll just... I'll just get out of your hair. Are you coming too?" she asked Maria with a wave of her hand.

Maria looked to Paul for a translation, and then just gave Elsie a rather sly smile before shaking her head gently. Something about her expression flustered Elsie, and she gave an awkward smile and wave as she hurriedly left the cabin and began ascending the stairs.

Arthur was situated above her at the controls, a confusing mess of levers, wheels, knobs, and all kinds of mechanical nonsense ensconced at the front of the steering deck. Elsie observed with some interest that Arthur worked them stiffly, his arms rigid whenever they weren't moving to grab another lever, pull another knob, or turn another wheel. He seemed much less comfortable with steering the ship than Paul, who was all easy grace as he guided the *Heart*. It was, however, relatively smooth sailing. Over the edge of the ship, Elsie saw the landscape rolled out in an endless flat plain. It was not an unnatural flatness like the Wastes of Gorand, where man had devoured the landscape and reduced it to nothing but rock and dirt. This was a natural flatness, with occasional dips and rises, broken up here and there by scrub brush or low-lying standing water.

"Come over here, kid," Arthur snapped.

"You can call me by my name, you know!" Elsie replied. She crossed to his side, wincing as she felt the wood creak beneath her shoes. "What do you want?" she asked, crossing her arms against the wind and watching him warily.

"I want to show you how an airship works," he said somewhat defensively.

"I'd like to know how it's even airborne!" She looked around at the sorry state of the ship.

"You should see the engine room," Arthur said grimly. "Now, this lever here is what controls the speed of the starboard side rear propellors..." He began to drone on, and Elsie found herself listening with fascinated attention as Arthur expounded the mechanical wonders of the airship.

Once Elsie had closed the door, Paul turned to look at Maria. She crossed the room in a businesslike fashion and latched the door smartly, before signing coyly to Paul, '*You know that they're right above us...don't you think we should wait until we're back in town?*'

Paul had a strange, determined look about his eyes that did not dissipate when he smiled at her. '*We are going to have a lot more time when we get to Bolden.*'

'*What do you mean?*' Maria asked.

'*I'm leaving Arthur,*' Paul said as he crossed the room to the bookcase. Miraculously, the gramophone machine had survived, unlike a great deal of the room's contents. He rifled through the discs that were lying in a pile on the floor and smiled as he selected one. "My Love in Your Heart" was the title on the sleeve.

'*Leaving Arthur?*' Maria signed, her gestures at first slow and uncertain, then gaining speed as his words sunk in. '*You mean that once we get to the next skydock, we'll be rid of him for good?*' She did not mean for the grin that split her face to be so eager but she could hardly believe it.

'*Yes. I don't know if he'll ever change, Maria. I thought...*' he waved his hands, erasing the former statement. '*I wanted him to be better, Maria. But every time I think he's made a step forward he seems to—intentionally, mind you—take two steps back. We can start a family out there. We cannot around Arthur.*' He hung his head, his shoulders slumping as though releasing a great weight, before meeting Maria's eyes again.

'*Did you tell him? Is Elsie safe out there alone with him?*' Maria asked frantically, starting towards the door before Paul stopped her gently with a hand on her shoulder.

'*I haven't said anything to him about it yet. Cadbury mentioned something about Helena to him. He's almost back to the way he was after the* Formidable. *But I'm not worried that he will hurt her. She reminds him of her, I think, in a way. And he didn't hurt me.*' He signed it emphatically, though she could see in his eyes that he was lying.

Not physically, maybe, Maria thought bitterly to herself. '*So that's what had him in such a foul mood. What are you doing?*' she asked as Paul set the record down onto the gramophone and began to crank it to life. When he had finished cranking the machine, he gently set the needle down onto the spinning disc.

'*So we can dance,*' Paul told her gently. He crossed the room deftly and put one hand on her waist, taking her other hand in his. She was surprised suddenly by how handsome he was, his deep brown eyes seeming to take all of her in with a single glance, his kindly face set off by the well-groomed sideburns she loved so much.

She pulled her hand free, a smile on her face. '*You know I can't hear it, right?*' she signed before reaching up to cup his cheeks with both hands.

'*But I can. And I'm a terrible dancer with music. Think of how bad I would be without...*' Maria interrupted his signs with a kiss, pulling his face down to meet hers almost a head lower. It took only a moment, but it was one of the happiest moments of her life.

32
LOOSE CANNON

Jacik felt like an animal trapped in a too-small cage. He'd tried pacing, but there was barely room for him to walk two steps in the cramped cell. Eventually he gave up, assuming a deceptively relaxed position leaning against one of the cold metal walls. He'd given his whole life to serve the king, and even more to be by the princess's side, and now he could do nothing to protect her.

Jacik had every confidence in Yvonnia's judgment. The king, however, had clearly been cornered politically and in his panic made a very unwise move, sending his only surviving heir into a foreign land full of brutes and barbarians. It was clear to Jacik that Baron Schulhard had never intended to welcome the Sialis or assist them in any way. Instead, he had decided to use them as scapegoats for Odol's inability to quell Greyer's rebellion. Whether Lord Cadbury had really destroyed an outpost of the rebels Jacik couldn't be sure, but he was positive that the rebellion itself was still alive and well, despite whatever losses Cadbury had inflicted. He had seen this denial tactic used by both the Holanites and the Ryokans in the civil war to save face, but it always backfired.

In any case, Yvonnia, Enya, and himself were about to be sacrificed on the altar of saved face; but whether that face was the baron's, or the emperor's, or even Cadbury's, it made little difference to him. All he could think of was that their journey would soon come to an end in Odolia, their captor's capital city, where they would be tortured for false confessions and then publicly executed. He stood up and began pacing again, nervous energy crackling through his limbs. Perhaps Yvonnia would be spared the torture, but he and Enya would not be, and it was a fate worse than death to know that it would be his false words that finally condemned her.

"If you don't stop that, you'll wear a hole in the floor for us to escape through," Enya said dryly from her bunk, "If it doesn't just lead to our death from falling a thousand feet, of course. Why don't you just sit down and rest?"

"I cannot rest while the princess is out of my sight," Jacik said grimly, not even pausing for an instant.

Enya slid down and perched on his bunk instead. "Why don't you just come over and sit with me?" she asked, pouting her lips and looking up at him through her dark lashes.

It took all Jacik's strength not to audibly groan. "Why can't you stop acting like a lovesick adolescent?"

"But I am a lovesick adolescent." Enya grinned.

Jacik rolled his eyes and pressed his lips together. It would be in Odol's best interests to have two of the three Sialis at each other's throats, rather than putting their heads together to think of a way of escape. Not that Enya had much of a head on her shoulders for such a dull task... He glanced at the girl again, and an idea struck him. He stopped pacing abruptly and sat down on the edge of the cot resting his chin in his hands as he thought quickly.

"I see you are ready to join me," Enya said coyly, leaning towards him so that her shoulder brushed his. Then, seeing his knit brows and fiercely concentrated expression, she frowned. "What's wrong?"

"I have a plan. You need to get us out of this room."

Enya laughed. "I suppose you think I could just use one of my hairpins to pick the lock or something."

"No. You are going to seduce that man out there." Jacik pointed at the heavy metal door.

"What?" Enya pulled away from him, her dark eyes wide. Jacik massaged the bridge of his nose. The idea sickened him, but the men here were barbarians, and it should be easy for a girl of her charms. Yes, he could still recognize them, even after all he'd been through. And she would be perfectly safe; he would see to that. If the brute laid a finger on her, he would kill him.

"Only convince him to open the door, and I shall deal with the rest," he told her.

"You're insane. I'll tell Yvonnia you suggested that," Enya said, her cheeks flushing as she looked at him incredulously. "Just as soon as she gets back."

"You suggested as much earlier," Jacik said, getting to his feet, "Tell her when we reach her above." The discussion was over. She had her orders. Whether she followed them was up to her. Enya sat on the bed for a few moments more, staring dully at the dusty floor. Then, with an expression of resignation, she rose and smoothed down her cropped black hair, moistened her chapped lips with her tongue, and crossed to the door. She glanced back at him, and Jacik gave her a firm nod. He stationed himself in one corner behind the door, and shut his eyes, waiting, listening.

"Sir?" Enya rapped on the metal door, the Odolian speech forming haltingly on her tongue. "May I speak to you?" She spoke as clearly and loudly as she could, putting all her effort into the strange words.

"What is it?" The small slot in the door slid open and the guard's eyes appeared, swiveling back and forth to take in the cell. Jacik was unsure if the guard could see him from this angle, but he noticed with gratitude that Enya stepped closer to the door and met the guard's gaze unflinchingly, filling his field of view.

"I could use some air," she said lightly, "And some better company than Jacik. The princess has been gone for so long…" She tilted her head. Jacik could imagine her lowering her gaze only to glance up disarmingly through her dark lashes.

"You know I can't open this door for anyone, sweetheart," the guard said. "Where's the bodyguard anyway?"

"He's sleeping. Don't worry about him, he can stay in here for all I care." Enya's voice was haughty with false contempt. She hesitated for a moment. "I'll...make it worth your while."

Jacik's mouth went dry. The words stung his heart, and he knew how much it must hurt Enya's pride to do this, despite her earlier bravado in Yvonnia's presence. Flirting with him was one thing; sucking up to their captors and executors was quite another. But it must be done.

The guard was silent for a moment, and Jacik heard him speak quietly to someone outside the cell. His heart skipped a beat. Was there a second guard? He had only seen one when they'd been put into the cell. "It had better be damn well worth it, sweetheart," the guard whispered at last. "If the baron finds out, I'd lose my head..."

Jacik heard the keys clink and turn in the lock. The hinges creaked, opening outward ever so slightly. His strong arms shot out above Enya's head and slammed the steel door back into the guard's face with as much force as he could muster. Pushing past her, he burst out into the corridor, glancing once to confirm that the guard was unconscious on the floor. As he had feared, a second guard stood on the other side of the doorway, clutching a musket with a stunned expression on his face. As Jacik spun towards him, the man raised his musket and Jacik saw the glitter of the sharp bayonet. Thinking quickly, he ducked down beneath the man's reach and tackled him to the floor.

With the skinny man pinned beneath his bulk, Jacik pulled his arms free, wrapped his fingers around the man's throat, and squeezed. He saw movement behind him and whipped his head around, but it was only Enya, her hands clutched to her mouth, staggering out of the cell. He felt the man's body go limp beneath him, but held on for a moment more before letting go and rising to his feet. He turned towards Enya, looking to make sure that the other guard was fully unconscious, but he was interrupted when she struck him on the cheek.

"You can do that next time if you want to escape," she cried in a hoarse whisper, tears welling up in her eyes. "I'm never degrading myself like that again."

Jacik looked past her at the unconscious guard, unable to meet her gaze. "Thank you," he murmured, "For freeing us."

"We're not free yet," Enya snapped, crossing her arms tightly over her chest and glaring at him as he picked over the body of the first soldier. He discarded the flimsy saber at once; to him it appeared almost decorative. He picked up the fallen musket instead. The guard had not fired it, so he thought it must still be loaded. Good thing, as he hadn't a clue how to use the weapon, much less reload. He hefted it in his hands, testing the weight. It would be awkward to use as a spear, even with the glittering bayonet, but as a bludgeon... He smiled. The wooden handle was heavy and solid. He turned it around in his hands and gripped the barrel as though it were a club.

"Follow me," he said. "Quickly."

He had no idea where he was going, but moving forward was better than staying still.

They hurried down the narrow corridor, Jacik ducking his head to avoid the low ceiling. The hallway was lined with doors, but they all looked about the same as the one they had just come out of: sealed metal with tiny slits that could be raised to look inside. Jacik thought that they must be in some lower part of the ship, near the great engines; he could feel them rumbling beneath his feet, causing the entire corridor to vibrate slightly. Enya kept close behind him, skirts gathered up in her hands. When he glanced back to check on her, he saw that her eyes were wide and glassy with unshed tears.

At last, he spotted an intersection ahead but came to an abrupt halt when he heard the coordinated tramp of feet. Enya bumped into him from behind, letting out a little gasp. He hushed her at once and plastered himself to the wall behind a protruding bulkhead, pulling the girl with him. He was just in time. A file of soldiers marched past briskly, eyes ahead, oblivious to the escapees. Within seconds, they had disappeared down the intersecting corridor.

Jacik peeled himself from the metal wall and peered around the corner in the direction the marines had come from. Another long, empty hallway stretched out several hundred feet before terminating in a T-junction. He listened, but heard nothing besides the thrum of the engines, the fading clatter of the soldiers, and Enya's ragged breathing. He looked the other way and saw the last red-coated soldier disappear around a corner ahead. He reached back, grabbed Enya's tiny hand, and pulled the girl after him into the wider corridor.

"What...?" she began, but he glared so fiercely at her that she shut her mouth at once. They started off again, moving quickly but quietly, tailing the soldiers as best they could. Jacik's mind raced, wondering where the squadron could be headed in such military fashion. Perhaps there had been an attack upon the ship, or even a mutiny. Wherever they were going, though, he thought it would be much more useful to follow men who knew their surroundings, rather than wandering endless corridors without guidance. The soldiers ahead turned once more, and Jacik and Enya followed behind at a safe distance, stepping out into the intersection.

"Stop right there, prisoner!" shouted a harsh Odolian voice behind them. "Drop the gun." The shout echoed down the corridor, alerting the company they were following.

Jacik froze, then turned to see who had spoken. A second company had come up behind them unawares. The captain stood in front, holding an elaborate flintlock pistol. A second was holstered at his belt, beside a wicked looking rapier. The first company was already turning, coming slowly back up the corridor towards the confrontation, muskets leveled.

"Drop the gun," the captain of the second company said. "Slowly, or we will fire." The men behind him fanned out on either side, guns at the ready; the corridor here was just about wide enough for three men to walk abreast. Enya pressed against Jacik's side, trembling as her eyes darted back and forth. They were pinched in a vice between the two companies.

Jacik met the captain's gaze and slowly began to lower the rifle to the steel mesh floor, crouching slightly. The dozen or so guns that were pointed directly at him didn't move. Jacik shifted the musket into one hand, as though he was about to drop it, and then in a flash of motion he dove to the floor, back into the corridor they had just stepped out of, shoving Enya to the ground with him. She screamed as a dozen gunshots echoed off the metal walls.

Pale smoke filled the corridors in either direction, creeping through the air towards them as Jacik rose to his feet, gripping the musket in both hands once more. Judging by the cries and groans from the marines, his plan had worked. A bullet had grazed his shoulder as he dropped, but he had no time to nurse the pain. He rushed to the left, swinging the musket like a club, cracking those who were still standing across the head with the wooden butt of the gun. As the haze began to clear, the men behind him rushed forward, filling the air with angry shouts.

Jacik hooked his musket across the neck of the fallen captain, pulling him up from the ground just in time to use his body as a shield against the next volley. Only a few of the men from the second company remained, and their bullets all struck the dead man or whizzed past Jacik as they shot wide. Without their captain, and with no time to reload, the marines devolved into poorly trained cowards, and instead of reaching for their swords or affixing their bayonets, they all turned tail and fled in the other direction. Not willing to run the risk of an alarm being sounded, Jacik dropped the limp corpse of the captain and rushed after them, cracking each one neatly across the skull with his musket.

When they had all been incapacitated, Jacik stopped for a moment to catch his breath. Over the rumble of the dreadnought's engines, slightly fainter now as they had moved further into the ship, he could hear the steady dripping of blood through the mesh floor onto the ducts and pipes below. *That's a sound I'd not soon get used to hearing,* he thought grimly. His ruminations were interrupted by a desperate cry from behind him, and Jacik spun back to face the carnage that littered the corridor. One of the marines had risen from the ground, wounded by the friendly fire but still able to stagger forward. He was wise enough to have drawn his sword, but not wise enough to remain quiet as he advanced. Still, Jacik was put on the defensive.

The man, more of a boy really, was white-faced and desperate. His swings were wild and unpredictable, and he rushed at Jacik with surprising speed considering his injury. As he fought to regain his bearings, it was all Jacik could do to fend off the sword strokes. Then he caught sight of Enya coming around the corner towards them. He opened his mouth to warn her, but with a cry she flung herself forwards and wrapped her arms around the young soldier's legs, causing him to stagger beneath her weight. It was enough to throw him off balance, providing an opening for Jacik to go on the offensive. With final horrible *crack,* he laid the boy out unconscious on the floor.

Standing up shakily, Enya brushed off her skirts and reached up as though to straighten her veil, forgetting for a moment that she had lost it. She settled for patting her hair into place instead. She shot Jacik a grim smile.

"Are you alright?" Jacik asked, not waiting for an answer before dropping into a crouch to search through the bodies of the soldiers. If Enya was able to stand on her own, she was well enough to not require his immediate attention.

"I'm...nauseous," the girl admitted, pressing a hand to her stomach as she looked around distastefully at the fallen marines. "There's...a lot of blood."

Jacik grunted in acknowledgement of her sentiments. "No sane man likes fighting," he said, sifting through the fallen weapons. He was shocked that Odol could fight a war at all with how poorly made their swords were. Out of the dozen or so soldiers who lay around him, only one sword was unbent or unbroken: that of the boy who had attacked him. He drew it out, testing the weight. It was a thin blade and didn't seem made for fighting. Still, it could pierce the uniforms of the Odolian soldiers, which was the important part. He threw the musket down.

"What do we do now?" Enya asked plaintively, wincing as the gun clanged against the steel floor.

"We press on," Jacik said, stepping towards the fallen captain on a sudden hunch. He set the flimsy sword against the steel wall and began to search. In the breast pocket of the captain's uniform, he found a folded piece of paper, covered with thin lines that outlined the form of the dreadnought and labeled in tiny Odolian text. Jacik's written Odolian was rusty, but he knew enough to decipher what he needed, and reading blueprints was a task not entirely unfamiliar to him.

"What's that?" Enya asked, staring wide eyed as he unfolded the tiny square of paper into a much larger map. Jacik ignored her, studying the lines and diagrams with extreme concentration. Enya edged towards him, peering around, trying to see what he was looking at. "Is that a map? I'm great with maps." Jacik grunted and turned away, orienting himself within the corridor as his eyes traced a path through the blueprint. After a moment longer, he folded the paper crisply and tucked it into the pocket of his own uniform.

"Follow me," he said briskly, snatching up the sword. "We have no time to lose."

Seeing no one in the corridor beyond, Jacik put his shoulder to the grate and forced it open. He and Enya crawled out of the duct into a quiet, clean, empty metal corridor, far from the thrumming engines and fallen marines. Enya coughed, and Jacik shushed her once, glancing around as he replaced the grate as best he could. It was slightly bent and fit poorly, but at a glance it wouldn't matter. They were drawing near to the end of their journey.

The ducts that fed into the captain's lounge and cabin were too small for a man to squeeze through, which was a wise decision on the part of the engineer who designed the dreadnaughts. But the ducts that snaked through most of the rest of the ship were large enough, in a pinch. The shoulders of Jacik's uniform were scuffed and torn, and his back ached from scraping against the tight metal walls and rows of rivets. But they had at last arrived in the corridor outside the captain's cabin, and Jacik was gratified by his own cunning.

He forced the last door open and rushed in, sword drawn, only to find the lounge empty. Two places had been set at the table, wine already sparkling in the fluted glasses, filling the room with its heady scent. Jacik began to look around, inspecting everything with expert eyes. He went to the polished timber door that led to the captain's bunk, but that room was neat and empty as well. Turning back, he saw that Enya was sniffing one of the crystal wine glasses intently.

"She's not here," the girl said, setting the glass down untasted. "Do you see anything?"

"They were in a hurry to leave," Jacik said, gesturing to the uncorked bottle and expectant table settings. "Perhaps..." His sentence was interrupted as the entire room lurched. Enya and Jacik grabbed hold of the solid table for support as the ship shuddered and righted itself once more.

"What was that?" Enya gasped, still clinging to the table as fear widened her dark eyes.

"The ship may be under attack..." Jacik began, but he was interrupted once more as the dreadnought heaved again, sending the crystal glasses and half-empty wine bottle spilling to the floor with a crash. The room tilted further this time, and objects slid out of the built-in shelves on the far wall as their doors flapped open. Jacik caught sight of a long, curved blade sliding across the carpet and stopped it with his foot as it passed him. It was his sword. Jacik grinned and snatched the blade up in one fluid motion as the ship righted itself once again. Here, finally, was a weapon he could use.

33
TEMPEST TOSSED

As Elsie was listening to Arthur, she heard the faint sound of music from beneath her feet. It was a slower song, and there were the fainter, thinner strains of someone singing, but through the wood of the deck it was impossible to hear the words. At that moment she knew that if she ever got any money in life, she would spend it all on surrounding herself with music.

"...this gauge is one of the most important, so you can't forget it. In fact, it's one of the only things that remains consistent between the smaller designs and the dreadnoughts. Kid...kid, are you paying attention?" Arthur barked, pulling Elsie back to reality.

"Oh, sorry," she said, refixing her eyes on the dashboard in front of her. "The music caught me off guard. It's a lot to take in, huh." She studied the dials and knobs, but much of her interest had evaporated.

"Music? What music?" Arthur muttered. "Anyways, the air preasure gauge..."

Elsie's mind drifted. She raised her head from the controls and saw something ahead that made her heart lurch. The sky in front of them had darkened, black clouds thickening rapidly above the rolling plain below. In the air between the earth and the clouds, she could see lights flickering sporadically. The low roll of thunder came to her over the whine of the airship's engine, drowning out the music.

"...kid? Kid, you have to have a greater resistance to distraction than that," Arthur told her. Elsie cleared her throat.

"Arthur?"

"Yes?"

"I think there's a storm ahead..."

Arthur turned from facing Elsie and stared straight over the prow of the ship, his eyes narrowing as he took it in. The entire horizon was now shrouded in darkness, and the sun had vanished behind the clouds.

"A pretty bad one too," Arthur replied slowly. Elsie's heart began to race and blood drummed in her ears, but Arthur remained deathly calm. "Kid, go fetch Paul and Maria. We need all hands on deck."

As Maria leaned her head against Paul's shoulder, he tapped her on the back to let her know that the record was finished and he needed to go and change it. She didn't care, of course. To her, it was two-and-a-half to three minutes of bliss, punctuated by Paul either turning a disc over or replacing it with a new one. All that changed was the rhythm with which he stumbled through the steps of a dance. He truly was a terrible dancer, often stepping on her toes and on more than one occasion tripping and nearly knocking the two to the floor. It didn't help that the wind continually shook the airborne ship, making sure-footedness an impossibility.

It was paradise.

Paradise was abruptly interrupted by Elsie. She slammed the door open and scrambled into the room, grabbing Paul's arm just as he was about to lower the phonograph needle. She was speaking so frantically that Maria couldn't decipher the words forming on her lips.

'*Paul, what's wrong?*' Maria signed as soon as she'd got his attention.

She did not like the expression on Paul's face. It was the same detached, resigned expression he got when he was about to acquiesce to one of Arthur's absurd plans. '*The ship is about to enter a storm,*' he signed slowly and firmly. '*Arthur needs me out there with him. You two stay here.*' He turned to speak to Elsie, likely to tell her the same thing.

Elsie was not having it, however. She was visibly frustrated with Paul, her brown eyes flashing as she shook her head defiantly. Maria smiled grimly. *Atta girl. You stand up to him and take no such silliness.* Elsie's words were lost in the barrier of sound, but through her annunciated lip movement, Maria could pick up the general idea. '*I'm not just going to wait here for you and Arthur to crash this ship! We are helping. Besides, he said* all *hands on deck, not just you.*'

Maria tapped Paul's shoulder and began signing to him before he'd turned around. '*Yes, you big oaf. You have to steer the blasted ship; you'll need someone else out there to maintain the deck and check the ropes. I say we turn right around and head back north. This rattletrap won't last a minute in a storm.*'

Paul frowned and shook his head. '*No friendly skydocks in that direction. But we do need to get somewhere else quickly. Bolden shouldn't be too much further south…*'

Ignoring him, Maria grabbed a stray uniform coat and threw another to Elsie. It wouldn't do much in a storm, but it was better than nothing, especially with the girl still laced into that prissy satin dress. The three of them stepped out onto the deck, wind whipping and tugging the door out of Maria's hand, slamming it shut behind her. Already, droplets of rain were beginning to fall, and ahead the clouds were rapidly darkening.

"We have to hit it at full speed!" Arthur shouted from the steering deck, his eyes wild as he braced himself and clung to the controls. Behind him, a bolt of lightning split the sky, arcing between clouds.

Elsie gripped the staircase railings with both hands, her knees threatening to buckle as the ship rocked, buffeted by a sudden gust of wind. Paul and Maria followed close behind, Paul gently pushing past Elsie up the stairs to the deck, Maria patting her on the back as she ran to secure some loose piece of equipment. Elsie felt rain sting her cheek as she steadied herself against the bottom of the stairs, though the huge cloth balloon seemed to be keeping the worst of it off the deck. Thunder boomed around her, only adding to the confusion.

Arthur was shouting orders at Paul, who took over the controls. At last, Arthur pushed himself away from the helm and turned to look down at Elsie, shouting something that she could not hear. The sprinklings of rain had become a deluge, echoing hollowly off of the cloth balloon, punctuated by the flash of lightning and the roar of thunder. Elsie could see nothing past the edges of the ship now. They had been swallowed up by the storm.

"...you even listening to me? Kid, I need you to get to the bow!" Arthur shouted as he limped heavily down the stairs, growing audible as he drew closer to her. He was pulling on his red overcoat, though his shirt was already plastered to his skin. "Kid, are you listening to me?"

He strode past her, beckoning her to follow with a sharp motion. Even his limp did not seem to impede his confidence; he walked with his back straight and his head high, impervious to the rain and wind. In fact, Elsie almost thought he was enjoying himself.

"What?" she managed as she fell into step beside him, keeping close in case the wind should threaten to bowl her over.

"I need you at the bow to make sure none of the ropes come undone under the strain. If even one of them comes loose, we'll all likely crash to our deaths. Maria will get the ones near the stern by

Paul, and I'll run back and forth here." He gestured to the network of ropes fastened to either side of the middle of the ship, holding the enormous balloon in place. "Just make sure you don't stand between the ropes and the edge," he added. "If one of them snaps, you'll be lucky if you just get a few broken ribs and aren't cut clean in half."

"What, are you serious?" Elsie exclaimed, looking up at him in disbelief.

"You'll do great," Arthur said, putting a hand on her shoulder and looking her full in the face for what felt like the first time. "You really saved me back on Veturi, kid. You'll do fine here."

His confidence, his confidence in *her*, stirred up a strange self-confidence in response. She felt like saluting. Instead, she nodded, turned, and set off running up the length of the deck to the front of the creaking airship, the wind shoving hair into her eyes and spattering stray raindrops across her face. As she reached the front of the ship, the spatters turned into a constant deluge of rain that quickly soaked through the flimsy uniform coat. *So much for Odolian military might*, she thought bitterly, surveying her surroundings.

Half a dozen thick hemp ropes, fastened to brackets on either side of the bow with complicated sailor's knots, shot up into the air on either side of her, pulled taught by the force of the balloon as it strained skywards. Above, they branched out into a complicated lattice that held the balloon in place. The entire network stretched and strained in the wind, the ropes creaking audibly, but it seemed to be holding fast. She scanned for any sign of fraying or deterioration, though unsure what she would even do if she found it. Arthur's instructions had been rather vague on that point.

She turned back to shout at him, but at that moment the entire ship jolted. Elsie cried out as she was flung sideways against the railing. The flimsy, splintered wood held for a moment, and then fell away beneath her weight.

Elsie flung out her arm, grasped the rope beside her, and shrieked again as her shoulder was jolted in its socket by the force of her fall. Her feet scrabbled for purchase on the slick deck, but as the ship was rocked again by turbulence she lost her footing entirely and found herself dangling from the rope, her hand locked around it by sheer force of will and adrenaline. She couldn't have pried her fingers loose if she tried.

The wind pressed her against the side of the ship, tearing at her hair and the heavy skirt of her dress. Her shoulder screamed. She struggled to drag her other hand up from her side, seeming to move in slow motion as she reached up, battling the wind and the fear and the pain. She grasped the rope with her other hand.

"Arthur!" she screamed with all her might. "Paul, Maria, help!"

Her words were lost in the fray, torn from her lips by the roaring wind and flung into the tailwind of the ship. Tears forced their way out of the corners of Elsie's eyes as she clung desperately to the rope. Maybe this was the end. Maybe she would fall to her death. Maybe it was all for nothing. *Please, please don't let me die. Don't let this be the end.*

"Kid!"

She looked up and saw Arthur, rain soaked and defiant, his burgundy overcoat billowing about him like a cape, his rough, sailor's hands reaching for hers. Behind him, the sky tore as they broke free of the storm clouds for a moment, golden sunlight piercing through the gloom. Then they were back in the thick of the dark and the rain.

"Kid, grab my hand!"

Elsie's grip tightened reflexively on the rope. Gritting her teeth, she made a great effort and let go, grasping wildly for Arthur's extended hand. His fingers fastened around her wrist, and he pulled her desperately up over the side onto the deck. For a moment she lay sprawled across his knees, her entire body trembling, shoulders throbbing with dull, heavy pain. Then Arthur scrambled back, dragging her away from the broken railing, and got to his feet.

"You alright?" he asked, reaching down to help her up. Elsie didn't want to move an inch. Blearily, she looked up and saw the sky flash golden once again as the ship barreled free of the storm, the clouds suddenly illuminated from without by rich evening light. With a great effort, she peeled her shoulder off the deck, reaching for his outstretched hand. As her hand once again touched his, she felt a searing pain and withdrew, staring at her palms. They were red and raw, not from dye this time, but with angry rope burns. She had been so intent on holding on for dear life that the pain never even registered.

"Those look nasty. You're lucky, kid, that was a close one." Arthur smiled grimly as she got slowly to her feet, shielding her hands close to her body as the stinging pain increased, no longer blocked by adrenaline. She looked up at him, opening her mouth to speak, but was stopped by the sheer beauty of what she saw.

Behind the ship, a huge mound of dark clouds hung suspended in the air, crackling every now and then with flashes of lightning. The rest of the sky was flooded with the glow of the setting sun, extending in broken fields of blue and white clouds as far as the eye could see. She saw the ground stretching out beneath them, smeared dark beneath the mass of the storm, but clear and crisp where the rain did not reach.

Arthur turned to see what she was staring at and grinned. "We've broken free!" he shouted, scrambling across the deck and taking the stairs two at a time. "Paul, you're a genius."

Paul stepped back from behind the controls, wiping moisture from his brow with a sleeve, a satisfied smile on his face. "That was a doozy," was all he said.

Elsie watched in awe as Arthur flung his arms around Paul's shoulders and engulfed the man in a hug. Maria joined them, struggling to shove Arthur out of the way as she reached for her husband. For a moment, they were more than comrades, or even friends. They looked like family. Elsie averted her eyes. The moment seemed too private to watch. *And that's why they stick with him, even when it seems like he's lost his mind,* she thought. She looked back at the wall of clouds, still fascinated by the impossible sight.

A shape caught her eye from within the mass, something large and dark looming just at the edge of sight. She squinted, shielding her eyes against the sun, trying to decipher what it could be. Then the storm parted suddenly as the shape broke through, shedding wisps of vapor from its hull as it blotted out the golden clouds.

Elsie's mouth dropped open. She had never seen anything so massive, nor so terrifying. The *thing*, the ship, did not look like any other airship she knew. It was built around a metal mound in the center, like a balloon but rigid and heavy, its angular hull bristling with cannons and walkways and cables. She saw figures climbing up and down, appearing antlike in comparison to the massive structure. Black smoke billowed out behind as it lumbered through the air towards them.

"Arthur," she said, her voice almost a whisper at first, then rising into a shriek of terror. "Arthur!"

Arthur broke from the embrace and ran down the stairs to join her on the main deck, his grin erased by a look of grave concern. She pointed breathlessly at the enormous ship, her hand trembling in the air.

"What is that?"

Arthur stared, his face falling into an indecipherable mask as he took it in. At length, he spoke.

"Kid, *that* is an imperial dreadnought."

34

FINAL FLIGHT OF THE *HEART*

Elsie gaped at the dreadnought in awe and terror. It appeared too large to fly, and yet it was airborne, moving in heavy-bellied flight through the clouds with a strange sort of elegance and precision. Its shape was unlike any other ship she had seen, angular and streamlined, without the awkward form of a balloon above to slow it down. She stepped closer to Arthur, feeling a curl of dread in her chest.

"Paul, which one is it?" the captain shouted to his helmsman. "I can't see from here!"

Elsie looked up at Paul, who shielded his eyes from the rays of sun which pierced the rolling clouds. "It's the Gorandi standard, sir! Could only be the *Redoubtable*."

"Turn to starboard!" Arthur barked, turning away from her to shout up at the steering deck. "Paul, tell Maria to get the cannons ready!" He pulled out one of his pistols, the engraved one with gold inlay, and aimed it in the direction of the steel monster. He closed one eye, adjusted his aim, then swore and spat on the deck. "No chance. Paul, get me closer!"

Paul nodded slowly, let go of Maria, and stepped back to the controls. He took the ship in a wide arc, swinging around through a bank of clouds back towards the approaching dreadnought. For a moment, it vanished from view.

Maria was furious. Her round cheeks were bright red, and her face was twisted into the meanest scowl Elsie had ever seen her give. She stomped down the stairs, grabbed the billowing tails of Arthur's military coat, and yanked him toward her. Then she slapped Arthur across the face and let her hands fall to her sides as she regarded him with a look of utter contempt.

Arthur snarled, jaw quivering as the veins stood out on his forehead. He glared up at Paul. "Get your wife to cooperate. We'll be blown out of the sky if she doesn't man the cannons!"

"What are we doing?" Elsie shouted, her eyes darting in confusion from Paul to Arthur to Maria and back again. The dread had coiled down into the pit of her stomach. She didn't have to ask. Arthur meant to destroy the dreadnought or die trying, and he was willing to bring them all down with him.

Arthur ignored her question, merely shouting at Paul to get them closer. The *Heart of Resistance* plunged downward toward the massive ship, breaking out of the clouds once more as it drew level with the dreadnought's upper decks. All Elsie could do was watch in horror as the Odolian ship opened fire.

A hail of cannonballs and musket shots flew past, some of the smaller bullets punching holes in the great balloon overhead. Elsie heard the hiss of air escaping. Arthur ran up beside her and leaned out over the railing, his blue eyes burning with hatred as he stared out at the steel monster bellying through the clouds. He looked back over his shoulder and shouted so loudly it hurt Elsie's ears.

"Paul, will you get Maria to help me or not? I can't fight on my own. Paul, get me closer!"

Elsie ducked as she felt a bullet whiz past her ear. She looked up at the helm and saw Paul, his face unusually serious, hands still on the controls. Maria was standing with her arms crossed, her back planted firmly against the door of the captain's cabin, regarding

Arthur and Elsie with a look of resigned disappointment. Arthur wrenched himself away from the railing and stalked across the deck towards the staircase, seething.

"Paul, you're being insubordinate. I swear, when we get out of this I'll..."

His eyes never leaving Arthur's face, Paul pulled one of the levers. The ship veered away from the dreadnought with a lurch. With several more adjustments of the controls, Paul turned the engine over. The whirring of the propellers and clatter of the engine rose to deafening heights as the ship mounted vertically into the clouds.

Scowling, Arthur turned back and fired vainly in the direction of the diminishing dreadnought. He tossed the pistol to the ground and dashed up to the helm, shoving Paul away from the controls. Paul stumbled back, caught by surprise, and the engine stalled momentarily. Arthur turned the ship around so tightly that Elsie was flung to her knees. She scrambled up and chased across the deck after Arthur, mounting the stairs two at a time. Maria tried to catch her as she passed, but Elsie ducked out of her reach and climbed to the steering deck as Paul regained his balance and grasped Arthur's arm, trying to pull him off the controls.

"Arthur, we can't fight them," Paul pleaded, wringing the fabric of Arthur's sleeve. "Not today, not like this. Please, you must be reasonable." His eyes caught sight of Elsie standing breathless by the stairs and his voice gained a new sense of urgency. "Elsie, stay back. Get below with Maria. Let me handle this."

Arthur ignored his navigator, throttling the engine and driving the ship back down toward the dreadnought. "Tell the crew to make ready to board. We may not have the firepower to take it from the outside, but if we could get inside..."

Elsie saw Paul's face sink. "Maria is right. You're mad."

"What?" Arthur roared. "You're mad for not listening to orders, Kauisol! Get to your post at once."

Paul shook his head, stepping back from Arthur as though releasing him from some bond. "No. I can't let you endanger Maria and Elsie any longer. You're mad, and you're going to kill us all if you don't come to your senses."

Arthur's face was blank. Elsie was uncertain if he could even hear Paul's words at this point. Maria had stepped away from her post to see what was going on at the helm. Elsie stared too in horrified fascination, even as another hail of bullets struck the ship broadside, tearing at the splintered wooden hull below.

"Arthur, I've been by your side through thick and thin," Paul said calmly, his voice barely rising above the noise of their flight. "I've done things I didn't think possible. I've hurt people for you, Arthur. I've killed for you. I am not going to let you kill us as a reward for my loyalty. Step away from the controls."

Arthur didn't flinch. Even as a cannonball rocked the ship, tearing another chunk out of the disintegrating hull, he remained ensconced at the helm, eyes glazed over as he pulled the levers seemingly at random. One of them stuck at the halfway position, jolting his arm. Arthur growled in frustration and yanked on the lever, only to pull his hand away with a cry of pain. The lever had cut a gash across his palm. Arthur grimaced, clenching his hand as blood leaked through his fingers.

Taking the opportunity, Paul shoved Arthur aside and seized the controls. He cursed under his breath and tried pulling at the stuck lever, to no avail. Maria was coming up the stairs, eyes blazing, fixing Arthur with a gaze that could kill.

There was a splintering crash, and the entire ship shuddered with the final exhale of a dying leviathan. Elsie was flung down onto the deck with such force that her vision went completely dark for an instant. Over the ringing in her ears, she heard a high-pitched voice screaming Paul's name before she finally blacked out.

Yvonnia had never experienced anything like the command tower during a storm. As the clouds grew thicker and darker, the world seemed to close in until the little glass-walled room was the only thing in existence. For several agonizing minutes, Yvonnia stood miserably in the center of the room until the baron practically threw a stool in her direction. "Just sit down, you Siali whore," he roared at her. "If you get in the way of one of my men, I'll have you thrown off the ship."

Wind and rain lashed across the windows, and nothing else was visible beyond the glass save when a flash of lightning briefly illuminated the roiling clouds. As they plowed forward into the storm, the ship began to buck and lurch, rattled by the wind as it steered frantically to avoid arcs of lightning that bloomed across their path. At one point, Yvonnia almost fell off the stool, only saving herself by bracing one leg painfully against the smooth metal floor.

The incessant tapping of the telegraphs nearly drove her insane. It was punctuated now and then by orders being given, messages being read out, or even the baron shouting about something or other, but the tapping itself formed an endless background chatter that grated on her nerves. One message, however, broke the monotony of the storm.

"Baron, I have a message," one of the telegraph men called, pressing his headset close to his ear as he listened to the incoming taps. "Prisoners loose, stop. Thirteen men killed, more wounded, stop. Need..."

Yvonnia scrambled to her feet, hardly daring to breathe. While the rest of them were distracted by the message, she bolted for the stairs, heart hammering in her chest. She would probably never make it, she knew, but she was grinning all the same as she clattered down the tight spiral. *They're alive! At least Jacik is, and he'd die before he let anyone get to Enya...*

As she reached the bottom of the stairs, the door was thrown open with a wash of chill wind and rain. A soldier staggered in, a long coat haphazardly thrown over his crimson uniform. Blood had seeped down his face from a gash near his hairline, dripping onto his collar, staining the uniform an even deeper red. He didn't have time to react before Yvonnia shoved past him. The door slammed shut behind her.

A wall of wind-blown water hit her body, soaking her to the skin in an instant as though she'd just plunged into the icy waves of the ocean. She staggered, the breath knocked out of her, and flung an arm over her face to protect her eyes. Even so, she was unable to see anything except random glimpses of the deck, quickly erased as water flooded her vision, forcing her to blink. Bent almost double, she pushed forward, praying she could find the air tank in the center of the deck and use it to guide her back to the staircase that led below. She had to find Enya and Jacik. If they were together, loose aboard the ship in the chaos of the storm, maybe they could find a way to escape.

Her foot caught on something she could not see, and Yvonnia tumbled to the cold metal deck in a heap, her cry of pain and fear lost in the howling deluge. In a blink she saw fierce lightning clash into one of the tall poles which surrounded the air tank, briefly illuminated hundreds of yards away through rain and cloud. Then it was gone, and she was forced to blink again as rain stung her eyes. She'd been heading in the wrong direction, but she thought perhaps now she had her bearings. She struggled to rise again as wind tore at her skirts, needling her skin through the thin silk fabric.

Even over the roaring of the storm, Yvonnia heard the angry bellowing of the baron behind her. Looking back over her shoulder, she saw the rain dash the ridiculous powdered wig from Schulhard's head. His shiny bald crown reflected the orange lamp-light from the command tower door.

"You fool! You imbecile wench! You'll die out here." He stamped over to where she lay, his heavy boots gripping the slick deck with ease.

"Better out here...!" Yvonnia's retort was cut short as the baron grabbed her roughly by the wrist and dragged her to her feet, wrenching her arm in his harsh grasp. She bit her lip so as not to cry out.

"I have half a mind to kill you right now! Get your bastard to stop killing my men this instant, or I'll cut your damn throat."

Yvonnia stared cooly back into his flaming blue eyes, suppressing a smile. "I couldn't stop him now," she said coyly, "Not when I'm in danger."

The baron drew an ornate pistol from his belt and pushed the barrel up under Yvonnia's chin. "You will stop him, or you will die here," he growled impatiently. "Now turn around before I blow your head off!"

She heard the sound of gunshots and the cries of dying men. The baron turned her to face the cacophony. The rain was thinning from a solid sheet into a spray whipped across the deck by the wind. Ahead of her, down the deck, she saw a tall dark man in modern Siali uniform, dancing swords with two marines for a moment before cutting them down with a stroke. This time it was not the desperate, dying dance he had put on in the ballroom, surrounded by overwhelming odds. This time, Jacik was confident in his chances. He could see a way clear to freeing his princess.

"Over here!" the baron bellowed.

Yvonnia saw Jacik raise his dark eyes to them. And then the dreadnought finally burst free of the storm and the sun seared across her vision, brilliantly illuminating a clear blue sky. Everyone seemed to pause for a moment, their breath and attention caught by the sudden ceasing of the storm. And then reality swept back in like a tide. Gripping Yvonnia's shoulder, the baron raised the cold barrel of his flintlock to her temple.

"Move an inch closer, and your beloved princess dies," he shouted. "Drop the sword."

A company of soldiers, most of them wearing the blue sash of the marine corps, filed in behind Jacik in a neat line, leveling their muskets at his back. The huge man stood frozen mid-action, his eyes fixed on the baron in a furious glare. It was an impossible situation; Yvonnia was certain that the moment he dropped his sword, he would be shot dead where he stood.

"Jacik, don't!" she called, but the wooden handle of the pistol struck her face with such force she felt a tooth loosen in her jaw. She cried out, barely remaining upright as the baron readjusted his vice-like grip on her shoulder.

Helplessly, Jacik clenched his fist on the hilt of his sword. "Strike her again and you die!" he shouted in his thickly-accented Odolian.

The baron laughed coldly. Yvonnia heard more men marching in behind them, and yet more lined up behind the bodyguard, amounting to two or three dozen soldiers, all with their muskets trained on his back. The standoff was hopeless. Either Yvonnia or Jacik was going to die, and at this point it might be both. The image came to her mind unbidden: Jacik's body twisting in the air as it was punctured by a dozen Odolian bullets...

"Baron! My lord, look!"

One of the sailors was shouting, pointing wildly off the starboard side. The baron's attention shifted, and he lowered the pistol from her temple as he stared. Yvonnia's eyes were drawn magnetically along with the rest of the deck's occupants.

A single ship, a dilapidated sky schooner, had appeared out of the clouds beside them. For an instant as Yvonnia saw it, she was filled with hope, but the feeling quickly withered away into fear, then despair. The ship was a shambles, its balloon heavily patched and the wooden hull pocked with holes. Smoke poured from the engine, which hung half exposed in the stern. She was shocked that it was still airborne, and even though it was hundreds of yards away across a vast pit of sky, she could tell that there were only half a dozen or so men on deck. It was far from the salvation she'd been praying for.

"What ship is that?" the baron asked one of his subordinates. "Someone with a glass, find the standard!"

A young soldier took a spyglass in hand and scanned the new ship, then shook his head. "It flies none, my lord! It hardly has a crew! The name on the side is the *Heart of Resistance.*"

"The madman," the baron said in a low growl which sent shivers down Yvonnia's spine. "Only one man would fly a ship like that." Schulhard turned and began shouting orders wildly. "That's it! That's the one. All men, fire on that ship! At once, you hear me?"

His cries were drowned out by the thunder of guns responding to his command. He withdrew his own pistol from Yvonnia's head entirely and aimed it futilely at the ship. Cocking the hammer back, he pulled the trigger to a barely noticeable *snap*. The gun had misfired. Momentarily distracted with frustration, Schulhard loosened his grip on her shoulder, just enough that Yvonnia was able to turn her head and bite down on his hand.

Jacik saw the opening he needed. The soldiers behind him turned as one man and fired on something beyond the ship, as did those in front. What they were looking at he could hardly imagine, and he didn't care. He needed to get that disgusting man off his princess. She was beautiful, even bruised, battered, and soaked to the bone, a symbol of everything he was willing to die for. And she was in danger. But now the baron was giving his full attention to whatever was out there, and he had his chance.

He saw the pistol misfire. As the man struggled with his gun, Jacik watched Princess Yvonnia twist her head and bite down on the man's hand, hard. The baron threw her aside at once, blood dripping from his fingers, and turned towards where she lay on the deck. The soldiers were ignoring Jacik, reloading their muskets to fire again on the new distraction.

Jacik rushed forward at the baron, his sword brandished and a Siali battle cry on his lips. The man reacted surprisingly fast, however, dropping his flintlock, which set off the charge harmlessly on the deck, and drawing a rapier from his belt. Schulhard parried Jacik's first strike with surprising skill. Jacik could almost find something to admire in the baron; his strategy was competent, his tenacity was almost admirable, and he did try so very hard. But he was *not* a swordsman. His swings were wild and frantic, and although Jacik was thrown off balance at first, he knew in just a few moments he would have the baron on the ground begging for mercy.

"FIRE!"

Jacik's right shoulder burned before he heard the echo of the gunfire, but he knew at once he'd been shot. But he also saw blood begin to drip down the side of the baron's bald head in a sharp line, spattering on his left epaulet. Schulhard let out a roar of pain and pawed at his head. Jacik could take a bullet, but the baron collapsed to the deck in a puddle of rapidly bloodying water.

"Hold your fire!" the baron called shrilly, throwing up his hand. A few more scattered gunshots went off, and then all were silenced. The baron looked up, sweat and blood streaking his face as he spat. "Don't just stand there, imbeciles! Get to the cannons and bring that airship down!" He seemed for a moment to ignore Jacik, who had stepped forward and leveled his blade at the man's throat.

"My lord!" called another voice. Jacik saw the man who had escorted Yvonnia, Lord Hollis, running across the deck towards them. He came to an abrupt halt when he saw the situation and staggered back a few steps, mouth agape as he struggled to make sense of what was going on.

"Hollis, you bastard, get the men to the cannons *now*!" Schulhard roared. He did not even look at the other man, fixing his beady eyes on Jacik. His mouth split in a sneering grin. "Well, you have me," he drawled. "Why don't you just kill me? Or aren't you man enough?"

Jacik pushed the sword further, parting the folds of the lace ruff at the baron's throat. "Let the princess, her maidservant, and myself go," he said thickly.

The baron scoffed. "Over my dead body."

As the cannon fire began to roar around them, a large shadow passed overhead, throwing Jacik and the baron into momentary twilight. Out of the corner of his eye, Jacik saw something inexplicable: a woman falling from the sky, landing with a heavy *thud* on the deck of the dreadnought. And then he looked back and saw what was coming towards them, and ran, scooping Yvonnia's limp body off of the deck, scrambling as fast as he could away from the bewildered baron.

Maria came up the stairs as quickly as she could, instantly spotting that Arthur, to her relief, had stepped back from the controls. His hand was bleeding heavily. *Good for you, Paul,* she thought, though she had no idea what had happened. The important thing was that Paul was back at the controls. Arthur had finally lost his damned mind, and she wasn't going to put up with it anymore. As she began signing fiercely at the captain, her eyes locked with Paul's. He smiled, crinkling the corners of his tired eyes, and she found herself smiling back despite her anger.

We're going to get out of here. It's going to be alright.

There was a flash of smoke and flame as the cannonball, measuring nearly two feet in diameter, smashed into the helm of the *Heart of Resistance.* Maria was momentarily blinded as soot and ash and splinters from the deck bombarded her. She threw up her arm, wiping over her eyes, and stared at the wreck. The engine had caught fire beneath their feet, and the ship's controls had been reduced to a heap of twisted metal and gears. Paul's name was torn from her throat in a ragged yell she could not hear.

The ship had already begun to lose altitude, dropping directly toward the dreadnought below. Arthur stood near the stern, an idiotic look of shock on his normally stern face. Maria's eyes followed his, and she saw Paul, laying in a heap of shattered wood near the remains of the helm.

She ran to him, leaping desperately over a hole in the deck. Dropping to her knees by his side, she gripped his hand with all her strength. It was pale, streaked with dark red blood. Her eyes fell to his torso, and her heart clogged her throat. Tears burned in her eyes as she took in the sorry state of her husband.

He managed to give her hand a single squeeze.

Maria shook her head sharply as she felt his hand begin to loosen in hers. Tearing her eyes away from Paul's body, she lifted them to Arthur with a glare of rage. She wanted to scream again, but her throat had constricted so much from the smoke and the pain that it was impossible. She rose to her feet slowly, dropping Paul's hand, and took a knife from one of the belts at her waist. It sailed through the air, just past Arthur's shoulder. Arthur didn't even flinch. His face was blank. He merely stood, staring with glassy eyes, clutching his bleeding hand.

Maria ran to him and grabbed him by the lapels of his stupid uniform coat. She shook him, speaking words aloud that she did not comprehend. Even if she could have heard them, words would never be enough. She had lost Paul. She had lost all meaning, lost her entire world, and Arthur refused to even react. Gone was the determined gaze in his eyes, replaced with a stark vacancy that terrified her. She shook him again, still shouting, but there was nothing she could do to make him respond. Beginning to panic, she pushed the captain away and went to the helm, searching desperately amid the twisted metal for anything she could do to salvage the situation. Nothing, not even a single lever, presented itself. Looking up, she saw Elsie crumpled on the ground by the staircase. Elsie! She had to at least save her. But before she could do anything, another cannon blast shook the ship from below, causing it to lurch violently, and Maria was flung over the railing.

Falling. She had never fallen from such a height before. She was hundreds, perhaps thousands of feet above the earth. She'd seen men fall before, but it hadn't frightened her. It was a common accident, especially aboard the *Formidable*, where she had first met Arthur and Paul all those years ago in the war. She had been one of the ship's cooks and would often meet secretly with Paul in the storerooms off the galley.

Her body hit the steel deck of the *Redoubtable* with a jarring thud. Dozens of Odolian marines surrounded her, their blood red uniforms streaked by blue sashes. She tried to push herself off the ground but cringed in pain as she realized that multiple bones had been shattered on impact. Through the haze of pain and tears, she saw a large man with dark skin standing over the body of another, a captain or general by the look of his uniform. *Baron Schulhard?* she thought dully. The other man looked up, then turned and ran, scooping up the body of a Siali woman from the deck as he went.

Her eyes went to the sky, and she saw overhead the flaming mass that had been the *Heart of Resistance* falling directly toward them. She said a silent prayer, unable to do anything more even as two marines grabbed her shoulders and dragged her to her feet. Smoke billowed from the falling wreck, obscuring her vision as she searched for any signs of life on board.

As the ship crashed straight into the baron, who was still lying prone on the deck, Maria saw Arthur standing at the helm, straight and proud even as smoke enveloped him and red flames licked at the tails of his heavy coat. The ship ground against the steel dreadnought for a moment before it fell away, plummeting over the side towards the earth along with a chunk of the deck. The balloon had caught fire, and there was no hope now of the *Heart* remaining airborne. The best Maria could hope for was that Elsie would survive the crash. Whether Arthur did or not, she didn't care.

That was when the marines dropped her to the ground as they scrambled in all directions. Maria let out a cry of pain, and with a great effort turned to see what had caused the commotion on deck. The huge mound in the center of the dreadnought had caught fire. The air tank which kept the thousand-ton monstrosity airborne was burning, pouring oily black smoke into the air as tarps and sheet metal shredded from the heat, whirling into the sky on the updraft. The *Redoubtable* itself plummeted towards the earth as marines and sailors tried in vain to smother the blaze.

Maria said one last prayer and clung helplessly to the rigging.

35

AFTER THE STORM

Elsie awoke to the throbbing in her head. She'd never felt quite so bad before. She coughed, heaving up thick phlegm, her lungs heavy with smoke and ash. Her eyes struggled to adjust as she scanned the area. She was lying on her side, her head propped up slightly, and she could see that they were in a strange place. The landscape was choked with dead trees and brambles. A pond, covered in sickly green algae, sat a few yards away, lapping gently at a low muddy shore. She pitched forward and coughed again, this time into her hands. They came away stained red. Numbly, she wiped them on the skirt of her filthy dress.

Elsie glanced to her right and saw that Arthur was sitting in front of an embering fire. It was night, though the horizon glowed orange. The air stank of putrid industrial smoke.

"Arthur?" she groaned, endeavoring to sit up. "What happened? Where are we?"

"Somewhere," Arthur said absently. "South of the Gorand Wastes. Midland Marshes, I think." He mumbled something to himself and poked the fire with a stick, causing a few sparks to fly up and settle in the mud.

Elsie sat up in sudden alarm. "Where's Maria? Where's Paul?"

Arthur's face fell, but his eyes were void of any emotion. "Maria? Likely dead. And…" He motioned vaguely. Beneath the twisted trunk of a tree, a mound of dirt had been piled about six feet long and two feet wide. Elsie's throat knotted, and she pressed a hand to her mouth as tears spilled down her cheeks.

"He's dead? How?"

"Cannons will do that," Arthur mumbled. "And Maria fell from the ship. Onto the dreadnought."

"Where is the ship?" Elsie asked, glancing quickly about.

Arthur wordlessly indicated the space behind Elsie. She turned gingerly around and saw something that was unrecognizable. The mound of splintered wood and metal was half covered by a heap of charred fabric that had once been the balloon, pierced by dozens of tears and holes. Besides these twisted effigies, there was nothing left of the *Heart of Resistance*. Elsie felt the knot in her stomach tighten.

"How did we—I mean, what did you do to-"

"Why are we not dead, you mean?" Arthur said disinterestedly. "Luck, I suppose."

"Luck?" Elsie cried. Despite the pain in her lungs and side, she stood up and crossed the muddy shore to Arthur, joining him beside the dim fire. From an upright position, she caught sight of something on the horizon, and her breath caught afresh. Through the dead branches of the mangroves and oaks, she saw a looming shape consumed in flame, pouring acrid black smoke into the sky in a towering plume. "What on-"

"What remains of the *Redoubtable*," Arthur said flatly, not even turning his head. "They probably caught fire in the storm. Schulhard must have been so focused on whatever prize he was chasing that he failed to notice the central blimp was compromised."

Elsie searched him for any sign of emotion: happiness, sadness, anger, regret, anything. Any sign that he was taking in what had just happened. But no, Arthur said each word with precisely the same lack of feeling behind it, as if he were reading the weather off a telegraph ticker tape. Elsie's blood began to boil as her eyes landed on the makeshift grave where Paul was laid to rest.

"Do you have nothing else to say?" she shouted. "You're just going to sit there and analyze your enemy's strategy, when your friend is dead and your ship is smoldering? What are we going to do now?"

"What can we do?" Arthur intoned flatly.

"Find civilization! Finally find those rebels I've heard so much about and join up with them. All this time we've been together you've tried to do things on your own, and damn it, it hasn't worked. Not at all! I'm still in this dress..." She looked down in distaste at the sodden blue dress, torn and filthy from hem to bodice. "...and that is all I have to my name. That and my own mind, and for crying out loud, that's more than you have! What were you thinking back there? We should have turned and flown as far from that dreadnought as possible. Maria was right to slap you, and I would do it too if my hands weren't burned, bruised, and battered, thanks to you."

She carried on, her voice rising in pitch and volume as he continued to stare into the fire. "Arthur Pendington, you and only you are to blame for what happened here. Paul was your friend, and in the end, you fought with him because he was trying to protect his wife. And if Maria is still alive, she's a widow now. Have you never considered what it does to other people, what you do?"

Her voice cracked as the words continued to tumble out of her mouth. "Think of all the people *we* hurt on Veturi! That poor man you punched because we broke into his shop. Those men who didn't get to work in the factories for their families, because we took their place. Captain Marjen! That's her ship," she pointed furiously at the wreck, "those were her phonograph records, her possessions, and now they're destroyed! All you do is leave destruction in your wake. And then you can't even enjoy the fact that technically you're victorious? You've destroyed everything, Arthur. Everything! And you're not sad because of it, and you're not even happy that you won. Feel something!"

She shouted it at the top of her lungs, though she had seen no change in Arthur's expression throughout her tirade. She hoped that there would be some spark of remorse or change. Instead, he just poked at the dying embers one more time.

Her shoulders slumped in exhaustion. She was about to turn away when she heard his voice, so low it was barely audible.

"You're right, Elsie."

Elsie blinked. Hearing her name from his mouth was bizarre.

"What did you say?"

"You're right," Arthur muttered, "I was an ass. I should have retreated."

Elsie huffed. "That's not important now. What's next? Where do we go from here?"

"Bolden, I think. I have... history there."

Elsie shrugged. It sounded as good to her as anything. She walked to the edge of the pond, staring numbly at the still, scum-coated water. A huge, rusted lead pipe was spilling foul-smelling liquid into the pond. She reached down and touched some of the green moss that flourished rampantly on the edge. "How will we get there?"

"I suppose we start in the morning," Arthur said briskly, sounding a little more like the man she'd traveled with on Veturi. "We will have to walk. We'll find one of the rail tracks and follow it on foot. Stow away on one of the trains if we can. I have a plan, don't worry."

Arthur stood, pulling his coat up about his shoulders. For a moment, Elsie caught a glimpse of his bright blue eyes. He hid it well, but she saw something in them she hadn't seen before.

She saw that he had hope.

EPILOGUE

Janna Tulli cursed and kicked a stray rock that was in her path. Her stomach growled, and it was only the hatred of Arthur Pendington which kept her feet moving forward. Her dry lips smacked at the mere thought of water, though it had never been her drink of choice. The food she'd purchased in Locend had run out two days ago, and after seven chill days and seven unbearable nights, she could take it no longer.

She hadn't seen a single person since she'd left Locend. The mining town was miserable and she found that she would probably starve to death in poverty before she got past the work lottery and onto Veturi. Instead, she used what money she had earned repairing some of the town's equipment and set out into the desolation of the Gorand Wastes. It was arduous and boring, with nothing in her sight except more flat earth. Occasionally she had to clamber over muddy streams and move around windswept dunes of dirt, but otherwise she simply had to move her body over the unbearably flat landscape.

Wearily, she gazed up at the hazy gray sky. The late autumn clouds rendered the sun invisible for most of the day, which made navigation difficult. For all she knew, she could be going in circles. At last, she collapsed to her knees from exhaustion. *I can't move another muscle,* she thought grimly. *I suppose I am going to die out here.*

Cursing Arthur silently, Janna hitched the empty pack off her shoulders and set it carefully beside her. As she laid her throbbing head on the sorry excuse for a pillow, her stomach growled, cramping as she curled onto her side. The bare rock and packed earth was just as miserable as it had ever been. *Does dying have to be such a damn nuisance?*

Her aching eyes wandered the endless wasteland, fixing on the horizon, where a tiny dark spot appeared for a moment, then vanished. It appeared again and Janna rubbed her eyes. *I'm losing my vision too.* She blinked, but the spot only grew.

Janna's heart began to race and she scrambled to her feet once again, ignoring the pain in her injured leg, waving her arms as the object drew closer. It was an airship.

She began to holler and scream, staggering forward, hoping against hope that they would notice her before it was too late. In her first stroke of good luck since she met Arthur, the airship slowed, changing course slightly and coming to a halt right over Janna. It hovered fifty or so feet overhead, propellors creating a huge updraft that whipped her tattered braid and sent the dust swirling around her.

A rope ladder was thrown down, thudding against the dirt a few paces to her right. A young man scampered down and reached out his hand to Janna. "You're a long way off from anywhere, ma'am!" he exclaimed. "The captain would have you aboard until we get to Bolden."

Janna felt her heart leap. "What's his name?"

"Captain Brenforth of the *Skyhook*! He's an honest man, won't no harm come to you ma'am!"

"Could I speak to him once I'm aboard?"

"Sure thing ma'am!" the boy said, a smile brightening his face. "What about?"

Janna took the young man's hand and began to climb the rope ladder. "I'm wondering if he has any use for an engineer."

Arthur and company will return in

The Hope of Rebellion

Coming Soon

GLOSSARY

Odolian Citizens

Arthur Pendington – Formerly a landed lord of Bolden, Arthur became captain of the Imperial Dreadnought *Formidable*. He is presumed dead since the dreadnought went down.

Paul Kauisol – Arthur's navigator and only friend. He served aboard the *Formidable* and has since aided in his captain's more incendiary efforts. He is married to Maria Kauisol, and acts as her interpreter.

Maria Kauisol – Formerly a cook aboard the *Formidable*, she fell in love with and married Paul Kauisol. She is deaf, and is a more-than-competent fighter, cook, seamstress, and jack-of-all-trades.

Janna Tulli – An experienced engineer, Janna is the only daughter of Greyer Tulli. Since leaving her father's rebellion, she has sought work in the skydocks of Gorand and drink in its many pubs.

Greyer Tulli – Deceased leader of Karlsban's rebellion against Odol.

Elsie – An orphan who was taken into Threadbury's Textile Workhouse at a young age after her father died. She is employed in the dyeworks.

Cattia – Elsie's friend. She was born in Threadbury's Workhouse and never knew a world outside of it.

Hanna – Elsie's friend. She grew up on the streets of Gorand and prefers the relative safety of the workhouse.

Mister Threadbury – The owner of Threadbury's Workhouse.

Madame Harban – An overseer at Threadbury's Workhouse. She is known by the girls as being cruel, and even those content with their lives in the workhouse dislike her.

Captain Lucille Marjen – Captain of the merchant airship *Worker's Chance*.

Rye – A native of Gorand's undercity.

Clemen – Former quartermaster of the dreadnought *Formidable*.

Baron Brandomir Schulhard – The tyrannical lord the city of Gorand and its surrounding province.

Theodore Schulhard – Baron Schulhard's son and heir.

Lord Oskar Hollis – An official in his Imperial Majesty's government who is often dispatched to deal with troublesome situations.

Ulysses Cadbury – The head of security on Veturi.

Lady Genevieve – A noblewoman of Veturi.

Lady Eritula – The governor of Veturi.

Siali Citizens

Yvonnia Holani– The Princess of Sial, she is the surviving heir to her father's throne. Due to her father King Holan's grief over his children slain in the Siali Civil War, she has taken many of the responsibilities of the monarchy on her shoulders.

Jacik Kivian – Yvonnia's loyal bodyguard. Raised a soldier, he climbed the ranks until he dedicated his entire life to protecting Yvonnia.

Enya – Yvonnia's personal handmaid, she takes her responsibilities lightly and being a nuisance very seriously.

Holanites – Those who acknowledge and support the reign of King Holan. The Holanites believe that peace can be negotiated with Odol.

King Holan VI – King of Sial. Holan is descended from those that usurped the throne and massacred the Basra family a hundred years ago. All his sons were killed in the Siali Civil War, though he still has a single heir in his daughter Yvonnia.

General Kachik Vasada – The last loyal Holanite general.

Thunats – Followers of an old monastic tradition, Thun appeals to those wanting an entirely peaceful approach to diplomacy.

Lama Fanq Nakazo – The spiritual leader of the Thunats.

Prince Balik Kalika Basra – An inactive pretender to the Siali throne and follower of Thun.

Lord Resna Kaliman – A Siali nobleman and follower of Thun.

Lord Manik Kaliman – A Siali nobleman and friend of Theodore Schulhard.

Ryokans – Followers of an ancient martial tradition, Ryokans reject the legitimacy of King Holan and fought against him in the Siali Civil War. Lead by nationalist generals, they also hate and fear Odol, and have made moves to exterminate the western colonists.

General Silander Rhela – A former Holanite General, now loyal to the Ryokan movement.

General Pretav Ozerov – A mercenary general from Ynarus, a nation north of Sial. Currently loyal to the Ryokans.

General Nayan Gera – The most fanatical Ryokan general.

Princess Menava Basra – A pretender to the Siali throne.

Locations

The Odolian Empire – Also known colloquially as Odol. Originating in the Townlands of Odolia, the Odolian Empire began three hundred years ago with a marriage alliance between the Odolia and Bolden provinces. Soon it expanded north and southeast, before finally looking across the southwestern mountains to Karlsban. It now comprises the Townlands of Odolia, the County of Bolden, the Duchy of Palande, the Barony of Gorand, the March of Vintine, and the Caliphate of Karlsban.

Gorand – Capital city of the Barony of Gorand, ruled by Baron Brandomir Schulhard. The only usable port on Odol's rough eastern coastline, Gorand monopolizes international trade and communication with Sial. It is constructed in three layers, with lifts and sky skiffs traveling in between.

The Undercity – A name given to the portion of Gorand's lowest layer which lies directly beneath the higher levels. Perpetually dark, it is filled with crime and vice.

Threadbury's Textile Workhouse – A women's textiles workhouse whose purpose is to shelter and give useful work to impoverished girls from Gorand. It is one of many such institutions.

The Wreckage – The area immediately surrounding Gorand, where all the refuse and waste from the city is dumped.

The Wastes – Or the Gorand Wastes. The area to the south and west of the city of Gorand where the land has been stripped of all resources, leaving a flat desert.

Locend – A mining town in the Gorand Wastes.

Bolden – Capital city of the County of Bolden. The center of Odol's continental empire, Bolden is where all roads and railroads lead. It also holds Veturi's monumental roundhouse.

Veturi – "The City of Light and Splendor," Veturi is a city that travels by rail. Sporting a population of over 50,000 people, it is built on top of massive train cars which hold rudimentary housing for the poorest citizens, as well as various industrial enterprises.

The Kingdom of Sial – An ancient country with a rich history on the eastern continent, currently ruled by King Holan VI. It is divided by factions who contend over what should be done about the Odolian colonists that have begun to settle its land.

Aldia – The capital city of Sial. It has been under the Holanite Dynasty's influence for a century. Previously, it was ruled by the now defunct Basra dynasty.

Airships

Sky-schooner – A type of airship with a single armed deck and midsized cargo hold. Sky-schooners are small, fast, and nimble. They can be manned by a barebones crew of 6 or 7, but will accommodate a crew of 14 or more.

Sky-skiff – The smallest type of airship, analogous to a ship's boat or sailing dinghy. They are used in a similar fashion, as transports between ships, escape vessels, or for covering very small distances. A skiff can easily be manned by one or two people.

Imperial Dreadnought – The largest flying warships in the Odolian sky navy. Only six were ever built. They are constructed around a single rigid air tank filled with highly pressurized hot gasses and boast hundreds of guns, plus firebombs and other weapons. Crews consist of well over a thousand men, not including marines and officers.

Heart of Resistance – Formerly known as the *Worker's Chance*. A sky-schooner equipped with an enviable twenty-four rate engine and half a dozen six pound guns.

Imperial Dreadnought *Redoubtable* – One of the five remaining Imperial Dreadnoughts, captained by Baron Schulhard.

Imperial Dreadnought *Formidable* – The sixth dreadnought, formerly captained by Arthur Pendington. It crashed following the destruction of Greyer's rebellion.

Historical Events

The Twenty Years' War – When Odol had conquered all of the other nations on the continent, Empress Crysalia II turned her gaze across the southern mountains, to the Caliphate of Karlsban, and sent her armies to conquer it. First, she sent a naval invasion through Karl's Bay, but the fleet was destroyed in short order. When airships were invented, Crysalia had a new fleet manufactured. Karlsban responded in turn with guerilla warfare, which bogged the war down into an uncomfortable stalemate. Finally the engineers in Vintine created the dreadnoughts, which ended the war within another year.

Greyer's Rebellion – Following the Twenty Years' War, Greyer Tulli, a partisan from Karlsban, led a violent rebellion against Odol, which lasted until he was killed by a dreadnought. Disorganized pockets still remain throughout Odol.

Siali Civil War – When General Nayan Gera razed a colony of Odolian settlers, King Holan VI tried to punish him, but instead Gera formed the Ryokan faction, which opposed Holan's "weak" reign. The ensuing war between the Holanites and Ryokans was resolved in a tentative ceasefire.

Currency

Odol's system of currency consists of coins once used by the nations it annexed, which have been restandardized according to the following values:

The Talent is the largest form of currency and is the envy of the world for its buying power. It is made of platinum and bears the face of emperors past and present.

The Granz is a solid gold coin, worth exactly half of a talent.

The Sept is a gold-plated silver coin that is worth 1/7th of a talent.

The Decat is worth a tenth of a sept, and 1/70th of a Talent. It is a small silver coin with an edge of gold.

The Kent, or half-decat, is just that. It is fairly common in basic transactions. It is a flat silver coin.

The Dul is a copper coin that represents 1/13th of a Kent. There are also variants that are worth two, three, five, and half a Dul.

Acknowledgements

There may be only one name on the cover of most books, but that belies the fact that it takes many, many people to bring a book from idea to publication. The authors would like to thank just a few of the amazing people who made *The Heart of Resistance* possible:

Shout out to Madde, who was the first to offer feedback on the beta draft, as well as Rebekah, Kathryn, Andrew, Ethan, Isaac, Selah, and Jennifer.

Thank you to Tony, Patrick, Marty, Kelly, and Martha of the writer's group, who provided feedback on the first chapters (and helped kill many Marconi-isms.)

Special thanks to Samantha, who was the first to hear the new blurb and be hyped. Hope the book lives up to your expectations!

Thank you to our editor David and our proofreader Anna. Your insightful critique and typo-catching made this book better than we ever could have on our own.

To Addison Horsell, who brought our cover art to life just as we'd imagined it, and to Cheyenne Van Langevelde, fellow indie author, who created the title typography and advised us much: thank you for lending your skills to this project.

Thank you to the members of the Write for Life Discord server, who provided assistance, community, encouragement, and hype.

The authors are also creatively indebted to the works of Charles Dickens, Jules Verne, C. S. Forester, Hayao Miyazaki, Kaoru Mori, Shinichirō Watanabe and the Sunrise team, Ken Forsse, Robert Fripp, Tony Levin, Thom Yorke, and numerous others. Thank you for the inspiration.

For our families, who had to endure much discussion of the book while it was still in fledgling stages, as well as assisting us in numerous ways, including childcare, help at our bookstore, transportation, food, hospitality, and general advice and kindness: thank you all from the bottom of our hearts.

We would like to thank Ellie for being adorable and for listening to mommy and daddy read this book aloud to each other and correct it as they went, without (much) complaining.

Thank you to Randy and Christine for believing in us.

Thank you to the patrons of Griffeys' Book Emporium in Delaware, Ohio, who supported our original dream of bookstore ownership and have now supported our dream of publication. We know half of you half as well as we should like.

Thank you, dear reader, for completing this work.

Last, but certainly not least, we want to thank the Lord and the communities of Grace Presbyterian Church, Holy Cross Orthodox Church, and St. Mary's Catholic Church. Thank you all for being the hands and feet of Jesus in so many ways. God bless you and praise Him.

About the Authors

Aria and David Griffey are a husband and wife writing team who love to create fantastical worlds grounded in historical detail. When they aren't crafting new stories, Aria works as a mom, artist, and bookbinder, while David works as a restaurant manager, miniature painter, and music nerd. They live in Central Ohio with their daughter and a lot of books. This is their first novel together.

Website: www.adgriffey.com

Facebook: www.facebook.com/ariadavidgriffey

Instagram: @ariadavidgriffey